On the Force

by

Margo Hoornstra

Brothers in Blue, Book 2

On the Force

Contact Information: info@thewildrosepress.com

Cover Art by *Diana Carlile*

The Wild Rose Press, Inc.
PO Box 708
Adams Basin, NY 14410-0708
Visit us at www.thewildrosepress.com

Publishing History
First Crimson Rose Edition, 2018
Print ISBN 978-1-5092-2214-8
Digital ISBN 978-1-5092-2215-5

Brothers in Blue, Book 2
Published in the United States of America

"You do realize this changes everything."

After a brief swallow, he pulled back some, but didn't let her go.

I realize all right. "But, we're still the same people. Inside."

With a quick twist, she wrenched away from him then walked over to the other side of the room. "You just don't get it, do you?"

She was talking, but he obviously wasn't hearing what she had to say. "What do I not get?"

He'd lied to her, and she was pissed. Any idiot would understand that. But her calmly controlled reaction held the undercurrent of more. Something was wrong, very wrong. That he knew for sure. What exactly and why, he had no clue.

"You're a cop." Her voice was low as if she spoke to herself yet needed to have the words out in the open before she could process exactly what they meant. "And I'm sorry to hear that. Very sorry to hear that."

His stomach clenched. "What the hell is that supposed to mean?"

"Exactly what I said."

"Sydney." He approached slowly and brought his palms to rest on already tensed shoulders that tightened even more at his touch.

"Vince." The strength of her shrug dislodged his touch.

Though his hands dropped away, he refused to give up. "Can we talk about this? Please?"

"We can." She twisted around to face him, and her voice grew tight. "Though I'm not sure it will do much good."

Praise for Margo Hoornstra

ON THE SURFACE: BROTHERS IN BLUE BOOK 1

"If you like a heavy helping of romance with your suspense, this book is for you."

~Romance Author Alison Henderson (5 Stars)

NIGHT STARS AND MOURNING DOVES:

"This is a well-done, quick read that will appeal to any reader who has battled life's obstacles and emerged victorious."

~The Romance Review (4 Stars)

ONLY IF YOU DARE:

"…this author has used a difficult subject to create believable characters, and a charming, easy-to-read, sweet romance."

~Long and Short (3.5 Stars)

HONORABLE INTENTIONS:

"Every page is packed with emotion and action, and this is a story you will find hard to put down."

~The Long And Short Of It (4.5 Books)

Dedication

To my husband Ron. For the ideas that sparked this book. Then for the support, encouragement, and love to see it through to The End.

Chapter One

Detective Vince Miller slid forward on the chair, his head bent toward the laptop open on the table in front of him. The clamor of a busy coffee shop at mid-day buffeted him from all sides. Dishes and silver clattered into bus pans while enthusiastic baristas called friendly greetings as new customers entered. A well-greased cash drawer dinged open then shut as money exchanged hands. Murmured conversations from occupied tables clashed with New Age Musak droning from ceiling speakers.

Running surveillance was such a bitch.

Doing his level best to ignore the din, Vince made a show of tapping his fingers on the built-in keyboard. A chaotic stream of letters, symbols and assorted numbers flowed across the screen in even black lines.

Pssssttt!

From behind the counter to his left, an irritating hiss spewed forth as machine induced steam swirled into a container of God knew what.

Psssttt!

He closed his eyes in frustration, then pulled in a breath he blew out low and slow. Ironically, he didn't particularly care for coffee. Especially those spruced up concoctions prepared here at Anton's Bistro in suburban Detroit.

Psssttt!

Teeth clenched, Vince squinted to focus on the gibberish filled screen. *A necessary price to pay for using freelance writer as a cover.*

Good thing he wasn't a budding author for real. No way could he produce anything of literary value in this madhouse.

"I brought you a refill."

A friendly female voice penetrated the tedium that had overtaken his brain. Apparently, his constant presence in here the past two weeks afforded him a certain measure of familiarity with the staff. A smooth, well-manicured hand reached in to remove the half empty ceramic cup at his elbow then returned it there a few seconds later. Filled to the absolute brim with more caffeine loaded brown beverage.

"Thanks."

"Are you getting a lot done?"

He lifted his gaze. A bright grin on the pleasant face eased him out of a dour mood. The server, identified by the red on white name tag attached just below her right collarbone as Teri, reminded him of his kid sister. Same ready smile. Similar blonde hair and wide trusting eyes.

"Sure am." So what if his response was a bunch of bull? The smile he flashed back was genuine. "Tons."

"What are you working on?" Sidling closer, she angled toward the exposed PC.

Vince had the screen lowered before she got near enough to see anything. "A manuscript."

"Really?" Interest sparked in bright eyes. "What kind of manuscript?"

May as well throw it out there. "I'm a writer."

"That's so cool." Her enthusiastic nod sent short

blonde curls bouncing. "What do you write?" He had yet to open his mouth when she answered for him. "A murder mystery, I'll bet."

"Why do you say that?" He kept a possessive hand in place on the lid.

Tilting her head to one side, she studied him with an appraising gaze. "You seem like the type. A man who's no stranger to danger."

He pushed up the sleeves on his worn gray sweatshirt. "You think so?"

"Absolutely! In the literary sense, of course." More curls bounced on a second nod. "The outfit is a dead giveaway. Jeans. A leather jacket." She put her hand on top of the short black coat draped over the chair across from him. "A guy in leather wouldn't write romance."

Brow furrowed, he considered her assessment. "I'd have thought a tweed blazer with elbow patches and a pipe would be a dead giveaway."

Wrinkling her nose, she shook her head. "You don't look like the pipe smoking type."

"Now there's a correct assumption on your part." *This one is for real.* As a former amateur boxer, he cared about his health. "Can't stand smoke of any kind."

"Me either." She took a step back then pursed her lips as she gave him a bold up and down inspection. "It shows you take care of yourself."

"I'll take that as a compliment."

"Figured you would." Her lips curled into a satisfied smile. "The dark hair and nice eyes don't hurt your cause either."

Now she's just messing with me. Even so, it felt good to smile back as she turned to walk away. "That one too."

"You're welcome."

His smile faded as he leaned back in the stiff wooden chair and snapped the laptop completely shut. An all-day rain kept up a steady barrage against the front windows. Accumulated drops slid down the glass in murky streams to obscure anything that lay beyond. No big deal. *For now.* A seasoned investigator, he didn't need a clear visual of the other side of the street or the building he'd been watching. He peered through the watery blur at the foot high marque he knew spelled out *The Argentile Gallery* in shining golden script.

Supposedly, an upscale art gallery and auction house. Currently owned and operated by one Randall Curan who came complete with a typical rich kid's resume. Heir to a food industry fortune. Private prep schools, an Ivy League college education, and a six-figure management position in a subsidiary of the family business waiting for him when he got out.

To think I've been assigned to find something wrong in this particular mix.

A widespread and sophisticated counterfeit ring was wreaking havoc in the international art world. All high-end galleries were suspect and to be put under temporary surveillance. In cooperation with the feds—correction—at their *direction.* Suspicion was all they had to go on. *Typical government operation. One or two bad actors in a group, and they're all corrupt by association.*

He opened the laptop, and its screen sprang to life.

Just a damned wild goose chase the chief has sent me on. His butt parked in here was more a favor to his mentor than anything else. The product of blue collar roots and proud of it, what the hell did Vince know about art galleries anyway? Except that they usually served a certain privileged segment of the population. Those with an abundance of extra money at their disposal and way too much time on their hands.

"You still doing okay?" Teri paused as she passed by his table.

"Fine, thanks." *Not!*

Over two weeks on this case and he hadn't accomplished much of anything except to learn the owner drove a Porsche—no surprise there—and kept pretty regular hours. Along with a handful of employees. The place didn't have many deliveries either, and only the occasional arrival of customers.

"Just checking."

"Thanks." *May as well offer some bait to see if she nibbles*. "Interesting building across the street. You ever been in there?"

Her gaze followed his toward the window. "The art gallery? Never." She bent to wipe off a nearby table as she conversed over her shoulder. "How about you?"

"Me, either."

Though not about to share, he'd had a bad feeling about this case from the get go. Not in the traditional sense of a bad feeling. More of the *why in the hell are we even bothering to investigate* kind of feeling. Right now, he was expending a lot of time to turn up nothing. Time that could be spent doing what he was supposed to. Chase down the *real* criminals.

Not the made-up ones.

Desperate for something, anything on this case, he continued the fishing expedition. "Any of the staff from there ever come in here?"

"Not that I know of. Why?"

Vince gave a shrug of the well-practiced, non-commitment variety. "Just wondered."

A deafening crack rattled the walls. The outside gloom exploded into a flash of light. A huge electric bolt sizzled and sparked as it hurtled downward. Water sheeting on the windows glimmered and glowed. Conversation ceased as heads lifted. Thunder rumbled then roared, like some ferocious beast prowling the city streets.

Eyes wide, Teri straightened and drew in her shoulders. "That was close."

"Sure was."

"Scary." With more shiver than shrug, she swiped a white cloth across one last table then disappeared into the back.

Nature's display over, the chatter resumed. Vince studied the laptop screen and worked to retrieve his make-believe concentration. The cursor's vertical line blinked back at him in a slow, monotonous rhythm. *Just shoot me now. Please.*

"Medium coffee." A distinctive feminine voice, at the same time lilting yet controlled, caught his attention.

He brought his head up, and his gaze landed on a woman in a tan trench-coat who stood by the counter stuffing a scarf into her left side pocket. Distracted by the storm's commotion, he hadn't seen her come in. It didn't take long for him to make up for what he'd originally missed. Starting at black, open-toed heels, he scanned the short length of navy dress pants to the hem of her coat. Belted at the waist, the thing did wonders to show off some darned appealing curves. Brown hair flowed in thick waves beyond her shoulders to hit mid back at the bra line.

Any chance Vince had to refocus on the laptop was toast, and he sat back to enjoy this newest view.

"Medium coffee. Is that all you want?" Teri's co-worker spoke from behind the counter. Her brightly painted lips pursed as if she was somehow offended by the simplicity of the order. "Any flavor shots?"

"No thank you. Just black."

The lady had a face made up of both character and beauty. High cheekbones. Large brown eyes. Full lips.

"How about a pastry with that? Maybe a cookie?" This one wasn't about to back down.

"Not today, thank you." Long hair swished as she shook her head. Several strands turned golden in the overhead light.

The barista shrugged then smiled. "Here you go, then."

"Thank you."

Taking the ceramic cup pushed her way, the striking woman turned toward the line of self-service urns at the far end of the counter. Only a few short steps away for her, and Vince made the most of every single one with his gaze firmly locked on the sway of one fine ass beneath that coat.

"Hey, Sydney." His little waitress friend carried out a large thermos she set behind one of the others.

"Hi, Teri. How are you?"

"Okay, I guess."

Vince pretended he could care less as the two women exchanged some pleasant small talk. *Sydney.* The name suited her. Strong. Purposeful. Elegant. Extremely hot. He fought to turn his attention back to the laptop. *Let's not get carried away while you're working. Take it as an eye candy treat. Nothing else.*

As it happened, this Sydney chose the table beside his, bringing along the fragrance of light musk and exotic flowers. She slipped out of the coat she settled on the back of her chair. As she sat, a filmy red blouse draped nicely over appealing curves. Ignoring her coffee, she pulled a cell phone out of her purse, studied its screen for a moment, entered a few notes or something with deft fingers, then set the thing down. Bored as he was, Vince was about to figure a way to engage her in idle conversation. To pass a little time if nothing else. A sudden vibration against his hip ditched that idea.

He had his cell out and to his ear in two seconds flat. "Yeah. Miller."

"You get a copy of that newspaper I told you about?"

At Chief Lambert's gravelly voice, the corners of Vince's mouth curved up then down again. A vision of the stern, round face of his current boss slid to mind. Deep, penetrating cop eyes beneath a lined forehead set in a continuous scowl.

"I did."

"Have you read that article about Curan yet?"

"What there was. More pictures than anything else."

"Anything in it you can use?"

Vince shook his head. "I'm not sure."

"Not sure, huh?" An exhale vibrated the line. "Read it again. The federal boys are breathing down my neck. We need to give them something."

"What if we've got nothing to give?"

A heavy dose of silence answered. Coming up empty wasn't an option.

"I get it you're a little frustrated, Miller."

"More like a lot."

"Hang in there. You been watching the local news?"

"Not lately." *I've been too busy watching what's going on around here, which is nothing.*

"The channels are eating up that embezzlement thing with the On Trend clothing chain."

"Now there's something I could really sink my teeth into." Regardless, he knew better than to come right out and ask for a change in assignment.

"Since that one is shaping up to be a bank fraud issue, Feds are swarming in, and we're swamped with their…assistance."

"Is that what you really mean? Their interference is more like it."

"Ain't that the truth? At any rate, stay with what you're doing. Hopefully, we can close this gallery thing out sooner rather than later."

"Okay." Vince drew the phone closer to his mouth. "Except I'll refrain from getting up to do a happy dance."

"Nice." A labored sigh blew through the connection. "I can do without the sarcasm."

Here it comes.

"Look at things from my side. The gallery case is still suspicion only. We can't even do a knock and talk over at that Genitalia place to fish for anything even remotely illegal."

"It's Argentile, not Genitalia." Vince deadpanned the correction. "Thanks for putting the word in my mind. Now you'll have me saying it. That is if I should catch a break in this case and actually get inside."

"The point is these feds don't want us to arouse any suspicions."

"I hear ya. That would be way too easy."

"Too risky. We went over this before you hit the field, Miller. Applying for a job or anything else at that—whatever the hell it's called—to get close to Curan is out of the question. At this point, the investigation is preliminary. Not official enough to warrant the trouble of establishing a new identity for you that will stand up to a background check. Plus, you show who you really are, my guess is we'll be referred to some fancy law firm in nothing flat."

Resting his elbow on the table, Vince massaged two fingers over his forehead. "Copy that."

"Hang in there, buddy." The chief's voice took on an appeasing tone. "Go over that article again. Keep at it. Something is bound to turn up."

"I'll do my best."

"Yeah, I know you will."

Vince disconnected the call with a thumb swipe then returned the cell to his pocket. True to his word, he spread out the newspaper he'd bought that morning and opened to page three. Chief was probably right. Best to keep his mouth shut about a case transfer. Details aside, assignments were assignments were assignments. Get the one he was on solved and go on to the next. Just another day at the office. Maybe he should have balked at being on loan just now to the Manderfield Township PD from Waterton, his home precinct two burgs over, but hadn't. It simply wasn't practical to work UC, pretend to be someone you weren't, on your own turf.

Too many chances to be recognized, which in some cases, could be deadly.

He glanced down at the motionless laptop again. *Not that I'm currently in any immediate danger.*

"So, Sydney." Teri was back at work in the dining room to clear away dishes and wipe tables. With a white cloth hanging from one hand, she stood with her back to Vince. "How's the job search going?"

"Absolutely underwhelming." A definite fatigue, even hopelessness, colored Sydney's reply. "It seems like I've been pounding the pavement forever."

Teri rested one hand on the back of an empty chair. "That's got to be tough."

"I'm not used to being unemployed."

"A lot of people these days are in the same boat." Their friendly server extended an arm. "I was lucky to get this, at least until I earn my degree. Don't worry. You'll find something."

"I hope so."

Vince took the chance for a side-long glimpse. Those beautiful eyes creased at their corners as Sydney offered what he took to be a brave smile. Lest he be caught staring, he focused his wandering gaze on the paper to read, once again, what was printed about Randall Curan. All six short paragraphs under the headline *'More Than Just a Pretty Face.'* Upright citizen. Philanthropist. Community leader. The accolades went on and on.

Drawing his lips into a frown, Vince shook his head. *Nobody was that noble.*

With both forearms flat on the tabletop, he leaned in to pour over an extensive layout of full color photos of Curan at various events around the country. A minor league baseball game, ultra-formal charity ball, the ribbon cutting of a municipal playground. *Nothing but warm, fuzzy, feel-good fluff.*

After another run through of the news item as instructed, he hadn't learned one damned thing new. Except the guy had an eye for the ladies. In each picture, Curan had a woman either on his arm or sitting very close by. A different and incredibly attractive woman each time. Blonde, brunette or redhead, didn't seem to matter to Curan. The dude boasted a broad, Cheshire Cat smile with each one. Although Vince did have to hand it to the paper for being equal opportunity. Under each picture, the women at least got their names listed. Provided they were spelled correctly. Beverly Hartford, Elaine Queens, Shanna Martin.

Sitting up straight, he folded the paper into quarters then set it on one corner of his table.

Hands clasped at the back of his head, Vince pushed his elbows apart to stretch out a number of the kinks that had taken up residence along his neck. *Nothing wrong with appreciating the company of a pretty woman.* One thing he and this Curan seemed to have in common. The *only* thing Vince had in common with the man, being he was no stranger to feminine attention either. He even acted on the female summons when the mood struck, and the time was right. Neither of which was happening at the moment.

The front door swung open. Echoes of unrelenting rainfall and car wheels whooshing across wet pavement swept in.

Teri immediately straightened to turn toward the entrance. "Welcome to Anton's."

An elderly couple, hands entwined, glanced up as

one unit. "Thank you."

The old guy kept hold of his companion as they approached the counter.

Vince rubbed his hands together as he squared up in front of the laptop. Even the seniors were getting some action these days.

Glad someone is, because it sure isn't me.

"Excuse me. Are you done with this?"

"What?" He glanced up.

The silky red blouse was at eye level. He forced his fingers not to touch, and his field of vision upward to settle on full lips. Taking in a quick breath, he lifted his gaze farther to connect with the prettiest brown eyes he'd seen in quite a while.

The neat brows above them rose in question. "The paper. Are you finished reading it?"

"Sure." He added a smile to the eye contact as he handed it over. "Be my guest."

"Thank you." The smile she offered in return was gracious. Period.

With the daily in hand, she quickly reversed direction to return to her seat. Vince concentrated hard to keep his gaze forward and *not* follow her movements. Paper rustled as she leafed through the pages.

"Anything?" Teri stopped between the two tables, a full bus pan balanced on one hip.

"Not in here." After a short sigh, she collapsed the tabloid into her lap.

"Don't get discouraged." Her tone grew light. "You'll find a job soon."

"I'll try to absorb some of your enthusiasm."

"Do that. It's on the house."

"Thanks." Any semblance of a pleasant expression vanished the second Teri left. Her gaze lowered, she pressed her lips into a narrow line. Smoothing then refolding the newspaper back together, she set it on the table. As resignation seeped in to settle in her eyes, she rested her chin in one palm.

Blame it on his upbringing, sexist or not, Vince never could stand to witness a lady in distress. Without thinking much about it, he vacated his chair and slid into the one opposite her. "I don't mean to intrude."

She was quick to glance up, eyes wide. "What?" Her surprise was short lived. Definite appreciation lit her gaze.

Hands at his sides, he was careful not to invade her space more than he already had as he went on. "I overheard you're looking for a job."

Caution swiftly overtook appreciation. "Did you?"

"My—uh—friend is desperate for help at her daycare, if you're interested." Actually, the woman his little sister worked for was the one looking. Too much information to share with a stranger.

The corners of her mouth curved up as her eyes brightened. "Nice of you to mention it, but truth is, I'd rather do almost anything than change dirty diapers."

"Sorry my paper wasn't more help."

"Don't be." Long, thick lashes brushed smooth cheeks. "My time wasn't completely wasted. There's an interesting article on page three about Randall Curan."

"Yeah, I saw that." He held in what he wanted to say next. *A complete and total waste of my time.*

"He's the owner of the art gallery across the street from here and is one of our most prominent local philanthropists. He also happens to be a very nice man."

Well, holy shit! Vince darned near lifted off the chair. Who knew spreading a little encouraging cheer, he'd hit the information gathering jackpot. "You know him?"

"As a matter of fact, I do." She made the admission proudly, as if the connection was some badge of honor.

Vince flicked a hand toward the building across the street. "You're a patron of the arts?"

She didn't bother to look over. "Not really."

He waited in silence while she took a sip of coffee. Lowering the cup, she slowly ran her tongue over soft lips.

Shifting his position to ease a sudden, and inopportune, tightness in his jeans, Vince cleared his throat. "How do you know him, then?"

"He's my neighbor."

A fleeting image of Chief Lambert sporting a rare smile sailed to mind. *Told you something would turn up if you waited long enough, Miller.*

"Really? Must be quite a place where you live. According to the article, this guy is loaded."

She leveled an even gaze on his. "There are different tiers of luxury. We live in the same general complex."

Vince nodded as if he knew exactly what she was talking about. "Probably the place he keeps in town. Away from the mansion."

"Probably."

When she set her cup to one side, he immediately noticed it was almost empty. Where the hell was Teri with one of her complimentary refills? He was running out of time. Before he could figure out something else to talk about, his one and only source on an otherwise dead end case stood and began to pack up.

"Thank you for thinking of me for that job." She slid into her coat then stared down at him for one long moment. "Mr. um…"

"Reeves. Vincent Reeves." As the phony last name came to him, he stood, too, and extended his hand.

This offer of his she accepted as she laid incredible warmth and softness in his palm. He wrapped his fingers tight to keep her there. If only for another second, maybe two.

"I hope your friend finds a suitable candidate."

His brow creased as he looked up at her. "Candidate. Yeah."

With a slight jerk, she pulled her hand free. "For her daycare."

The topic of their initial conversation swooped through to take hold in his suddenly clouded brain. "I'm sure she will."

"I admire your confidence. Nice talking to you." She cinched the belt on her coat and incredible curves bloomed.

His attention followed the motion. "My pleasure." *I wish.* "Nice talking to you." With a hasty smile, he nodded, then let his gaze stay with her all the way to the door.

Once there, she paused to pull the scarf from her coat pocket, and something fell out to hit the floor. Vince didn't move as she lifted the scarf onto her head and tied the ends under her chin. She opened the door to the patter of lingering raindrops and swish of a passing car on drenched pavement. In the distance, a darkening sky lit up. A few seconds later, thunder rolled low.

The storm was moving on.

Chapter Two

"Miss Raines. I have a few questions."

Sydney slammed to a halt just outside her local Marty's Market grocery store, blindsided by the microphone wielding man who stood in her path.

"William Fosmore WWTT-TV." His words cut through the cool, morning air of early fall. "Aren't you the former Chief Financial Officer of the now defunct On Trend chain of clothing stores?"

He thrust the hand mike forward and grazed her lower lip.

"Yes." She glanced up as his bearded accomplice shouldered a camera he aimed at her face. "What do you want with me?"

The wiry man with thick dark hair pulled his mike back. "One day all eighteen greater Detroit stores were open, supposedly doing a thriving business. The next day was a total one-eighty. Employees arrived for work to find doors locked and the lights off. That was ten days ago, with no explanation from Brock Richardson, the owner. Our viewers deserve to know why. Can you explain what happened?"

She scrunched her mouth in distaste as he shoved the mike at her again. "I can't. I don't know what happened." Exactly what she'd told the workers who called her at headquarters that awful day, panic rampant in angry voices, when their paychecks bounced. "I was as surprised by the closures as anyone."

"Some would find that hard to believe. Wouldn't you? Surely you know something." He went on to grill her, snapping the microphone back and forth like a miniature juggernaut. "A lot of our citizens were thrown out of their jobs."

Like I wasn't. She kept the smart retort to herself.

People going in and out of the store lingered near the shopping carts lined up by the automatic doors. Curious onlookers who'd paused to witness her public humiliation. After she spent the last week pounding the job availability pavement to no avail, Sydney had ventured out on a Saturday to pick up a few necessities.

Only to run into this.

"How can you say you were surprised?"

"Because it's true. I really don't have any answers." A heavy rain from the day before had left its mark. She side-stepped some murky, standing water in an attempt to push by him. "If you'll excuse me, please."

He sidestepped right along with her. "Surely you aren't completely in the dark. You had to know some of what went on."

"Honestly, I didn't. I wasn't in the loop." She left it at that. No need to share she'd practically given her soul to a position that dissolved without warning. "I'm in the same situation as so many other employees."

"Don't you mean former employees?"

She cradled her brown bagged groceries in her left arm then clenched her right hand into a fist she took care to keep at her side. "Former employees, if you must."

"I must." He flashed a decidedly plastic smile as

determination glittered in suddenly darkened eyes. “You worked at company headquarters, as Chief Financial Officer no less, yet claim to know nothing about any of the company’s financial problems?”

The unavoidable truth made her stomach tighten. She winced before lifting her gaze to look directly into his. “No, sir. I didn’t.”

Once considered by some to be top in her field, should she have known what was about to happen? Suspected *something* when her boss brought in Belinda Simms as his new assistant? Fresh out of grad school with her shiny new MBA and, based on the non-stop smiles Brock began to sport shortly after her arrival, a profound eagerness to please. Which undoubtedly went both ways. It still irritated her that Brock bought Belinda a similar necklace when she admired the one Sydney always wore.

All things too late for her to care about now, with the company’s assets gone and the happy couple conveniently MIA.

“What’s next for you, then?”

She glanced down. The microphone was back near her chin. “I have no idea.”

Only half true. She refused to waste time lamenting the unfortunate turn of events and had hit the ground running. Honing her networking skills to perfection, she’d put them to the test amassing the names of potential employers. All safely entered and secure in a convenient data app on her smartphone. Her electronic version of a little black book, contained detailed information on various companies she’d learned about either online or through former business contacts.

Those, that is, who still took her calls.

"No idea at all?" Had his tone softened, or did her desperation for a break of some kind have her imagination playing tricks?

None. "I'm sure the authorities who have launched an investigation may soon have answers for you and your viewers."

He jerked the mike away. "An investigation? You've obviously been contacted. What did they want to know?"

Once again, the mike was thrust under her chin. "I have no further comment."

She'd said too much already. The bag of groceries she held had grown heavier. Securing its entire weight in front of her, she made another try to push by him.

He stood fast. "I have a few more questions."

"Sorry, I have no more answers."

"How can you say that when…Miss Raines. Sydney! We're not done here."

Speak for yourself. Lowering her head, she sprinted off toward her car. Unless the idiot grabbed her from behind, she'd make an escape.

"The public deserves to know." His breathless voice went on from behind her.

Dodging random puddles in the parking lot, she kept going. With any luck he wouldn't have the stamina to talk, dodge and run after her at the same time. Practically diving head first into her Mustang, she dumped her solitary bag on the passenger seat, slammed the door, then fumbled to insert her key in the ignition.

That's when her luck ran out.

"You owe the public an explanation." The unappeased reporter rushed up to pound on the driver side window like a starving grizzly after fresh meat.

Back off or I'll run over your toes! Holding in the shout, she pulled her car forward with a jolt then cranked the wheel and sped out of the parking lot. Driving like a woman possessed, she somehow managed to stay within the speed limit. In case he followed her, she took a few necessary detours through some of the more up-scale Manderfield Township neighborhoods, repeatedly flicking her gaze up to the rear-view mirror.

Her palms started to sweat as she noticed a big, white late model Buick was on her tail, similar to the one her ex drove. Which was, no doubt, repossessed after she quit making the payments. With a quick blink, she re-focused on her driving as she steered down another tree-lined side street.

Now I'm just being paranoid.

Blame it on her roots. Veering through a small traffic circle, she glanced in the mirror again. The only car in view was a huge, red Cadillac that promptly turned right into a wide driveway.

Taking no chances, she drove around for a while longer, then gunned it up her own driveway when she finally arrived home. She immediately turned off the ignition, then didn't start breathing again until the automatic garage door closed all the way down behind her with a thump. The cooling engine ticked as she sat in the blessed dark. With her heart still pounding, it took a moment before she could peel her hands off the steering wheel as she continued to seethe.

By God, she'd show that William Fosmore and so many others just like him, put her anger to good use and devote all her efforts to finding another job. Surely she had a few promising contacts to revisit. One by one, she pried her fingers free. After dropping the keys into her purse, she collected her purchases and climbed out of the car. Entering the back door of the high priced Winsome Gate condominium she could no longer afford, she dumped her groceries on the counter as she came through the kitchen, then walked to the front door and stuck her head out only long enough to collect her mail.

"Oh, Sydney. Good, you're home." Ida Flannery, her elderly next-door neighbor, called over from her adjoining porch. Her prized pet Orson, slanted green cat eyes in a fluffy ball of white angora, held securely in both arms. "I just saw you on the news."

Envelopes and assorted junk mail in hand, Sydney brought her head up. *That didn't take long.* "They must have streamed it live. How'd I look?"

Ida sent a compassionate smile her way. "You looked great. You always do." The reassuring smile fell. "Too bad those folks won't leave you alone." Her kindly neighbor was one of the few people she knew who believed Sydney was innocent in the whole ugly debacle. A fact she shared with all who would listen, along with details she *thought* she knew about Sydney's lack of involvement.

"It's not easy being a scapegoat." She wrapped her velour sweatshirt more tightly around her middle.

The on-line media threats received now and then she could handle. Losing a once sterling business reputation; not so much.

"You looked cute with your hair pulled back like that in a high pony tail. Younger."

"Thank you." She touched the band around her

chestnut hair. At almost thirty, she often thought it was high time to give up on the youthful hairstyle. For whatever reason, she never did. "I was out running errands. I never expected to be broadcast on live television."

"You sounded rather frazzled."

All she could manage was a weak shrug. "He caught me off guard."

"That was obvious."

Even as Ida seemed to expect more, Sydney wasn't up to any further sharing. "How's Orson doing? Home for a change, I see."

Though frowned upon by the Winsome Gate hierarchy, Ida usually allowed Orson free rein around the hallowed grounds. And the crafty feline took full advantage.

"Yes, he is." Ida strolled over then came to a stop beside her. "I have no idea why, but when this little rogue decides to come home, he insists he wants in your townhouse not mine."

"Bless his misguided little heart." Sydney stroked under the animal's fuzzy white chin. "It's partially my fault. The first time Orson stopped by, I gave him some tuna I had."

"That makes me feel somewhat better." She hefted the portly cat more securely in her arms. "Be warned, though. Once you start feeding him, he's yours for life."

For the first time that day, Sydney was able to smile. "The companionship might be nice. At least until I find a job."

Absently leafing through the stack of window envelopes, mostly bills, she worked to shut out images of being old, gray, and still very broke.

Ida put a hand on her arm. "If nothing else, you could do what I did, honey. Find a man who's loaded. Then working wouldn't be an issue for you."

Sydney's depressing thoughts scattered at the advice, though she retained the presence of mind to nod. "That's true."

From previous conversations, she'd learned the woman's late husband Bernie owned a highly successful chain of taco restaurants. Past tense. Not one who cared to get her hands dirty—to quote Ida directly—she'd sold the results of the man's life work for a hefty profit shortly after his demise.

"It's really not a problem supporting myself." She kept up the smile hoping Ida wouldn't take offense. "I'd go crazy if I didn't have work to keep me busy."

Though she had to admit she didn't totally miss the stress and pressure of being one of the first women CFOs in a once prosperous national chain. During her break up with Mark, work had kept her sane.

"To each his own, I suppose." Ida sniffed through a well made-up, buffed, and polished nose as she turned her attention to Orson.

"I suppose." Sydney's congenial attitude began to fail.

There was no question her father would allow her to return under his roof while she got back on her feet—even welcome her with opened arms. As she thought of her sole living parent, another smile formed, only to quickly disappear. *Not an option.* Though she loved her dad dearly, along with all he stood for, no way could she bring herself to return to that particular fold.

Mindful Ida continued to stare, she forced

optimism into her voice. “I have made one connection recently at a local pet store. They seemed interested in what I had to offer.”

“Well, that sounds promising.” Ida absently stroked Orson’s back. “If not that, something will come along for you soon.”

Though her heart wasn’t totally in it, Sydney nodded. “I appreciate the well-wishes.”

Lest she seem too needy, she chose not to share that the HR head at one of On Trend’s closest competitors was very encouraging when Sydney took a leap of faith and contacted her by phone.

“I saw that official looking vehicle out in front of your place the other day.” Ducking her head, Ida stepped closer and lowered her voice. “I wasn’t surprised you alluded to being contacted in your television interview.”

Sydney blew out a breath. *They were back to that.* An idle comment made under duress already returned to haunt her. There was no sense lying to Ida. One way or the other, she’d find out the truth. “I have.”

“What did they want to know?”

“If I knew anything.”

“What did you tell them?”

“There wasn’t much I could tell them.”

She’d been courteous to the officers who came by. The ones who grilled her on the details of Brock’s disappearance, then did their best to not scoff at her blank stare response. How was she supposed to know where the company owner was? It didn’t take a financial genius to determine the books had been cooked. Obviously a completely separate set from the ones Sydney was responsible for. That hardly spared her from an extensive, and very official interview. The worst was she detested having her honesty and integrity questioned by anyone.

"What did they say about that?"

Sydney gave Ida a half smile. "Not much. Except to inform me I was a person of interest."

"That sounds serious."

"Person of interest is another way of saying they had no real leads in their case."

"I see."

"Well, I really need to get back to my job search." Sydney didn't try to stop it when her voice fell. "Such as it is."

Ida's comforting hand rested on her arm. "You'll do fine eventually. I'm sure of it."

"Me too, Ida. Good-bye, Orson." Sydney backed through the door she closed tight then clicked the deadbolt into place. Turned back into the room, she flicked her wrist. "Take that!"

The offensive stack of letters sailed upward then drifted to the floor as she fought the urge to rip the damned things into a thousand tiny shreds. Better yet, she'd turn on the gas-powered hearth and reduce the paper to worthless ash.

"Who am I kidding? I'm no deadbeat." She owed these creditors and, somehow, would figure out how to pay them.

Suddenly on a mission, she scooped up the envelopes she slapped down on the end table then strode to the kitchen. Snatching up her purse, she rifled through its contents for her phone. *Oh no!* Her breath caught, and her stomach knotted when she came up empty. Undeterred, she tossed her purse aside and made a beeline for the front hall closet. Once there, she yanked open the white louvered door, rummaged through various garments hung on the rod until she found her trench-coat, and slipped her right hand into the pocket on one side then the other. *Nothing!* Ice water filled her veins. Forget the phone. That could be replaced. Her precious stash of potential employers was gone to who knew where.

"Probably in a trash heap somewhere about to be bulldozed under." Her spine went rigid, and she stood stock still to breathe deep. Right now, she didn't have time to give into the sheer panic about to claw through her.

"I absolutely refuse to be forced back to square one in this damned job search I've been thrust into." She shut the closet with a thud. "Refuse. Do you hear?"

The irritation in her tone echoed in the spacious room. Closing her mouth, she glanced around. *Does who hear? Who in the hell am I talking to?*

"Real good. Alone and talking to yourself. Not a good sign. Complete insanity must be just around the corner. Keep it up and the men in white coats will come to haul you away."

Plopped down on the plush gold loveseat, an heirloom of her grandmother's, she retrieved her laptop from underneath.

Square one, here I come.

At this point, all she could do was try to rebuild, from memory, the list of potential employers she'd worked so diligently to create. Failing that, there was no other choice but to scour the internet for the hundredth time in search of all possible job opportunities.

"Maybe even at a daycare if I get desperate enough." Her fingers stilled on the keyboard as her thoughts strayed to the guy from Anton's Bistro she'd met the day before. *The drop dead gorgeous one with a definite compassionate streak.*

"If nothing else, it might give me a chance to get to know him better." A small smile escaped as her doorbell chimed. "Don't tell me it's Ida again."

Pushing to her feet, she walked toward the front door. Thanks to the one-way security glass along the right side of the entrance, she could scrutinize visitors with anonymity. Living alone, she did so on a routine basis. Except, her first glimpse out the special glass hardly revealed her elderly next-door neighbor, and she let out a gasp. The man who'd recently inched into her thoughts was on the other side of her door. For what, she couldn't imagine. But, there he was, standing in front of her. With his head up and his eyes directed forward, he appeared to be a man who had a keen awareness of his surroundings.

Who's definitely in charge.

Taking a step back, she shook her head. Not that she really cared for that particular trait in members of the opposite sex. *However...* She did have to smile. *Despite that one personality flaw, he sure is good looking. Dark hair and, incredible blue eyes. Strong chin with the hint of a rather appealing cleft.* She indulged in a lingering survey down the rest of the package. Those jeans on him were just snug enough to ignite any woman's imagination. A red Henley shirt, two buttons opened at the neck, stretched across a solid chest. Similar to the way his black leather jacket hugged extremely broad shoulders.

The doorbell dinged a second time. After a quick blink, she shut down her assessment. With one hand on the knob, she bit her lower lip. The man had a name. Brow furrowed, it took a moment for her memory to kick in. Vincent, he'd said. Vincent Reeves.

Keeping the chain in place, she opened the door as far as the links would allow. "Yes?"

Not only was his smile immediate, those captivating blue eyes of his lit with definite approval the moment they landed on her. *Correction.* Whatever he could see of her through a tiny crack in her door.

"Do you remember me?"

Her heart struck a definite upbeat rhythm. *The real question—could I forget?* "I remember you."

"Great!" The smile expanded to a full-fledged grin that brought out some charming laugh lines around his eyes.

She put a hand flat against her stomach at an unexpected flutter. A physical sensation she hadn't experienced since way before Mark left.

Check that, since I kicked the selfish SOB out.

"I was hoping you would."

Glancing up at the flesh and blood male in front of her, she shut down all recollections of the past. "Why are you here?"

"I thought you might need this." He handed an item she immediately recognized through the meager opening.

"My cell!" She snatched her phone away from him first and remembered her manners next. "Thank you. Where did you find it?"

"It fell—you must have dropped it at the coffee shop."

"The coffee shop, of course."

The last time she remembered having her phone was at Anton's where she sat alone, feeling oh so very sorry for herself. For once in her life, she appreciated being rescued.

"I found it on the floor after you left."

She hauled herself back from fantasies of conquering heroes and maidens in distress as she unlatched the chain and swung the door wide. "My itinerary for next week is in here. Future interviews I plan to line up." Desperation leaked into her voice, and she shut her mouth.

Cold calls I must make.

"Sounds like you're moving right along with this job search of yours."

With a tight hold on the precious phone, she spoke before thinking. "Would you like to come in?"

"Sure."

Surprised at herself making the invitation, she hastened to tack on a brief qualifier. "For a minute, anyway."

After all, how much impact could he actually have on her life if she offered him some hospitality for only a minute.

He didn't waste any time taking her up on her offer as he stepped over the threshold. The man was definitely taller than she expected.

With an effort, she again remembered her manners. "Can I take your coat?"

"Thanks."

As his buttery soft jacket landed in her arms, she slid her hand along the satin lining. Her fingers lingered for a moment on its warmth, before she hung it in the closet and turned his way. “How did you find me?”

“To be honest, it wasn’t all that easy.”

“My number is listed.”

“It wouldn’t have mattered. All I had to go on was your first name. When I asked our friend Teri if she knew your last, I got a deer in the headlights reaction.”

She had to smile at that picture. “As friendly as they all are in there, we never seem to get beyond the superficial.”

“Sydney. It’s a unique name for a woman.” His gaze roamed down to her toes and back.

A definite heat blossomed through her in the wake of his stare. “I think my father wanted another boy. That was all you had to go on?”

“Back at the coffee shop, you mentioned you were Randall Curan’s neighbor. Since he’s essentially a public figure, his whereabouts were relatively easy to track. I thought I might luck out just heading over this morning.” His gaze lowered to the floor before he looked up again and met hers. “Unfortunately, your doorman wasn’t exactly eager to help. In fact, he did everything to avoid helping but plead the fifth. I was lucky he slipped up and admitted you lived here when I first asked.”

“Glenn can be a p…” She stopped herself with the word pain on the tip of her tongue. “Pretty full of himself at times.”

His brow quirked in question. “Why’s that?”

“He can be a little possessive.” Lips pursed, she shook her head. “He’s one of those who considers himself God’s gift to women.”

“So he’s not a boyfriend or anything.”

A laugh slipped out she didn’t try to stop. “Not

hardly. And definitely not him."

"I'll have to remember that." He stepped slightly forward as he spoke. "At any rate, despite his lack of cooperation, once I found the right residential complex, all I had to do was start knocking on doors. Simple trial and error."

"You did all that for me?" Appreciation swelled in her chest. She put a hand over her heart to hold it there for a moment. "You're very resourceful."

"It's my . . ." He shrugged. "The lady next door just now was very helpful."

"Really?" At the knowledge he'd talked to ready and willing to tell all Ida, a flash of dread struck fast and deep.

"She's quite a character."

"She is that. I was going to make myself a sandwich." Sloughing off what remained of some nagging unease, her gaze flicked to the cherry wood clock on the mantel above the fireplace. "It's almost noon."

Why the hell was she offering to feed him? That usually led to unnecessary involvement. Case in point, Orson. Once you started, you'd never get rid of them.

"I planned to fix tuna salad."

"One of my favorites."

"Make yourself at home." Turning toward the kitchen, she had no clue why she said that.

Shrugging the thought away, she went immediately to the refrigerator to open the door.

"Anything I can do to help?"

She caught a sharp inhale at that deep voice so close and pulled her head out. Only a few feet away, he leaned against the serving island in the center of the room.

Commander Andrew Raines, Michigan State Police-retired, Sydney's over protective father, would have an absolute stroke if he could see her—rather them—now.

Don't trust anyone you don't know. Never invite a stranger into your home.

"Get the bread out of the pantry, if you would." With her hands full of a jar of mayonnaise and container of relish, shutting the refrigerator door with one shoulder, she angled her head toward the full-length cupboard to his right. "It's on the top shelf."

"Got it." He'd already lifted down the loaf of bakery fresh sourdough to set on the counter. "Knives?"

After another head incline from her, he found the silverware drawer on the first try. It was as if he belonged here.

"You saved me some wear and tear stress on my psyche, worrying about what I was going to do next." The items she carried made light thumps as she set them on the counter. She glanced up at him. "In my never-ending job search."

"You seem pretty self-sufficient." As their gazes locked, his encouraging smile revealed more irresistible laugh lines around the edges of his eyes.

"I try." She turned her full attention back to lunch preparation.

By the time she had the sandwiches made, sliced in half, and put on plates she set on the table, he had discovered the jar of sweet pickles in the refrigerator door and the gallon container of milk on the shelf just below. Moving fast, she pulled two clean glasses out of another cupboard to the left of the sink before he beat her to that, too. One in each hand, she set them on the table beside the plates.

"Do you want a full or half?" He had the milk container poised over the empty glass in front of her.

Though she opened her mouth, it took a few seconds for any words to form then come out. "Half, please."

He poured her glass exactly half full then put twice as much into his. "I'm the oldest of five, three sisters and another brother." Walking over to the refrigerator, he put the container back where he got it. "Guess I just naturally take over meal preparation. Force of habit." He returned to take the seat across from her.

"I would have guessed you were the oldest. You act like a true caregiver."

His initial response was a nod. "I've heard that before. What is it you do? What kind of job are you looking for?"

"Something in finance. My background is as a comptroller, CFO. That kind of thing."

"A far cry from changing dirty diapers." He nodded again. "I can see why you weren't interested in what I had to offer."

The smile he tacked on at the end sent a second definite flutter through her. He put both arms on the table and relaxed his shoulders. Immediately, he appeared incredibly harmless. And just as incredibly appealing. A vision of *him* changing dirty diapers streaked into her mind.

He'd probably be good at it.

"Though I may keep your offer in mind." She picked up her sandwich then took a bite.

"I'll remember that."

With a polite nod, her attention strayed out the window while she chewed. A couple of blue jays swooped down onto the bird feeder on her back deck, causing a small flock of sparrows to scatter. After she swallowed, her gaze returned to meet his.

"Getting my phone back is a true Godsend. I was about to be forced to pick up where I was at the beginning of the fiasco called losing my job, making cold calls. Not to mention the expense of replacing it."

"How long have you been unemployed?"

"Almost two weeks, although with the struggle I've had, it seems more like two years."

"That's got to be extremely difficult."

"You have no idea." She warmed to the sympathy he offered. "I was the CFO of the On Trend Corporation."

"The stores that went belly up?"

"More specifically down like so many dominoes."

"Tough enough to lose a job. The way losing yours happened had to be especially hard."

She idly munched on her sandwich before she spoke. "The chain sure didn't close peacefully. The local press is having a field day covering the human interest angle of a story that struck close to home for so many." The fact he seemed willing to listen prompted her to keep talking. "The way my old job ended is the biggest obstacle to my finding another one. Apparently, the owner of the company set up a dummy corporation then cooked the books to cover it up. I had nothing to do with that." She set her sandwich down and went on. "As CFO of the corporation, I was suspected of wrong doing. Guilt by association."

"Yeah. I—" On an abrupt stop, he cleared his

throat. "The situation got some pretty extensive notice in the media."

He turned his attention to devouring the food she'd given him.

That he was aware of some background surrounding the current misfortune in her life brought an odd sense of comfort. "Not something I ever expected to go through."

"If I hear of anything like you're looking for, I'll be sure to let you know. Maybe do what I can to help."

Moistening suddenly dry lips, she met his gaze and swallowed. "That's nice of you."

"You seem to have pretty good instincts." Though he smiled, his gaze shifted right.

From out of the blue, the horde of warnings and cautions she'd grown up with about talking to strangers flooded into her brain. Add to that, she wasn't used to getting close to people—especially men—at this fast a rate. Time to send the well-fed stray on his way. Nicely and politely, of course.

"I'd offer you dessert, but I'm afraid my cupboards are more than a little bare lately."

"Not a problem for me. I rarely eat dessert, anyway."

She stood to collect their now empty dishes, except for the glass he still held on to, and headed for the sink. If she managed some degree of separation, surely he'd take the hint. Rinsing the plates and her glass, one by one she loaded them and the used tableware in the dishwasher as her mind worked out a fitting scenario.

Next, she'd shut the door then straighten to rest her hands on the counter for a second.

When she turned around, he'd have stood too.

She'd thank him again for coming to her rescue. In the figurative sense.

His response would be to thank her kindly for the lunch…and leave.

Chapter Three

In the process of draining the milk from his glass, Vince froze. *This was it.* The inevitable kiss off.

Thanks for your trouble and good-bye.

He shifted his gaze to the right as he moved to rise and nearly choked on his latest swallow. Sydney bent to access the opened dishwasher. Smooth, well-worn denim tightened around her hips to caress some damned fine curves. He helped himself to a long, brazen look at one incredibly nice ass. *Round. Inviting. And…*

"I do wish I had more to offer you."

As she turned around, he jerked his attention to her face. At the cool gaze leveled on his, with her brows quirked in expectation.

Ball's in your court, Miller. Don't screw it up. "Good luck getting another job." The chair legs scraped as he stood then held up his near empty glass. "Here's hoping you find one to suit you."

Give me the facts as you know them, and I'll move on.

His job was to gather relevant information. One of the—correction—*the* main reason he was here in the first place. To talk with friends and neighbors of the suspect, in this case Randall Curan. Get a handle on who and what he was. All of which he could pretty much perform in his sleep. Yet hadn't accomplished any of it by now because?

Because so far, I haven't done much more than admire Sydney's ass.

"I appreciate you taking the trouble to find me and bring my phone back."

At the lady's voice a second time, he mentally skidded back to the here and now. "Just doing what anyone else would have done."

Leaning against the counter, she crossed her arms. "Not everyone. I have to tell you, I had visions of my cell being lost forever."

"Obviously that didn't happen."

"No. It didn't."

Move it along, Miller. Interrogation 101. "So how long have you lived here at Winsome Gate?"

Her raised brows lowered, and she blinked. "I bought this townhouse going on two years ago."

"Two years." Her statement confirmed what her next-door neighbor had said.

"I was transferred around so often at my former job, renting was just easier."

He could certainly relate. Having lived in the same sterile high rise for close to ten years now, he had nothing more to show for it than a massive collection of rent receipts.

"Sometimes jobs can be a pain." He took her weak smile and nod as signs of agreement. "With what they demand, we tend to identify what we do with who we are. Let our jobs define us." *Or take over our lives.*

"When I was finally brought here to the company's national headquarters, I wanted something permanent, so I purchased this."

"I can understand why." Vince nodded. Two people on the same philosophical page. "Good to put down roots."

"I thought so at the time." Lowering her arms, she clasped her fingers together. "That's why I'm determined to find another job in the vicinity. I don't want to relocate again."

"Can't blame you for that. This is a really nice place you have. These Winsome Gate Condominiums are first rate." *Now or never, Miller. Get the job done.* "You mentioned Randall Curan lives around here, too?"

Her chin lifted. "He does."

"To be honest, I'm a writer." Setting down the glass, he took a step toward her. Just one, then stopped. "I do freelance work."

"That must be interesting."

"It has its moments." Despite a sudden tug of regret, he forged ahead with the lie. "My current work is extremely so. Interesting, I mean. I'm doing a magazine article on him. I snagged an assignment from *Trending Art Magazine,* a relatively new publication." *So new, getting the assignment was a snap.*

"Why did you choose him?" A more intense gaze settled on his face.

She's got me there. He shifted his weight. "You said it yourself when we met. He's a philanthropist and a very nice man. People like reading about things like that. Gives them hope."

"That's as good a reason as any, I suppose."

He brought his hands up, palms open for emphasis. "It sure would help if I could get to know him."

"Up close and personal?"

"Yeah."

She broke eye contact to glance past him out the window, where her attention remained for a very long time.

Probably thinking a man with an ulterior motive. Can't blame her for that.

"I believe people like Randall deserve their privacy." She brought her gaze back to catch his as she spoke. "Surely there's enough information about him out in the public domain you can use? Remember that newspaper you let me borrow?"

"I do."

"Perfect example."

"Old news. Common stuff. I want to write something different. Unique." He stopped talking to swallow. "That's only possible if I get to know the—"

"Man and his habits?"

"Exactly."

"Which is extremely personal." The eye contact didn't waver. "And intrusive on your part, don't you think?"

Vince opened his mouth then shut it. The last thing he needed to do was argue. Come on strong and spook her out of any further cooperation.

Time to back off. Appear non-threatening.

Like when he'd posed as the bait to flush out a mugger who terrorized a local mall. Slowly, he lowered his gaze at the same time as he let his shoulders slump. "You're right there. Everyone has a right to privacy. Especially on their own turf."

"I'm glad you agree."

"You make a strong argument." His most charming smile would work well here. He brought it out full force.

Her unchanged expression told him she wasn't impressed "I read somewhere that only a small percentage of freelance writers make enough from their writing to support themselves."

He kept up the smile as he made sure to look her in the eye. "Until I write and sell the Great American Novel, these magazine articles help pay the bills."

"What else do you do?"

He licked his lips then swallowed. *What the hell is going on?* He'd worked UC a good part of his career. Detective Vince Miller was legendary among his peers for his ability to blend in—to become his cover identity—for God's sake. Where was the all-important detached indifference he'd come to depend on? A talent that had always served him well in the past.

He cast around in his recent history for a vocation he'd know something about. Help him talk intelligently. The memories he pulled up came from a time prior to his police days. P.I. work, along with washing dishes in a high-end restaurant, paid the bills when he put himself through the academy.

"Investigations." Once the word came out of him, he had no choice but to run with it.

"What kind of investigations?"

"Private. Insurance frauds. Divorce. More accurately pre-divorce, getting the goods on the wandering spouse."

"You're the guy who rats out the cheating husband to a suspicious wife."

"You'd be surprised how many times it's the other way around." Warming to the subject, he rested his palm on the countertop. "Most of the spouses I've dealt with pretty much know what's going on. They hire me to provide proof positive. Evidence they can take to court."

"The work you do must be very lonely."

Her sympathetic tone along with the suggestion of compassion, blindsided him. Talk about hitting the nail on the head and she didn't even know it. For the next few nanoseconds, all he could do was clam up and mull over her comment. The law enforcement job had taken a toll on him over the years. In the early days, what with the excitement in pursuit of the bad guys, he'd been too busy fulfilling the oath he'd taken to serve and protect to think much about being alone.

A series of musical strums from the other room interrupted his thoughts.

"That's my cell." Pushing off from the counter, she wiped her hands along the outside of her thighs and headed on a run toward the other room.

Vince took time to deposit his glass in the sink before he followed. She held the phone to her ear and had her back to him when he reached the living room.

"No, that's okay." Though the voice was strong, her shoulders sagged. "I totally understand your position. Of course. It was nice of you to call and let me know. Thank you again." With a quick sideways flick of her wrist, she tossed her phone to the couch. "For nothing."

Dropping her chin to her chest, she whooshed out a long, low breath just before her whole body began to shake.

Vince stepped up close behind her. "Bad news?"

With a slight jolt, she lifted her head. "You could say that."

"I take it you didn't get the job."

After a hasty look over one shoulder, she pivoted to face him, eyes glistening with tears. "You're very perceptive."

He indicated her phone with a tilt of his head. "What did they say?"

"Same as usual. They couldn't get beyond the circumstances surrounding my previous employer. The suspected criminal actions still pending." For the first time since he'd known her, her voice faltered. "All the creative accounting at On Trend that's now being investigated took place at some dummy company, *after* it left my control. Except no one wants to believe that." She took in a shaky breath and aimed her watery gaze toward the ceiling. "There's something inherently unfair about giving your all to a company for years only to be cast aside."

"You weren't cast aside. Your job was yanked out from under you."

She brought the back of one hand up to swipe at each cheek in turn. "At first I was in denial. I figured losing my job the way I did was a fluke. A huge mistake, and my position along with my reputation, would be restored once the whole unfortunate misunderstanding got sorted out. Then irritation set in, to be quickly followed by anger and frustration." The small laugh she let out rang hollow and empty. "Right now, I'm just plain scared."

"Hey. Something will turn up. You only need one."

Her still damp gaze swung away to take in their surroundings. "Tell that to the bank who holds my mortgage."

Damn! He hated it when a woman cried. A few random tears and he was toast.

"Look. It can't be all that bad." He took a step back then clenched his jaw and moved close again. "Nothing lasts forever. Everyone deserves a break. You'll get yours soon enough."

Platitudes? All you've got here are platitudes?

As if acting on its own, his hand came up to rest on her shoulder. He slid his palm down her arm before he took her hand in his. Twining their fingers together seemed second nature. He ended with a squeeze of reassurance. Without much thought, he brought his other hand under her chin to tilt up her face.

She raised her gaze to meet his. Brown eyes glistened behind a new supply of tears. "If nothing else, I appreciate your optimism."

Vince could have sworn his heart skipped a beat, maybe two. The trust swimming in her gaze was unmistakable. Trust he didn't exactly deserve just now.

Unable to look at her straight on, he took the next best course of action and lowered his lids to shut out visions of despair he was powerless to make better. Guilt bore into him like a well-tightened screw. He did his best to ignore the neat little wound. The next thing he knew, his mouth brushed over hers, taking a sample of incredibly soft lips. Warm. Inviting.

Her tiny sigh of acceptance spurred him on. The hand under her chin slid along her throat to caress the back of her neck. His other hand released hers to wrap around her waist and draw her into him.

Compassion, concern, empathy, support. The motherlode of caring emotions flooded into him, one after the other after the other. So many and so fast, he was at a loss to process them all as they blew through.

Gentle arms circled his neck then stiffened to clasp together as she clung to him. Heat from their kiss ignited sparks of tiny electric currents to zip along his veins. Once shallow and relaxed breathing caught up in no time to the rising tempo of his heartbeat.

After a few incredible moments, and no time at all, she drew away and brought her hands up to rest flattened palms on his chest. Taking the hint, he dropped his arms to let her go, fully expecting to be clocked in the jaw. She'd be justified.

"That doesn't happen often." Her eyes shining, she released a nervous laugh.

"I'll say."

"As a rule, I don't let my emotions get the better of me."

"Yeah. Me, either."

Jesus, Miller, get a grip.

He did his damnedest to bring erratic breathing under control. "I'm sorry. I just…I don't know." He straightened and took a quick pace back from something that should never have occurred. Sure as hell couldn't take place again.

Raising her gaze to meet his, she favored him with a broad smile. "I can't tell you how much I needed that."

His eyes grew wide. "Really?"

"More than you know."

Damned if she didn't get me again. "Glad I could help." Instinct ordered him to move closer. He resisted.

She's not issuing an invitation for more, asshole. She's simply being honest.

The grin about to sneak out of him waned. *Honest.* Too bad he couldn't return the favor. Not yet anyway.

Can't be helped. Out of my hands. Duty before anything else, and all that crap.

"I wish you the best in finding another job, but

right now I really have to leave." Resigned he'd have to find another way to get close to Curan, he plowed through a sudden jumble of emotions to produce a half-assed smile. "Again, thanks for lunch."

"My pleasure." A wicked grin erupted. "Thanks for the kiss."

Despite better intentions his blood heated. "My, uh, you're welcome."

Time to get the hell out of here. He made a move toward the door.

"No wait!" She gazed out the window beside the front entrance, then hurried around him and had the door open before he got there. Instead of stepping aside to let him by, maybe slam it shut as he left, she peered out. "You're in luck."

"What?" He craned his neck to see what was going on. There was no traffic on the street that ran in front of her townhouse. A couple of teenaged girls jogged along the opposite sidewalk toward a man with a dog coming the other way.

"Mr. Curan's outside right now. Walking Buffy."

"Buffy?"

"His prized Irish Wolfhound. Come on, I'll introduce you." She reached back to take a firm grip of his hand then tugged him behind her.

What else could he do but follow? "Why the sudden change of heart? Or should I say, remind me to kiss you more often?"

She said nothing at first. Only her laughter, deep and true, floated back to surround him. "You said it yourself. Everyone deserves a break now and then. This is yours. We'll have to hurry, though, before he gets too far way. They're going at a pretty fast clip."

Vince and Sydney hit the bottom step still holding hands. A hearty gust of cool afternoon air slapped him in the face. Even without it, his cop instincts flooded in to take hold and assess the situation.

A man about Vince's height, maybe a little shorter, traveled along the sidewalk. A tall and slender gray dog on a leash padded beside him with its head up, gait steady. The subject's full length, tan leather coat swished from side to side, practically dragging the sidewalk. *Plenty of places to hide a weapon. Too many.*

He tugged on Sydney to slow her down then caught up again to walk beside her. She called a swift greeting when the joggers passed by. He gave a curt nod.

"Mr. Curan." She hauled on Vince's hand to move faster. "Wait a moment. Please."

"Yes?" He stopped and turned around, looping the leash and dog to his other side. "Yes? What is it?"

Vince retrieved his hand from Sydney's loosening grasp as he scanned Curan from head to toe and back while they approached. Unbuttoned, the coat flapped open in the wind. In full cop mode now, it took Vince a millisecond to complete a once over of the subject's lower extremities. Sandals! The dude wore sandals of all things. With socks, but still. *No worry about a weapon there.* His professional analysis continued. Tight fitting athletic pants in black, and an equally tight turtle neck. White. Damned near transparent. No evidence of a firearm there either.

"What can I do for you?" Curan's eyes remained distant, his expression notably vague. Up until his gaze slid from Vince to Sydney.

As they halted in front of him, she spoke first, "I'm your neighbor from across the way." She made a wide arm gesture toward her place. "We met once at a reception for the Friends of Forgotten Animals. My boss at the corporation I worked for at the time was a big contributor like you." She extended her hand toward him. "I'm Sydney Raines."

"Sydney, of course." He clasped gloved hands around hers as his eyes lit up. "How could I forget?"

Vince's gaze settled on the top of Curan's head and moved downward. Blond hair, blue eyes. What could be termed a pretty boy nose and mouth. Hence the women at his beck and call.

"Mr. Curan." She groped for Vince's arm and connected. "I'd like to introduce you to my friend Vincent Reeves."

Vince was already moving forward. "Great to meet you, Mr. Curan. I'm a huge fan."

The man's gaze shifted his way. Only because Vince made sure to quickly grab one of those gloved hands.

"Mr. Reeves is writing an article about you."

"A piece for a magazine." Vince stored more information away. Curan didn't make eye contact as they shared a brief handshake. *That doesn't mean he's not an art thief.* "You're an interesting figure."

"Hardly worthy of public attention." Despite the humble words, Curan's head rose a little higher, and his nostrils flared. The corners of his mouth twitched up.

Smile in place, Vince resigned himself to more necessary ego stroking. "Your gallery is fast becoming one of the largest in the country."

Which is what drew the attention of the feds in the first place.

"Of contemporary works." Curan let the leash sag

as his dog dutifully sat down beside its master.

"Your dog is beautiful." Sydney offered a palm, allowing the animal to take in her scent. "Buffy, right? I've heard you calling him."

"That's right. Short for Buffington." Curan's attention shifted her way.

In fact, his gaze roamed her body as if he owned it. With her focus on the dog, she missed the hasty once over. Vince didn't.

On instinct, he made a move to step between them, then tamped down on the overprotective urge and stayed put. *Easy. She's an attractive woman. Who wouldn't want to look?*

As Sydney knelt to befriend the dog, Vince zeroed in on the owner. "I'd appreciate the opportunity for an interview."

Curan dragged his attention away from Sydney's ass. "I could probably accommodate that. Who is it you write for?"

"*Trending Art Magazine*. It's very new. Online mostly. Circulation growing."

"I'm always glad to help the up and coming." His gaze left Vince to glide over Sydney again.

Might as well get things going. Vince willed his clenched jaw to loosen then retrieved the always present notebook and pen out of his breast pocket. Sydney glanced over with her brows drawn down but just as quickly looked away.

Vince sloughed off the action as irrelevant. "To get me started, if you don't mind." He glanced up wearing another congenial expression. "What first got you interested in art?"

"A woman."

The unlikely answer seemed to startle the man who gave it. Bringing his head up with a jerk, confusion settled in his eyes. Then a faint smile played around his lips as if he reviewed some internal memory. "I was in college."

"What woman?" With a final pat to the dog's head, Sydney straightened. "I'm sure she'd be flattered to learn she was your inspiration."

Curan's pupils dilated, the blue in his eyes flickered, became shadowed then cleared. "I doubt that."

"Where do most of your paintings come from?" Vince figured he may as well get the answer first hand.

The man quickly turned toward him. "To answer your second question, we dabble in the higher priced items for our customers who require it." He waved one hand in a dismissive gesture. "My real passion is helping young, untried artists achieve their dreams of recognition and possible wealth."

Sydney's gaze brightened. "That's a very noble ambition."

"Not an ambition. That suggests something to strive for not yet achieved. As I said, it's my passion. If I do say so myself, I'm very successful at it."

Vince shifted his weight and wrote more information in the notebook. "Exactly the angle my editor is looking for. How do you find your clientele?"

He cast Vince a look that bordered on disbelief. "Surely you jest. They find me, of course."

Jesus. Talk about overreaction. He nearly raised his lids in an elaborate eye roll then remembered to keep serious control. "Good point."

"Would you like a tour of Argentile, Mr. Reeves?"

Vince didn't need to force an enthusiastic smile. "A tour would be great."

Though he spoke to Vince, Curan's attention slid to Sydney. "The gallery is open from ten to eight. Every day but Monday, when we're closed."

Tell me something I don't know. He jotted the info down for show. "What day works best for you? When are you least busy?"

Curan gave a self-satisfied nod. "That's a tough question. These days, we're always busy." The smile grew as he turned toward Sydney. "Happily busy."

Vince pushed forward. "So?"

Curan looked over. "To be honest, Wednesdays can be a little slow."

"Wednesday." Vince made a final entry and put the notebook away.

"If that would work for you." Curan shrugged.

"That works fine for me."

"I wouldn't mind a tour myself." When Sydney spoke up, both men turned her way. "If neither of you mind."

"Mind?" Curan lifted both brows, and his eyes lit up again. "I certainly don't."

Though Vince sure welcomed the chance to see her, he was careful to do no more than nod. "As long as our host is on board."

"I'd love to have you." He blinked as his gaze swung from Sydney to Vince then back. "Both of you."

Vince resisted a sudden urge to tuck Sydney under his arm and escort her back to her door. He was making way too much out of a harmless, impromptu lip lock. An offer of comfort on his part taken to the extreme.

Save the over active protective instincts for those

who really need them.

Now that he'd made initial contact, though, the important thing was to keep it going. *All in due time.*

"Guess I should head out and get to work on my article." He put the pad and pen away then rubbed his hands together as if in anticipation of the event. "While my notes are still fresh."

Sydney turned to look up at him. "Thanks again for bringing back my cell."

"You gave me lunch, so we're even."

Curan came forward, hand extended. "Nice meeting you. Reeves, right?"

"Right." Vince made direct eye contact. "Curan."

"Yes." The hand fell away.

Vince flexed taut fingers as they stood face to face. Wild goose chase or not, there was something about this guy he didn't particularly like. He'd figure out what it was eventually. He always did.

After all. Wasn't that his job?

Chapter Four

Sydney steadied her cell phone between one ear and a shoulder as she fluffed up the throw pillows on her loveseat. "What is it now, Mark? And be quick. I have things to do."

"Hello. It's nice to talk to you, too." The charming—more like snake charming—voice of her ex slithered over the line. "We haven't done that in a while."

"What do you need?" She made no effort at all to conceal her irritation.

Since she'd just gotten off the phone after a late morning conversation with Vince, she wasn't about to give up the resulting good feelings for anyone, especially someone who meant nothing to her anymore. Her lips curved up at the previous memory. He'd forgotten his jacket the other day and wondered when it would be convenient for him to come over to pick it up. She'd countered with a breezy *anytime is fine*, to which he'd replied, 'How about six, then I can take you out to dinner?'

Despite who was on the other end of the phone this time, she held on to the smile from Vince's invitation. One more item to add to her growing list of good fortune coming her way.

"Are you ready to listen to reason?"

Her thoughts scattered. "What kind of reason?"

Already knowing what would come next, she asked anyway. Why, she had no idea.

"As I've said before. I want your wedding ring back."

"So, you do admit the ring belongs to me."

"You know what I meant."

"Unfortunately, I do." *More even than maybe you realize.*

"Still bitter, I see. Aren't you, Syds?"

Her jaw clenched at the long ago endearment. "Don't call me that. Please."

"It's getting chilly over there."

She rolled her eyes as she picked up the dust rag she'd set down when he first called. Mark had a laissez-faire attitude toward life. The complete opposite of the rigid, sometimes smothering environment where she grew up. At one time, that made him exactly what she sought in a soul mate.

Until his laid-back attitude went to the extreme.

"We had something good together once, Syds."

"Apparently once wasn't good enough to last forever."

"Too bad." An exaggerated sigh came over the line. "I've written a song we're trying to record. Studio time costs money, you know."

"Find a garage with decent acoustics and have at it."

"Don't tell me that ring is your most coveted piece of jewelry."

Okay. I won't.

On her knees, and busy rubbing polish into a table top, she offered no reply. After all, she had been raised to be a lady who swore only under exceptional circumstances. Sitting back, she set the dust cloth aside. As if on its own, her hand found the way to her cherished sapphire solitaire with its setting and chain of solid 24 karat gold. A birthday gift from her dad and brothers. Which probably cost much more than their family could afford at the time.

"Thought I'd give you a chance to reconsider."

She glared at the ceiling. "Not likely."

"Why are you being so negative, Syds?"

Though she said nothing, her blood pressure eked up a notch as she snatched up the dust cloth she ran vigorously over the table edge and down all four legs.

"In my mind I'm not asking for much." He never could stand the silent treatment.

"In my mind, you are."

"You could at least return the diamond I bought and paid for."

"And gave to me as a gift."

"I'm guessing you're not wearing it anymore."

"You have that right." She splayed her bare left hand out in front of her. "Why would I?"

"So why not give it back? That diamond didn't come cheap."

"For the first time since you called, I agree with you. I'm well aware of the expense, since I had to finish paying the bill for it." When he had the decency not to argue, she went on. "Just because I don't wear the ring anymore doesn't mean it's not important to me. In case you've forgotten, the setting that diamond is in belonged to my grandmother. That is my sole reason for hanging on to it."

"I should have gotten a smaller stone in a different setting."

"You should have maybe kept working." The breath she paused to take stuck in her throat, and she coughed.

"That's not fair."

"I think it's more than fair. I understand you moved around with me and the job I had, but when you finally landed a job of your own that paid well, plus offered benefits and a pension—security for the future—you walked away one day because…" She moved on to vigorously scrub the matching end table to a decent shine. "What was it again?"

"You never understood my dreams." His voice grew louder. Par for the course when reality intruded on his life. "Let alone supported me in fulfilling them."

"Oh, but you're wrong. I did support you. Literally. I worked while you sat home all day to await the 'arrival of the muse'." She quoted the term he always used to justify simple laziness. "While I worked to pay the bills and put food on the table."

Her voice elevated in volume as she lamented one of the many problems that had finally scuttled their extremely short marriage. She craved security in her life. He didn't. The sad part, she *would* have stood behind his dreams. If he'd only made some effort to plant at least one foot in reality—worked somewhere, making something—while he sought to fulfill them.

Or so she believed. Until he crossed a line he never should have. Did what no man had a right to do to a woman.

"You're an unreasonable bitch!" When all else failed he always resorted to name calling. Or worse.

She wasn't about to take the bait. "You're entitled to your opinion."

"Half of what we earned in our marriage is mine. I don't care what that damned judge determined."

"I'm not going to argue with you over an issue we both know will never be resolved." Hard as it was to do, she kept her voice slow and soft.

He hadn't made any real effort to understand her the entire time they were married. It was a sure bet he wouldn't try at all now that they weren't.

"This isn't over, you know. If I have to sue you for what's rightfully mine, I will."

Clamping her mouth shut, she closed her eyes to breathe deep and count to ten. "We're done here, Mark."

"Don't think I won't."

"Good-bye." She disconnected with a finger punch and tossed down the phone. "Knock yourself out. Because I have more important things going on."

For the next couple of hours, she cleaned house with a vengeance. All her furniture and floors got the attention she hadn't had the time, or inclination, to give them for quite a while. A grin stretched her mouth as she stowed the vacuum in the hall closet and headed for a shower. Things certainly were looking up for her these days.

Because of a man who'd come into my life so wonderfully unexpected.

****

Savory scents of tangy tomato sauce, rich cheese and warm bread swirled in the air of the quaint Italian eatery as Vince and Sydney followed the fast-moving hostess into the main dining room.

"Pacelli's has always been my favorite spot to eat since the first day I moved here." Enjoying the warmth of his palm on her back, she glanced toward him as she spoke.

"Decent food and a pleasant atmosphere." His voice rumbled close to her ear.

"Here you go folks. Hannah is your server today." Their heavy-set hostess set two menus on the table edge before she hurried away.

Vince nodded his thanks then turned his attention back to Sydney. "Pretty much all you can ask of a restaurant."

"It is." She slid into one side of the booth then half expected he'd sit beside her.

He paused for a split second as if he thought about it, then took a seat across from her. "Not to mention good company."

Warmth from his compliment surged into her as the sweet and mournful strains of an Italian love song floated around them. A lone musician strolled nearer with a violin tucked beneath his chin, the bow sliding lightly over the strings. The tall man's eyelids were lowered, and his lips turned up as if he were in a dream as he swayed to the music and wove his way among the tables. In their immediate vicinity, couples with their heads inclined toward each other conversed using intimate tones.

Vince picked up one of the menus. "Have you been here before?"

"A couple of times." *But never like this.* She glanced up at him, and a sense of optimism filled her heart.

"I've been here too. Both times with friends." He studied the contents of his menu without further comment.

Just as well. Sydney had no right to ask who, exactly, those friends might be. Still, she gave into a touch of curiosity.

Had he brought a woman here before?

Not that she felt inclined to share who she was here with either—let him wonder like her. Ben, the IT kid from work, along with a few others from there, hardly qualified as dates. Usually, for her, it was dinner alone. More times than not, a single serve pizza from take-out, since the place was walking distance from her condo.

Picking up her water glass, she watched him over the rim. Vince was such a very nice guy. Someone she might want to get to know better. Maybe have a future with. *Thank God, he's not a cop.* She'd seen what that did to her mother and then both of her poor sisters-in-law.

A small chip of ice came with her next sip. She shivered as it slid down her throat.

"Seems as though I lost you for a moment there."

His voice drew her out of her thoughts. Setting down her glass, she clasped her hands on the table and smiled over at him. "Just taking it all in."

"What can I get you?" Their server arrived at the table, and Sydney had yet to open the menu.

Vince glanced up. "We need a few more minutes, please."

"Sure thing." The redhead walked away with a smile.

With the menu before her at last, Sydney shifted her attention from the list of appetizers, past the available drinks to the light fare dinner options.

"What's your favorite?"

She glanced up. Vince had set his menu to one

side. From the center of their table, a white candle in a fluted globe reflected a delicate glow off the sharp planes of Vince's features. Its single flame danced in his eyes where heat shimmered low and deep, causing more warmth to spread through her.

"Word is they have the best chicken marsala on the planet." Sydney closed the menu she pushed aside. "That's my choice."

"Sounds good to me, too."

Exactly what they ordered when their waitress reappeared a short time later. The woman didn't look up from her pad. "A Moscato or Chardonnay would go nicely."

Vince glanced Sydney's way. "Do you have a preference?"

Sydney didn't have to think twice. "Chardonnay. Always Chardonnay."

They took turns choosing the rest. House salads with vinaigrette and warm bread rather than garlic toast. The only difference, Sydney asked for her dressing on the side.

"Coming right up." With a bright smile for her customers, the attendant hurried away.

Sydney took the cloth napkin off the table to drape over her lap. "Randall Curan has offered me a job."

Vince shoved his napkin bundled silverware aside and leaned toward her. "Do you plan to take it?"

Something in the proprietary nature of his tone bothered her. Unsure why, she let it pass. "Of course. It's a terrific opportunity."

"Do you think that's wise?"

Had he just totally ignored my response? Maybe against her better judgement, she let that go as well.

"Why wouldn't it be?"

A few days ago, she'd served him lunch. To reciprocate—he'd said—he invited her to dinner. None of which gave him the right to second guess the decisions she made in her personal life. She should have handed over the leather jacket he originally came for and left it at that.

"Don't the man's actions strike you as odd?" He sat back as their salads, bread and wine were delivered.

"His entire demeanor strikes me as odd. All true patrons of the arts are quirky by nature, I suppose. He's no different."

Vince broke off a chunk from the soft loaf he dipped in some red marinara sauce. "That gives him a license to be eccentric?"

"In a way." Though she didn't bother to share, eccentric was a refreshing change from the demands of the up-tight, self-serving boss she'd left behind.

"Maybe it's all just an act." He wiped his fingers on a napkin.

"You definitely have a suspicious streak."

"Let's just say I'm cautious."

Try extremely overprotective, or over intrusive.

She drizzled dressing over her salad and decided to change the subject. "Galleries are constantly pitched display and review requests from not yet established artists."

"Everyone wants their work noticed." Vince started to take a forkful of lettuce, then picked up a crouton he popped in his mouth. "Even me."

"Part of my job will be to schedule interviews for those I think have merit. The final decision whether to showcase the work will be Randall's."

Before he could respond beyond an eyebrow quirk, the wandering violinist approached their table to share more of his beautiful music. The will to argue seeped out of her as she rested her elbows on the table, then cupped her chin in one hand to let the stirring melody wrap around her. Leaned forward at his waist, the virtuoso drew his bow over the strings one final time in a slow and methodical sweep, until the last mournful note drifted to silence.

Sitting up, Sydney joined Vince and a few other nearby diners to clap in appreciation. "That was lovely. Thank you."

"*Mille grazie!*" The violin and bow lowered to his sides, the man bowed in her direction then lifted his attention to Vince. "Senor, you are a lucky man."

Vince's response, a brief nod, was only a slight disappointment she quickly shook off as the musician left the table. "I'm excited at the prospect of taking on something new. Travel will be a big part of my position." She'd decided to counteract some of the negatives he was throwing at her with all the positives she could come up with. "That should be exciting."

"Exotic locations?"

"Maybe eventually. Right now, we're going to concentrate on Michigan talent and branch out from there."

"Not the art capitals of the world? Paris? Rome? Madrid?"

"That would be nice. As I said, eventually."

Silence became the norm as their entrees were placed in front of them. "Here you go, folks. Enjoy."

As the waitress left, Vince pulled his gaze away from the steaming plate of chicken smothered in mushrooms atop of fettuccine noodles. "I'm happy you got the job. I'm sure you know what's best. It's your life."

"Yes, it is." She made sure her tone was emphatic. "You know all about travel though, I assume."

"What?"

"Don't freelance writers like you get to travel around a lot?"

"Not necessarily." He seemed to almost grimace, then was quick to look away. "I have yet to travel much out of North America."

"Really? I've been to Europe once. A graduation gift from my father. He and one of my brothers came along, of course."

"That must have put a bit of a damper on your freedom."

You have no idea. "But didn't stop me from enjoying myself." Picking up her wine, she savored a sip of the tartly sweet liquid. "The other day at my place you mentioned being from a large family. What was that like?"

A grin flashed. "Aside from the general chaos and noise on those rare occasions when we are all in the same room, most of my upbringing was relatively drama free. An intact, two-parent home with all the benefits that kind of environment allows." Pride entered his voice, and his eyes sparkled. "As for my siblings, two of my three sisters are married with two girls each. They and my brother all live out of state. My kid sister, Becca, is a senior in high school. She, obviously, still lives with my parents. How about you?"

She thought of her mother gone from complications of diabetes two days after Sydney turned twelve. A father who, while totally out of his element at home, did his ultimate best with a grief stricken pre-pubescent daughter. Two older brothers right in there with him, trying to make up for what all of them had lost. Bringing gentle fingers to her neck, she lovingly touched the precious jewelry she still wore nearly every day.

His eyes narrowed as he noticed. “The necklace you’re wearing. It’s nice. Unique.”

“A gift from my dad and two brothers for my sixteenth birthday.” She let her hand fall away as she prepared to answer Vince’s original question. “You’re one up on me with the intact, two-parent home.” She shared a few details of her youth. “Not a horrible way to grow up. Just not the kind of normal you had.”

“That must have been rough. I’m sorry.”

Reaching across the table, he brushed her knuckles with gentle fingertips, and her tightened fists loosened. Opening his palms, he captured her hands in his.

“Both my brothers are the strong, silent type. Not a lot of chaos around them. My dad was, still is, quiet, too. Even more so after my mom died.”

She detailed a few circumstances for Vince’s benefit and was surprised when her voice cracked. “It hurts to talk about my teen years sometimes. Sorry.”

“Don’t be.” Though he didn’t elaborate, his tender squeeze of the hands he still held told her all she needed to know. “It’s okay to still miss her.”

“You’re right. But not to dwell on.” Tucking fond memories of her mother back into the special place in her heart, she blinked to clear a watery gaze and cast him a small smile. “Another down side, as the only female in our house, the chores of being chief cook and bottle washer usually fell to me."

"Another reason why you shied away from the day care idea I had for you."

"That's very possible." She glanced at him as she took another swallow of wine.

For the next hour or so, they talked, ate, sipped some wine, and talked some more. Vince shared some humorous incidents from his childhood and she disclosed a few she recalled from hers.

Finally, Vince set a used napkin on his empty plate the waitress cleared. "Any nieces and nephews for you?"

She shook her head. "Both my brothers are childless. By choice not design. Their wives are sweet and loving. Totally devoted to their husbands." *Too devoted.*

"What are your hobbies? What do you do in your spare time?"

Her eyes widened. Not an unusual question, but for the first time it dawned on her she was stuck for an answer. What with a failed marriage and, as a result, devotion to a job that disappeared, she hadn't allowed herself a carefree moment in a very long time.

"Me either." He spoke up when she didn't.

She let out a small laugh at how his situation mirrored hers. "I like that you're honest."

"Many of my friends claim I'm married to my job. Guess that would explain why I never married for real."

"Oh. I married for real, all right." She held a half empty glass of wine in front of her mouth. "In my mind, if not his."

"Another tough break in your life." His gaze locked with hers. "Sounds like you deserve to have some good luck for a change."

"Maybe." She took a sip and smiled. The man had a definite knack for making the bad goings on in her life more bearable.

"Here's your check, folks." Their server stepped up, and Sydney's reverie ended.

Vince glanced at the tab then took his wallet out and put some bills on the tray. The palm of his hand stayed sure and firm in the middle of her back as he guided them to the exit and outside a few minutes later. Fall was making its arrival known through cooler evening breezes, and the inevitable earlier arrival of dusk. Twilight darkness was doing its best to encroach, but a slow lowering sun wouldn't allow it quite yet.

She turned her face up to his and smiled. "That was wonderful. Thank you."

"The food or the company?" He reached down. Her palm and fingers fit perfectly into his as they descended the steps.

"Both of course."

They turned to travel down the street, and he firmed up his grip. "Good to hear."

The man had a low key, easy way about him, helping her relax. Enjoy herself. He held tight to her hand as a car passed them close to the curb.

"More rain yesterday definitely came with cooler temperatures." Sydney brought up the small talk topic as they walked along. "A couple of times I was sure it would turn to snow."

"I'm not ready for winter." As if to punctuate his words, he circled her shoulders with his arm to subtly pull her closer.

They approached her condo where wide bare

sidewalks gave way to well-kept grounds filled with hardy yellow Marigolds and deep purple Mums. Several trees lined the curving walkways, offering the added beauty of subtle color changes of their leaves from green to amber, red, and gold.

And all along the way to Sydney's porch, Vince kept his arm comfortably around her.

"Lovely night for a walk." Ida raised her free hand as she called out the greeting. She was coming down her front steps with Orson attached to the other end of a thin, pink leash. The cat skulked over to a low bush then glanced over one shoulder to scowl at its owner.

"It is that." Sydney marveled at how true her statement was.

"Nice to see you again, Ida." Vince nodded at her neighbor.

Poised to make introductions, she stopped. "I forgot. You two know each other."

Ida dragged her gaze away from Sydney's escort. "We met the other day when he was looking for you."

"I'm not sure he agrees it's such a lovely night." Sydney pointed at a subdued Orson. "I don't think he appreciates being on a leash."

Ida regarded her pet as she strolled over. Orson, who was headed toward one of many stone planters by the street had no choice but to follow. "I'm trying to impress upon him he needs to stay in his own yard."

"Maybe he'd prefer a blue leash instead of pink." Letting Sydney go, Vince bent down to provide a few consoling strokes along the feline's back. "If he's a guy and all. I know I would."

Ida threw her head back to laugh out loud. "I'm sure you would. However, I can't imagine anyone having the guts to put you on a leash. I know how males of all kinds simply have to be able to carouse. Until they find a reason to stop and settle down."

Vince only gave a self-conscious smile at her comment as he glanced up. Ida's beaming expression left no doubt she approved of the company Sydney kept. *That makes two of us.*

"Have you thought about using a GPS device?" Standing, Vince took Sydney's hand.

Ida cocked her head to one side. "GPS device?"

"Global Positioning System. It pinpoints the location of a subject anywhere. In this case your cat. Like an ankle bracelet the police use on someone under house arrest."

Ida's eyes grew wide. "Wouldn't something that big hurt my little man?"

Vince shook his head on a small laugh. "Just get one small enough to attach to his collar."

"I have one of those to help find misplaced keys. A gift from my dad last Christmas." Sydney glanced over at Vince then back at Ida. "Actually two of them came in the package. You could try one to see if it would be worth buying."

"That's a good idea, dear. I'll get that from you. But not right now. I have a gentleman friend coming over soon."

Sydney wondered which of the many suitors Ida attracted was tonight's companion. "Is it Jonathan?"

"Ah, Jonathon. He took me to the symphony last week. I invited him in when he brought me home afterward." She fanned a hand in front of her face. "He's quite the looker and beyond, if you get my drift."

Sydney certainly did get her drift, not to mention

the picture that went with it.

"But I'm not going out with Jonathan tonight. Today it's Albert."

"Albert." Sydney nodded at the name she didn't recognize. Most of Ida's men friends she knew by first name only. Could be Ida did too.

"What is it the two of you have been doing this evening?" Ida made no secret of her open interest as she scanned Vince top to bottom.

"We just finished dinner." If he was bothered by the inspection, he didn't show it.

"How nice for you. Well, I really should go shower and put on my party clothes. Albert will be here soon." Despite what she said, Ida didn't move.

Orson sat on the sidewalk. Rolled to one side, he batted aimlessly at the leash. With a sudden claw strike, he clutched the thin band between his paws and started to gnaw with gusto.

"Orson! No!" Ida bent down to scoop him up.

Sydney took advantage of the distraction and pulled Vince toward her door. "Have a nice night, Ida."

"You too. Enjoy your evening."

"Bye, Ida. Have fun on your date." Vince called out as he slipped an arm around Sydney's shoulders.

"Oh, I intend to." A suggestive giggle drifted back. "Stay in touch, Vincent."

Sydney indulged in a backward glance. Was she inviting Vince to remain in their lives? *My life?*

They reached her porch and stood, face to face while Ida remained on the sidewalk below, staring. Smiling.

Sydney turned with a sigh to unlock the door. "We obviously won't be alone unless you come in."

"Works for me." Vince followed her inside then closed the door behind them.

"Ida can be something else. She is also quite the social dynamo as you heard."

"She is that."

Sydney decided she may as well be honest. "Call me old fashioned, but I prefer one relationship at a time."

"Same goes for me." Vince nodded as he spoke.

A one woman, man. Another point scored in his favor.

"Makes life easier." As they stood in the entrance, she automatically slipped off her shoes.

"My mother always had us do that." Vince was soon out of his shoes he slid to the corner with the side of one foot. "She was as stickler for a clean house."

She smiled at the homebody in him as she hung their jackets in the closet. "By all means, make yourself at home. Not that I'm so much a stickler, to use your words. I've just always been more comfortable in my stocking feet. Barefoot is even better."

"Casual but neat. I like it."

She considered his comment for a moment. "Can I offer you something to drink?"

He lifted his gaze from an intense study of her lips and blinked. "What are the choices?"

"Hard or soft. Your call. Beer or wine for the former, plain bottled water or pop for the latter."

"We had wine at dinner." He draped an arm around her shoulders as they entered the living room and kept going. "Too much of the hard stuff tends to dull the senses."

"That's true."

Once they got to the kitchen, she reached for the container of ice at the bottom shelf of the freezer. When she straightened, her shoulder blades came to rest against the solid warmth of his chest. He wrapped his arms around her to pull her even closer. After a few fumbled moves, she set the ice container on the counter and exhaled on a sigh as his lips touched the skin on the back of her neck. Goosebumps along her flesh met with the heat that rose from within, somewhere near her heart. She lowered her head. Warm muscles flexed as he tightened his arms around her and used his mouth to do marvelous things to her nape. Tiny electric jolts skittered across her skin everywhere his lips made contact.

Then he lifted them, if only momentarily. “On second thought, I’m not the least bit thirsty.”

“Hungry then?” The words whispered from between her lips.

“Oh, yeah. Very hungry.” His soft breath rippled over her ear.

A series of shivers rushed in waves down to her toes as he slowly rotated her to face him. She had no idea which one of them stepped forward first, only that in the next moment she was securely wrapped in Vince’s arms. And, only being there was what was important. That and the pressure of his lips, warm and firm yet incredibly gentle as they closed over hers. Her eyelids fluttered shut as he worked an incredible magic over her mouth. Heat slid through her as he teased her lips apart with the tip of his tongue. She swallowed a silent gasp as he ventured inside. Wondering for a moment if this were simply a good night kiss, she was slightly flushed, nicely heated, and extremely turned on when he finally let her go. If the simmer in those deep set blue eyes was any indication, his sentiments were remarkably similar.

Once more his lips sought hers. This time, he kissed her so hard, and for so long, she feared any minute now she'd no longer be able to remain upright. Just when she was sure to collapse into him, he released her, took his arms from around her and twined their fingers.

"There has got to be a more comfortable place for this than up against the refrigerator."

She opened her eyes and blinked twice. Only after he said something did she realize her spine was pressed against the cool, flat surface of the appliance. "There definitely is. Let me put the ice away first."

"I can do that." Pulling her gently away from the door, he replaced the tray then turned to again twine his fingers with hers.

They walked hand and hand into the living room without speaking. Once there, and settled close on the loveseat, her palms slid up rigid biceps and across broad shoulders as his lips found hers again. The tempo of his breathing spiked. Hers accelerated to keep up.

Her hands clasped together around his neck as she rose up to accept all he seemed to offer. More determined than ever to give back to him certain promises of her own.

Chapter Five

The entrance of the Argentile Gallery reminded Vince of a large, upscale hospital. Spotless and clean. Impeccable and sanitary on the outside, while hiding the unpleasant but necessary procedures that went on behind the scenes.

Its stark white walls had a shoulder high border of darker marble accents. Variegated marble floors were polished so bright, track lighting from above reflected off it in dazzling shimmers. As he strolled through the wide corridor in search of Sydney's office, Vince was tempted to shade his eyes from the glare.

Could that much marble be genuine?

He passed under a high archway decorated in elaborate scroll designs and more marble inlays. What he personally termed Early Gaudy Decadence. Coming into a wide, atrium area, he pulled up short. A massive tree, plush, shiny green leaves and all, was planted smack dab in the middle of the building and rose three floors high.

Unbelievable!

Several hallways spread from this first-floor hub like spokes on a massive wheel. The floors above were more like balconied hallways with an abundance of wall space and very few doors. He mentally catalogued the location of each entrance, then resisted the urge to pull out his notebook to sketch a floorplan. Something he'd do from memory once he left. Or use his cell.

"How do you like the gallery, Vince?" Sydney's voice reached out from behind to stroke the back of his neck. "These staircases on either side take our visitors to what they call the primary viewing areas."

Unable to suppress a smile, Vince turned around. "Impressive."

Impressive was right. And he hadn't even bothered to check out the staircases she mentioned.

"It is, isn't it?" Her initial smile of greeting, radiant yet polite, grew as their gazes locked and she drew nearer. Low heels tapped the floor with each step.

"Very." It took no effort to return her smile. In fact, he was amazed at how truly happy he was to see her. Especially since the last time they were together he'd left her place after only a few incredible kisses. In reality, he'd wanted to share so much more with her.

Like, maybe, who I really am?

He pushed the thought away, then didn't move as she stopped in front of him. Just stood and stared in thorough enjoyment. A pale pink business suit with strategically placed ash gray accents underarm to hem and across the waist, hugged places he'd give anything to caress. Her skirt flowed over those perfectly shaped hips to stop just above the knee. Pale, glimmering stockings did wonders for long, sexy legs.

"Maybe a little over the top by most people's standards." She was close enough, so he could hear when she lowered her voice. "But the clientele seems to like it."

He consciously closed his mouth as he scanned opulence unlike anything he'd seen before. "What's not to like?"

To take her in his arms for a lingering kiss of welcome wasn't appropriate. *Was it?* He settled for clasping hands when she offered both of hers.

"You're here for the tour."

He frowned at the quick arrival of her strictly business attitude, then chalked it up to her being here with a job to do. *Like you are, remember?* "And to see you, of course."

"I would hope so." The small laugh she released echoed off the slick walls. "Because I was looking forward to seeing you, too."

Her brown eyes sparkled with fine copper flecks as she held his gaze again. For Vince, the huge overpowering room ignited with a true sense of hospitality. Again, he contemplated possible consequences of taking her in his arms for that kiss.

"Mr. Reeves. Vincent. Welcome."

His amorous thoughts vaporized like steam from icy water splashed on heated rocks. Randall Curan, minus the leather coat and dog, hurried over from some obscure hallway. Vince hadn't detected the owner's approach, and his suspicious side emerged full force. *Had the man been standing out of sight on one of the upper tiers? Watching? Listening?*

Embracing the sudden return of his cop persona, he glanced over at Sydney. Like it or not, he was here for reasons that didn't necessarily include her. Quick to look away from the woman who filled his thoughts when he was supposed to concentrate on other things, he extended his right hand toward their host. "Thank you for inviting me."

"My pleasure." Curan dropped the hand shake after a couple of weak pumps, stepped back, and glanced to his right. "And Sydney. You'll be joining us, of course."

"Of course." With a definite smile, her gaze slid off her boss and onto Vince. "If that's what you'd like."

Like? I'd love nothing more than to spend some time with you. Vince kept his expression serious as his mind took off on a trip to fantasyland. He pulled it back to the here and now. "Sure. Why not?"

"Always a treat to be in your company, Sydney my dear. Oh, by the way." Curan cast a smile as weak as his handshake Vince's way. "Excuse us a moment, please. I need to touch base with my newest assistant about something else."

"Of course." Vince nodded, then made it his job to pay attention as the two stepped away to converse. Though he couldn't make out whether they spoke of gallery business or not. Eyes narrowed, he studied Sydney. Her smile remained intact, while some of the sparkle in her eyes, evident when he'd first arrived, was no longer there. Or was he simply lying to himself?

Should have checked that raging male ego at the door, man. She's working here. Something he hadn't wanted her to do, so she'd be out of the way of this wild goose chase he was on. *Then you wouldn't have an excuse to see her again.* His rational side stepped up with a counter argument, and he had to agree.

"Where would you like to begin, Mr. Reeves? Our interview or the tour?"

Though it wasn't exactly easy, he shut down all inappropriate thoughts at his host's question. "Whatever works best for you."

"A tour then."

Vince pulled his phone out of his jacket pocket he

held up. "I'd like to record our walkthrough, so I'll have everything intact for my article. Do you mind?"

Curan eyed the cell before he gave a curt nod. "Not at all. Not at all." A smile emerged as his regard fell to Sydney. "This is perfect. As my personal assistant, you'll need to know this place inside and out." Curan eased his arm over Sydney's shoulders as he started walking toward the first of many hallways. "What better way for me to kill two birds with one stone, as they say. Take care of both of you at the same time."

"I have been holed up in my office for the past couple of days." To her credit she side-stepped away from the physical contact to move closer to Vince. "The gallery has a huge gala coming up. I've been deep into the planning details."

"Our goal is to showcase some of our newest acquisitions set to be delivered tomorrow." Curan spread his now empty arms wide as his smile dimmed considerably.

Vince did his best to shake off all thoughts not related to the task at hand. "This is such a vast establishment." *Cue appropriate awe and interest on the face.* "I certainly can't wait to learn more about it." With *his* left arm draped heavily over his host's shoulders, Vince swept out his right. "Lead on please."

"Of course." His expression polite, save for still narrowed eyes, the man slid away from Vince much as Sydney had done with him, then turned to walk ahead of them. "Follow me."

"We certainly will." Vince spoke under his breath as they started out.

Sydney made no sound as she fell into step behind him. She simply reached out to briefly take his hand for a squeeze before letting go. Hard as it was to not think about the woman who'd enabled his being here, Vince brought his focus back to the limited number of doors off the main hallways. Doors that led where? And held what behind them?

All questions he was confident he'd figure out in due time. *Because that's my job.* If he didn't exactly turn in a spectacular performance when it came to most everything else in his life, he was good at his work. Especially when he went undercover.

They spent the next hour or so viewing various paintings as Curan explained some of the background on each. He obviously enjoyed hearing himself talk. With various nods at what he deemed appropriate intervals, Vince remained aware of the structure that housed the gallery, and mentally logged the comings and goings of what appeared to be a rather small staff. He could probably be discreet and get a list of names and job descriptions later from Sydney.

A pang of guilt at his necessary deception struck like a poison dart near the center of his chest to make him wince. When this was all over, sooner rather than later if he lived right, he'd make it up to her.

I swear I will.

"As you can see, all of our paintings are in indistinct frames to better showcase the art."

At Curan's voice, he returned his attention to where it belonged. "Interesting."

"It is. We carefully place each one at three or four foot intervals to allow our patrons plenty of space to pause, step back, and enjoy them."

"Fascinating." Vince pulled his gaze away from a side exit door and brought up his cell.

An MO of the art theft ring was to smuggle higher priced paintings in and out of the galleries within the thicker frames of less prominent works. Vince stroked his chin as he feigned deep concentration on *the art*. Not happening here unless the more valuable works were painted on tissue paper. He tilted his head to get a better look at the mountings this gallery used.

Nope. Not even then.

"Over here is something I find rather unique." Curan spoke, and Vince glanced his way.

Once again, the trio was off down another hallway. A few more minutes in, Vince figured he'd better slip back into character. He stood back a pace as they stopped before the portrait of a young girl in a sundress and bonnet looking out the window at a deserted beach.

"This is nice." In his opinion, it truly wasn't half bad.

"You have good taste, Mr. Reeves."

Who knew? Vince made sure to keep all traces of surprise from his face. "You think so?"

Sydney came to stand beside him. "That beach does look very tempting."

"It does, doesn't it?" He looked down at her, and his fingers twitched with wanting to touch her, caress her…

"This particular painting is one of my favorites."

At Curan's voice, Vince ditched the untimely thoughts. "Why's that?"

"I was drawn to the artist long ago. Would you believe this stunning piece was created by an ingénue only nineteen years old?"

"It is beautiful." Sydney stepped forward to further study the portrait. "Hard to believe someone so young would have such talent."

Curan nodded. "The subject is actually the artist's identical twin sister. A new take on a self-portrait, you could say."

Vince went back to his pat response. "Interesting."

Curan didn't take his eyes from the painting. "Repose, as I've titled this work, isn't for sale. It's one of the first pieces I ever acquired. At a very great price."

In Vince's mind, there had to be more of an explanation for such a strong, emotional reaction besides an art lover's personal choice. "It seems very special to you." He held back his next question. *Why's that?*

"I've found talent abounds in the young." Taking Sydney's hand with the nonchalance of someone who had every right, Curan led the way along a rounded corner to the next series of paintings.

All Vince could do was follow with his doubts unanswered, and a lousy phone the only thing in *his* hand. Curan had creep written all over him. Which in and of itself wasn't a crime.

Easy. She belongs here now. You don't.

He shook his head at the undeniable truth. "Most of the works you acquire aren't necessarily what would be termed by masters I assume."

Curan raised his fingers in a fluttering motion. "That would depend on one's perception of what a master is. In my opinion, monetary success does not a master make."

Vince nodded, struggling to keep his eyes from glazing over. "Makes sense."

Like hell. All he could do was videotape everything

and get his pals at the precinct to help him figure it all out. Together, maybe they could write a decent article he could turn in. Or have one of the admins at the station do it for him. He had a feeling Curan would be looking for it.

"*Ms. Raines, call waiting, please. Ms. Raines. Call waiting.*"

The computer generated female voice echoed down the hallway.

Sydney glanced up. "Excuse me for a moment. I'll be right back."

Both men turned as she hurried away.

"Already she is a definite asset to us." His head tilted to one side, Curan's gaze followed her retreat as he crossed both arms. "Truly an asset. She will help bring us much success."

Unsure how exactly to respond, Vince did no more than nod as he pulled his gaze away from the sway of tantalizing hips that had captivated him since day one.

"You're fortunate to have found her." He made the comment in the most off hand manner he could conjure up. At the same time, something unnerving took hold of him at the idea he was the catalyst that had brought the two of them together.

"I am that."

He shook his head and touched Curan on the shoulder. "Shall we take a break and get to that interview?"

"Yes. Of course." He indicated a modernistic shaped bench across from a bronze statue of a dog with a stick in its mouth.

As his host perched at one end then crossed his legs, Vince made it a point to straddle the other as he stole a look at his watch. Two hours in and near as he could tell, he'd pretty much seen everything Curan had to offer. Before his arrival at the gallery, he'd gone over e-mailed pictures of the missing artwork. So far there hadn't been any traces of any of them around here, and he had a feeling there wasn't going to be. Art thieves made their money selling stolen objects to eccentric, private collectors. Who in their right mind would steal a well-known painting for public display?

"What would you like to know?"

At Curan's inquiry, Vince scrapped a probe of what he was really after and went for the basics instead. "Tell me a little about yourself. In your own words."

"Well…"

Itching to have his pen scratching over notebook paper, Vince held up the phone to tape much of what he already knew. *Let the wild goose chase continue.* He blinked twice and came up with an expression of pure interest as he listened to Curan drone on about his Ivy League education and subsequent business ventures.

"I've had many, many financial triumphs."

Vince let a half smile escape as he nodded obligingly.

"Most people don't understand, I didn't have it as easy as one would think growing up."

Vince picked up on a definite bitterness in Curan's tone. His alter ego cover pretended he hadn't heard anything out of the ordinary as he kept his gaze steady. "Why's that?"

The other man's eyes became virtual slits as if he contemplated the answer before he gave it. "Various reasons. When you have money you've inherited, people don't expect you to be especially bright and business savvy. I take great delight in proving them wrong."

In the next instant, he curved his lips up and his eyes brightened. Just like that, his sullen attitude was a thing of the past. Unnerved by the hasty mood change, there was nothing Vince could do except catalogue this additional bit of behavior as he compiled a profile of his suspect.

And ignore the subtle lift of some hairs on the back of his neck.

Still in character, he nodded. "And this gallery will help you do that?"

A faraway cast took over Curan's gaze. "Perhaps."

"Another issue resolved." Both men stood as Sydney walked toward them then filled her new boss in on some details of the call she'd just taken.

A pending shipment mix up and how she'd handled it. Feigning a study of the dog across from him, Vince listened. Nothing was mentioned about incoming paintings or other possible contraband. This shipment was track lighting and other hardware supplies that was delayed.

"I called the electricians and postponed the installation. He said that would be fine. We'll still have the new features set up for the gala."

"Perfect." The original concern on Curan's face cleared, and he was on the move again with Sydney in tow, tucked under one arm. "Already you're irreplaceable to me."

Vince gripped his phone a little tighter rather than intervene. A few kisses and a couple of dates… He winced as he was forced to correct himself. One date he'd initiated. Motivated by gratitude, with guilt thrown in after the fact.

As they made their way along another series of paintings on the second floor, Sydney tolerated Curan's grab and go for about three steps before she slid out from under his arm and away from him. As he continued moving forward, she discreetly fell behind.

If Curan was bothered by the understated slight, he didn't show it as they circled back, then came to a stop a short while later in the main atrium.

"Well, I think I have enough information to do an article justice." Vince put the cell in his pocket.

"You're sure you don't want further biographical information?"

Vince declined with a slight head shake. "You've been very gracious. I'm sure I have more than enough to use."

"Very well."

When Vince nodded this time, Curan turned to Sydney. "Before you leave for the day, there's one more thing I wanted to go over with you."

As boss and employee conversed about more gallery business, Vince excused himself for what he termed a restroom break. On his own private tour of the back hallways and behind a few doors, he didn't come up with much more than dust, cobwebs, and a couple of large extension ladders. If this gallery was fencing stolen goods, an accomplice somewhere was twiddling his thumbs for lack of action. Though not a particular fan of Curan, Vince had to admit the guy appeared to be clean. Quirky as hell, but clean. Making his way back to join Sydney and her boss, he considered what to put in the report he needed to file. More importantly, the most diplomatic way to word the conclusion he'd drawn.

Suspicions unfounded. Case closed.

"And now you have an idea of the inner workings of Argentile." Curan stopped talking to Sydney and turned toward Vince as he approached. Arms crossed over his chest, he glanced around like a monarch appraising his realm.

"Thank you for your cooperation."

"You're welcome." Curan looked at him then at Sydney. "It's been a long day for you, I'm sure. You can leave now too, my dear. We've thrown a lot at you so far."

Vince made certain his relief didn't show either in body language or expression. "I'll walk out with you."

She glanced over with a smile. "I have to go get my coat."

"I'll wait."

"Goodbye, Mr. Reeves. See you tomorrow, Sydney, my dear." Not waiting for either to answer, and with a slight bow, Curan hurried silently away.

When Sydney came out from her office wearing the mid-length trench coat a few minutes later, Vince fell into step beside her, but waited until they were outside to speak. "Your new boss is a little over the top, don't you think?"

"Oh, I don't know."

Even though maybe he wouldn't like the answer, he had to ask. "You appreciate all that touchy-feely stuff from Curan?"

They walked in silence for a time after his question. For so long, in fact, he began to wonder if she planned to answer. As he glanced down at her, she looked up at him. Their gazes caught and held for a moment before she pulled hers away.

"Not really." More silence followed her brief reply.

Vince had to concentrate to keep his mouth shut. For his part, he didn't like it at all. Not that *his part* mattered…much. Except, in his mind, he and Sydney had something going that could turn out to be good if they'd let it. *What would that something good look like exactly? When you knowingly deceived her and used her to further your latest case?* He closed his mind to accusations he couldn't deny.

"But, thank you." Her words came at him from out of the blue.

What in the hell had he done lately to deserve her thanks? "You're welcome. But, what exactly are you thanking me for?"

"For not stepping in to tell Randall to stop putting his arm around me or touch me in any way."

She was thanking him for giving her space? "It wasn't my place."

"My father and brothers would have literally been all over it…rather him." She looked at him for a second before her gaze fell away.

He glanced over at her and frowned. For someone who claimed to be appreciative, she wasn't doing much to show it. With her head lowered along with her voice, she seemed more saddened than pleased. All he could do was shrug. Far be it for him to try to figure out the inner workings of a woman. Even with his sisters to practice on all those years, he still wasn't very good at it.

"I believed you could handle yourself." *Even though I sure didn't enjoy watching.* More truth made it to the tip of his tongue. Just in time, he stopped it from coming out.

"I can, and I will." Despite what she said, disappointment seemed to flash in her eyes. "All my life I've had my battles fought for me. Though my father gave lip service to the idea, I was never allowed to stand up for myself. Before I'd even had the chance to decide whether I wanted to do something, it was done for me. I plan to let Randall know myself that I didn't appreciate the physical contact."

"Really?" Vince held back the sigh of relief before it slid out.

"Really. It would have only embarrassed him to take a stand in front of you. However, as I said, I do plan to tell him to back off tomorrow."

"What if he fires you over it?"

"Then it's his problem. Not mine." She studied a clear blue sky for a moment before she went on. "I have the utmost confidence in what I do and the way I do it. Mr. Curan recognizes that and pays me well for it. If he decides not to. As I said. His problem." Her eyes narrowed, and her lips tipped up as she met his gaze. "Because I'd sue his ass for sexual harassment."

A huge laugh burst out of him. "Sounds like a plan to me."

"It's my plan. For now."

Too soon, they came to a stop by Sydney's dark blue Mustang and turned to face each other. From what little he did know, women liked to talk. Obviously, Sydney was no different. He only had one problem. He wanted to take her in his arms and kiss her senseless.

"As I said, I appreciate you keeping your distance." She took hold of his hand and held tight. "Back there at the gallery, I mean."

His thoughts dropped away. If she wanted more talking, he'd talk. "Anytime. I'm happy for you. That you found a job."

She drew her brows down as her gaze homed in on his face. "But."

Caught off guard watching her mouth, he raised his gaze to meet hers. "But nothing."

The eyes studying him widened, but only slightly. "There's a definite hesitation in your voice. I can sense a qualifier coming on."

Lowering his shoulders, he gave his best attempt at a relaxed smile. "I hope this job is what you want and that it works out for you." Without thinking about it, he squeezed her fingers. "Makes you happy."

"It's going to pay the bills." Her face broke into a smile. "I'm very happy about that."

"That's good."

She retrieved her hand to place both palms on his shoulders. "But thank you for caring enough to ask."

"No problem."

Those delicate palms slid up to circle his neck. Her body followed the movement as a matter of course. As she drew nearer, then made shoulder to knees contact, her warmth spread into him then through to his soul. Despite what she claimed about her personal preference keeping a safe distance from her boss, she was getting awfully close to him.

"Touchy, feely has its place with the right person." Her voice was low. Sexy and suggestive.

The heat working its way through him spiked then did a swan dive to settle below his belt. "Curan's not the right person for you?"

"What do you think?" Rising on tiptoe, she shut

her eyes as she brought her lips up in search of his.

Vince was more than willing to accommodate her. Wrapping both arms securely at her waist, he pulled her close until the softness of her body molded to accept the pressure of his. Satisfied with her closeness, he lowered his mouth to claim hers. She tasted fresh and sweet, with a definite hint of forbidden fruit. Any warnings he'd given himself to keep his distance melted away like a candle touched by a flame. Hit with a blow torch was more like it. Soon he was lost to everything around him, focused only on Sydney in his arms and the kiss they shared.

The faint wail of a siren in the distance registered first. Vince took note and automatically stiffened. *Someone somewhere needs help.* That help, in the form of a fellow officer, was on the way. The unmistakable rise and fall yowl of its signal grew louder as the squad car drew nearer.

The change in Sydney's demeanor was swift and stunning. Her eyes opened. A once dreamy gaze cleared. "Police. Not fire."

He pulled back. *She recognized the difference?* Either way, he called up a necessary mask of disinterest. "I'm sure the police will take care of it."

"They always do."

Each remained silent as the approaching siren swelled. For Vince, the mood was irreparably broken. He struggled to rein in his instincts to provide backup as needed. Unsure what else to do, he kept Sydney close at his side. The siren screamed, wound down to a whir then dropped into silence. Near as he could judge, whatever was going down had to be less than a block to the north. Robbery or accident, there was no way to know. Poised to act, everything in him strained to bow to the internal adrenaline flow and become part of the fray.

And blow a carefully crafted cover in the process.

Jaw tensed, senses on high alert, he forced himself to breathe slow and even as he maneuvered Sydney behind him then stood to face, head on, what might come their way.

In the near distance, a car door slammed then another. Voices, alarmed yet controlled, rose into the advancing dusk.

"Stop! Police! Stop!"

The thuds of feet hitting the ground picked up speed.

"He's running! I'm in pursuit."

Footfalls grew louder as the pursuit advanced their way. A young kid in jeans crashed out of the bushes and Vince stiffened, ready to draw down. Arms pumping at his sides, the kid's hands were empty. *No weapon.* Tall and lanky with brown hair and a blue windbreaker flapping. Eyes wide and wild, he pulled up, his head swinging from side to side.

Certain Sydney stayed behind him, Vince advanced on the suspect, keeping his stance rock-hard. "Better do what they say."

The kid hesitated as he jerked his gaze to Vince. "What?"

"Do as—"

In the next instant, he landed face first on the pavement as a blur of dark blue tackled him from behind.

"Ooof!"

"Stay down!" A knee was driven into the kid's

back. With one hand used to restrain his quarry, the officer reached back with the other to snatch the cuffs off his belt.

Feet scuffled on pavement as, with another flash of blue, his partner arrived and slid down beside them.

"You son of a— Watch it, man. Oww!" More muffled protests rose up.

With the handcuffs clamped in place with a telling clink, the arresting officer lifted the runner to his feet.

"Let's go!"

One led him away as Officer Foley, Vince's contact at the Manderfield Post, turned to Vince and Sydney.

Familiarity flared for a millisecond as their gazes met then immediately disappeared behind a guise of indifference. "You folks okay?"

His expression clearing, Vince nodded. "We're good. Wow that was scary."

"We're fine, officer." Sydney spoke up from behind him, her voice high pitched with emotion. She took a step forward. "Stay safe."

Initial surprise struck Foley's eyes before a full out smile bloomed. "Thanks. I'll do my best."

"Good job, Officer." Vince's nod and smile of recognition spoke for what he couldn't say. *Nice take down.* "Thanks."

Sydney flattened her hand against the left side of her chest when they were alone again. "My heartrate's almost back to normal. How about you?"

He kept his eyes wide as if the shock and surprise still hadn't worn off for him either. "Mine's getting there. That was really something. The officers handled things like the pros they are. We were never really in any danger." Without a second thought, he pulled her back into his arms. "You sure you're okay?"

She rested her head on his shoulder. "I'm sure."

With her body pressed close, his blood heated to damned near boiling as it collided with the adrenaline surging back and forth in his veins.

Situation de-escalated. Suspect neutralized and in custody. Heart beat returned to normal? *Not a chance.* From his rookie days on, it always took Vince a while to physically de-escalate from any activity in the field.

Emotionally always took a little longer, too. The same was true of the woman in his arms. Emotionally, he had to de-escalate this situation, as well. Neutralize his involvement.

No matter what he had to sacrifice in the process, his duty was clear. Conclude his case and move on. Leave Sydney exactly as he'd found her.

God help him, he hoped he could.

Chapter Six

Sydney settled into her ergonomically fashioned red leather chair in front of the molded glass structure Randall Curan considered a desk to pour over submissions received that morning. When she'd arrived her first day, Randall sat down with her to explain ever so briefly what the job entailed then left her to her own devices. Not a huge issue, as she'd learned a job on the fly before. She was pleased to discover shifting papers and making phone calls proved to be downright cathartic. More important, the big bad wolf wouldn't be crashing through her front door anytime soon.

Jotting some notes about a vendor for the upcoming gala event she hadn't been able to get a hold of, she secured them in a folder she put into a lateral cabinet behind her. Turned back to the desk, she rested her elbows on its glossy top when Randall appeared in her doorway.

"How are things going with you?"

She assumed her most businesslike posture. "I have some lines on a harpist to play during the cocktail reception. Two actually." Noting a couple of names she'd been given by the local symphony association, she then went on to detail the virtues of each. "Both, I've been told, are equally talented, according to the literature the agency faxed."

"I'm sure you'll make the proper choice."

“I appreciate your vote of confidence.” She evened out a stack of materials on one corner of her desk. “The programs came out nicely. They sent prototypes before I order the full print run. You can look them over when you get a chance. Make changes if you want.”

“As I said. I trust you. So, we’ll either be the talk of the town or its scourge depending upon how the gala goes.”

No pressure there! “That’s true.” She’d had her fill of the work-related niceties. It was time to get the one problem she had off her chest. “Randall, we need to talk.”

He straightened then blinked. “Do we, now?”

“Yes.” She indicated the chair across from her desk. “Please. Have a seat.”

Without taking his eyes off her, he came forward. “About what?”

“About.” She cleared her throat. “The working conditions around here.”

Instead of sitting down to listen to what she had to say, he took hold of the chair back he hauled around the desk to position beside hers. He then maneuvered close enough, so their knees nearly touched when he finally sat and leaned forward. “What’s the problem?”

“This.” She slid her chair back. Confident she’d put sufficient space between them, she stood and walked around until the desk was once again a necessary barrier.

Beginning at her toes, he scanned the length of her until he settled a questioning gaze on her face. “This?”

“Your seeming penchant to be physically close to me at all opportunities.”

“You don’t like that?”

At his look of utter disbelief, she nearly laughed out loud. *How could he not get this?* "It makes me uncomfortable, especially in our office environment."

"If you don't like it, I won't do it." With both hands on his thighs, he sat straighter. "I thought all women…well, they obviously don't."

"Thank you for understanding."

"Not a problem." He rose, put his chair back where he found it, then came to stand beside her and extended his hand. "Thank you for speaking your mind."

"I may do so in the future, as well." She issued the veiled warning with a smile then returned to her desk as he walked out of her office.

Returning her attention to more correspondence, she hadn't been working long when high heels tapping across the hallway floor grew louder, then came to a stop.

"You must be the new kid on the block. Randall's latest assistant." A low, sultry voice in her doorway made Sydney glance up.

She immediately had a smile in place and her hand out in greeting. "That's right. I'm Sydney Raines."

The heels clicked again as the woman came forward, until beautifully manicured fingers folded lightly over hers. "Sydney is it?" A blatant one-two inspection accompanied the comment.

Sydney inhaled sufficient perfume to choke the proverbial horse then concentrated on the woman's perfectly made up face. "And you are?" With her hand pulled back, she tilted her head in innocent expectation.

"Nancy Parsons." The name was spoken in a rush, as if Sydney should really have the decency to know that already.

"Nice to meet you."

A heavily penciled brow shot up. "Yes. Of course."

With practiced poise, Sydney kept her lips tight together. The woman was something else.

This Nancy person angled her head and lowered fake lashes over skeptical eyes. "I certainly hope you're as competent as you look."

Sydney let a friendly smile hide a blossoming animosity. "We at the gallery have our customers' best interests at heart. Perhaps you'd like a tour? We have docents available and can also schedule private showings."

The thick, spikey lashes lifted a fraction of an inch. "I will say you have the schmooze lines down pat."

Her eyes widened. Sydney wasn't sure what an appropriate come back should be. That didn't stop her from trying one out. "You are no doubt a patron of the arts. We like that around here."

"Honey. I am *the* patron of the arts. For this gallery, at least."

"Oh." When her mouth stayed open, she made sure to close it. "You're a collector. What types of pieces do you prefer?"

The woman let out a delicate scoff. "My tastes aren't your concern. Randall has never mentioned me?"

Now we're getting somewhere. Sydney shook her head. "Although it's true I haven't been with the gallery for long. Perhaps…."

"Perhaps he should have explained to you who I was your first day. The rascal. I'll have to talk to him about that." Though her words, along with her demeanor were strong, a hint of disappointment seemed to push around the edges of her mouth. "You see, Ms.

Raines. Sydney. I'm one of your bosses, too." She watched Sydney for a moment before she went on. "Since I hold a significant share in the ownership of this place."

Sydney did her best to hide a wide-eyed surprise while she processed this latest bit of information. "One of the owners?"

"Exactly." The woman sat without being invited. "Sorry I missed your initial day here."

"It was rather uneventful. I'm sort of learning as I go."

"I was on a scouting mission. Seeking out new works for our gallery." She laid her palms flat on Sydney's desktop and leaned further forward. "I've e-mailed you two lists of contacts. Those who made the grade and those who didn't. Send out letters thanking those who didn't for their interest. You'll find a form letter in the files somewhere. Regarding those whose work had merit, prepare a letter to each, for my signature of course, giving them possible showing dates. Those are on the schedule posted in the group files." She glanced at a pad of paper by Sydney's right hand. "You are getting all this, right?"

"Of course." Sydney keyed in on the silent signal and, picking up the pad, started to take notes. If to do nothing else but appease.

"I'd like them sent out today." The woman stood then peered down at her.

Putting the notebook aside, Sydney stood as well. "It was nice meeting you." The hand she extended was ignored, and she let it drop to her side. "They'll be on your desk by three."

"Two would be better. As I have an off-site

appointment at three."

"Two it is, then." *Why argue?* She'd figure out this newest workplace dynamic after doing what was asked of her.

"I'll expect them." Spinning on her heel, the woman was on her way out when she snapped her fingers then turned back around. "One more thing. My time is extremely valuable." She went on to provide instructions on the proper way for Sydney to screen her calls. "For future reference, of course."

"Of course." Still standing, Sydney kept up a pleasant smile.

"I can't be bothered to listen to sales pitches from half-baked artists who really have nothing of quality to sell."

Then she was gone, leaving Sydney to wonder exactly how *she* was supposed to make a determination of visual quality with an audio phone conversation. Seated once more at her desk, Sydney shook her head and blew out a breath. She set aside the folder of gala details she'd pulled out before the woman's intrusion then opened the mainframe on the computer to check her inter office e-mail and seek out the appropriate data files.

Despite fielding several interruptions that afternoon, at five o'clock sharp she clicked the mouse in her palm to shut down her computer. She'd delivered Nancy Parson's letters, as requested, at two sharp, taking particular delight in the woman's apparent surprise at her efficiency.

Retrieving her purse from a small closet by the door, she pulled it over one shoulder, then pushed through the door to, literally, put work behind her.

The brisk fall air swirled up to meet her as she stepped outside, gently lifting the hair away from her face as it danced across her cheeks. Trials of the new job aside, all in all life was good, up to and including the prospect of having a man in her life. A kind and honest man by all indications.

As she approached her car with a smile on her face, the cell in her pocket strummed. Pulling it out, she checked the caller ID. Three letters—DAD.

She slid her thumb over the screen. "Dad. Hi. I didn't expect to hear from you until Sunday."

Sunday, their weekly ritual call at seven p.m., on the dot. And God help her if she was busy somewhere else and didn't answer. Lucky thing her dad lived four hours away up north in Traverse City, or he'd be on her doorstep every time he couldn't get a hold of her.

"Something's come up."

"I'm just now leaving work. I'll call you as soon as I get in my car."

She didn't bother to wait for his yay or nay response. Knowing him, he'd probably argue, so she disconnected but kept the phone in her hand as she hurried across the parking lot. Quick to unlock the doors, she got in, hooked up her seatbelt then hit the lock button and started the engine before making the promised return call.

When her phone hooked up to blue tooth, she sat back the minute he answered. "Hi, Dad. How are you?"

"Fine." The word came out short and anything but sweet. "That's not what I called about. But first, how's the new job? Do you like it? Are you comfortable there?" Code for, is it a safe place to work?

During their last Sunday night call, she'd filled his

ear with details about the gallery. Babbling on and on, maybe out of sheer relief she wasn't going to lose her condo after all.

"I checked the place out."

Of course you did. Like the virtual shakedowns of any boy in high school who was brave enough to risk the third degree from her father to ask her out.

Heaven help Vince, provided they got that far. Legal or not, the poor man's entire background, birth to present day, would be under scrutiny in no time flat.

Still, it was hard for her to suppress a smile. "What did you find out?"

"There was very little available." Frustration rang out loud and clear in his tone. Andy Raines wasn't used to being stonewalled.

Maybe you shouldn't be so nosey. She bit it back. "It's a relatively new enterprise."

"I figured that out for myself. Anyway, I'm calling about Doug."

Just like that, the topic became her older brother.

She gripped the phone harder. "Is he okay? What happened?"

"Nothing. He's fine."

She seriously wondered about that but didn't argue. Her oldest brother had been working undercover now for two months. So deep under cover, he could go a week or more with no contact.

"How's Amy holding up?"

"She's managing."

Translation. As his wife, she knows the score. "That's good."

It was just fortunate they didn't have kids.

"A local county commissioner up here is suspected

of taking bribes. Doug got work as a contractor looking to score a hefty government contract."

"Sounds relatively safe."

Her dad's silence made it a sure bet that might not be the case.

"They're going to report he's been hurt on the job to put him in the hospital, hoping someone will make a move on him."

Sydney ran a hand through her hair. "Try to kill him?"

"That's not going to happen for real."

How do you know for sure?

She bit her lower lip to keep from saying it. Her dad had such confidence in the other officers in her brother's department. He always insisted the capers, as Andy Raines liked to call them when either of his sons went undercover, were foolproof. *For his benefit, or mine?*

"Anyway, don't be alarmed at what you may hear on the news. Who knows what gets picked up these days and is broadcast all over the damned place. I just want you to be aware."

"It's only make believe." She called up the term he'd used when she was a child to explain his behavior when he worked his own undercover assignments.

"Exactly." He cleared his throat. "I love you. Talk to you on Sunday."

"I love you too, Dad. If you talk to them, tell my brothers I said stay safe."

"Can do. You, too."

With the engine already running, she flicked on the radio for company before she even put the car in drive. Anything to drown out the silence and prevent her thoughts from taking off.

Despite her father insisting nothing was going to happen, she knew better. Way better. Bad things happened to police officers all the time.

All the way home the radio wasn't helping her suddenly strung out nerves. Truth was, she didn't want to be alone just now. She fished for her cell as she pulled her car in the garage, got out and walked toward the door. Vince answered before she'd even turned the knob to go in.

"Hey, Sydney. I was just going to call you."

Lowering her head, she smiled. Exactly what she needed to hear. "Hey yourself. How would you like to join me for some pizza?"

"Tonight?"

"Yes. Tonight."

"Do I really know you that well?"

Her heart sank as her fingers loosened their grip on the phone. Had she been wrong? Read more into what she thought was a growing relationship than was there? "Well if you're busy…"

"That's not it. I'll only share pizza with you if you're not one of those crazies who insist on anchovies."

She laughed out loud at his teasing. "I'm not. Mushrooms and black olives are my passion."

"Smart woman. In that case, I'll pick one up to feed your passion and be right over."

"I'll be waiting."

After changing into jeans and a long-sleeved, V-neck sweater, she spent the next few moments straightening up. Picking up a throw pillow to fluff, she found herself humming in anticipation of seeing Vince.

Less than two hours later, a nearly empty pizza box remained open on the coffee table in front of Grandma's loveseat. Two half full bottles of light ale beside it.

Sydney leaned back against the cushions with a sigh. "I so needed that, and the company tonight." Reaching over, she placed her hand over his.

"Glad I could accommodate." Vince stretched his other arm along the back of the loveseat.

When he shifted to circle her shoulders, his fingertips stroking along her upper arm.

Leaning into him came as naturally as breathing, and she settled close. The contradiction of a sensitive touch at odds with the strength of solid muscle felt exceptionally right. For the first time all day, she relaxed. With only one problem. Although Sydney knew there was no way she could, she so wanted to share with Vince what weighed on her mind about her brother. After all, that was what people who cared about each other did. Supported each other, helped make things right.

Not when it involves our work. Never share with a civilian. They won't understand.

Time to talk about other things. "How did your week go? Did you finish your article?"

The strokes on her arm stilled for a second then continued. "Not quite. It's not due until sometime next week."

"Do you have enough information? If you need more, I could probably arrange for Randall to—"

"That's not necessary. I'm good." A tightness entered his voice. "But thanks, I'll keep your offer in mind. So how about you?" When he spoke up this time, the tightness was gone. "Your first week on the new job. How was it?"

She rested her head on his chest. "Tiring. Exhilarating."

His fingertips continued a light massage on her shoulder and upper arm. Such minor contact, but she was totally captivated by its strength.

"Did you enjoy it though?"

"There's a lot to learn. I have a feeling one woman I met today is going to make things difficult for me."

"I'm sure you're up to it. Hell, with your people skills, you'll soon be running the place."

Sitting up, she shifted to bring her gaze even with his. "After the day I've had, I really needed that vote of confidence."

Creases at the edges of his eyes momentarily deepened though his gaze never faltered. "Glad I could accommodate. You know me. I aim to please."

It felt so very natural as he again slid his arm around her and she settled more deeply against him. "You're nice to be around, Vince."

"Just nice?" His body twitched as he slumped slightly. "As in companionship nice?"

Even though she knew he was teasing her, a pang of guilt hit. "How about really nice?"

The comeback was lame. Selfish or not, she needed his physical presence right now. If only to help maintain her sanity. She hated the way worry about her father, brothers and their jobs took such a heavy emotional toll.

Vince tightened his arm around her. "I was kind of hoping for more."

Definitely! She held back sharing until she paused

to sort through her thoughts. *What was her true motivation tonight? The companionship? Or the more?*

"Me too. Hoping for more." Her response came out strong. A sure sign, despite her reluctance, the decision was already made. She sat up to face him again. "Now, about that aiming to please part."

Expectation lit his eyes, and a smile quirked his lips. "Something I'm good at. Especially with you."

Not waiting for a response, he closed his lips firmly over hers. When he folded both arms around her, she melted into his warmth. His hand skimmed along her back, urging her nearer. She clasped her hands at his neck then shifted her head to allow him better access as his lips traveled along her cheekbone to her jaw and on to the sensitive flesh below one ear.

Her breathing accelerated as she gave herself up to the wonders of his touch. His fingertips, maddening in their gentleness, slid beneath her top to press more warmth against her skin. Warm or not, she shivered as his palms rose over her rib cage then slid like heated velvet to cup her breast.

Lifting his mouth, he locked his gaze on hers. "Is there anything else you need from me?"

Everything you're willing to give.

She drew another quick breath at the thought and stared into eyes alight with desire. Before she could even exhale, his lips sought hers again. As their kiss deepened, he pressed her down on the cushions. When he tried to lie down beside her on the narrow loveseat, one leg dropped to the floor with a thump as he jockeyed for position.

Sitting upright, he pulled her back into his arms. "There has to be a better way."

With her head again rested on his shoulder, she yearned to fulfill the promise lingering between them.

"There is a better way, and I'll show you." Accepting a sense of resolve like never before, she stood then took his hand to lead him down the short hallway to her bedroom. As they passed through the door, her lips turned up at a random thought. *Good thing I changed the sheets.*

They stopped beside the bed as if of one mind. Without a word, he raised the hem of her sweater then pulled the fabric off her arms, shoulders and over her head. Hot, incredibly gentle palms slid along her rib cage to the clasp of her bra he unhooked with one swift motion. As both garments fell to the floor, she turned to face him. His gaze lowered to take in the sight of her and the clear blue of his eyes darkened to resemble a star lit sky at midnight.

"I have protection on me." His voice was low and raspy as he folded her in his arms.

His mouth neared hers, but she put a light finger to his lips. "We don't need it."

He pulled his head back at her words. "But…."

"I'm on the pill." Her lips curved into a smile as the confusion in his gaze cleared. "Unless there's a reason we need more."

With a slight head shake, he gathered her close. She splayed her hands open to cling to his back when Vince dipped his head to brush warm kisses on her skin. His hands spread on either side of her ribcage to keep her close as he edged her backward. When her calves came up against the edge of her mattress, he lowered her onto a plush softness of the bright blue down comforter.

Kissing, tasting, touching, loving, he settled into place above her and clasped his hands over hers to stretch both arms over her head as he dropped his mouth to her breasts. Both eyes closed in anticipation as her breath stalled somewhere close to her heart. On a sigh of acceptance, Sydney arched into his intimate demands, until the delicate sensations became almost too much to bear.

"Kiss me, Vince. I need you to kiss me."

"Whatever you want, sweetheart." Raising his head, the words were no more than a soft vibration against her lips as his mouth covered hers.

As he released their kiss, she was barely able to breathe as, with his hands and lips, he worked an amazing magic. Her body hummed under his touch as her mind recalled the charm of his words. *Whatever you want, Sweetheart.* When they finally came up for air, she positioned her hand between them then beneath the bottom of his shirt. Sliding her palms over heated skin and firm muscle, she raised the garment up over his head.

Desire and passion shimmered in the depths of the eyes staring into hers. "It is getting warm in here."

He drew away from her then stood only long enough to unzip the pants he dropped to the floor. Separated briefly to shed what little clothing remained between them, they slid back together with incredible ease. Braced above her, their legs meshed perfectly as if designed to do so as Vince settled firmly into the cradle of her hips.

She gasped then smiled as he merged two into one. Hands at her sides, she fisted the sheets as he pushed them further into the depths of the mattress and pulled her into a world of sensations and pleasures she shared with him alone. In that moment, all that remained of her reality disappeared. Vince Reeves, strong and sure as he rocked into her then away, became all that mattered. The heat between them strengthened and flared until she was positive her soul was scorched to bear forever the mark of this man.

Chapter Seven

Vince spun the padlock to open his locker in the basement of the headquarters building of the Waterton PD. Operative words, *his locker.* Not a catch all loaner two burgs over. It felt good to be home, if only temporarily. For a moment, he simply stood there to stare at the contents in front of him. Family pictures taped inside the door. His little sister, Becca, mugging for the camera with an ear to ear grin after she'd kicked the game winning goal in her first ever high school soccer game. His mom and dad standing on either side him the day he graduated from the police academy. Below that, the black and white academy graduation picture of his birth father beckoned his attention.

"Hope I'm not dishonoring all you stood for."

And all I stand for now because of you.

Images of what he'd done the night before replayed in his mind. His overtures to make love. Sydney's nod of acceptance. The thrill and passions of discovery.

Vince raised his eyes to the maze of copper pipes crisscrossing the ceiling. Reliving bittersweet memories of what could never happen again.

"Well look who's here." Patrolman Luke Simms sat his bare ass down on the molded plastic bench that ran along the bank of lockers and ruffled a skimpy white department issue towel over wet hair. "You finish that UC?"

I wish. "Not quite."

Luke peeked out from the cover of white terry cloth. "What brings you back then?"

Vince rummaged in his locker as an excuse to keep his face hidden. "I needed a reality check."

"I hear you. It's damned difficult working undercover."

"You can say that again. This case is turning out to be a whole hell of a lot harder to process than I expected." *Pretending to be a friend, then becoming lovers with a woman I'm ultimately going to betray.*

"It's not a drug op or hard core crime case where you're constantly walking the line between upholding and breaking the law is it?"

Vince shook his head. "Nothing like that."

"Isn't it easier with the softer, white collar stuff?"

"In some ways dealing with spaced out druggies might be easier." Lowering his head, Vince mumbled the answer.

"Say what?"

He glanced over. "With them, you know where you stand. They're the bad guys, and we're the good." *Thing is I'm not exactly feeling like one of the good guys at the moment.* He straightened to pull his shaving kit off the top shelf. "Hard core or fluff doesn't necessarily make the job any easier."

"It should. With white collar crime, you don't have to stop thinking like a good guy to start thinking, then acting, like a bad one. Pretty much a victimless situation."

"Not always." Vince shrugged as he spoke darned near under his breath. *Victimless, like hell.* Though he had to consider the possibility when this whole situation with Sydney played itself out, if the victim might well be him.

"What have you got so far?" Luke stood and dropped his towel on the floor.

Vince glanced over as those thoughts scattered. His colleague was asking for the straight facts like the ones he'd eventually put in his report. No emotions involved.

He took a breath. "I had that art gallery under surveillance for a while and didn't see anything out of the ordinary. All very normal comings and goings. No suspicious looking deliveries or unmarked vehicles. Pretty much just the gallery owner and his staff and customers. An underwhelming number of those."

Luke pulled on briefs then a pair of jeans he zipped up. "The very thing that could be an issue in itself. If the place doesn't seem to be making money, it could mean it's a front for something else."

Vince shook his head. "Not likely." He shared the highlights of Curan's bio. "Money doesn't appear to be a big issue one way or the other."

"Or motivating factor, unless it's ego to warrant criminal activity."

"We did our own background check of Curan when this whole thing with the feds started. Which still leaves me with a lot of nothing there either." He pressed his lips together. *Nothing there but her.* "Worth reporting, that is."

Luke scoffed. "Take heart, my friend. It's a fed initiated operation, right?"

Vince nodded. "It is."

"If there's nothing there like you say, they'll eventually lose interest and move on. They always do. Then you're out of there and none the worse for wear."

That remains to be seen. "Maybe." If there was anyone he could confide in, about Sydney, it was Luke. So why wasn't he rushing to do it? "As I said, I ran surveillance on the place and got nothing. Then out of the blue—" *more appropriately the storm* "—I got a personal introduction to the suspected perp."

Luke's face lit up. "An in with a known associate? Lucky you. How'd that come about?"

"Not exactly an in." Quick with that reply, Vince gave an abbreviated version of his initial encounter with Sydney. Leaving out one highly personal detail. "Then she connected me with Curan."

"Sounds like one lead led to another."

Did it ever! He shook off invading memories of Sydney Raines. The taste of her lips, feel of her curves beneath his hands.

"So, what's your next move?"

Another roll in the hay? Vince shuttled the uncalled for thought away as he worked to banish the image of soft brown eyes and full lips. "I'll know better once I get inside."

Luke remained mum, no doubt waiting for more of an explanation. Too bad Vince didn't have one.

"Not working out as you'd expected?"

"You could say that." He rubbed a hand over his chin. "What's been happening around here that I've missed? What's going on with you?"

"Me?" Lips tight, it took a moment for Luke to meet Vince's gaze. "For one thing, I'm on desk duty."

"Again?" Vince dumped his shave kit in his duffel bag.

Luke was famous for bucking the system, or as he preferred to say, doing what was necessary to get the job done.

"Temporarily." He pulled a navy blue T-shirt out of his locker he pulled over his head. "Too bad you're UC these days. I was hoping the chief would let me out to ride with you. You being such a straight arrow and all."

"Being with me, you can't screw up?"

"I guess."

Vince pursed his lips in thought. *So maybe you won't screw up your career. What I do with mine remains to be seen.*

"Back in our academy days did you ever expect the job would end up like this?" Luke shook his head. "So many damned rules to follow?"

"We all need to adhere to the rules."

"I have no problem with that."

At his colleague's comment, Vince said nothing, just tilted one eyebrow as he shot him a look.

"I mean, I just never expected so damned many of them."

"We can't pick and choose which ones to go by." Though he didn't really want details, Vince had to ask for them. "What happened with you?"

Luke looked to one side then up at Vince again. "The way it went down, I got all macho on Chelsea."

"The woman you're supposed to marry in what? Six months?"

"Something like that." Luke took a deep breath and sat taller. "Anyway, they broke us up as partners when we moved in together."

"Seems like an oxymoron but go on."

"They paired Chelsea up with Amanda West."

With a slight grunt, Vince nodded. "West is a ten-year veteran who really knows the ropes. Chelsea could have done worse."

"Maybe." Luke's eyes widened as if a light had just popped on in his head. "That's right. You know West and then some. Aside from a professional perspective, you could say."

Vince stuck his head back in the locker again. "You could."

Truth was, Vince became highly familiar with the female officer's 'and then somes' when they'd dated a few years back. Though nothing really serious ever developed between the two of them beyond a few romps in the sack. Not that he necessarily would have acted on it if anything had.

"In fact, you two had a real connection for a time."

Saturday night sex while going their separate ways Sunday morning was a connection? "We were never actually that close. Then once I was promoted, to comply with regulations, we broke it off. Turned out she was fine with that."

"She's married now. West is. Kept her maiden name."

"Doesn't surprise me."

"Me either. But, pairing Chelsea with another woman? That's just not right."

"What, are you prejudiced?" Something made Vince smile as he spoke. "Sergeant West has proven herself time and again as a top-notch officer in the field."

"She sure proved that to be true the other day. Sorta showed me up in the process."

Again, it wouldn't be fair not to ask. "How so?"

Luke took a breath. "West and Chelsea were out

responding to an unknown assailant, possible domestic that sounded like it was about to go south. I was only a few blocks away, so of course I went in when dispatch called for backup." After another breath, he went on. "Given the situation, I arrived on scene with my firearm drawn, only to discover the responding officers had the situation under control and everything secure before I got there." He shook his head. "Way before I got there. Neither one of them appreciated my efforts. West said they were, and I quote, overzealous and unnecessary. I'm sure Chelsea would have backed me up and kept it all to herself. Her partner not so much."

"Why doesn't that surprise me?" Despite the serious circumstances, Vince couldn't suppress a laugh. "Amanda can be tough to deal with."

"All women can be tough to deal with."

Vince glanced over. "Chelsea, being a fellow cop, should know better, huh?"

"You'd think." Luke put both hands on his knees and hung his head. "That's not the worst of it."

Vince closed the locker door and looked down at him. "There's more?"

His buddy sighed. "Chelsea's still mad at me too. Real mad. She hates when I do that macho stuff. Says it undermines her as a professional."

"So why did you?"

"I don't know. Thinking she was in danger, I saw red." Luke fisted both hands. "I didn't think of possible consequences. Quite frankly, I didn't think of anything but a need to protect her."

"Happens to all of us."

"Guess I better figure out a way to get back into her good graces before the wedding."

"Probably wouldn't hurt."

"Easier said than done." Luke shrugged. "I have a feeling I really blew it this time."

"Maybe. Maybe not." Admittedly lame, but all Vince could think to say. Truth was, Luke deserved more.

"At least she hasn't thrown me out."

"That is something."

Luke's hardened look softened. "It is nice living with someone you love. Gives me a sense of belonging."

"I can understand that."

Ironically, this is exactly where I belong was the first thought to strike him that very morning when he woke up in Sydney's bed. Then a second thought took over and held.

What the hell was I thinking?

That's just it. He wasn't thinking. Turned out being with Sydney tended to do that to his head. He sidestepped over to put his arm around his friend. "Hang in there. You two will get it figured out."

"Here's hoping." He shrugged. "So, you hook up with Ned Foley over there at Manderfield yet?"

"I did. He's my official contact. I've gotten to know him some. We've met a couple of times for breakfast. What a character."

"I'll say." Luke chuckled. "That guy has been around forever."

Vince let out a silent sigh of relief. This was good, talking about something else to take his mind off the woman he was forced to mislead. "He must have graduated from the academy sometime in the Dark Ages."

"Still working the roads, chasing taillights."

"Doing what he loves."

"He's got to be pushing sixty. Word is he passed up promotion after promotion simply to stay in the field for no other reason than because he wanted to."

"Gotta respect him for that." Vince was getting comfortable with the neutrality of their conversation. Anything to quit discussing a case that was taking him, and his career, down one hell of a dangerous path. One he'd never trod before. Maybe never would again. "In fact, I ran into him the other day, almost literally. He was after a kid for shop lifting I later found out. I happened to be walking down the street. Somehow the kid took off on him and damned near ran right into my arms."

"You helped with the arrest then."

"Couldn't." He ducked his head back into his locker to rearrange a pair of boots on the floor.

"Why not?"

Straightening, he filled Luke in on some of what he termed extenuating circumstances. "Would have blown my cover with her."

"Can't do that."

"Nope." *No matter how bad I want to.* Vince glanced up at the unbidden thought.

"Sure are a lot of crazies in the world." Luke's brow furrowed.

"Guess we should consider that job security."

"Some pretty nasty stuff going on. Sitting at my desk the other day." Blatant sarcasm ripped into his tone. "I got so damned bored I read every stinking bulletin that came through from some other departments. Crime these days ranges from grandma robbing her local PTA to a gruesome John or Jane Doe body discovery."

"ID unknown?"

"Somewhere down south I think. Found in a car. I should say burned out carcass of what had been a car. Couldn't even tell if the victim inside was male or female. That's how bad it was."

"Jesus."

"He wasn't there that day, apparently."

Vince was suddenly sick of some of the gory details of police work. Metal clanged as he shut the locker door and spun the dial. "I'm off to whatever the rest of this investigation might bring."

Even as he said it, Vince had no real idea what that prophetic bit of bullshit meant. But he sure as hell had an idea he'd find out soon enough. Pushing away the thought, he shrugged into his coat.

"Don't sweat it, Detective Straight Arrow, I'm not worried about your case. You always manage to figure these things out."

"You think?"

"As for me, all I know is Chelsea means the world to me. I gotta figure out how to get back in her good graces."

"As bad as you've got it, you will." With a nod over his shoulder, Vince smiled. "See you later."

"Wish I had your confidence." His friend dropped his gaze briefly then looked up. "Good luck with your case."

"Thanks. I think I'll stop by the gallery before I go home."

"Always working." Luke shook his head. "Enjoy."

"Here's hoping." The irony of their exchange

wasn't lost on Vince as he stepped outside.

A gust of unusually warm air greeted him, and he unzipped his jacket then took it off to throw in the backseat before he climbed into his car. Sitting there for a moment, he peered out the windshield at a squad car parked by the back door of the station. *Waterton*, in bold royal blue was lettered in a circle. Enclosed in the center was a badge of gold with the words *Police Department* emblazoned across the top. In large, solid type along the back, side panel was the proclamation: *TO SERVE AND PROTECT*.

Vince averted his gaze as he stabbed his key into the ignition. Right now, he was doing a piss poor job achieving either. Not to mention being on track to bring Internal Affairs raining down on his head, and his career, big time.

He flipped the key to on. As the engine took off with a growl then hum, he made a vow to himself, and to Sydney. Before this was all over, he'd come clean to her about who he really was and why he had to do what he did. Somehow, he'd find the balls to apologize to her. Moving the gear shift into reverse, he glanced out the back window before he hit the gas. The untruths, the deceit, he'd take responsibility for all of it. Even for making love to her.

With the nose aimed at the exit, he put the late model Chevy loaner car in drive then scanned the street and pulled forward at a break in the traffic as he hit the accelerator.

Oh, yeah. I take FULL responsibility for the pleasure of making love to her.

God help him, no way could he bring himself to apologize for that.

****

The receptionist desk up front was empty as usual when Vince first wandered into the Argentile Gallery. Not exactly disappointed, he walked unaccompanied, back to Sydney's office.

For the moment, he took his focus off the what and how of his case he planned to discuss with her and concentrated on what went on around him. Which was, on a mid-week afternoon, a lot of nothing, save for some low voices coming from one of the other hallways. Not the customer traffic one might expect for a supposedly thriving business operation.

Sydney was on the phone when he arrived at the doorway to her office.

"Thank you for your interest in the Argentile Gallery." Her tone was polite and professional as she spoke into the receiver. She wore a smile to match. "Good-bye."

"Another happy customer, I assume." Leaned against the door jamb, Vince pushed off and moved toward her.

"Vince." The moment she lifted her gaze to his, Sydney's face lit up, and the smile broadened to make her eyes sparkle. Her regard dipped to the phone. "They are now. They had a delivery issue that was easy to solve."

Advancing into her office, he couldn't take his eyes off her as a comforting heat spread through his chest to surround his heart. "I got off, uh, finished up earlier than I expected. Hope I'm not interrupting."

"You're not." She leaned back in her chair. "Even if you were, it wouldn't matter. I'd never turn you away."

Tell me that when you learn the truth.

Before he'd totally registered the full import of that idea, she came around her desk, glanced at the door, then hit him with a light kiss.

"It's good to see you." He had his arms around her and dipped his head, ready for more. Things didn't get far before she pushed at his chest and he felt obligated to let her go. "You're at work. Sorry."

"I'm not. Sorry that is." As she slid away from him, the original brightness in her smile dimmed as she looked up at him. "I'm afraid Randall isn't here just now. He won't be around tomorrow either. He's out of town."

Not willing to release her entirely, he kept his hands on her waist. "Just out of curiosity, out of town to where?"

May as well make a pass at working the case, while I'm here.

She shook her head then shrugged. "I'm not sure. Something that needed his attention. Somewhere. He didn't elaborate. Sorry."

"Not a big deal, since he's not my first priority for coming around anymore." The sheer truth of what he said rang in his ears. "I thought we'd go somewhere together after work. Maybe grab something to eat."

Her bright expression turned downright dismal. "Oh, Vince. I can't."

The optimism he'd arrived with took a hike. "Why not?"

"I have to work."

"Tonight? After the gallery closes?" *Easy.* It wouldn't do to seem too possessive. "Doing what?"

She frowned at him then stepped back and

straightened. “Attending the Manderfield Township Council Meeting.”

“Why?” Since her initial refusal to go out with him, he was just full of questions.

“There’s a proposed zoning ordinance on their agenda. One that could adversely affect the gallery. Randall wants to make sure he has all the facts about it, and since he’s out of town…” She ended on another shrug.

“Couldn’t he send a lawyer or something? Instead of you?”

“Probably.” She pursed her lips then glanced down. “At a much higher price than he’s paying me.”

“I thought with rich people money was no object.”

“Whether that’s true or not, before he left he asked me to go in his place and I agreed. Now I wish I hadn’t.”

About to lodge another protest, Vince stopped himself and took a breath. Why not make the most of what little time they did have together today? “I guess you had no choice.”

She pulled her gaze from his to look at her desk. “The meeting doesn’t start until seven, though I wanted to get there early. Maybe talk to some of the council members before things actually begin.”

“I wouldn’t want to hold you up.”

“I’m not worried about that. We probably have time to stop for something light. Maybe at Anton’s across the street?”

He opened his mouth and shut it again as her offer took him by surprise. It probably wasn’t the best idea to be seen with her in a place the chief already knew about. “Sure. Sounds good.”

"I have a few more calls to make before I leave."

"I'll let you do that. Maybe I'll talk with a few customers. Get more insight into my article. Then wait for you in the front entrance."

Less than half an hour later, Vince was doing just that. Waiting. While he tried his best not to pace. Work off the frustration that had taken over once he left Sydney's office. His interview with a couple of Argentile patrons did absolutely nothing to further the case. If this place was involved in the art theft ring the feds were probing, Vince was a…

"Ready to go?"

At Sydney's voice, he spun around. "Sure am."

The second she fell into step beside him, his arm was around her shoulders, and he pulled her close to his side. Heat seeped into him from the contact, and any residual tension he'd been holding on to slid away. If nothing else, he was determined to make the most of what little time they did have tonight.

She turned slightly his way as they walked across the parking lot. "Have you been busy today?"

Her question made him drop his thoughts. "Sort of."

"Doing what?"

He damned near miss his footing as they stepped up on the curb. "You know, the usual."

Smooth, Miller. Really smooth. He opened the door of Anton's for her, and they walked inside.

"Hello and welcome to Anton's."

They both glanced up at the barista's greeting. Giving their orders, making small talk with the staff, then picking up their drinks and selecting a table made further private dialogue between the two of them impossible.

When they finally sat down across from each other, Vince made sure to direct their conversation to how her job was going, what the weather was supposed to be the next day. Anything to avoid answering her initial question. Somewhere in there, he took hold of her hand. If he couldn't follow through with what he wanted to do, be truthful about who he was, physical contact was the next best thing as she told him about her day at Argentile.

Curan's been running you pretty hard. He was quick to ditch the first words to come to mind. No way did he want to sound judgmental. "Have you had a chance to get acclimated?"

She took a sip of her latte then set down the white porcelain cup. "Not really."

The truth of her answer caught him off guard, and he ditched his next knee jerk response. *What can I do to help?* "Things around the gallery moving pretty fast?"

"It's not so much that. In fact, things are moving a bit slower than on my previous job." Keeping her hand beneath his, she sat back and smiled. "Which is a welcome change."

"But you still feel a little unsettled."

Her smile disappeared, and she studied him with her brow furrowed. "Very perceptive of you to notice."

He was careful to produce an off handed shrug. "Guess I'm more tuned into you than maybe you realize." *Or I should be.*

Though the creases on her forehead cleared, her eyes widened before she gave him a shy smile. "Maybe I'm the one who needs to become more perceptive."

The things he wanted to share with her stacked up

in his mind like rush hour traffic halted for a second round at a stop light. He squeezed her hand instead of speaking right away, as his heart sat in his chest like a dull, inactive blob. "I'm sure you'll learn the ropes soon and get into a comfortable routine."

"I'm sure I will too." Pulling her hand free, she twisted her wrist to check her watch. "I suppose I should get going." She glanced across the table at him with her lips pressed together. "I wish I didn't have to."

"Me too, but that's fine." Vince stood, his tone a hell of a lot lighter than he felt. "We can get together for longer some other time. Tomorrow night maybe."

"I'd like that."

"Me too." His heart woke up enough to complete a spry little back flip.

"Call me." There was no shyness in her reply, just comfortable familiarity.

He put his arm on what had become its customary place around her shoulders as they walked back out the door. "I'll call you."

"Okay."

When they reached the parking lot behind the gallery, she got into her car, and he got into his.

Glancing over at her before he even thought about firing up the engine, he lifted his right hand. With quick waves exchanged through their respective side windows, he and Sydney went their separate ways.

Chapter Eight

"Hey, gorgeous."

"Hey, yourself." Sydney smiled into the phone as warmth seeped in then crept around her heart. "How are you, Vince?"

Dragging through the door after another long day at the gallery, all she needed was to hear his voice to receive a quick surge of energy.

"I'm good." He stopped a moment to clear his throat. "I wanted, uh, what are your plans for tonight? Anything important going on?"

Her smile grew. "No. I just got home from work."

"Have you had dinner yet?"

"I hadn't gotten that far." Glancing up, she took in the disarray that was her living room. The pile of mail on the table in the entrance she hadn't had a chance to go through in a week. "What did you have in mind?"

Another throat clearing came over the line. "Just that I'd like to…thought maybe we could get together tonight like we talked about."

At his hesitation her smile dipped. She'd never known the man to be anything but direct and straight forward. "I really don't feel like going out tonight. Why don't you just come over? I'll throw together some broccoli cheese soup."

"I'll pick up a salad mix and some wine." His agreement was swift. "See you soon."

"Sounds good, Vince. See you."

There was a definite spring in her step as she hung up the phone and headed into her bedroom. She even indulged in a quick shower before changing into Capri length jeans and a maize and bright blue University of Michigan T-shirt. Once in the kitchen, she pulled a carton of chicken broth off the pantry shelf, then bustled around collecting the rest of the necessary ingredients for the soup. She'd just closed the refrigerator door when her cell rang. In anticipation of another call from Vince, she hurried toward the counter where she'd left it.

Had he changed his mind? Wiping her hands on a plaid dish towel, she shook her head. Why would that be her first thought? *Because I have it bad for this man and I'm not sure his feelings are as strong as mine?*

Stilling the butterflies threatening to take flight in her stomach, she glanced at the Caller ID, read *Winsome Gate Condominiums*, and screwed up her nose.

"This is Sydney Raines."

"Hey, Sydney. How you doin'?"

"Hey, Glenn." Her nostrils flared on a grimace at his hokey impression of a guy on the make. She forced civility into her tone. "What do you need?"

The reckless question was out before she thought about it. The grimace deepening, she braced for his inevitable response.

"You." The suggestive chuckle that followed made her skin crawl. "Since you took the trouble to ask and everything."

Never in a million years. "That's not what I meant."

"Actually, I'm just doing my job. Checking in to make sure my tenants are safe and secure. All part of this protect and serve profession of mine." A self-indulgent sniff came over the line.

It took a boatload of concentration to not laugh out loud. Even given her limited experience, without a doubt, she knew a lot more about the profession than he did.

"You doing okay?"

"Peachy. Thanks." Dead air was the response to that remark, prompting her to speak up again. "So. Duty fulfilled here. I'd be the last one to want to keep you from safeguarding the others in this complex."

"There is one other thing."

"What's that?" Lifting her hand, she absently massaged two fingers over her forehead.

"I accepted a package delivered for you this morning. Thought it might be important."

She rested the phone between her shoulder and ear as she went back to lining up her soup ingredients. "I'm a little busy right now. I'll come over to pick it up as soon as I can."

"I'll be here until nine. Looking forward to it."

That makes one of us. "I'll be over in a little while." She slipped the phone into her palm to hang up with one thumb, then tossed the device back on the counter and reached for an onion.

Soon, the savory aroma of chicken broth, broccoli and sharp fragrant cheese filled her kitchen. Setting the burner to low, she left the soup to simmer while she went to retrieve whatever package awaited her.

Fall was definitely in the air as she stepped outside. Despite a cooler breeze, low sunlight fell warm and welcome on her shoulders as she made her way down the porch steps. High in the elms and maples, birds not yet traveling south twittered and chirped as they flitted in and out of plush green leaves with the beginning tinges of red and gold. She followed the curved walkway toward the curb.

"Well hello, beautiful." Glenn glanced up with the greeting before Sydney got fully through the door of the management office.

"Hi." In the name of etiquette, she made a polite attempt to match his wide smile. "You have my package for me here?"

"I do."

"Where is it?" She crossed her arms over her chest.

Glenn remained behind the long, high counter that separated them, occasionally glancing at several television screens aimed his way. The sound of conversation then a laugh track floated out from one of them. He stood then sauntered over to stand beside her. "How's your day going?"

"Busy." The cologne he'd slathered on assaulted her nose, and she fought the urge to back away. "How about you?"

"It's been pretty quiet today." He glanced her way with a wink. "Civilians are behaving themselves."

Seriously? "I hope the package isn't too big to carry. I walked over."

His blank stare lasted a couple of seconds before he blinked. "Oh, yeah." He turned to duck under his desk then pulled out a six-inch square box he handed over. "I thought it could be important."

Sydney glanced at the brown paper covered cube with California Cosmetics as the return address. "This is a company I've ordered from before. Probably a free sample. They're always sending me those. Thanks for taking it in for me." She tucked the package under one arm without looking up at him.

"Anytime." He didn't move from where he'd planted himself between her and the door. "I tried that restaurant you recommended. The little Italian place."

She nodded as she started to edge around him. "They do make a very good pizza."

He sidestepped along with her then stepped back and leaned against the door jamb with a casual ease. "You just say the word, little lady, and we'll go there some time."

At the crudely issued dinner invitation, she met his gaze. To politely refuse, yet again, would be pointless. As would being rude. Neither had deterred him in the past. "I don't think the man I'm currently involved with would appreciate that."

"Oh." The revelation knocked his bravado down a notch or two as bold confidence fell from his expression. "You're seeing someone?"

A smile bloomed as she nodded. "I am."

"Oh."

"For quite some time now." Nothing wrong with using a little white lie to strengthen her case.

"Is it serious?"

Even though she opened her mouth, no words emerged. Mainly because she could think of none. Was her relationship with Vincent Reeves serious? Neither had made mention of a commitment unless lovemaking counted.

For her it did. "Yes. I'm afraid it is." *Afraid?* "Thanks for the package. Bye."

She'd already pushed through the door before he had a chance to detain her any longer. *I'm afraid it is?* What kind of answer was that? Talk about a telling word choice. Or was she, as usual, overanalyzing? What exactly *was* she afraid of? Vince or the commitment? Taking a firmer grip on the package, her mental quandary continued as she stepped off the curb.

The engine roar caught her attention first. In the instant she took to look up, it was too late. The package flew out of her hands as she tried to backpedal out of the way.

A solid mass of fast traveling metal clipped the back of her thigh just below her hip. She arched backward from the blow. In an attempt to keep her balance, she lurched forward, momentum kept her limbs flailing with nothing to grab on to and she stumbled. The unforgiving pavement bit into her knee. Somehow, she twisted her upper body enough to land the rest of her on the newly mowed grass. Every ounce of air in both lungs jolted out of her as she hit the unforgiving ground. Mouth gaping like a fish out of water, she put a hand to her throat as she fought to inhale.

"Stay down!" A male voice shouted at her as she rolled to climb to all fours.

Still struggling to draw a breath, Sydney flopped to her back and glanced up. Birds flew in haphazard patterns, silhouetted against a blue sky scattered with clouds. Without warning, her vision blurred, and she brought an arm up to shield watering eyes.

"Don't try to move." Urgency filtered through Vince's voice.

Cool palms covered her cheeks as she lowered her

arm. A gray haze took over her vision, and she blinked. *I'm okay.* Intending to speak, with her breath still basically AWOL all she could do was mouth the words. Vince was on his knees beside her. His palms remained on her cheeks to keep her head in place. Judging by the mixture of stiffness and aches in her limbs, she figured her arms and legs must still be intact.

"Don't try to move. Lie still." His palms slipped from her face.

Unable to even nod, all she could do was stare up at him. For whatever reason, Vince's mouth was the first thing she noticed. Lips pulled rigid, their corners drawn down in concern.

"I'm okay, Vince. Really." Raising her head, she managed to get the words out.

"Oh my God! Oh my God! Oh my God! Sydney, are you okay?"

She recognized Randall's voice as scuffling footsteps rushed toward them. "I don't know what happened."

"You did this?" Vince's words were bitten off short.

The approaching steps pulled up, his feet mere inches from her head. "No, of course not. But whoever did so simply drove off."

"Did you get a description of the car?"

"It was a light color." The force of his voice became shrill. "That's all I saw."

Vince grunted then shook his head as his full attention returned to her. "Sydney. Look at me. Open your eyes."

She lifted her lids as best she could to the concern in his gaze.

"My phone rang, and I glanced over to reach for it." Randall spoke again. "When I glanced back, the car was speeding off, and Sydney was flying through the air."

A door slammed, and more footfalls scuffed on concrete. "What's going on?"

"Did you see anything?" Vince called out to whoever approached.

"No. I was in my office and heard the commotion, but don't worry. I have everything under control."

"Nothing? You saw nothing?" Jaw rigid, his eyes flashed dark and intimidating just before he glanced up.

"No, but I'll handle this." Glenn skidded to a stop at her other side. His knees jabbed into her side, and he nearly toppled on top of her as he knelt down. "Are you okay, Sydney? Let me help you stand up."

She turned her head without thinking then winced as Glenn's hands closed over her shoulders.

Vince strong armed him off of her. "Back off. It's not a good idea to move her until we're sure nothing's broken…or out of place."

Glenn reared back up after being pushed to his haunches. "You don't understand. I'm the law enforcement around here."

"Then you're surely versed in proper first aid procedures." Vince hit him with a steely gaze. "Right?"

Mouth dropped open, the condominium hireling blinked. "Yeah. Sure."

Contrary to what he said, Glenn did no more than sit back and watch. With a cool and professional touch that would make any experienced EMT proud, Vince checked Sydney's head and neck for injuries then moved on to test her limbs.

"You're sure you're okay?" Randall's shaking voice rose. Standing above them, he continued to lament the situation in fits and starts of an ongoing monologue. "It was partly my fault. I pulled out and he swerved to avoid hitting me."

"It was a male subject driving the car?" Vince spoke in a low tone. "That's something."

"That's all I saw, though." Randall shook his head.

"You're sure you didn't see what happened Mr. Law Enforcement Around Here?" Vince glanced over at Glenn. "Could that be what happened?"

The man remained wide-eyed as he shook his head. "'Fraid I can't answer that. I was…uh, busy watching my monitors."

One side of Vince's top lip curled back. "Didn't think so. Did you at least call an ambulance?"

"No." Sydney spoke up before Glenn had a chance to. "That would cost even more money that I don't have." She struggled to sit up to prove further medical attention was unnecessary. "Really."

"You're more important than money." His voice softened.

She laid a still trembling hand on Vince's arm. A muscle twitched beneath her fingertips. "No ambulance. I'm fine."

"You don't look fine." Fresh pain was reflected in the depths of his eyes as if he suffered right along with her.

"It's okay, Vince. Really."

"Nothing seems to be broken."

She opened her mouth to agree when Randall swooped in again, moving his hands in erratic patterns as if he directed some bizarre orchestra. "Do let me know if there's anything I can do. I'm so sorry I was partially responsible. I was texting. A new order is coming into the gallery…"

"Shit happens when drivers aren't paying attention." Vince's response was guttural at best. "We'll let you know."

Her grip tightened on Vince's arm. "I'll be okay. I'm sure of it."

"I'm not." The comment rumbled out from under his breath.

Dampness spread over the top of her left calf as she sat up and she glanced down. Droplets of blood seeped out of her knee from a number of scrapes. "I'm just a little skinned up is all. My knee came down first, then I fell sideways, and my butt absorbed the brunt of the impact." She raised her slightly bruised derriere as she met his gaze to offer a half-smile he failed to return. "I just need to get inside and sit down."

"In my opinion, you really need more than that, but it's a start."

Randall kept up his frenzied bobbing around them. "If you need to go to the hospital, incur any medical expenses. I'll pay for everything. Money is no object."

He was so terribly upset, so flustered, Sydney actually began to feel sorry for him. "It was an accident, Randall. I understand that."

"I sure as hell don't." Vince's voice, low so only she could hear, vibrated with anger.

Sydney glanced at her boss.

His eyes remained wide and wary as he continued to babble on with promises of support and compensation. "I am so very sorry."

"She doesn't seem to be seriously hurt." Vince's

voice came out deep and measured.

“As I’ve said.” Randall leaned toward him, his expression equally grim. “I’m sure it was an accident.”

The reply was a shrug as Vince helped Sydney to her feet. She automatically leaned into him, savoring his strength. All she really wanted to do was to wrap her arms around him and hang on for dear life.

“I’ve got you.” His arm tightened at her waist as his hand cupped her hip. “Let’s get you inside.”

She curled her hand around a firm and solid shoulder. Another half-smile she tried for never materialized as Vince turned her around.

“Ow!” With a wince, she stumbled. Putting weight on the knee shot pain clear up from her shin to the top of her thigh. Even though he supported her, Sydney hobbled along beside him for a few more steps.

“This is going to take forever.” He stopped to put one arm behind her knees then cradled her shoulders with the other to lift her off the ground.

Relieved to no longer have to walk on an obviously injured knee, she rested her head against his shoulder and closed her eyes. Vince said nothing more until they got across the street to the sidewalk that led to her porch and front door.

“Damned dumb idiot! Owns a car like a Porsche, then is criminally inattentive in a God damned residential area. Jerk.”

“He’s my boss. I’m not going to press charges. Anyway, it was more or less an accident.”

“Accident or not, you could have been more seriously hurt, even… Dumb ass!” A muscle along his cheek flexed as his jaw clenched. Vince shifted her closer against him as he carried her up the last stair to her porch.

"He said he was sorry."

Vince took the key she pulled out of her pocket to hand him. "Whatever."

"Now that I think about it, the other car looked a lot like one Mark used to drive, but…"

"Mark. Who's Mark?" The words burst out.

"My ex-husband. We may have issues, but he wouldn't try to hurt me. Or maybe I just imagined it."

Choosing to say no more, she rested her head down as he carried her inside then over to the couch. She unwound her arm from around his shoulder as he lowered her onto the cushion.

"Put your leg up. You need to elevate that knee." He slipped off his jacket he slipped under her injured leg.

"Don't!" She pushed the make shift pillow away. "You'll get blood on that."

With one swift move he deflected her hand. "Easier to wash this than an entire couch."

Accepting his logic, she rested her head on the tufted arm and closed her eyes. "You win."

"Figured I would." For the first time since her accident, the hard edge of his tone lessened.

Rather than banter back, she let out an audible sigh. "Thank you for taking care of me. If you hadn't come by when you did…"

"It's what…" When he had her injured joint settled to his satisfaction, he straightened then stood back as if to study his work. "Did you hit your head when you fell?" A deep scowl had frown lines etched across his brow and along the corners of his mouth as he touched her forehead.

"I don't think so. Nothing hurts up there."

"Are you sure?"

"To be honest, I'm not absolutely sure of much of anything." She cautiously explored her skull.

He circled her wrists to pull her hands away. "That doesn't necessarily mean all is okay."

With incredibly gentle fingers, he probed her scalp and the back of her neck then slid his palm around to cup her cheek.

"Everything happened so fast." She relaxed under his touch.

The cushion dipped as he knelt beside the couch. "I need a flashlight of some kind."

"Kitchen drawer. By the refrigerator. A small one."

"Perfect." He got up and headed out of the room. "Band aids and or gauze and tape in the bathroom?"

"Yes. In the cabinet over the toilet."

"Disinfectant in here too?" Amid some rummaging sounds he called out the question.

"Should be."

"Got it. And your bottle of ibuprofen."

It wasn't long before he returned with the various items he'd mentioned in hand. Dropping everything on the coffee table, he cleaned and bandaged her knee first then picked up the pen light he clicked on. With the same delicate touch he'd shown her outside, he spread her lids wide then moved his face nearer. So close, she could inhale the minty scent of his breath. Even as the tiny beam hit her pupils, it was hard for Sydney not to squirm. She gave her best effort to remain still, then swallowed to moisten a dry throat and licked her lips. When she blew out the whisper of a breath, Vince's gaze slid to her mouth where it lingered for a moment.

Deep furrows on his forehead cleared, and his expression softened as he set her penlight on the end table. "I'd hate to have something happen to you."

In the next instant, he had her secure in his arms. As his breathing evened out, he simply held her.

"I'm okay you know." Her words were muffled against his chest.

He released a sigh then pulled back only far enough to meet her gaze. "I don't want to lose you, Sydney."

She stroked his lips with light fingertips. "I don't want to lose you either."

"Seeing you lying on the grass, not moving as Curan stepped out of his car. For a second there, I'm convinced I saw the son of a bitch smile. Then he caught sight of me and went into his 'I'm so sorry' routine."

"It was an accident." Her response was mildly insistent before she bolted upright. "My soup!" She lurched off the couch and hobbled to the kitchen. "I forgot all about it."

Vince was right on her heels. "Where the heck do you think you're going?"

She didn't answer until she got to the stove. "Our soup. I left it to simmer while I went to get my package. It's only supposed to cook for about twenty minutes tops. This has been on the heat much longer." She pulled the pot off the front burner with one hand while turning its dial to off with the other. "A few more minutes and our dinner would have been ruined."

"I would have been happy to go somewhere to get us take out."

"If I keep stirring we should be okay." She worked

the wooden spoon slowly through the bubbling soup.

"If you keep putting weight on that injured knee of yours, you won't be." Hauling over a bar stool, he situated the seat near her butt then pushed down on her shoulder. "Sit. Take your weight off that knee. If it's sprained at all, you could end up with some real problems."

"Such as?" She didn't look at him as she spoke.

"Such as some real stiffness and swelling. Or worse, you might have cracked your knee cap. Which we won't know for sure since you refused medical treatment."

"That sounds like something my father would say." Though she remained seated to satisfy Vince, Sydney glanced at their dinner. The spoon she swirled slid over the pot bottom without sticking. At least nothing was too badly burned. "I didn't need medical attention. I never blacked out. I was able to move around. Plus, I had you to take care of me." She raised up again to peek into the pot. "Which you did especially well, I might add." Banging the spoon handle on the pan edge, she turned to look at him. "Why's that do you think? Why are you so skilled?"

His immediate response to her question was a shrug. "Let's just say I was a Boy Scout. And a darned good one."

"I'll bet you were. Hey!" Before she knew it, Sydney was back in his arms like a bride being carried over the threshold.

"Now that you've saved the soup, time to return to the couch and elevate that knee." Once he had her re-deposited in the living room, he lifted her leg onto his wadded up jacket then went back to the kitchen.

Letting her head slump back, she stared at the ceiling as drawers opened and shut. Soon, he returned, sealing up a zip lock bag full of ice he then wrapped in a dish towel. “Twenty minutes on, twenty minutes off.” With great care, he laid the cold pack over her injury. “While you’re doing that, the wine and salad I brought are still in my car. I’ll look for your package while I’m out there.”

“The package. I forgot all about that.” Though she chose not to tell Vince, her knee had begun to throb.

He didn’t look back as he rose to head for the door. “Did you?”

After he left, she laid her head against the cushion and closed her eyes as cooling relief leached into her joint. Within minutes, Vince returned. Refusing to allow Sydney to do anything but sit still and rest, he served their dinner. Along with a couple of pain pills he had her swallow. Even as they ate, he kept checking with her to make sure she was comfortable and not hurting too much.

Leaving each of them with another glass of wine, Vince collected their empty bowls and salad plates. “Tomorrow is Friday, I assume you’re taking off work.”

“Probably. Put everything in the sink. I’ll load the dishwasher in the morning.” She spoke to his retreating back as he disappeared into the kitchen.

“It’d be just as easy for me to do it now.”

“Suit yourself.” The white wine winked and swirled as she brought it to her mouth. Taking a healthy sip, she rolled the tasty liquid around on her tongue then swallowed. *Who am I to argue?*

By the time Vince returned to the living room,

she'd drained the final few drops and set down her empty glass.

"How does your knee feel?"

"Better. Much better. Thank you."

He sat down behind her then situated her to lean against him. "Keep the ice rotating on and off it for a few more hours. Promise?"

"Whatever you say." Settling into the comfort he offered, she readily agreed, then decided to go for a friendly little poke. "If you think I'm competent enough to take care of myself."

"I have no doubt you can take care of yourself. However, now that you mention it, just to be sure, maybe I should spend the night. Just to be sure you're okay."

"Sounds like a good idea to me." She gave the response without thoroughly thinking it through, then decided it didn't matter.

The important thing was to have Vince with her tonight, all night.

What transpired in their future, she'd deal with when it arrived.

Chapter Nine

"And that's a recap of what I have so far on the Argentile Art Gallery case." Vince resumed his seat in a well-worn chair at the conference table.

The conference room upstairs at the Waterton PD headquarters remained quiet for a moment as papers shuffled. A few attendees in the meeting cleared their throats. His fingers circled the small Styrofoam cup half full of what had become tepid coffee. He'd left Sydney that morning to come to work simply because he had to. His appearance at this briefing was mandatory. An undocumented absence would have definitely been noticed. He'd served some coffee and toast to her in bed and made her promise to take it easy. All of which would have to do until he could get back to her.

Thoughts of Sydney retreated as murmurs of a low-key conversation reached his ears from the two federal agents who sat across from him. Jenkins and Murphy. From what Vince had been able to learn about them, two lifers. The presentation he'd given them, like the report he planned to file, was detailed and comprehensive. No evidence of criminal activity found. No reason to continue with the investigation or his involvement in it.

Which, for Vince, sure was a double-edged sword.

Professionally he was off the case. Duty fulfilled. He opened his fingers as the cup he held cracked from the unintentional pressure. Personally, he remained in deeper than he ever dreamed possible.

"You're sure there's nothing going on there?" Jenkins, the older of the two spoke first.

Vince sat forward to make eye contact. "No evidence of covert activity at all."

The man chewed on one side of his bottom lip. "Nothing being sold or illegally traded at this Argentile place?"

"Nope."

"Counterfeit paintings? Priceless statues?"

Vince continued to shake his head. "Nothing. Near as I could tell the place was clean. More a local gallery looking to further the careers of local talent. All on the up and up. Like a number of business ventures Randall Curan has been involved in over the last decade."

Jenkins leaned forward too. "All in this area?"

"Not hardly." Vince shook his head. "Countrywide. Real estate deals ranging from shopping mall development to single dwelling construction. Retail and restaurant franchises. You name it, he has a vested interest in it. Or did at one time. He once owned a health spa and workout center near Denver, a chain of coffee shops in San Francisco and two shopping malls. One in Seattle and one near Houston."

"In other words, quite the mover and shaker." Jenkins nodded. "Interesting."

"It might not hurt to continue to track his movements." Murphy, the quiet one, made it a point to speak only to his partner.

The other guy nodded. "Which would definitely be a good idea if Miller here had found something, anything."

Vince refused to bow to what he decided were touches of sarcasm in their tones. "You're looking for famous paintings." He again made direct eye contact with each of them in turn. "Curan caters to up and coming, not yet famous, talent."

"If that's what we got, that's what we've got." Chief Lambert walked to the front of the room. "I can tell you, Miller is one of our premier investigators. If he says there's nothing there. You can be sure there's nothing there. In a nutshell, like he said, our careful review of the facts and data collected regarding one Argentile Gallery and Emporium indicate no further investigation required."

Case closed, so let me get the hell out of Dodge.

"That pretty much sums it up." Vince backed up his boss. "I've watched the place since I was first put on the case and saw nothing to indicate anything illegal. Then I procured an entrée to the owner, which confirmed my initial findings." He drew a breath and tapped a foot under the table like mad, he so wanted out of there. "I witnessed nothing to indicate Argentile is part of the international theft ring you guys are chasing."

Jenkins made a move to stand. "If we feel the case should be reopened, we'll let you know. Otherwise, for now we call it quits. We do appreciate the thorough and comprehensive work of Detective Miller here."

Vince gave a nod to the two federal agents. "Always a pleasure."

"On behalf of the Director, we thank you for your service." Jenkins reached across the table.

Rising, Vince accepted the hand extended to him. "Maybe you'll find your mastermind at the next one."

"If you ever need our help in the future, just call and we'll again loan you our best." The Chief's hand landed on Vince's shoulder.

The other agent's stern expression matched his partner's as he offered a cursory handshake. "We'll do that."

"What's next?" Vince stood face to face with his boss as their federal counterparts walked out.

"For starters, take the weekend off. I'll see you again on Monday. But before you go answer me this. What's bugging you about this case?"

As he brought all internal turmoil under control, Vince made sure he showed the old placid exterior. "What makes you ask?"

"You read body language as well as I do. That whole meeting you were bobbing and weaving like a rookie in his first firefight. Bouncing your foot like crazy. A sure sign of someone who wants to escape."

"Not escape so much as the desire to quit wasting my time…and the department's."

"No real skin off your nose." Lambert crossed his arms over his chest. "You write the article like your cover persona promised. Or get someone to write it for you. Have it published under your alias, send this Curan character a copy, forget this particular case and go on to the next one."

As the instructions from his superior went on, Vince's gut squeezed tighter and tighter.

"Same as you've done over and over for…how many years you got under your belt?"

Clearing his throat, Vince stood taller. "Thirteen and counting. I started when I was twenty-two."

"Twelve more and you get to retire with a decent

pension." As Vince said nothing, the chief assumed his trademark scowl. "I'm taking your silence to mean you agree. As I said, take the weekend off. I'm sure by the time roll call comes around Monday morning, there will be plenty for you to do."

Drawing his lips down, Vince nodded. "Fair enough. I'll see you then."

"Yeah. You will."

As the Chief went back to his office, Vince headed for the locker room. Thoughts of Sydney and cases and duty collided in his mind as he took the cement stairs to the basement. Hitting the landing on the first floor, he swung around the railing to make his way down the next staircase.

Time to come clean with Sydney. He caught a quick breath as a sudden surge of emotion seized up his gut. Doing his best to shake off all of it, he pushed through the locker room door.

"Hey, look who's here." Always smiling, Adam Hollingsworth aka Adam Pride was the only one around when he entered the dimly lit space. "Welcome back."

Along with Luke, Adam was about as close a friend as Vince had. If ever he needed one, it was now.

"That should be my line." Vince walked over to shake hands. "You just fly in from Hollywood?"

Leaned down to unzip the duffel at his feet, Adam stood then opened the locker in front of him. "We were on location in Montana."

"Beautiful country as I understand."

"If it was, I didn't get to see much of it."

"You mean to tell me moonlighting as technical advisor to the stars isn't all it's cracked up to be?"

"Not really. When I fell into the job after the

protection detail on that Hollywood big wig, I expected a little of the glamourous lifestyle would come my way, too. This time out I spent most of my days at a shooting range the studio rented, showing inept and clueless glamour boys how to shoot. Guess I'm good at it. They got me flying to so many locations so often I've had to cut my police duty hours to part time. Not sure how much I like that. Makes me wonder why I just accepted a bit part in one of the episodes I'm working on as the tech advisor."

"As what?" Vince glanced at the picture of his dad as he opened his locker then retrieved some folded clothes from the top shelf.

"I play a patrolman."

He stared over at his friend. "Typecasting at its finest. If you're not careful, you'll have your own series."

"Wouldn't that be great?" He deadpanned the comment as he transferred the contents of his duffel to the locker floor. "Before you answer that, let me. It wouldn't. As much as I enjoy the attention, especially of the female variety, I don't think I'd really be happy for long." The grin vanished as he grew serious. "My heart still lies with police work. I don't think playacting full time would be all that great."

For a fleeting second, Vince had to wonder which one of the two of them was better at playacting. He sat on the bench then looked over at Adam. "All kidding aside, you ever think maybe Luke is on to something?"

"As far as what?"

Vince was quiet for a moment. "Settling down. You ever think about it?"

"With one specific woman?"

"That's kind of how it's done."

"You been thinking about it lately?" He eyed Vince as if he knew something was up.

"Maybe. Luke does paint a pretty nice picture."

"Someone to come home to at night. Share your life with. Confide in."

Leaning forward, Vince started to busy himself in his locker then stopped. *I have to get this off my chest or, swear to God, I'm going to burst.* "Truth is I have thought about settling down."

Adam's eyes grew wide, and his mouth dropped open. "No shit? Anyone I know?"

Vince shook his head. "Nope. Not yet, anyway."

"So, she's a civilian?"

"You could say that."

"Oh, oh. Why am I getting vibes like I'm talking to Luke and he needs a way to get back into Chelsea's good graces?"

Vince sat up to look Adam in the eye. "You're pretty perceptive."

"Oh, man." With a huge smile, he grabbed Vince by the upper arms. "Has that old straight arrow behavior of yours finally hit a curve?"

Though he really didn't want to, Vince smiled back. "You're loving this, aren't you?"

"Not unless you let me in on the details."

Vince released a sigh he'd been holding in damned near all day. "It's going to be a relief to tell somebody."

"So get on with it."

"It all started at a coffee shop called Anton's Bistro."

"In Manderfield. I've driven by the place. Never been in there."

"I have. Have I ever."

Adam didn't interrupt once as Vince went on to provide the details of working his former assignment. Up to and including his unintended involvement with Sydney.

He put his hands out, palms up, when Vince finished. "As I see it. You haven't really gone outside department policy. Hardly went rogue or anything."

"That part isn't my problem. I've gotten myself pretty deeply involved in this relationship with her." He stopped to take a breath before he revealed the part he could hardly believe himself. "She doesn't know I'm a cop."

Adam's long, low whistle ran like nails on a chalkboard along his third nerve, but he kept a direct gaze on his friend.

"You're kidding, right? Please tell me you're kidding."

Vince let the stoic expression he held on to speak for him. "You plan to help out or not?"

Another grin flashed before he became serious. "Sure. What do you want me to do?"

His gaze fell. "Damned if I know."

Adam slung an arm around his shoulders. "Exactly how deeply involved in this relationship are you?"

"Bottom line? About as deep as it gets."

Adam regarded him quietly. "Walking away without a backward glance isn't an option?"

"Not hardly. In your opinion, what is an option?"

"Man up and tell her the truth." Adam gave his shoulder a slap. "Take your lumps if there are any, salvage the relationship as best you can. If you can."

"And if I can't?"

Releasing him, Adam shrugged. "If you can't. Move on. But only if you really can't find anything to salvage. If there's no common ground." He crossed his arms, leaned his head back and studied Vince with a piercing stare. "If that stricken look on your face is any indication, you have a bad ass case of true love going on."

"Is it that evident?" Vince closed his mouth. Had he become that transparent?

"Ha!" An unexpected hand slap landed on his shoulder. "You look like a kid who's just been told there's no candy. And on Halloween no less."

"If only I felt that good." Vince glanced down as he mumbled. "I don't mind telling you. This one's pretty tough."

"If you're in as deep as you say, whatever is supposed to happen will. But you gotta start with telling her the truth."

Vince let out a grunt at the certainty in Adam's tone. "Tell me something I don't know."

"Think I just did."

About an hour later, Vince held on to Adam's words as he drove over to Sydney's house. No matter what, he was determined to come clean about his true identity once and for all. Getting to her door was easy enough. Then he had to knock a few times before she answered.

"Vince. What are you doing back here so soon?"

"I wanted to check on you to make sure you're doing okay."

"As fine as I was when you left me a few short hours ago."

Just to make sure, he scanned her from head to toe.

She wore old jeans and a soft T-shirt. He itched to touch what was underneath.

"That's good." He took her in his arms for a kiss of welcome.

She smiled against his lips then held on to his shoulders when he released her. "I'm still a little stiff. That hasn't changed from this morning either. But my knee feels a lot better."

"Your boss gave you the day off?" He kept an arm around her as they parted. "That's good."

"He was still very shaken up about what happened when I called in this morning. I assured him I didn't suffer permanent damage. That I'd be fine to go to California."

Dumbfounded, he stared at her as his mouth dropped open. "California?"

Nodding, she stepped back then chewed her bottom lip. "We leave tomorrow."

No way could he initiate the important discussion he'd come for now. "Tomorrow?"

"Afraid so. In fact, I'm packing now, and I should get back to it. Come with me and we'll talk while I do."

He noticed she hardly limped at all as he followed her into the bedroom where a large suitcase lay open on the bed. "Anything I can do to help?"

"You can keep me company. Actually, I'm almost done." She went to the closet, slid a few clothes along the rod then pulled out a couple of shirts and some pants. Returning to one side of the bed, she removed their hangers.

"When did all this come up?"

"It was in the works before I got there." Folding the pants in half, she rolled them into a tube shape she fit along one side of her bag. "Unfortunately, I'll be gone for the next few days."

"How many exactly is a few?"

She lifted her head then paused as if to calculate the precise number. "Seven. A full week. We fly back from California on Saturday, a week from tomorrow."

At the idea she'd be that far away from him, uncomfortable sensations he couldn't quite get a handle on swirled in his gut. "Fly back from California?"

On a quick nod, she resumed packing. "We drive to Grand Rapids to attend, ArtPrize, a huge show devoted to the arts. Visual, performing, the whole spectrum. We stay there for two days, then we fly out to sunny California." The subdued tone she used hardly matched her upbeat words.

"Another art show?"

"Not an official one. For scouting potential talent." She straightened but didn't turn to face him. "The reception and exhibit at the Argentile Gallery is the following week. I shouldn't be going out of town again until sometime after that."

"Promise?" He stepped up behind her to slide his arms around her waist.

She wrapped her fingers over his forearms to hold on and rested her head against his chest. "As much as I can promise at this point."

"Guess it is what it will have to be." Holding her tighter, he buried his face into her neck to take in the scent of her.

Whatever garment she was in the process of folding slipped to the bed in a heap. "Do you remember the conversation we had a when I first started working at Argentile about how travel would be a significant part of my job?”

“Um, hum.” He brushed his lips against her soft warm skin.

As he kept on with the kisses along her neck, she shifted her head on a sigh. “When I said I was looking forward to it, I had no idea I wouldn’t…” Her voice trailed off.

“Yeah.” He raised his mouth just long enough to get out the single word, then went back to feathering kisses on her nape.

She dropped her head forward. “This is definitely one thing I’m going to miss. Not to mention I’ll miss you even more.”

As she turned and wrapped her arms around his neck, her warm breath floated along his cheek and she closed her eyes to offer her lips. An offer he was more than willing to accept. Anything, to hold on to the woman who had come to mean so much to him.

Deepening the kiss, he pulled her more securely into his embrace. Spurred on by the sheer joy of having her in his arms, he didn’t hold back. Couldn’t have even if he wanted to. With one arm wrapped tight to keep her close, he shoved her suitcase to one side with the other. His lips still on hers, with some minor maneuvers he lowered them both to the comforter. Without another word, she settled into place beneath him, and he raised his head to gaze down at her. Warm brown eyes, already narrowed in passion, returned his stare.

Her lips parted, then turned up at the corners. “Give me something to remember you by.”

For a moment, he simply buried his face in her hair and hung on. “My pleasure.”

Clothes became no more than an annoying barrier

to be quickly dispensed with, and he briefly lifted away from her to shed his. He craved skin to skin contact. When he returned to her side, she was on her knees working to lower the zipper of her pants. Nudging her down, he pulled the material off her hips and legs. As he turned back after depositing them to the floor, she lay naked, except for the ever-present sapphire and gold necklace. Against the smooth backdrop of her skin, facets of the smoky blue gem caught the light and sparkled.

With her arms outstretched to him, she smiled. "I'll miss you, and this, for the next week."

"No more than I will." He took care to kiss her lips, her cheeks, the hollow of her throat.

His mouth traveled from her neck to her shoulders, across the swell of her breasts, yet he couldn't get enough of her. Braced on his forearms, he watched her face. Her eyes were closed, and her lips opened on a sigh. As he eased into her, her hips shifted in welcome. Using his knees for leverage, he pushed further in. She gasped and clutched his back, then arched up to match him stroke for stroke as they found their own unique tempo. His breathing, and hers, accelerated as their pace quickened.

Nothing else mattered, nothing else existed, except for the two of them alone. Together.

Sweat broke out to trickle between his shoulder blades as she folded warm and moist around him. His breaths became soft gasps, as he settled into a smooth and vigorous rhythm she easily accepted and returned. Her grip on his back tightened. He winced slightly as nails bit into flesh, but the sweet pain drove him on. Delicate lips were light and warm against his neck. A moan escaped her, a mere whisper on the air, to vibrate along his throat. She cried out his name, squeezed her knees to clutch him tighter and arched into him. As he held her snug against him, she bucked and shuddered.

Blood thrummed in his ears as he hit the crest along with her. Then he buried his face in her neck, reveling in the scent of her as, together, they slid down the other side. Breathing ragged, he slumped away from her to lie on his back. The arm he draped over her stomach moved with a dwindling rise and fall as her breathing returned to normal.

"That was quite a…that was something." She spoke in tiny gasps. "Amazing."

Turning toward her, Vince pulled her close. She draped one leg over his.

He relaxed into a throw pillow he propped behind his head. "Life with you is good, you know. Unbelievably good."

"Outside of the bedroom, too?" She sat up with a smile and spread an arm out.

"Way outside." He reached up to pull her back down beside him and held on.

"I know you wouldn't just be saying that to lure me into bed, since that's sort of where we already are." She snuggled close and nipped at the side of his neck as her laughter died away. "Life is good with you, too, Vince."

His lips touched hers, and he suddenly became a weary traveler arriving home. There was no way around it, Sydney Raines filled in the blanks in his life. If only he could be sure he did the same for her. This woman he wanted to be with for the rest of his life.

Chapter Ten

"Enjoy your stay with us, ma'am." Standing as stiff as the starched red and black uniform he wore; the lanky bellhop gave a short salute with a white gloved hand as he backed out of Sydney's suite.

"Thank you. I'm sure I will." She glanced over one shoulder as the door shut with a soft click. "How can I not?"

Turned back into the room, her voice trailed off as she scanned her little corner of the Amway Grand Plaza Hotel. For the next few days anyway.

Billed on its website as an elegant Five Diamond property, the *ultimate in luxury* rating certainly delivered on the pledge of unparalleled comfort and stunning opulence. With an emphasis on the latter. In the sitting area, pristine blue brocade fabric covered a small loveseat and matching chair, both studded with accent pillows in rich, dark blue velvet. A gleaming mahogany desk with upholstered spindle backed chair was tucked in a corner by the window. Floor to ceiling drapes, also in blue velvet, covered most of one entire wall.

Randall Curan lived the high life and had no problem sharing.

She strolled over to open a brown leather book on the desk and read through several available, and tempting, amenities. Early bird breakfast, and various other room service menus, premium label, fully-stocked bar, in room massage.

All printed in elegant cursive script, the list went on for two full pages. Apparently, the upscale décor was just the beginning.

With a resigned sigh, she closed the cover. As nice as her surroundings were, she couldn't manufacture much enthusiasm for being here. A nagging sense of being oddly unsettled and alone had been with her since she left home. It didn't take much effort at all for her to figure out why. Bottom line, she missed being with Vince.

More than I ever thought I could.

Walking over to where the bellhop had left her suitcase, she pulled up the handle to angle it on its wheels and tow behind her toward the bedroom. She didn't get far before her cell chimed, and she dropped the handle to dig in her purse. Vince had wanted to know when she expected to arrive.

Her lips tipped up as she brought the cell to her ear. "Hello."

"Good, you got there okay."

A smile that had stretched her cheeks slipped away. "Hi, dad."

"You said you should get to your hotel about this time. I wanted to make sure you did."

"We did." She cupped the cell loosely and made her way over to the loveseat. "It's only about a three and a half hour drive from Detroit to Grand Rapids."

"I know that. Did you drive alone or what?"

"No, I traveled by limousine." She could almost see those salt and pepper brows lift at that bit of news and went on before he could collect himself enough to comment. “We had some things to work on that couldn’t wait. Randall said riding with a driver would be conducive to that.”

“A limousine?” The eyebrows had to be buried somewhere well into his hairline by now.

“His preferred method of transportation. Not necessarily mine.” Still standing, she stopped for a moment to mull over the undeniable truth of that statement. “Mr. Curan has a first-rate business, and my new job certainly pays well. Retirement benefits, too, if I choose to take advantage of them.”

“That’s some ways in your future.”

“Speaking of pensions, how are you enjoying retirement?”

“It’s not worth a damn.”

She half smiled, half frowned at the abrupt response. “Why’s that? I thought your pension more than paid the bills.”

“It’s not always about the money. I’m thinking about going back to work.”

“Doing what?” Sydney tucked the receiver between her ear and shoulder as she sat and settled back into plush pillows which weren’t nearly as comfortable as they looked. “Security? Court system?”

“The department up here has made me an offer for one quarter time. Pretty much as a consultant.”

“Are you going to take it?”

“I already have. Starting Monday.” He took a breath. “Unfortunately, I may not be able to come down to take you out to dinner later next week like I planned.”

“Well that’s too bad. Though I understand.”

“We can always reschedule.”

Sydney put her feet up on the coffee table. "That little Italian place I told you about will still be there."

"Leave it to you to find an Italian restaurant close to home."

"They make an eggplant parmesan that'll knock your socks off."

"That was always your mother's favorite. So. Anything else important going on in your life? Besides the job?"

"What?" Sydney did a fast replay of their conversation so far. Had she given anything away? She hadn't mentioned Vince. Should she?

She shook her head. *Too soon.* He'd no doubt come up with questions she wasn't sure she could answer just now. Then what?

"Are you making any friends at work?"

"A few."

Dad. There's this guy. You'd like him. Honest. Caring. Although not a cop, which may be a deal breaker for good old Dad. In her book, one of many positives about the man.

"I have another call coming in. It may be the department. I need to take it. I'll call you Sunday."

"Bye. I love you."

"Love you too…" The phone cut out.

Setting the cell on the table, she stood to take a grip of her suitcase handle and entered the bedroom where she flopped onto the king-sized bed. She needed to change before the luncheon meeting with her boss and Nancy Parsons. Figuring her absent enthusiasm wasn't about to appear any time soon, she dragged herself off the bed.

Chandeliers sparkled down on cloth covered tables

set with precision in the elegant dining area when Sydney entered. Murmured conversations and the occasional clinks of cutlery on china swirled around the room. She spotted Nancy right away, alone at a round table off to one side. Before she even had a chance to sit down, the tuxedo clad waiter approached, a white gloved hand cradling a chilled bottle of what was certain to be expensive wine. Sydney offered a polite smile and slight head shake as she took her seat then covered the stemmed glass in front of her with one palm.

Nancy waved him off as well. "We have work to do." With no further preamble, she started in with a list of tasks she expected her to complete before they returned to the gallery.

Sydney pulled a notebook from the briefcase she'd had the foresight to bring with her and jotted the instructions. Burying the thought this woman's power grabs at her time were beyond irritating, she glanced over and smiled. "Of course, Nancy. Provided Randall doesn't have other, more important, plans for me."

The woman sat up with an abrupt grimace. "You're not capable of doing for both of us?"

Sydney kept her smile in place at the subtle challenge to her abilities. Making demands on her already full schedule during a trip that was busy enough made the woman's condescending attitude worse. "We'll see what happens."

"Yes, we will." Nancy finished the remark with a wrist flip to check her watch. "When did Randall say he'd be here?"

Sydney sipped from the water glass that had been set in front of her. "One o'clock."

"Oh." The grimace had become a permanent fixture to mar her face. "It's nearly ten after. Where in the world could the man be?"

"Sorry to keep you ladies waiting." As if he materialized as a result of her demand, Randall appeared to slide into the chair beside her. "It's such a lovely day, I toured the gardens and lost all track of time."

"Not a problem." Nancy spoke up before Sydney had a chance to.

With a lifted hand, Randall summoned the waiter who immediately arrived at their table. "Champagne all around, my good man. The best you have."

A broad smile erupted at the request. "Right away, sir."

"We have reason to celebrate." His expression beaming, Randall faced Nancy and Sydney again. "I finalized the acquisition of some popular contemporary pieces."

Nancy's eyes lit up. "Randall, that's wonderful. Congratulations."

"But, there's more. So much more." His grin grew to colossal proportions as he gave them a run down of his day. When their server returned, he waited until all three glasses were filled, raised his, then indicated the others should do the same. "Plus, I've discovered another young talent to mentor. We'll introduce her work in a private showing sometime next month. With the artist in attendance, of course."

"Congratulations." Returning his smile, Sydney clinked her glass with his.

Nancy snatched hers back. "You did what?"

"Agreed to mentor her." He took a gulp of

champagne. "We need to make transportation and living arrangements."

Sydney took a quick sip then set down the glass to raise her pen above her notebook. "What are the particulars?"

"Does it matter what the particulars are?" Mouth flat, Nancy studied Sydney. Only after she glanced away and across the table did the hint of a smile reappear. "Randall, dear, I thought we agreed not to focus on a particular artist, but to welcome everyone with real talent. To further our initial reach rather than put our resources into specific individuals."

"There's no reason we can't do both." His smile disappeared as he spoke in a short, clipped voice. "We need to accept opportunity when it comes our way. Don't you think I know what I'm doing?" The volume of his voice rose as he leaned forward.

Nancy narrowed her eyes. "This is not how we agreed things would proceed."

As the two owners entered a low key, but heated conversation about the immediate future of the gallery, Sydney set down the notepad and pen, then did her best to not listen in as she waited for them to finish.

"Mr. Curan. A picture, please. For the ArtPrize website."

Engrossed in *not* paying attention to her tablemates' argument, Sydney hadn't seen the blond man approach their table, a couple of expensive looking cameras draped from leather straps around his neck.

"Of course, my dear man."

"Yes. Please."

Immediately, a couple of scowling expressions transformed to pleasant smiles as the verbal combatants separated and posed as if part of a finely choreographed production. Randall stretched his arm Sydney's way until she had no choice but to slide closer and lean in to become a part of the shot.

"A couple more, please." The shutter clicked several times as lights flashed. "That's great. Thank you."

Standing, Randall produced a card from his shirt pocket. "Send some to the Argentile Gallery, please. Along with an invoice, of course."

"Can do." The photographer palmed the card and left.

His amicable expression gone, Randall started right in on Nancy as he retook his seat. "You think he would have bothered to come over if I hadn't been at the table? I'm the reason Argentile is a success. You need to remember that. Now shall we?" He made a show of lifting his champagne her way.

Her answer was a disgruntled stare before she raised her glass to comply. For her part, Sydney did her darnedest to keep from doing a fist pump.

After their initial blow up, the rest of the meeting, and lunch, progressed with minimal bickering between the two. All Sydney had to do was alternately take notes or sit quietly to listen. No way was she going to speak up to offer an opinion and risk bringing the wrath of either one of them down on her head. She wasn't sure whether to be relieved or not when, after they'd eaten and talked some more, Randall pushed his coffee cup to one side and turned her way.

"When we determine the exact course we plan to take in our, rather my most recent acquisition, your duties will be adjusted accordingly."

"With my input, of course." Nancy leaned forward to be heard. The woman would not give it up.

"Yes. Of course." His grudging response was accompanied by a sidelong glance toward his partner.

Without a word, she turned away to lift her purse from the floor then dug into its contents. Sydney could hardly believe her eyes when the woman produced a cigarette she held between two fingers. *Who did that anymore?*

"I don't think you can smoke in here." Just as Sydney spoke, a soft yet distinct click made her glance over.

Randall slipped something silver back into his pants pocket then brought his hand back to rest on the table. "She's probably right."

"Very well." If Nancy had been irritated before, Sydney expected white hot smoke to blow out of her ears any second now. Without another word, she tossed the unlit cigarette on to the table.

Her boss didn't seem to notice, or even care. "Tell me, Sydney, have you experienced the spa yet?"

At the unexpected question, she shook her head. "No, I haven't." Though she *had* checked out the brochure in her room, seeing the exorbitant prices listed, she hadn't pursued a visit much beyond fantasy.

"You must go. On me."

"No really. I couldn't expect you to pay."

He put up a hand to demand silence. "All the better when you don't expect what comes your way. No arguments. Consider it a business perk."

Nancy's now constant grimace deepened as she regarded her, but after a telling glance from Randall, she held her peace on the issue.

"A business perk. That's what you're calling it now?" Sarcasm evident in her tone, her narrow-eyed regard slid over Sydney.

"I'd like that. Thank you." Rather than continue to argue, Sydney easily gave in, only because her desire to get away from her two feuding superiors overrode any reluctance or guilt at taking in a little luxury on the company dime. "See you both tomorrow morning."

Making a hasty exit, she walked the short distance to the hotel spa. If the comforts of her room were lovely, the services she received were nothing short of heaven. Accepting a manicure, pedicure and facial, she declined the full body massage and Turkish towel wrap. Even at that, never had she been so pampered, and Sydney allowed herself to enjoy every minute of it. The French milled soap they used felt absolutely exquisite on her skin, and Sydney fell in love immediately. Lavender scented with the texture of pure silk, she simply had to take some home. Though she nearly choked on the fifteen dollars a bar price, she bought two.

As Sydney picked up the tiny ribbon-handled bag, the attendant helping her lifted a larger sack onto the counter. "With Mr. Curan's compliments. A generous sample of each of the items we used on you today. Plus, in here, we also have some of our one of a kind merchandise."

Brief yet elaborate descriptions of each luxurious product followed.

"Thank you." Rather than make an issue and refuse, and with only a small touch of guilt remaining, Sydney collected both her bags and briefcase then left.

The Plaza Essentials Gift Shop and specialty men's

clothing store lining the lobby promenade bustled with late afternoon activity as she passed by. Keeping her gaze focused on signs for the elevators that would take her to the tower and the solitude of her room, she dodged around coming and going customers. Many, like her, loaded with packages. The carpeted hallway she turned down was empty except for a lone figure coming toward her. With the bags in one hand and cell in the other, she kept her head down as she checked to see if she had any messages.

"Well, well, Syds. It really is you."

Hearing her name called out by an all too familiar voice stopped her dead in her tracks. She jerked her head up. "Mark?"

Her ex's gaze met hers. "Unbelievable."

Her mouth fell open as she stared back at him. Unbelievable was right. If only she'd paid attention to where she was going, she may have been fortunate enough to have seen him first and avoided any contact.

She didn't flinch as he took his sweet time to study her from head to toe.

Hard to believe she'd once surrendered her heart and soul to this man with the longish sandy hair, playful blue eyes, and a ready smile. At one time the combination had sent her desire for him into overdrive but did nothing for her these days.

That didn't mean she couldn't at least attempt to be civil. "How are you, Mark?"

"I'd answer that if I believed you really cared." His voice dripped with disdain.

She chose to ignore it. "Suit yourself."

Any trace of congeniality his face carried vanished as he eyes grew hard. "Looks like life's been good to you lately."

"Only because of my own diligence and determination I found a position to fit my skills."

"And pays pretty darned well, I'd say." Holding his mouth rigid, his gaze strayed to the bags she held.

She shifted them to get a better grip and slipped the cell in her pocket. "I'm comfortable."

"Lucky you."

"I've been fortunate."

As he continued to stare at her, the hard edges of contempt around his eyes were ill-concealed. "I'll just bet you have."

"I'm gainfully employed, if that's what you mean." She was pleased with what came out next. "And you?"

"Getting by." He produced a predatory smile. "Thanks for asking."

"What are you doing on this side of the state?"

"The art fair, of course." He referenced the guitar on his shoulder with a slight tilt of his head. "And you?"

"Same thing." She shifted the bags to her other hand as a sigh escaped. "I'm here with the art gallery I now work for."

"Who would have guessed we'd end up with something in common after all." The smile that at one time set her heart fluttering emerged. "Maybe that means there's a chance we could get back together."

She was shaking her head before he finished speaking. "Not in this lifetime. Especially now that I'm dating someone."

His eyes widened at that bit of news as he stood straighter. "That didn't take you long."

"It's been two years, Mark. Plus, our marriage was

over long before the divorce papers were signed." *Our marriage was over the first time you raised a hand to me.*

It took clamping her mouth shut tight to keep from throwing out that particular truth. In the relative safety of a public place or not, she knew better than to antagonize the man.

"You're here performing?" Wanting nothing more than to be away from him, she had no desire to ask for specifics.

"I'll be at ArtPrize all week. Not that I can even begin to afford to stay here. I figured I'd at least stop by to see what I was missing." When she didn't comment, he went on. "We take one of the main stages tomorrow. Our set probably starts about three."

"Too bad I'll have to miss it." He wasn't the only one who could do sarcasm. "Couldn't make it even if I wanted to. I have interviews seeking new talent scheduled for much of the upcoming week."

"Busy. Busy, huh?"

"Exactly."

"Like that job you had before. The one that took so much of your time away from us?"

"It's called paying the bills. Plus, there was nothing wrong with being successful at my career."

"You lived and breathed that damned job."

"When I was home nights, you were out." An older couple walked by and glanced over. She lowered her voice. "Then there was the time you spent our rent money on a new set of strings or whatever for that thing."

"As I recall it was a joint account."

"It was joint all right. With one of us making

regular deposits and the other merely withdrawals." Taking a step back, she pressed her lips together. As always trying to reason with him was a total waste of her time. "Why do I bother?"

"You got nothing to show for that old job of yours now. Or do you? Maybe a cut of that other money to say, look the other way?"

She stood straighter and kept her right arm against her side, fist balled. "What's that supposed to mean? No. Don't even say it. If your question was worthy of an answer, I'd produce one." He didn't deserve the chance to respond. "We're done here."

"You really think you can blow me off that easily?" Mark shifted his weight to stand taller.

Sydney's first instinct was to take a step back. She returned the wrath in his stare instead. Visions of the vehicle that nearly ran her down emerged, and with it, a new ration of anger. "Don't threaten me, Mark."

"Or what?" As another couple passed by, he lowered the volume of his voice, but not the warning in his message. "You'll send that posse you call a family after me?"

At the reference to her dad and brothers, she simply glared at him. This was one battle she'd fight alone. "Leave my family out of this. I'm talking about the restraining order against you that I still have in effect."

"You think that's going to make a difference? A piece of paper is going to keep you safe?" His face contorted as he advanced toward her.

It took all she had to not retreat as she foolishly swung her packages between them. A lot of protection those were going to be. "We really are done here,

Mark."

"I don't think so." In one motion, he lurched forward and clamped his hand, hard, on her upper arm. "I said I wasn't done talking to you."

Though her flesh burned from his grip, she refused to give him the satisfaction of crying out. "I'm done talking to you." Using a pinwheel movement, she wrenched free. "And do not put your hands on me again." Festering ire made her voice deep, her words distinct. "Ever."

Pushing past him, she stalked down the hall toward the elevators. Once she got to her room, she gave the door a satisfying slam, and let out a long breath. This was turning out to be one hell of a crappy day. Her packages landed with a crackle and swoosh as she dropped them by the entrance and headed straight for the bedroom. With eiderdown pillows propped behind her back, she reclined on the bed and gave herself a hug. A poor substitute for the strength of Vince's arms around her.

Until she returned home to him again, memories would have to do.

Chapter Eleven

Vince made his way down a grassy slope to the wreckage then crouched on all fours beside the burned-out vehicle to get a better look at the body inside. Check that. More like the blackened and charred shape of a torso, two arms, two legs and a head. Which was where any chance of a positive ID ceased. Race, age, gender were all tossup questions for now.

Hot bile rose to the back of his throat, and he kept his head down then swallowed until the unseemly brew dissipated. Arriving on a deceased at the scene call was never easy. This one was worse than most. In an effort to calm a queasy stomach, he raised up to rest one arm on his thigh and lowered his chin to his chest.

Taking air in through his nose and out from his mouth, Vince kept his breathing slow and steady. No way did he care to lose it and puke his guts out all over the taped off scene on this remote stretch of rural highway. After all the years doing this, he was supposed to be hardened. Used to this kind of atrocity. So many under his belt, and he still wasn't immune.

Hell of a way to end the week.

Snapping on a pair of latex gloves, the medical examiner took up a position beside him. "Well, well. This is quite the crispy critter we have here."

He scowled at the jackass. "Show some respect. This was a person at one time."

"Sorry. Didn't mean to offend." The ME shrugged then used low tones as he spoke into the tape machine held in his palm.

"It never gets easier, does it?" A hand landed, firm and welcome on Vince's shoulder. He turned toward the grim and sullen face of Luke, his temporary partner.

"Sure doesn't." He blew out a labored breath, confident, for now he wouldn't embarrass himself like some unseasoned rookie. He sought out the ME again. "Any way to know if the victim was alive prior to?"

"The fire?" He spoke with the nonchalance of one who dealt with dead bodies on a routine basis. "All things considered, it's very possible."

"Jesus." More bile surged up to singe his throat, and he coughed then spit to get rid of it.

"What's this?" Using small metal tongs, the physician lifted something off the body then held it up to the light, squinting as he examined it. "That may explain one thing."

Vince also squinted at the charred item, with no idea what he was looking at. "You find something?"

He released the specimen into an evidence bag he sealed shut. "I won't know for sure until I run some analysis."

With the crunch of tires on gravel, a news vehicle pulled up, spewing dust as it jerked to a stop. Two men scrambled out. One fisted a black microphone. The other hoisted a camera on to his shoulder, flicked the lens finder down and started filming.

"Get as much footage as you can." The first man spoke to his companion as they hurried toward the taped off scene.

"What can you tell us? What happened?" He

leaned over the barrier of yellow tape.

Vince ducked down to further examine the wreck. The last thing he needed was his face splashed on the news. This was not the way he wanted Sydney to discover who he really was. "Handle that for me, will you?"

Luke cast a startled glance his way. "Me?"

"Yeah, you. Now go!"

Surprise lit his eyes at the request, but he didn't protest further. "Sure. What do you want me to say?"

"Just that the accident, and do refer to it as an accident at this point, remains under investigation."

"Got it." Luke strode over to where the intruders stood, stretching the yellow police tape in their effort to get closer to the scene.

"Guys! Guys! Back away. Please. This is a restricted area."

"Can you tell us what happened?"

"Negative. We just got here ourselves. For right now we ask that you stay back behind our perimeter and not broadcast any of this until we've had a chance to contact the next of kin."

"Our greater Detroit viewers deserve to know." The reporter wasn't going to go away quietly.

"Shut your mike off, please. Now." The volume of Luke's tone rose.

"What if I don't?" A firm, challenging voice answered.

"Right now, if we wanted we could arrest you for hindering an ongoing investigation."

"You'd do that?" By now the other voice had lost some of its daring.

"Damn right I would. Now, you, put the camera

away too."

Vince smiled at Luke's well played bluff.

"When we're ready to tell you something we'll let you know."

"What not to do on a Friday night, huh?" When the reporter made the offhand comment, Vince could only surmise he'd done as he was asked.

"You got that right." Luke's response was spot on.

The guy was buying the freak accident scenario. Who were they to argue?

"I'll give you whatever I get as soon as I get it." Luke's voice grew louder still as he left the intruders and got nearer. Coming to stand beside Vince, he shook his head. "That should buy us some time. How the hell did they get here so fast?"

"The power of technology, my friend. Running their radios on our frequency twenty-four seven, sometimes they know where a call's going out from before we do."

Luke snorted. "It's all about the blood and guts these days. Tape the gore they broadcast to the world with no regard for the souls who might be suffering."

Kneeling down again, Vince cast him a sidelong glance. "Aren't we philosophical today?"

Luke squatted next to him. "I prefer realist, but you think what you'd like."

"Amazing sometimes what civilians get themselves into." Resting an arm on one knee, Vince surveyed the landscape, a smooth expanse of several acres planted in soybeans, a sea of yellow foliage growing low to the ground and swaying in a southwesterly breeze. All untouched by the nearby, and spontaneous, grass fire and residual ash from the burned-out metal carcass in its center. “What are the chances that a vehicle like this would travel off the road at this particular spot?”

“Then burst into flames.” Luke kept his attention on the wreck.

“Say one in a million?”

“If that. Unfortunately.” Luke scratched his head. “This kind of thing really does happen all the time. Someone who’s been drinking gets behind the wheel and starts driving. Takes the back roads to avoid getting caught.”

“Miscalculate a curve or gets cocky, and speeds way over the limit.”

“With horrific results. Do you think that’s what happened?”

“Hard to say.”

Vince stood, hands on his hips, to complete a visual of the rest of the area. A solitary farm house, white two-story with a wide front porch sat about a half mile beyond the field. Even if whoever lived there was home at the time of the crash, chances were slim to none that any of them would qualify as an eye witness.

“Doesn’t look promising, does it?”

Vince broke off his survey to glance over. “Sure doesn’t.”

“Still have to at least make contact for possible witnesses, don’t we?”

“That depends. What’s this?” Pulling thin plastic gloves out of the fanny pack clipped around his waist, Vince stretched them over one hand then the other. Careful to brush aside some dirt and dried grass, he picked up a twisted piece of metal.

“Could be something. Could be nothing.”

“I’m counting on the former.”

"You would." Properly gloved like his partner, Luke separated the top of the plastic evidence bag he sealed shut after Vince dropped the unknown object into it.

"Let's sweep the area to see what else we can find, if anything."

"Sounds good."

Metal of a different kind clanged as the ME and his assistant loaded the body into their van then climbed in the front. The doctor stuck his head out the passenger side window. "If you don't need us anymore, we're headed back to the morgue."

"We'll be in touch." Vince punctuated his response was a hasty wave as he continued to comb the ground for whatever the scene would turn up.

Back at the squad car about an hour later, Vince removed and disposed of his gloves. "You might know we'd get nothing more."

As he did the same, Luke nodded. "It may be this is one we won't be able to solve."

Standing side by side, they each coated their hands with disinfectant, front and back, then rubbed them together.

Vince simply nodded his agreement. "Might be."

Physically he'd cleaned off any contaminants. Unfortunately, nothing created by man was strong enough to wipe the grisly scene he'd been called to from his mind. Images that stayed with him as he and Luke climbed into his unmarked squad car.

Neither talked much as they returned to the station and went inside.

"Another day in Paradise." Luke sat at his desk. The chair squeaked as he wheeled himself closer then looked up. "You go home. I'll dictate the preliminary report."

About to shrug out of his jacket and sit across from him, Vince remained standing. "You don't have to do that."

"I know. It's not a totally unselfish move on my part. Chelsea's on the night shift this week. It'll give me a chance to see her when she arrives."

"Who am I to get in the way of that." Vince dug out his keys, wishing Sydney was in town. "Thanks. I owe you."

"And you know I'll collect, too." Luke gave a quick wave as he opened a drawer.

Off duty and in his own vehicle a while later, Vince sped up as he entered the I-696 expressway. Cruising along, he flicked off the car radio as a news flash about the latest discovery with the 'victim as yet unidentified' disclaimer was announced. He didn't need to hear it spelled out for him.

Too soon, the exit to Forest Meadows and his apartment loomed ahead. Vince cranked a hard left. Taking advantage of the official use only turn around lane in the median, he pulled onto the freeway going the other way and brought the car up to the speed limit a few seconds later. Trees and landscapes became a blur as, almost on its own, his foot pressed harder on the gas pedal if only to get him away faster.

But away to where?

Eventually, he'd have to go home to the emptiness of his apartment. Pushing the phone button on his steering wheel, a low chime echoed inside the car. He spoke clearly when the computer asked who he wanted to call, then concentrated to regulate his breathing as he waited on the line.

"Hello."

A smile emerged when his little sister answered. Little to him. Even though she'd soon be all of eighteen.

"You're home. What a concept." The last few times he'd called, she'd been out with her friends. Typical teenager.

"Only because Mom asked me to fix her latest computer issue."

"The important thing is you're home." A place he so needed her to be just now.

Where I'd give anything to keep you.

Guilt stabbed at him for wanting so desperately to make sure those close to him remained safe. Even if the measures he chose would interfere with her life.

"You haven't been around in a while. I miss seeing you."

"I've been working." He slowed from the bat out of hell speed he'd been traveling.

"I know. Mom told me you were undercover."

"Not anymore."

"Really?" A lightness entered her tone. "So, if and when I see you on the street, I can acknowledge that I know you?" The question was direct. Matter of fact.

He supplied an answer in a similar voice. "You can. Even that we're related. Unless you'd rather not."

"We'll see how I feel at the time." She reacted exactly as he expected to his effort at comic relief.

"What's been going on with you?"

"Not much. Mom and Dad are taking me to visit some colleges in the next few weeks."

He found himself smiling at the idea she had her

whole life ahead of her. "That's great. You still want to be a teacher?"

"Sure do. Maybe special ed."

"You'd be good at it."

"You think so?"

"With your sense of caring, I know so."

"Ooops. There goes my cell. Amy and I are going to head for the mall."

"Be careful."

"Mom's reaching for the phone. She wants to talk to you, anyway." She either didn't hear his words of caution. Or chose not to acknowledge a warning that she undoubtedly believed didn't pertain to her. "Bye, Vince."

"Bye."

He didn't have to wait long before his mother came on the line.

"Hello, Vince. How are you?"

The mere sound of another familiar voice, and more calm washed over him. Even with the question he didn't care to answer honestly.

Almost immediately conflicting emotions rolled back in. "I'm fine. How are you?"

"Are you still…on assignment?"

He took a breath. "No."

Her sigh of relief reached out to him over the connection. "You're back on regular duty."

"I am."

"Your father will be glad to hear it." The woman was a master at deflecting her emotions. "What do they have you working on now?"

One of the most gruesome scenes I've ever been called to. "The usual."

"You know you have an open invitation to dinner any night you can make it."

Though he was relieved she didn't ask for details of *the usual* another pang of guilt hit. He hadn't been home to visit in a while.

"One of these days. Soon." He made the promise without thinking much about it. "When I do get there, I may bring a guest."

A measure of silence met that remark. "Anyone I know?"

"Not yet. But I think you'll like her."

"Her?" Something in her voice lifted. She no doubt liked hearing the feminine pronoun. "If you like her, I'm sure I will too."

He had no idea what made him share, even obliquely, anything about his involvement with Sydney. What if he came clean to her and she told him to take a hike? *I'll simply tell Mom it didn't work out.*

"Squirt says she's in the process of picking out colleges." He automatically used his pet name for his little sister.

"Hard to believe she'll be out of the house soon too." His mother's tone took on a wistfulness he wasn't used to. "You all grew up so fast."

More guilt to deal with. "And now you and Dad can enjoy those well-earned retirement years."

"Your Aunt Sophie has been after us to go on a cruise. She and Frank go every other year or so. Guess your dad and I could go on one with them one of these days. Every time we get together with them, they rave about how wonderful cruise ship travel is."

His foot let up on the accelerator as their conversation turned to normal subjects. "You and Dad always talk about seeing Australia. Why don't you start there?"

"We could look into it. Provided the trip isn't too expensive."

They shared more ordinary, everyday back and forth chit chat and the tightness in Vince's shoulders eased.

"Oh, there goes my timer." This time, his mother's voice took on an urgency. An ordinary, everyday urgency, which was fine with Vince. "I have a cornbread in the oven for dinner."

An immediate mental picture came to mind that made his mouth water. *If only I were there to share it with you.* "I'll let you go then. I'll call before I bring…before I come over."

"Just to make sure we're here. Love you, Vince. Bye."

"Bye, Ma."

"Call ended." The computer made the announcement as he depressed the disconnect button on his steering wheel.

Vince glanced around to get his bearings. He'd traveled about ten miles the other way while he talked to his family. At the next turn around opportunity he came to, he cranked another hard left. There was no avoiding it any longer. It was time to go home. Alone.

He opened the back door of his one bedroom, one bath and little else apartment a short time later, just as his cell phone rang. *Sydney?* He flicked his keys onto the kitchen counter and dug in his pocket.

Flipping the mobile out, he hit accept on the screen. "Miller."

"Hey, it's Brad."

"Hey yourself. How's it going?" A quick and automatic greeting among friends, but where Brad was concerned, he truly wanted to know.

"Good. Life is good."

"Glad to hear it." Vince meant that, too. He'd never totally accepted the path this pal from their police academy days had taken. "What's up? How's the bounty hunter business?"

"Can't complain."

Despite the hitch in his buddy's voice, which Vince took to be unmistakable evidence of doubt, he refused to utter what sat on the tip of his tongue— *When are you coming back to the force?* "Chasing another judicial no show?"

A chuckle was the immediate response. "Two of them. Married couple arrested for passing bad checks. If they're smart, they've split up."

"Can't be that smart if they got caught in the first place."

"Good point."

"What do you need?" This brother of his wasn't one to get a hold of him simply to socialize.

"A favor. If you're up to it." Brad was quick to launch into the real reason for his call. "I need some information about the pair I'm hunting and was hoping you'd help me out. It'll take me too long to go through regular channels."

"I hear you. And I will." Vince wouldn't bend the rules for anyone else.

Brad cleared his throat before he spoke. "When you get around to it."

As he walked into the living room, Vince unbuckled his shoulder holster, slipped it off and laid the whole apparatus on the end table along with his department issued cell. “Not a problem.”

“I appreciate that.” Brad’s voice was somewhat muffled by the connection. “There is something else.”

Vince bit. “Which is?”

Another breath rasped out. “After I take care of this one, I’m coming back.”

“Back where?”

“Law enforcement. This couple snatch is going to be my last as a bail recovery agent.”

“Well hot damn!” His first good news of the day. “What changed your mind?”

“Brad, I have those two rooms aired out upstairs.” Before his friend could respond, a woman’s voice from somewhere in the background came over the line. “But I need help with that darned stuck window in the back room again. When you have a minute.”

“Be right there.” The response was momentarily muffled. “Hey. I gotta go.”

“And leave me hanging?” Vince couldn’t curtail his curiosity. “Who was that?”

Brad answered with a chuckle. “Her name’s Jenny, and we’re getting married. I’ll explain. Later.”

Vince smiled for the first time since he got home. “Think you just explained all I need to know.”

“Guess I did. Thanks for all the help.”

“Yeah sure.”

“Talk to you soon.”

“Soon.” Vince ended the call and immediately dialed again.

“I was hoping you’d still be awake.”

Any residual tension seeped out of him the second Sydney’s voice came over the line, and he smiled.

"Not even thinking of going to bed yet." *Not if it's alone.* A chaotic rush of all the things he wanted to share with her came together like a firestorm in his mind. Who he really was. What he really did for a living. How he hoped to God she'd accept him when he confessed how, and why, he'd deceived her.

Because he wanted, and needed, this woman in his life, no matter what.

He held in a sigh of regret. "How's the trip going? No cancel that, how are you doing?"

"I'm little tired. We've been going non-stop here in Grand Rapids. We take off for California day after tomorrow."

"At least going east to west, you'll gain a few hours."

"Only more hours for Randall and Nancy to fill with work for me."

Seated on the tan, cloth covered couch, he toed off his shoes and rested his feet on the matching ottoman. He could use an ice-cold beer right now but didn't have the ambition to get up and get it. "Maybe you need to get some sleep."

"I tried taking a nap this afternoon when I had some much needed down time. It didn't work. In fact, for what it's worth, I'm still in bed now. Have been for a while."

All thoughts of liquid refreshment scattered. "What are you wearing?"

Her laugh was full of life and enjoyment and made a dent in the armor he always built up around his heart when he tried desperately not to bring work home with him.

"My usual sleeveless, short nightgown." Her tone

took on a distinct playfulness.

As it occurred to him he'd never seen her in bed in a nightgown, or anything else, the blood fueling his brain headed south. "What color?"

"Pink."

"My favorite."

"You're telling me your favorite color is pink? I'm not buying it." A rich chuckle followed.

The armor fell away altogether. "Hey. Can't a man get in touch with his feminine side?"

"I've looked in vain for your feminine side. I know better."

Memories and images from the last time he'd held her in his arms merged to become one hell of a fantasy in his mind. At this rate, his brain didn't stand a chance in the blood supply department. "Okay. You got me. What I meant to say was my favorite color is whatever color you happen to have on."

Or I can happen to take off you.

"That's sweet. You're sure it's not just a come on?"

"Not a chance. You're too important to bother with that."

An unusual silence fell between them.

Ping!

His work cell let out an alert he had a new text message. As he picked it up to check, his heart lifted then sank. A positive ID on his 'accident' victim. Another fact he wanted to share with Sydney had to stay unrevealed.

"I miss you, Vince."

"I miss you, too." He set the other cell face down on the table.

"What did you have for dinner?"

"I didn't get that far yet. I just got home."

"It's almost eight o'clock. What were you doing?"

Took in a movie. Visited a children's ward at the hospital. Slaved over my laptop on that Curan article until my fingers bled. He immediately came up with all sorts of responses. Some of them appropriate. None of them true.

He stroked his forehead with an index finger and hoped she'd accept a generic response without question. "Working."

"Did you get your article done?"

"What? Oh. Pretty much."

"Why do I get the idea you had a harder day than you let on?"

Because already you know me so well. I only wish you knew me better. "It wasn't all that bad." He glanced over at his firearm on the table.

"If you say so." The sheets rustled.

Was she getting deeper into them? Or getting up? "What else have you been doing?"

"Meetings with applicants, mostly."

At the fatigue in her voice, all he wanted to do was take her in his arms. Lie beside her while she slept. "Any sales?"

"Some. But not nearly enough for Randall."

"What's on tap for you tomorrow?" In the next second he toyed with the idea of calling in some of his vast accumulation of sick time and making a day trip across state.

"More meetings. First one at eight in the morning. Then more of the same for most of the day. Lunchtime. Mid-afternoon. You name it, I'm booked."

"You don't sound too enthusiastic about it."

"Because I'm not." Her voice trailed off. "But I have no choice."

"There's always a choice." Unable to sit still any longer, he got up and went to the kitchen.

"Not with the expenses I've racked up the past couple of months. With no money coming in, my savings are pretty much depleted…"

When her voice trailed off again, he took advantage and spoke up. "Not if we shared expenses."

More silence fell. She must have been just as shocked as he was at the suggestion.

"How would that work, exactly?" Her tone was low, searching.

You in my bed every night. Beside me when I wake up in the morning. Be here for me to come home to. I'd do the same for you.

He gave up on the pipe dream as he opened the fridge and took out a cold one. "I don't know. Maybe it wouldn't. When do you fly back?"

"Saturday. Sometime in the afternoon."

"What time?"

She said nothing for a few seconds. "We get in around two, I think. Why?"

"What's the flight number?"

"Randall usually has his limo driver take all of us home from Metro."

He hardly waited until she finished speaking. "I'll pick you up. What's the flight number?"

"I'm not sure. It's a Delta flight."

"I'll find it. Is he giving you Sunday off?"

"Not this Sunday. There's the reception. The week after, he offered. I'm not sure I'll—"

"Take it. And, I'll pick you up when you get in."

"Okay."

Doing his best to quell the jumble of thoughts vying for his attention, he streamlined the various chunks of data into a straight forward and cohesive plan. Come hell or high water, the next time he and Sydney were face to face and alone, he would confess to every detail that stood between them. Bare his soul.

Then hope to hell she could accept him for who he really was.

Chapter Twelve

"It's so good to be home, Vince." Sydney was caught up in his strong, capable arms the second they spied each other at the airport.

"Yeah. It is." Caring blue eyes stared deeply into hers, and he offered a brief smile before capturing her lips.

Tucked into the comfort of this embrace, she relished the solid pressure of his body accepting hers, the light rasp of afternoon whiskers on her upper lip and chin. The stress and tension that had kept her body rigid for most of the flight from San Diego to Detroit drained out of her in a flood, when it struck her what being home really meant.

With her eyes closed, she let the unique scent of him she'd missed so much surround her then wrapped her arms around his neck and held on. "You are so good for me."

He flexed his arms to keep her close, buried his face in her hair, and released a sigh. "It's good to have you home."

"It was nice of you to pick me up. Randall and Nancy were in rare form this trip, bickering like a couple of school children on the playground. Only worse. I don't think I could have taken another minute of it on the drive from the airport." She ran a hand through her hair. "Then to top it off, I ran into—"

Wonk! Wonk! Wonk!

The low blast of a horn erupted from nearby. With a thump and whir the luggage carousel they stood beside started to rotate.

Vince lifted his head. "Looks like the baggage handlers are on top of things."

"Good for them." Unable to resist the sarcasm, Sydney was reluctant to let him go as they broke apart. "Well what do you know." She stepped up to the circling conveyor as, wonder of wonders, her two maroon suitcases were the first items out of the chute. "These are mine." She glanced back at Vince.

"Let me." Grabbing one handle then the other, he pulled them to the floor. "I was able to park pretty close."

Close was right. In no time, they'd navigated the escalators and hallway leading to the attached parking garage and his metallic silver Jeep Laredo.

"Get in and relax." He placed both hands on either side of her face and brushed his mouth against hers before he ushered her into the front seat. "I'll put your luggage in the back."

"Okay." She did as she was told without argument.

With his hand still on her shoulder, he straightened but didn't let go. "You look exhausted."

"I am." Smiling up at him, she set her purse on the floor in front of her.

"Take it easy. I'll be right back." He shut her door and she immediately relaxed against the seat. Briefly.

Spurred on by his comment about her appearance, she sat forward then lowered the visor to peer in the mirror. Granted she didn't look her ultimate best. Though not creased or puffy, the skin directly under her eyes was a shade or two darker than the rest of her face. A grueling non-stop work schedule capped off by a cross country flight could do that to a person.

Chiding herself for the temporary bout of narcissism, she flipped the visor back up. She and Vince were beyond the need to have each and every hair in place for each other, like some couple meeting for the first time through a dating site. They'd known each other long enough.

Or had they?

How well *did* she know the man she'd been involved with for such a brief time? She glanced around the interior of his car. A half full water bottle sat in the cup holder of the console. Aviator sunglasses were looped over the rearview mirror and a black cell phone charger plugged into the outlet by the radio had its spiral cord left to dangle free. His leather jacket lay in a heap on the backseat. Some items in the vehicle were familiar, some not. All were a part of Vince. Though tempting, she refrained from snooping in the glove box. What she did know about who he was would have to be enough for now.

The back hatch thumped then clicked shut. Almost immediately, Vince climbed into the seat beside her, and a definite sense of peace and comfort washed over her. The fact she didn't know every detail about him didn't matter compared to what she did know.

"How was your flight?" He glanced over as he fired up the engine.

"The usual. Cramped seating. Crying babies."

"Curan doesn't spring for first class? That diminishes my opinion of him."

"I'm sure he would have. The flight for me was

booked after first class was filled. This has been a whirlwind trip."

"Are you hungry? Do you want to stop for something to eat?"

A smile crept over her lips at his thoughtfulness, and her growing love for him swelled up to fill her heart. Before she could think too much about the rationale behind the details of that particular notion, she shook her head. "I'm more tired than anything else right now. If you don't mind, I just want to go straight home."

"Straight home it is." He put the car in gear and glanced out the back window. "Why would I mind?"

"Unless you're hungry. We could—"

"I'll get you home." Taking a second to lay a hand over hers, he pulled the car out of its parking space and aimed for the exit.

As they rolled up to the toll booth, she reached for her purse. This time, he put his hand over her arm to stop her and, when she looked up at him, merely shook his head. Pulling some bills out of a cubby near the dash, he gave them to the clerk and they were off again.

"Thank you."

Settled into the sway and flow of a moving vehicle, her head drooped. In no time, she was sound asleep…

"Sydney. We can go in now." Vince's voice filtered into the darkness of Sydney's mind. With his hand, warm and gentle on her shoulder, he gave her a slight shake. "Morning, Beautiful. Time to get up."

Her eyes fluttered open to sunlight shining through the windshield. On a sigh, she closed them again. "Just a couple more minutes, please."

She ran her tongue around a mouth that still tasted

like the sweet and sour flavored snack mix she'd eaten on the plane, washed down with some ice cube loaded orange soda.

As he shut off the ignition, the engine went quiet then ticked a few times as its inner workings cooled.

He slid his arm around her shoulders as he moved closer. "If you want, you could sleep here all day."

His breath trailed along her cheek just before his lips touched hers. With her eyes still closed, a smile emerged against the mouth he lifted too soon.

"If you ask me though, you'll probably sleep better in your own bed."

"Only if you agree to join me. We've been apart for a long time."

"I thought you'd never ask."

His low chuckle reached in to heat her from head to toe, with stops at a few distinct places in between. A thrill of anticipation quickly followed. Swiftly brought wide awake, she yearned to get to it. She turned her head so their gazes could connect. The blue of his eyes darkened to the color of an autumn sky at dusk. He tipped up one side of his mouth and she curved hers up in return. Then he moved in to, once again press his lips down on hers.

Within seconds they were wrapped in each other's arms. On a sigh of acceptance, Sydney surrendered, parting her lips under the warm, sweet pressure of his mouth. Breaking the kiss, he spread his palm on the side of her shoulder to pull her close. As close as he could around the console. Its hard leather top came up against her ribcage.

"Now that I think about it, we'd both probably be more comfortable inside."

With a smile on her face, she took his hand to twine his fingers with hers before letting go. "You're right, as usual."

"About time you recognized that." Opening the door, he stepped out on the pavement.

She pushed off the seat to climb out on her side. "Maybe it's something about you I've always recognized, but just didn't care to admit until now."

"One more thing to love about you." Leaving the back hatch open, he came over to drop a quick kiss on her lips.

When he left to unload her luggage, she kept her appreciative gaze on his attractive backside, as his last words echoed through her mind. *...to love about you... to love about you.*

"Oh Sydney. Welcome home." Ida called out first, then waved from her front doorway. "How was your trip?"

"Tiring to say the least. It's good to be home." With Vince beside her once more, she suddenly realized the off-hand comment took on a new and very special meaning.

He'd hauled out her bags he set on the cement, then telescoped up the handle on one. "Hey, Ida."

"Vince. Nice to see you. Did you get a lot accomplished on your trip, Sydney?"

"I did." With a smile of thanks to Vince, she took charge of one of the suitcases. "We interviewed a ton of prospective artists and selected a good number of pieces to exhibit."

"That's wonderful."

"It was." Nodding as they walked up the sidewalk, Sydney went on to detail a few of the more unique personalities she'd met. "Some of their work was truly amazing."

"I hope you don't mind." Ida crossed her arms over her chest as she walked over. "I brought Annabelle and Rufus over here to my place."

"Annabelle and Rufus?" Sydney gave her a blank stare. Had Ida acquired additional pets? "I'm not sure…I." Giving up, she blinked. "Who are they?"

"Your Boston Ferns of course." She spread her hands out, palms up. "You did entrust them to my care. They seemed so sad over there at your place all alone, so I put them on a table in my front window."

"Oh. Them." It wouldn't do to be rude. "We'll be right over to bring them back home."

"Okay then." Ida nodded. "Don't tarry though. They've missed you."

"They've missed me?" She smiled up at Vince with a slight shrug.

"They'll be so excited." Ida laughed as she headed next door. "Don't bother to knock. Just walk in. I have a streusel ready to go in the oven I must tend to."

She disappeared inside before Sydney could reply.

"You're one of those people who gives names to their plants?" Vince pulled her suitcase up the stairs to her porch.

She singled out her door key then held it in front of her. "No. But, it's not that the pair of plants aren't important to me. I bought them when I first settled into my townhouse and craved some connection to home and family. My mother raised Boston Ferns. When I was still home, I made sure to keep them alive and thriving after she no longer could. I do appreciate Ida's efforts. It's just that, all I want right now is a hot bath and my own bed."

"I'm all for that."

Smiling at the tingles flaring below her waist, she unlocked her front door and stepped back as Vince set the luggage inside.

"Let's hurry." She glanced up at him and winked.

"Let's." He took time to grin back. "After all. Annabelle and Rufus are waiting for you."

The television was on in one corner of the room at Ida's when they let themselves in.

"She always has that station going." Sydney glanced over at the national news only channel Ida preferred. "I think more for company than anything else."

"Understandable." Vince glanced over at the rather small screen.

Some talking head commentator elaborated on one series of current events while other news of the day items, white letters on a red band, ran across the bottom of the screen.

"There are the kids." Sydney's two fluffy green ferns sat on the coffee table in the front window.

"Look who's here." Ida talked directly to the plants as she walked in from the kitchen. "Your mom, and she's here to take you home." Coming to a stop in front of Sydney, Ida put a hand to the side of her mouth. "It's good you got back here quickly. Rufus started to droop a bit."

"Oh no." Sydney did her best to generate some actual concern for the two pieces of vegetation she owned, although they were hardly on a first name basis.

"Hate when that happens." Vince spoke from beside her. "I hope he's okay."

"Me too." Sydney suppressed a smile.

"Don't worry. I nursed him back to health."

"Thank you for taking such loving care of him."

"To be honest, it didn't take much more effort on my part than bringing them over here. Orson was admirably respectful, I must say. At one point he tried nibbling on one of Annabelle's fronds, but when I scolded him, he let her go."

For the first time since she'd walked in the door Sydney looked beyond her immediate surroundings. "Where is Orson by the way?" By now he surely would have presented himself if he were home.

"He got out and away from me. Seems he's gone off on one of his carousing events." Ida glanced out the front window then went over to take a closer look outside. "I haven't seen him since some time yesterday."

"Oh, I'm sorry." Sydney made a move to collect her plants.

Vince glanced over at Ida. "You didn't put that little gps device on him yet?"

"I keep forgetting to give that to you." Sydney spoke up before Ida had a chance. "Sorry."

"No problem. You've been busy."

Standing, Sydney put her hands on her hips. "I'll bring it over tomorrow."

"That is sweet of you, dear."

"There's been a new development in the national On Trend clothing chain financial scandal." An anchor's voice caught Sydney's attention. "A body found earlier this week in a secluded area in Macomb County has been identified as that of Brock Richardson, Founder and CEO of the now defunct company. Dental records were required for positive identification since the body was discovered badly burned in a vehicle after what appeared to be a fiery crash. Authorities continued to investigate the exact cause of the accident."

Rooted to the spot, Sydney zeroed in on the report. "Oh, my God. That's awful."

Pictures of the accident scene followed. With close ups of the burned-out hulk of a car. Her stomach knotted and, putting a hand to her mouth, she glanced away as the voice over continued.

"You may remember that many of the stores…." The report went on to provide details of the chain's demise. Some of the information was accurate, but most was not. Sydney sure wasn't going to worry about that now.

"Isn't that the man you used for work for, Sydney?" Ida had stopped going on about Orson's wandering ways to listen as well.

"Yes." She returned her attention to the screen, half expecting her name to be mentioned at any moment. "It is. Brock wasn't there for long. I mean, on site at headquarters. We were always told he was working in other areas of the company." *Not to mention personnel.*

"Brock? You know him, knew him, well then." Ida walked over to grab Sydney's hands and squeezed tight. "I'm so sorry for your loss."

"Don't be." At Ida's wide-eyed surprise, she went on, "I mean, we really weren't close." She shut her mouth to swallow.

Brock Richardson came into the headquarters building with a bang. *And seems to have gone out the same way.* Even so, the news of his unfortunate demise still made her shudder.

Lips pursed, Ida shook her head, dropped their hands, and stepped back. “Still it’s very sad.”

Sydney kept her eyes and ears focused on the news program, whose anchors had gone on to a story about a five car train derailment somewhere in the southwest. More dramatic pictures flashed on the screen as the commentary continued. Though those from the latest accident scene weren’t nearly as graphic as the ones from Brock’s. *Or was the personal connection what caused her strong reaction?*

She had yet to move when Vince came up behind her. Without a word, she leaned against him. His arms circled her waist, and immediately she grabbed him to hold on tight.

“Such a horrible, horrible shame.” Ida made a *tsk-tsk* sound then shook her head. “Probably driving too fast.”

“Probably.” Vince uttered the comment as he let Sydney go.

“Well.” She indicated her plants. “Time to get Annabelle and Rufus home.”

“Oh, Vincent.” Ida glanced his way. “Before you leave. You know how it is when you don’t have a man around the house.” She issued the aside to Sydney with a wink before her attention returned to Vince. “My stove light seems to be burned out. I have a replacement bulb in the drawer. Could you change it for me, please?”

Vince looked at her for a second before he smiled. “Sure. Where is it?”

“This way.”

As he followed Ida toward her kitchen, Sydney walked over to the table holding her plants. “You do that, and I'll meet you at home…my place, when you're done."

"Sounds like a plan."

Sydney did her best to shake off a definite sense of unease at the news report as, with a plant in each hand, she walked the short distance to her house. Settling the foliage into place by her front window, she took hold of the handle of one suitcase she wheeled behind her toward the bedroom door. Turning the knob, she pushed inward. The door resisted then pushed toward her. She jerked her hand away and jumped back. The door seemed to open wider on its own. A flash of white at ankle level bounded by.

"Orson!" Right hand flattened on her chest, she turned as the cat, tail straight up and flicking, scurried away. "You scared the crap out of me."

Following close behind him, she hurried to scoop the animal up and headed straight out the door and over to her neighbor's.

"Guess who I found." When Ida happened to meet her at the door, she deposited him into her arms. "He came out of my bedroom."

"You're kidding. Bad Kitty." She made a gesture of admonishment toward the errant feline. "He must have gotten in when I went over to rescue…uh…pick up your plants."

"Probably."

"I don't remember him following me over there though." Creasing her forehead, Ida gave her pet a perplexed look. "Did you?"

Sydney was way too tired to argue about semantics. The way Ida kept track of Orson, how would she know for sure where he went?

"The important thing is he's home now."

"Let me know if he did any damage." Ida called out as Sydney headed back to her own place.

"I'm sure everything is fine. Thanks again for taking care of things for me, Ida."

"Any time."

Back at her bedroom door, Sydney picked up the handle of her suitcase. *So much for an uneventful arrival home.* When she stepped inside, she let out another scream then clapped a hand over her mouth.

"Oh, my God!"

All the larger drawers in her dresser were either pulled all the way out or partially so. The smaller top drawers were upside down with their contents strewn across the bed. The doors on her jewelry armoire beside the dresser gaped open.

Hands on either side of her face, she continued to survey the destruction. Her bedroom was ransacked far worse than even Orson could have done. Smart as he was, she doubted the wily cat could open the top bureau drawer, let alone dump it out.

What if whoever did this is still in here? Swinging around, she focused her gaze on the closet door swung wide open. The door to the adjoining bathroom was open as well. Dropping her hands to her sides, the initial terror that gripped her gave way to irritation that immediately blossomed into rage.

"Whoever did this is going to be so sorry."

Hurrying into the living room, she made a hasty scan around. Nothing in here appeared to be disturbed. Even the papers on her desk in one corner by the window seemed to be as she'd left them.

Suddenly aware she stood inside alone, Sydney ran

out onto the porch, then pulled out her cell.

"Nine-One-One, what is your emergency?"

"Someone broke into my house."

"What is the address?"

Sydney blew out a breath and answered.

"Are they still in there? Where are you?"

Closing her eyes, she willed herself to slow down. "No. No one is around that I can see. I was out of town and just returned."

Calmer now, she provided additional information as best she could.

"An officer will be there shortly. Wait outside, please."

Well, Duh!

The call ended, she dropped the hand holding the cell to her side. Starting to tremble, she raised her head and turned toward the townhouse next door.

"Vince, come here please, and hurry! I need you."

Chapter Thirteen

Vince caught Sydney as she scampered down the porch steps and launched into his arms. Rocked backward, he stiffened then steadied them both. "What happened?"

"Someone broke in." The words rasped beside his collar bone as she burrowed close and held on tight. "And ransacked my bedroom."

"It's okay, Sydney. It's okay." He rubbed his palm along her backbone. His whispered words of comfort continued. "You're not alone. I'm here. I've got you."

I'm never going to let you go. Ever.

Adrenaline bubbled up to flood through his veins, but he made himself remain solid and unwavering. "Are they still in there?"

"No." She pulled back slightly and shook her head. "No one was in there. The closet and bathroom were empty, too."

"You're sure?"

"I didn't see anyone."

A million what ifs and whens ricocheted through his mind. This was personal, but for Sydney's sake, he struggled to put the necessary internal protocols into place. *De-escalate the situation. De-escalate. Stay in control. Calm the victim.*

"Tell me what happened." He kept one arm around her shoulders, held her tight against him to share his warmth. “Take your time.”

“All I know is I went into the bedroom.” She burrowed more deeply into him.

“Did you hear anything before you went in?”

“No. Nothing. I turned the knob to push on the door and Orson flew out.” She raised her head to again glance up at him and tried for a smile. “Poor kitty. He must have gotten locked in there at some point.”

“Sydney! Are you all right?” Ida called over from the safety of her porch.

“I’m fine, Ida. Someone broke in while I was gone.”

Her neighbor slapped both hands on either side of her face. “You’re kidding.”

Sydney swallowed before she spoke. “If only.”

“It might be better if you went inside, Ida.” Vince did what he could to keep things under control. “The police will probably want to talk to everyone individually.”

“He’s right, Ida.” Sydney spoke up before Vince had a chance to continue. “Go back inside. We’ll call you if we need you.”

“Okay, I will.” Despite her words, the woman stood pat. “If you’re sure you don’t need me now?”

“We’ll call you if we do.” Vince made sure to keep his words slow and even as the woman did as he asked.

“I went back after taking Orson over to Ida’s and discovered the drawers overturned and clothes all over.” She shivered and took a breath. “Then I freaked out and immediately dialed in to report it.”

“You called nine-one-one?”

“Yes, of course. Manderfield Township usually responds to calls from here.” Her voice was stronger. A good sign she was coming off the shock.

"Manderfield Township." He kept his arm around her.

Being that there was no immediate threat, Vince would have preferred to handle the situation more low key. His way would be to bypass dispatch and the inevitable announcement on all channels, which would have been easier than Sydney calling nine-one-one. But, she had, and now he had to live with it.

"I explained to the operator this wasn't an emergency."

Sydney's voice scattered his thoughts. "That's good." *Hopefully.*

Duty mandated they stay where they were. They'd only complicate the situation, possibly contaminate the crime scene, if they went inside.

"It's better if we wait out here." He made sure his tone contained quiet reassurance.

She pushed away slightly to nod. "I know."

Vince had no choice but to stand beside her as a MTPD cruiser slowed at the curb then stopped. He caught sight of the numbers twenty-two on the side. Twenty-two was the squad car Foley usually drove. The uniformed officer in the front seat put his hat on over gray hair, and Vince didn't know whether to laugh or cry. *This could be good, or go very, very bad.*

Dispatch no doubt informed him the intruder was no longer on the premises, since Foley took his own sweet time before he even opened the door. *No doubt pausing to call in his arrival on scene.* Then the laid-back veteran had to unbuckle his seat belt and do more of who the hell knew what before he finally exited the car.

Nothing was an emergency to Foley. Nothing.

Vince's official contact at Manderfield squared the hat on his head and glanced up as he approached. When his gaze landed on Vince, recognition followed by unasked questions immediately flared. A subtle head shake from Vince was all it took for neutrality to take place in the depths of the older veteran's eyes.

"You folks okay?"

"We're fine, Officer," Vince called out for both of them.

All business and with his usual poker faced demeanor, Foley came up the stairs and offered his hand to Vince. "I'm Officer Ned Foley. I understand you've had a break in."

"The property belongs to Ms. Raines." Vince made a mental note to contact the man ASAP with any and all plausible reasons to *officially* explain why he was there.

Once he came up with some.

Sydney shook Foley's hand. "I'm Sydney Raines."

"Are you the one who made the call?"

"Yes. When I discovered my bedroom had been ransacked." She paused for a moment to stare at him. "You're the officer we encountered the other day."

"I am. I'd say it's nice to see you again." He sent a pointed look Vince's way. "But obviously not under these circumstances."

Sydney let out a slight laugh. "Tell me about it."

Vince kept his expression placid, despite the irony her words echoed in his thoughts.

"Let's get started." Foley took a notebook out of his right breast pocket to flip open, then felt around his torso for a moment before he produced a pen from another pocket. "That's all that was disturbed? Only the bedroom?"

"I assume so." When her voice faltered, Sydney cleared her throat. "Nothing else in the other rooms seemed to be disturbed."

"You left the premises immediately?" Brows furrowed, he concentrated on whatever it was he wrote down.

"Of course." She glanced toward the street. "Is it okay if we go in now for the rest of this? My neighbors have enough to gossip about without adding this to the list."

Both Vince and Foley looked where she indicated with her gaze. A small contingent of residents stood across the street, some vying for position to gain an optimal view of whatever was going on beyond the police vehicle.

"We can." Foley nodded. "But only as far as the living room."

"As long as we're behind closed doors." Sydney didn't waste a minute before she headed inside. "I think I know who did this."

Vince lifted a shoulder as he exchanged glances with Foley when they followed behind her. He pulled the door shut as soon as they all cleared the threshold.

"Mind if I look around?" Foley stepped in front of her.

Hands clasped on her stomach, Sydney looked over at him and shrugged. "Of course not. Be my guest."

Foley walked slowly around Sydney's neat as a pin living room. The TV, VCR, and PC were all where they belonged, still there and all intact.

Vince gave into a need to comment on that fact. "Lots of valuable stuff in here and none of it disturbed."

Foley jotted something in his frag notes. “We should dust for fingerprints on that doorknob.”

“It won’t do you any good I’m afraid.” She held up one palm. “I’ve already handled it.”

“Anything of value in the bedroom?”

Sydney shook her head. “Nothing really.”

“Anything missing?”

She shook her head again. “I didn’t really take the time to check.”

“Let’s do that now then.”

“Okay.”

With Sydney again leading the way, all three filed into her bedroom. Without seeking permission, Sydney stepped in to scoop up her scattered underwear, en masse, to return to a larger drawer she slammed shut. To his credit, Foley didn’t stop her.

Being the recipient of an over the shoulder and meaningful glance from the officer in charge, Vince took up a position against the doorjamb as Foley and Sydney started to comb piece by piece through the destruction.

“I’m telling you I think I know who did this. I’m sorry, Officer Foley.” She righted a large jewelry box that had been tipped on its side then sorted through some of its drawers that had been left open. “Nothing’s missing from here. My calling you was a mistake. Please can we all sit down and discuss this?”

“You think robbery wasn’t the intent?” Vince had to ask.

Foley turned to look at him through narrowed eyes but said nothing.

“Oh, I think robbery was the intent all right. Except what he was after wasn’t here. I took the ring he wants back with me."

"Ring he wants back?" Foley held the pen above his notebook as he repeated her words.

"I'm afraid so. Please." She indicated the doorway.

Nodding, Foley walked toward it. "Okay. Let's hear what you have to say."

Back in the living room, Sydney took a seat on the couch beside Vince, and Foley took the chair opposite. When Sydney rested her palm on Vince's knee, all he could do was put his hand over hers.

Pen poised over his pad again, Foley glanced up and definitely noticed the gesture, though he didn't write anything down. Whether or not he found it important enough to make note of later remained to be seen.

"You said you had an idea who would do this?"

"The first person to come to mind would have to be my ex-husband." With a quick glance at Vince, she leaned forward. "Mark."

Ned wrote the name down then looked up. "His last name Raines?"

"No. It's Stanford. I never took his name."

Vince catalogued the full name for future reference. An address would be easy enough to come by.

"You don't get along so well with him?" The officer on scene settled further into the chair.

Lips pursed, she considered him. "Does anyone really get along with their ex? I mean that's the whole point. Right?"

"Anything specific?"

"He thinks I owe him."

Foley gave a quick glance up, brows raised. "Like

alimony?"

She shook her head. "He tried for that and failed. No. Now he thinks he's entitled to the return of everything he ever gave me during our time together."

"What amount of time together is that?" He looked briefly at Vince who could only offer a half-assed shrug.

"Two years. We've also been divorced for two. The whole marriage was a mistake."

With another slight glance Vince's way, she ran a hand through her hair. "Mark lives in Warren off Eight Mile. At least he did at one time. I hadn't heard from him in a while, then he called a couple of weeks ago."

"You remember the exact date?"

"It was..." She turned her gaze on Vince. "That day, just before you arrived to get the jacket you left here, then took me out to dinner."

Unfortunately, he didn't have the luxury to not respond to that loaded piece of information. "Monday before last, whatever date it was I'd have to check."

Sydney nodded and rubbed her hand along the top of his thigh. "Saturday was the day you stayed for lunch and were so sweet to comfort me when I didn't get that job."

Thick, gray brows damned near hit the tip of an equally grayed hairline.

Foley sure was getting an earful.

Vince tried for a subtle side long look to see if any of this was being written down. It didn't seem to be. A sigh escaped he covered with a throat clearing. He had to hand it to the man for the way he kept his expression dispassionate at these juicy sound bites.

"Anyone else you can think of, Ms. Raines?"

"I'd like to think I have more friends than enemies."

"You probably do." He eyed her from beneath quirked brows. "Why don't you classify them all." His pointed gaze strayed briefly over to Vince. "We'll take it from there."

Sydney gave him a wry smile. "I'd expect nothing less."

Vince coughed into his elbow, then sat back to listen.

"Let's see." She ticked off points on raised fingers. "A rude woman where I'm currently employed and my ex. That's about it. Oh, I've gotten some nasty e-mails from some of the people I used to work with. A few blame me for what happened to them. That makes for a pretty deep suspect pool." She inhaled and sat straighter. "All of which is irrelevant."

"I'll be the judge of that." This time when Foley spoke he didn't glance up.

"Maybe. Maybe not." Before either of them could protest, she went on. "I ran into Mark in Grand Rapids last week." She glanced at Vince. "Before we flew to California. I didn't know he was going to be there as part of the art festival. He's a musician. I only saw him, briefly, in a hallway. Our encounter wasn't pretty."

Vince perked up, and his attention definitely peaked when she provided a few details of their less than friendly meeting. Then why hadn't she shared the information with him when she first returned?

"In fact, he as much as said he was going to do something to get even. Before I turned my back on him and walked away."

For his part, Vince wanted to know more, though

this sure wasn't the time or place for any questions he might have.

"Maybe he's just jealous of your success. Wants to strike out. Retaliate in some way." Vince had to speak up.

She looked at him for a long moment. "You both certainly have a police officer's suspicious DNA." Her gaze swept over to Foley then back to Vince as she gestured with one thumb. "Him I can understand."

Foley didn't respond to being pointed out. "How about those who like you?"

"You could say Glenn the security guard slash doorman around here likes me to a fault."

Vince sat back and refrained from clenching his fists as Sydney went on.

"My boss, my new boss, doesn't seem to have any problems with me. He took a chance and gave me a job when I needed it most. Then there's my next-door neighbor Ida and Orson. He really, really likes me."

Ned glanced up, one brow quirked. "Say what?"

With a smile, she lifted both shoulders then let them drop. "My feeble attempt at comic relief. Orson is her cat. He always seems to end up at my door."

While Vince's colleague may have been laid back to a fault, he was also known to be a monumental by the book type cop. Compared to him, Vince looked downright rogue. These days, anyway.

"Did you get along well with your former boss?"

Vince's attention peaked again on that one. If the media had the information about the clothing chain mogul's death, the area police departments did too. Although they weren't necessarily aware Sydney knew Richardson's fate as well.

"It's hard to say. Brock had only worked in our headquarters office for a month. He brought his own assistant with him. We didn't really have much one on one contact."

Again Foley glanced up. "How about outside of work. On a personal level?"

"Not a chance. He was too busy with the assistant. Her qualifications for the job seemed more personal, but maybe that was just my take."

A light bulb seemed to flash on in Foley's brain. "Did she maybe take the job you thought should be yours?"

Vince couldn't let that one go by unchallenged. "What are you getting at?"

"Just going where her answers are leading me."

"Please." Sydney put a hand up to stop them, then turned to Foley. "If you're suggesting I had something to do with his death, I didn't."

"So you do know he's deceased." With the writing materials in one palm, Foley clasped both hands in his lap then tilted his head and watched her.

Sydney flicked a hand toward Ida's. "We just saw a news report about it."

"Do you know of any of his enemies maybe?" Foley didn't so much as blink.

Teeth clenched tight, Vince shifted in his seat but didn't comment. *Jesus, Foley, stick to what you came here to investigate.*

Sydney shook her head. "As I've said repeatedly, we really weren't that close. Anyway, I was a few hundred then a few thousand miles away from Detroit most of last week."

"You have witnesses who can corroborate that?"

Sitting forward, she narrowed her eyes to focus on his face. "How many would you like?"

That comment didn't make him so much as blink either. He raised the pad and pen then started writing. "As many as you have."

"For right now, you can contact Randall Curan, my boss and another person who works there, Nancy Parsons. If you can wait until I get to the office on Monday, I'll send you an entire list of the potential clients I met with."

"That won't be necessary." Foley cast yet another pointed glance at Vince before he turned his attention back to her. "I'll take your word for it. Just trying to cover all the bases here." Closing the notebook, he stood.

Sydney rose with him then extended her hand. "Thanks for stopping to take the report."

Foley smiled as he accepted her handshake. "You do understand these are all questions I'm compelled to ask." His glance slid briefly over Vince. "Just doing my job."

"No one can fault you for that." Rising, Vince shook Foley's hand as well.

The uniformed officer shrugged then pulled a card from his breast pocket he handed over. "This has my personal cell number on it. Don't hesitate to call me if you need anything. Or if either of you remembers anything more."

She took the card to set on the table. "I may save you the trouble and confront my ex."

Foley shrugged. "Suit yourself. But you need to understand once we're called, we need to investigate and file a report."

Her gaze softened as she smiled. “I do understand that, Officer Foley. Thank you.”

Vince placed an arm around his colleague’s shoulders to steer him toward the door. “I’ll walk you out, Officer Foley.”

He was vaguely aware Sydney flopped back down on the couch. Obviously relieved to be done with all things law enforcement related for now.

“It’s just lucky your lady friend wasn’t hurt.” Foley kept a low, yet level tone as he spoke.

Vince opened the door and walked them out to the porch. “You got that right.”

Foley turned to face him, adding a sharp look. “I’m not sure what you have going here, Miller, and I’m not going to ask. As far as I know, you’re still in our jurisdiction working on a case from yours.” When Vince said nothing to correct him, the man lowered his voice even more. “I get how you want to protect a snitch. Any of us would.”

“Good you understand. Thanks.” Though it galled him to do it, Vince chose to *not* set Foley straight. By God, when this was over he’d set things straight with everyone involved. Especially, Sydney.

“It’s what we do.” Foley caught him with a level eyed stare. “Because that is what you’re doing, right? Why you’re here.”

“That’s it.” Vince held a steady stare down with his coworker. “I appreciate your, uh, cooperation. Working UC can get complicated.”

“Uh-huh.” His brows rose. “I can imagine.”

Vince dropped his gaze then brought it up again. “Though I should have the matter resolved soon.”

Wise eyes bore into him. “The case you’re

working."

"Yeah."

"Be careful. Don't ruin what I understand is a spotless reputation for nothing."

"It's hardly nothing." Just what it was, he couldn't wait to find out.

"This better be worth it."

"It is."

"We go back a ways. Based on that, I'll trust your judgement. Just don't screw yourself over."

"Never." Vince put his hand on the doorknob. "Thanks, Ned, I owe you one."

"Yes. You do." The response was terse before a firm palm landed on his arm. "It's hard as hell, but you can't make it personal."

"Easier said than done."

The hand fell away. "I know. But you won't do anyone any favors if you go off half-cocked."

Mouth a tight line, he huffed out a quick breath. "I'll do my best."

"Don't we all? I'm going to check with a few of the nearby neighbors. See if anyone saw anything."

"Sounds good."

"Take care now."

"You too, and thanks again." Coming back inside, Vince leaned against the closed door for a second before he returned to the living room. Sydney was stretched out on the couch with her eyes closed and one arm rested on her forehead.

She pulled her legs back so he could sit down. "I just feel so damned violated."

"I know. You get grief because some dumb bastard doesn't know the difference between right or wrong."

His brows drew down as he lifted her feet to set in his lap.

“I should never have called them. Bothered them.”

“Bother or not, your house was broken into. You had to at least get a police report on file. If only for insurance purposes.”

“I’ll bet you anything it was Mark. It fits, Vince. I ran into him in Grand Rapids before we left for San Diego. Stupid, I know, but I may have mentioned how long I’d be gone.”

“He wants the ring that bad?”

Her response was a small shrug. “Who knows? Maybe he just simply wanted to scare the hell out of me. He did a darned good job. Initially, anyway.”

“Harassment?”

“And then some.” She extended both arms over her head then closed her eyes. “So much for the restraining order I filed.”

“You gave them his name and number. They’ll check him out.” He picked up her foot and ran his thumb along its sole. “There’s nothing wrong with still being afraid, you know.”

Her legs went limp as she de-stressed under his touch. In that sense, he was doing his job.

“Nothing wrong with it, maybe, but it’s not for me.” Her tone became breathy as his fingers kneaded her foot, toes to ankle. “Fear and anger are too destructive.”

“Maybe.”

She let out a breath then squirmed and jerked. “That tickles.”

“Sorry.”

“It’s me, not you.” She relaxed her leg back toward

him. "I've always been super sensitive in that respect."

He cupped her heel in one palm and stroked up the underside of her calf. "So noted."

"I can't believe that cranky old police officer would think I had something to do with Brock's death." The cords at the sides of her neck tightened.

"He didn't say that specifically."

"He didn't have to. Damned suspicious cop minds anyway."

"Let's not think about that now. You're ruining all my hard work."

She smiled at his comment. "It's hard for me to not think about it, but with your help I'll try." As if proof positive, the muscles in her legs loosened to lay heavy on his lap. "I must say, no woman in her right mind would want to let a man like you go. With such capable hands, and the talented ability to use them."

He released the foot he'd tended to. Before he could pick the other one up to rub, she rolled onto her stomach then squirmed around for a moment until both legs were again extended and resettled in his lap. Her entire body was slack and relaxed as she sank into the cushions. He thoroughly enjoyed it as his gaze roamed all the way to the curve of her ass, and he ran his palms down her sides, paying particular attention to massaging her waist.

She tucked her arms beneath her to cradle her head. Pleased he'd been able to get her to relax, he returned his attention to her soft curves. Shifting toward her for better access, he stroked his palm along the entire length of one leg. Pausing at the sensitive area at the back of her knee, he drew tiny circles with two fingers.

At her contented sigh, his mouth spread in a

triumphant smile. "Feel good?"

Another sigh escaped before she answered. "Magical."

"I'm glad."

Kicking off his shoes, he rose up on his end of the couch then tossed the back cushion to the floor to give them more room as he swung one leg over until he straddled her from behind. Shifting his weight again, he rubbed both palms slowly up her thighs. She didn't move, exactly, just twitched slightly as his hands circled her hips, massaged over her rib cage then went on to do the same across her shoulder blades. When his hands came together at the back of her neck to knead away the tension he found there, she buried her forehead in the couch then turned her face to one side.

"Whatever it is you're doing back there, please don't ever stop." The muffled comment was released in a drowsy tone.

"Wouldn't think of it."

For a few minutes more, he kept up the rhythmic contact in silence. Under his touch, hunched shoulders eased, and taut neck muscles slackened. At one point her arm drooped toward the floor with her hand opened and relaxed. Aware of a few physical changes of his own, he was quick to deep six the untimely urges. *Yeah that was going to happen.*

"Don't think about anything right now. Just relax and try to get some rest." He sat back on his haunches with the intent to shift to a more comfortable position.

As if attune to an unspoken signal, Sydney turned over to face him. He gazed down at the eyes looking up at him. Soft, brown, and filled with trust. "Funny, but right now I'm not one bit sleepy."

Regret he had yet to tell her the truth ripped a fissure in his heart, as he leveled his gaze on hers. "You still need to rest."

Sitting up, she circled her arms around his neck then smiled just before she pressed her lips to his. For how long, he had no idea as he gave in to passions he had no desire to control. Leaving her mouth thoroughly kissed, he sought the softness of her neck with his lips, the warmth of her collar bone. Delicate fingers trembled over the sensitive flesh at the back of his neck and it was his turn to let go of a sigh.

"As nice as this is, rather was, I have work to do." She took her arms from around him and sat back.

For him, an uncomfortable emptiness was all that remained. "Which is?"

"Though it would be lovely to rest and forget, I can't. I won't be able to do any of it at all until I get the damned mess in there cleaned up."

"I'll do what I can to help."

"I'm going to selfishly take you up on that."

When she rose from the couch and headed for the bedroom, Vince was right behind her. It took them less than an hour before they had the place back into shape. She returned the contents in the drawers he put back into the dresser. At first when she started to dust the furniture, he protested then relented, not wanting to get into a pro and con discussion about the necessity of preserving the crime scene. What did it matter at this point anyway?

He even vacuumed the floor for her. When they finished, and she sat on the foot of the bed, he joined her.

Reaching over, she took his hand. "You know what

angers me even more?"

"What's that?"

"Mark ruined the welcome home I had envisioned for you. For us."

Tell me about it.

"But what with the cross-country flight and all the rest of it." She swept her arm around the room then tilted her head back to gaze into his eyes. "I don't think I'll be the best company tonight."

"No one says you have to be." Releasing her hand, he wrapped his arm around her shoulders then cradled her head against his chest. "I sure don't. Would you mind if I stayed anyway?"

Her hair brushed his chin as she nodded. "I'd like you to. I'm brave, but not that brave." Despite her words, she glanced around the room again. "I just want all traces of that creep gone." She dusted her hands on the sides of her slacks. "Now if I could only get the rest of the travel grime off me."

Grime or not, all he wanted to do was lay her down and make love to her right then and there. "You go get cleaned up, and I'll fix us something to eat."

As he headed for the kitchen, when the water came on full blast in the shower, Vince swore he heard Sydney's deep sigh of relief as she stepped under the flow. Guilt vied with sadness as he opened the refrigerator. Putting everything else out of his mind except taking care of Sydney, he searched for something they could eat.

"Whatever you fixed us, it smells great." Coming out of the bedroom about a half hour later, she brought the alluring scent of freshness with her.

"Finding something decent was definitely a

challenge."

She smiled at him as she sat down on one of the stools. "Grocery shopping was the first thing on my to do list tomorrow. It looks like you did all right though."

They both took in the spread he had managed to put together. Scrambled eggs with mushrooms, spinach and cheese and whole wheat toast they devoured without a lot of talking.

"You cooked, I'll clean up the dishes." She glanced over at him, then down at their empty plates. "You can take a turn in the shower if you want."

His mind keyed on the final word. "I just might do that."

"I was careful to leave you plenty of hot water. That's one thing about Winsome Gate. They install more than adequate hot water heaters."

As she went on to extoll the virtues of water temperatures, Vince gave into a wry smile. Right now, for him, anything between cold and frigid would serve him quite nicely.

Sydney was in bed when he emerged a short time later. Clean, yes. Refreshed, not so much. With a self-deprecating chuckle and head shake to match, he climbed between the sheets beside her. Immediately, she slid over against him. He had his arms open and ready to close around her before she even got all the way there.

Lying with Sydney, holding her tight, it soon became a toss-up where her breathing ended and his began. He nestled her body more securely against him.

Totally irrelevant.

Nothing mattered except the fact he held her. Period.

Chapter Fourteen

Sydney parked her car out in front of her townhouse and shut off the engine. No sense pulling into the garage since she'd be leaving again soon anyway. About to climb out, her cell chirped. Standing, she pulled the phone from her purse to answer as she slammed the car door.

"Hello."

"Sorry I had to leave early this morning." Vince paused as if he wasn't sure what to say next. "It couldn't be helped."

"That's okay. I understand. Duty called." A smile curled her lips as she remembered his kiss. "At least you said good-bye before you left."

"I didn't want you to wake up to an empty bed."

"Which you can fill again for me anytime."

"So noted. And appreciated. What are you doing now?"

"I had some errands to run and just got home."

"Are you inside yet or still out?" The light-hearted voice turned serious.

Her brow furrowed at the nature of his question. "Just coming up the walk. I parked on the street because I'm going out again in a few hours."

"Everything look okay? Nothing around the door disturbed?"

"Everything looks fine." She raised her head to do

a quick three sixty of her surroundings. "You remind me of my father, you know."

"Why do I get the feeling that's not necessarily a good thing?"

"Because it isn't." Arriving on the porch, she inserted her key in the lock. "However, he has an excuse for being overly suspicious. He's a cop. Comes with the territory, I suppose."

Dead air met her comment. Opening her front door, she waited.

"It's called being cautious."

"Yes. And he tried to make me cautious to a fault. I won't live my life in fear, Vince."

"No one's asking you to. There's a significant difference between that and being cautious. I'm just suggesting you might want to be a little careful."

"Consider me being cautious and careful, for you. I looked both ways before I got out of the car and walked up to the house." She shut the door then set down her purse and walked over to sit on the couch. "Anyway, I'm not concerned about another break-in. I put a stop to that possibility today."

"You what?" His tone became filled with concern. "Did Foley, uh, the police call you?"

"Nope. And as soon as I finish talking to you, I need to call them."

"You're not pressing charges?"

"There's no reason to." Even though he couldn't see her, she shook her head. "After you left this morning, I called my ex to confront him."

"At least you didn't go over there."

"Why should I? He's the one who started it. He's also the only one I know who's stupid enough to do such a thing. I promised if he told me the truth—"

"That you'd forgive and forget."

"You're half right. I told him I'd forget the whole thing. I don't intend to forgive." When Vince didn't comment, she went on. "He confessed without much effort on my part." She paused a moment to reflect on the one and only good thing about their former relationship. "The funny thing was, with all his many, many faults, Mark never could lie to me. An admirable trait in any man. Don't you think?"

Vince coughed before he answered. "An admirable trait."

"After he demanded the ring back the first time, I decided to keep it with me. Not that I'd ever wear the thing again. I shudder at the thought."

"I'm glad the case is solved."

"Me too. As I said, as soon as I hang up with you, I'm going to call Officer Foley and tell him to close their case."

"Are you sure you want to do that?"

"Why wouldn't I? If I choose not to file charges, he can do what all good police officers do as they endeavor to protect and serve." She couldn't keep the touch of sarcasm from her tone. "Leave innocent civilians like me alone and go find some bad guys to harass instead."

"It's your decision. I'm not going to argue. Just watch yourself. That's all I ask. I care about what happens to you."

She cradled the phone more snugly to her ear. "Nice to be cared about. Especially when your motives are pure." Smiling, she added the good-natured bit of teasing. A frown developed at the short silence that followed.

"And personal." Vince spoke at last. "Don't forget personal."

Her smile returned, and her heart warmed. "Of course. Personal."

"Got that right. What I called about was your open house this afternoon. Am I still invited?"

"Of course."

"I was hoping you'd say that. What time does this gala, as you call it, start?"

"One o'clock." She kicked off her shoes.

"Do you want me to pick you up?"

"You don't have to. I'll need to get there a couple of hours early to make sure things are set up right."

"And I'd probably be in the way."

"You'd be bored."

"If you say so. I'll see you there."

"Okay. Bye."

With the prospect of seeing Vince fresh in her mind and anticipation running roughshod over her heart, Sydney phoned Officer Foley.

"If that's the way you want it, I'll conclude with personal dispute resolved, no further investigation required." He seemed more than happy to accept her explanation. Then he went on. "About the other."

"Yes?" Running a hand through her hair, she grimaced at his thinly veiled reference to her continued status as a person of interest in some other investigations.

"Your witnesses checked out on that, too."

"I was sure they would."

"Except for your boss, Randall Curan. He never returned my call."

"He's a busy man. I appreciate all of your assistance." She made sure to insert some brightness into her voice. "Thank you."

"You're welcome. Call us if you need anything else."

"Here's hoping I won't have to." She'd run out of breeziness, even though she couldn't fault him for doing his job. "Thanks again, Officer Foley. Good-bye."

****

Sydney placed both hands on the hips of her gray and white sweater dress to survey the results of a few days planning. In and round all the travel on her job. With the elegant backdrop of the gallery's atrium area, fine china dishes were set on tall cocktail tables draped in white linen. Servers in black slacks and starched, white tuxedo shirts weaved through a decent sized crowd with trays of caviar and wafers, other assorted canapes, and stylish stemware flutes of both champagne and non-alcoholic sparkling juice.

Standing to one side, she clasped her hands in front of her and glanced around, nodding with small smiles now and again as her gaze landed on various guests. Thanks to her judicious work in sending out media kits, the gallery should also receive some very nice press from this event. Her gaze strayed to the archway leading from the front entrance where several more guests walked in. Some in couples, some in small groups.

None of them Vince.

"The displays you've set up are stunning – simply stunning." Edna Parker, a well to do patron ambled by with the help of an ivory handled cane.

Sydney produced a high-beam smile. "I'm pleased you like them. Perhaps you'll find something that appeals to you." Nothing wrong with reminding those present all the artwork was available for sale.

"We shall see." With a curt return smile, the woman kept moving.

A thin, dark haired man walked behind another crush of entering patrons. Glancing from side to side, he looked as if all he wanted in the world was to get in front of them. Once he worked his way through the throng, he marched directly up to her.

His hand jabbed out. "Howard Lancer. How are you?"

"Fine." Sydney accepted an incredibly limp grip. "Are you enjoying yourself?"

"Yes, of course. Nice party." Without further chit chat, he dove right in. "I've been trying to get a hold of Randall for some time now." He backed up slightly and blinked. "However, meshing two extremely busy schedules in any constructive way is proving more and more difficult."

Recognizing his name as someone who had called the gallery more than once since she'd been there, Sydney took a small step forward. Strange that he hadn't connected with her boss. "What would you like me to do?"

The man pulled a card out of his pocket to press into her palm. "I represent the US Continental Bank. Randall and I have business dealings to discuss. We've both just been way too busy lately to make time for each other. I'm hesitant to trying talking with him here. Perhaps if you send me a copy of his schedule, we can privately set something up."

Sydney lowered the hand containing his card to her side, not sure she wanted to be part of the odd request. "I'll see what I can do."

"That's all I can ask." His gaze roamed the room. "Oh, there's Nancy. Maybe I don't need to talk to Randall after all."

"Just let me know." By the time Sydney muttered the words, he'd already set his sights on the gallery's co-owner. *More power to him for that.*

"Argentile is coming together nicely, thanks to the addition of our latest exhibits." Curan's voice drifted over top of a small gathering from somewhere at its center. "Of course, when I put my mind to something, I can't help but be a success."

Laughter followed his comment, and Sydney shook her head at the monumental ego of her boss. Talking a good game if nothing else. Major success, sure. A money maker for its owner, not so much. If their disappointing trip to San Diego was any indication. As murmurs of conversation buzzed around her, she let the corners of her mouth droop. After smiling for so long, her cheeks were beginning to ache. Hopefully no one would miss her if she took a quick break.

The deserted hallway that ran behind and parallel to the main atrium was the perfect place to be alone. The door she'd come through shut with a soft click behind her. Taking a few steps sideways, she leaned against the wall painted a clean, bright white. Its coolness seeped into her back, and she rolled her head counter clockwise to ease out a couple of knots that had settled in her neck.

If Vince were here, he'd have these kinks worked out of me in no time.

Her eyes closed and a smile bloomed.

"Why of course we can arrange a time to get together. I welcome your input."

She jerked upright with a start and pivoted in the direction of Randall's voice. He must be walking through with a client, and she'd best appear on duty. When no one materialized in the hallway, Sydney waited.

"That really has nothing to do with it." His voice took on a tightness she hadn't heard from him before. Maybe Howard Lancer had finally gotten that meeting he sought. But why couldn't she hear him respond? More silence followed then stretched on, and Sydney strained to catch what might come next.

"It will be enjoyable to meet face to face." Randall's reply suddenly dripped cordiality.

That was it, he must be on the phone. He lowered his voice to a murmur as he said something else she couldn't quite make out.

"Yes. Yes. I look forward to it." A deep laugh rumbled out of him. "Good bye."

Whomever he'd been talking to, a girlfriend perhaps, it was none of her business. Ever the charmer, he was probably working to endear himself to either a lady friend or another customer.

"Sydney, dear. There you are."

Before she could stand up straight and make a discreet exit, her boss was on her.

"I just stepped out here for a moment to catch my breath." If she were lucky, he'd believe she wasn't eavesdropping. Flashing a smile toward him as he approached, she lifted her hands. "What do you think so far?"

"Exquisite! Perfect. Fabulous! And I don't *think* I *know!*" His arms opened in an all-encompassing gesture. "A fabulous success to be sure. What you've joined here is a one-of-a-kind enterprise, Sydney, my dear."

She nodded, unable to summon a similar amount of enthusiasm. "I know."

"Of course you do." He stared at her with a closed expression. "Shall we rejoin our guests?"

With another nod, she led the way back into the crowded atrium.

"Edna! How are you?" His face suddenly beaming, he hurried over to the wealthy matron.

Left standing alone, Sydney glanced around the throng, about ready to embark on some necessary mingling.

"Sorry I'm late." Appearing at her side, Vince took hold of her hand.

"Trying to be fashionable?" Despite her glib remark, she took comfort simply being beside him. His strong, low key demeanor was a welcome contrast to the over the top tendencies of the man who'd just walked away.

"Yeah. That's it. Fashionable."

"Thought so." She pulled back slightly to survey him head to toe, and her heart did a little flutter dance in her chest. The man certainly did an impressive job of carrying off business casual. Above the jeans she was used to seeing him in, he wore a red checked sport shirt opened at the neck, and a navy blazer. Broad shoulders were the key, she decided as her gaze rose to slide along the freshly shaven chin to meld with incredible blue eyes.

He drew a breath. “Truth is I couldn’t get off work…I got held up. Editors and deadlines. Unavoidable.”

“I understand.”

The hand holding hers squeezed. He shot her a half smile. “I knew you would. Can you forgive me?”

“I’ll think about it.” She scoffed under her breath. *Who am I kidding?* All was forgiven the moment she set eyes on him. She just wasn’t ready to let him know about it yet.

“That’s all I can ask.”

Her thoughts dissolved at his words. “I’m glad you could make it.”

His gaze left hers to study the room. “All the arduous work you put into this seems to have paid off.”

“I think you’re right. Are you hungry?”

“Not for food. To be alone, yes.”

Another smile bloomed at the vivid memories of what being alone with Vince had come to mean. “Let me tend to a couple of details first.” Starting to step away, she was slow to pull her hand from his. “I’ll be right back.”

“Promise?”

At the suggestion in his voice, she paused a second as she walked toward the service entrance. With a quick glance over her shoulder, her lips curved up. “Promise.”

His wink in response nearly made her laugh out loud. As it was, she wore a huge smile by the time she approached the head caterer and made quick work of providing a few additional instructions. Vince remained right where she’d left him when she returned.

“How’s the article going? Are you making progress?” She asked the question as they strolled away hand in hand.

"It's practically finished. I focused on the success of Argentile and its cultivation of talented, lesser known artists. I think Curan will be pleased."

"I'm sure he will."

As they wandered through the gallery and farther away from the crowd, murmurs of multiple conversations, tings of silverware on dishes and clinks of crystal faded to an indistinct hum.

Vince slowed as he turned toward her. "How long do you have to stay around?"

"Until it's over."

"Oh."

At his crestfallen expression, she hurried on. "The invitations said from one until four. After that I'm all yours."

She glanced up to reflect the promise of her heart in the gaze she locked with his.

"Exactly what I wanted to hear." Though he returned her smile, he lowered his eyes slightly. Creases of concern remained at their edges.

Having no idea why that would be the case, a wispy strand of unease threaded through her. "I took a couple of steaks out of the freezer before I left home. With baked potatoes and salad. Sound good for dinner?"

"Sounds perfect."

A slow and subtle instrumental drifted down from speakers in the ceiling. They walked for a time without speaking. The fact he'd spend the night after dinner, though unspoken, was already a given.

As they rounded a corner, a painting of a little girl standing in a field of flowers seemed to catch Vince's eye, and he stopped in front of it. "Do you ever wonder what the subjects in these paintings might be thinking? Or did at the time they posed?"

She leaned against him and rested her head on his shoulder as she studied the little girl in a yellow bonnet. "I like to think they didn't know they were being painted. Maybe the artist saw this or something like this and painted from memory. Or made the scene up altogether from a variety of personal experiences."

"Could be." Turning her toward him, he gently stroked her cheek with warm knuckles. "There are things you see or experience that stay with you for a lifetime."

Is that what we have going for us? Something for a lifetime?

She paused at the sheer enormity of the idea. Was it wise to even consider a lifetime with a man she'd only recently met?

"Or maybe the whole thing was staged," he continued. "The little girl placed in the center of a field of flowers and ordered to stay still."

"No. Let's go with the artist's imagination. Randall always talks about how human thought, belief, and imagination are materialized through art."

"Sounds like something the instructors would say in the art appreciation classes I took in college."

"Where did you go to college, Vince? What did you study?" She picked up his hand again as they continued down a side hallway.

"Good old state U."

"Michigan State?"

"Is there any other?"

She laughed out loud. "Not that I know of."

"Me either."

Each day she learned more and more about the man. Plus, the more she learned, the more she liked.

"What did you study?"

His back was to her as he led her behind him to a free form stone bench at the end of the hallway. "A lot of different subjects. Didn't end up getting a degree in any of them."

As he sat then pulled her down beside him, he kept his eyes averted though not enough to keep her from seeing the creases of concern had returned to their edges.

"That's why freelance writing is such a good fit for me." He cleared his throat then stared up at something on the ceiling instead of her. "I get to learn about all sorts of things instead of focusing on only one."

"I take it art appreciation isn't your chosen specialty?"

"Nope."

His answer was released quick. Too quick. A twinge of disappointment from out of nowhere channeled through her. She shifted just a little bit on the bench to place herself closer to him. "What is then? Not the investigations you told me about earlier?"

"That's just easy work to put food on the table between writing jobs."

"Oh really?"

"Really. What about you and college?"

"During my time in college at Central Michigan, I was pretty anal. Straight through for four years to study accounting and economics with a major in marketing, then earned an MBA and went from there."

"Someone who knows what she wants and isn't

afraid to go after it. Honest and direct." His voice faltered. "I like that. Especially in a woman."

"Do you?" As they continued to make small talk, all she knew was she needed something substantial from him right now. If not a full out declaration of love, at least an indication there was hope for something like it in their future.

"But beyond all that." He hurried on as if eager to get the words out. "You've become important to me in a relatively short amount of time."

A swift blush warmed her cheeks. Well into her thirties, she felt like a high schooler who had snagged the most popular jock at school for her own. "We did evolve pretty fast." She gazed deeply into his eyes.

"We did that." Sure and steady, he looked back at her. Then suddenly he blinked and looked away.

"I don't make a habit of sleeping around." Part of her didn't think saying that was necessary. The rest of her wanted him to know.

"Why would I think you did?" His hand came over where hers lay in her lap. "We're mature adults, Sydney. Not immature teenagers who don't know any better."

"I know that." She lowered her gaze to the strong fingers encasing hers. "I've been through a lot the past few weeks."

"Is this where you tell me you're vulnerable and maybe I took unfair advantage of that?"

Something in his tone, condescension maybe, got her hackles up. She pulled her hands away and sat straighter. "Absolutely not."

"I'm sorry. That was meant as a joke. Albeit a bad one." When he reached to take hold of her hands again, she allowed it. "I'm not the kind of guy who sleeps around a lot either."

"You've never been married."

"That's right." His nod was barely perceptible. "Never."

"Any serious relationships?"

His smile softened the off-hand shrug that came next. "Once and only once. It didn't work out."

"My marriage didn't either."

"Sounds like, as far as making relationships work, there's nowhere for either one of us to go but up."

"Sounds like it." Nodding, she didn't bother to tell him she couldn't agree more.

****

"I have to say that wasn't quite as painful as I thought it would be." Vince slipped his arm around Sydney's shoulders as they walked up the back entrance to her townhouse.

Since she'd parked in the one car garage, his car was in the driveway.

At the mercy of a light autumn breeze, several leaves of red, yellow, and gold skittered across their path.

She lifted the collar of her trench coat more snugly around her neck. "Thank you for staying until the bitter end. I appreciated the support."

"No problem."

The headache that was coming on full force when she left the reception had subsided somewhat. Given the flurry of activity that took place the last half hour, she was surprised the top of her head hadn't actually blown off.

"Who knew Nancy would try to initiate another

business argument with Randall. In the back office, but still at the reception of all things. The woman truly is a piece of work. Self-centered, opinionated and…" She paused, hunting for the right word. "Just downright ornery."

"She sounds lovely. I'm almost sorry I didn't get a chance to meet her face to face." Vince hit a button on the remote in his palm, and his silver Jeep beeped as the doors locked.

"No. You aren't." Digging in her purse, Sydney pulled out her house key. "Believe me, you didn't miss anything. I'm just glad she kept her shrewish behavior private. Waiting to confront him until he went back to his office when things were winding down. Regardless, she had no business doing even that."

He dropped his arm as she stepped onto the small portico ahead of him. "You did a great job running interference with the guests who were still there so they wouldn't notice what was going on."

"And you did great helping me charm the last of them out the door." About to put her key in the lock, she turned to face him. "I can't thank you enough for being there for me when I needed you."

"As I said. No problem." Bringing her into his arms, he brushed a kiss on her lips. "I'm glad I could be there when you needed me."

She hugged him tighter when he released her lips. "You always seem to be there for me when I need you. Why do you think that is?"

"I'm supposed to be?" The sigh he emitted shook them both. He straightened, stepped back from her embrace, then took her hand. "Let's go inside, sweetheart. There's something I need to … we need to talk about."

Chapter Fifteen

Sydney and Vince came through the back door of her condo and walked, without speaking, into the living room. He slipped the coat from her shoulders to hang in the closet then took his off and did the same. As he settled on her couch in the living room, she headed back into the kitchen.

"Is Chardonnay okay with you?"

"Whatever you have." Their choice of wine wasn't paramount on his mind just now. How to phrase what he needed to say to her was.

"I can't tell you how glad I am that reception is over." Her voice came at him from the other room.

That makes two of us. I think. "You have been putting in the hours lately. I hope that boss of yours knows how lucky he is."

"Whether he does or not doesn't matter to me one whit. What is important is I'm off work now and home. With you." Coming back into the living room with a stemless globe shaped glass in each hand, she stopped to stare at him for a moment as a sweet smile blossomed. "You and I. Together alone for a change."

Breaking eye contact, he set the wine she handed him aside untouched as his gut somersaulted and his mouth went dry. "Sydney, there's something you need to know."

"What's that?" She stepped to the end table to grab

a hummingbird coaster.

"My real last name isn't Reeves."

About to settle close beside him on the couch, the most important person in his life froze with her wine glass aloft. As she stood above him, he wasted no time launching into a detailed explanation of who he really was. Her silence remained while he laid out the basics of his UC assignment as neatly and succinctly as the written report he'd filed. Direct, clear, and concise. Giving his reasons, substantiating all his actions. Up to and including the inevitable conclusion. No criminal activity discovered.

Case closed.

Staying where she was, she said nothing. Just watched him as a wariness he'd never seen from her before clouded her gaze. "You're kidding, right?"

Guilt ate away at him as he stared at her but said nothing. He could hardly blame her for being in shock. The bombshell confession he'd just dropped into the middle of their still fragile relationship ticked ominously and was about to go off. To blow up and destroy everything they had going so far.

"Please tell me you're kidding."

"Right now, I wish I were." Sitting forward, he clasped his hands together between wide spread knees.

Any second now, he fully expected his face to be drenched in ice cold Chardonnay. Instead, like his, the bottom of Sydney's glass hit the table with a clink. Leery of making any sudden moves, he glanced up at her. Those beautiful brown eyes that had grown wider and wider as he talked, narrowed in a most menacing way now that he'd finished. The lush mouth he so loved to cover with his own gaped open in disbelief.

Amazing as it was, owning up to his true identity turned out to be relatively easy. He clasped his hands tighter. Awaiting her reaction after the fact was anything but…easy. At most, she should rant and rail about what a scum bag he was for having duped her. Go on to call him every nasty word ever created. Even make some up if she wanted. Threaten to call the police and have him arrested—as asinine as that concept was. At the very least, she could simply and politely ask him to leave.

What he hadn't counted on was her silence. Ominous and grim, it stretched wide and long between them, as if designed to push them apart.

That he wasn't sure he could handle. He released his fingers then clasped them together again. *May as well try to get the ball rolling.* Even if it turned out to be a wrecking ball. "I guess I expected more of a reaction."

Slowly, ever so slowly, she shut her mouth and she quickly opened it again. "Like what, Vince? What exactly did you expect? Steam to come out of my ears, lightning bolts to flash from my eyes and flames to shoot out of my mouth?"

"No. Of course not."

Though he didn't dare tell her, the truth was a show of blazing anger he could handle. This silence of hers was something else. Her control in the face of his deceit was unsettling as hell.

"What I want to know is why you took your own sweet time to…to…come clean with me."

Pulling his hands apart once and for all, he leaned back for a second then straightened. "At first I couldn't because—"

"It would have compromised the assignment."

After she finished the sentence for him, he nodded. "Exactly. The feds were involved. I couldn't do anything but keep quiet. Those guys don't take kindly to having civilians interfere in their operations."

"Interfere? Really?" Her tone deepened to one of disbelief. "And after the feds left the case?"

He took a moment to swallow. "We…you and I…never seemed to have the time."

"That is so lame, Vince. In all the alone time we did spend together the past couple of weeks." A fast breath huffed out of her. "You couldn't take five minutes?"

"Five minutes wasn't going to cut it. We've been at this a lot longer right now, and nothing's been resolved."

"You couldn't even try?" Tears moved up to tinge her voice. Even as she clamped her mouth shut, her chin continued to tremble.

"It's not that I didn't want to. Didn't think about it a lot." He lifted an arm toward her then, thinking better of it, let it drop. "You were always so busy with your new job."

"Seriously? You not being able to tell me the truth was my fault?"

"No. Of course not. I'm not saying that at all." Pressing his lips tight, he again broke eye contact. "It's no one's fault you had responsibilities. Out of town business. The reception Curan had you put on."

"You could have been honest with me. Not used me the way you did."

"I never used you." He pulled in a breath as he looked up at her. "It was my job, Sydney. I was just doing my job as I'd been instructed."

"Certainly you were. You're not a magazine reporter, you're a cop. One who was working undercover to bring a man to justice who, by your own admission, never did anything wrong in the first place."

With both hands at her sides, she drew them into fists she relaxed, then clenched tight again. Vince lifted his chin, half expecting her to clock him with a well-aimed right hook.

"That's not exactly how it is." Springing forward, he attempted to wrap her into his arms.

She brought her palms up hard and flat on his chest and shoved. "I know how it is, Vince. Believe me I do."

"I don't doubt that." Not knowing what else to do, he rubbed tensed fingers on his forehead.

Her eyes narrowed again, then darkened to signal a simmering anger. "I can't believe you did this to me." The tenor of her voice rose. "Initially maybe, but to carry on the charade for the past few weeks."

Ignoring the warning note in her tone, he immediately tried once more to pull her close and was somewhat amazed when she didn't karate chop his solar plexus. Even so, the warmth of her breath floated over the side of his neck. He closed his eyes to savor the moment for as long as it might last.

"You do realize this changes everything."

A definite chill took the place of any contented glow. After a brief swallow, he pulled back some, but didn't let her go.

I realize all right. "But, we're still the same people. Inside."

With a quick twist, she wrenched away from him then walked over to the other side of the room. "You just don't get it, do you?"

She was talking, but he obviously wasn't hearing what she had to say. "What do I not get?"

He'd lied to her, and she was pissed. Any idiot would understand that. But her calmly controlled reaction held the undercurrent of more. Something was wrong, very wrong. That he knew for sure. What exactly and why, he had no clue.

"You're a cop." Her voice was low as if she spoke to herself yet needed to have the words out loud and in the open before she could process exactly what they meant. "And I'm sorry to hear that. Very sorry to hear that."

His stomach clenched. "What the hell is that supposed to mean?"

"Exactly what I said." Her voice cracked.

There was only one light at the end of this seemingly no win tunnel he'd put himself in, and a small one at that. This relationship with Sydney, contentious or not, was one he was hell bent to preserve at all costs.

"Sydney." He approached slowly and brought his palms to rest on already tensed shoulders that tightened even more at his touch.

"Vince." The strength of her shrug dislodged his touch.

Though his hands dropped away, he refused to give up. "Can we talk about this? Please?"

"We can." She twisted around to face him, and her voice grew tight. "Though I'm not sure it will do much good."

Wrapping his fingers gently around her upper arms, he breathed a sigh when she didn't pull away.

Nor did she resist when he placed a gentle arm around still rigid shoulders to lead her back to the couch. He sat at one end and drew her down then laid his arm over the back cushion, waiting for her to settle in beside him. Instead, she immediately slid some distance away.

"Did you expect me to go all hissy fit psycho on you?" Before he could respond, she went on, "Simply because you did what, I'm sure, you were told to do?"

"No, but—maybe a little."

She turned slightly to look him in the eye. "Make no mistake. I know all about what a police officer must do to work undercover. Having to eventually mislead the people who trust them. It's never personal. It's always part of the job." Her gaze dropped as if in resignation. "Doing what needs to be done."

"Is it at all safe to say coming clean didn't change your feelings about *me*?"

"Right now, I'm not sure."

He kept his mouth shut as a chill ran across the back of his neck. The hairs there spiked up in response. For now, maybe it would be better if he refrained from speaking and waited for her to take the lead. He didn't have to wait long.

"I like you, Vince." Lifting her head, a clear and steady gaze kept hold of his. "I like you very much."

"That works. Given that I feel the same, where's the problem?" He attempted to flash a quick, reassuring smile. When his mouth refused to cooperate, he gave up. "At any rate, we can discuss this like two rational adults."

"Like two rational adults."

"Tell me one thing, so I at least have a fighting chance. Do you think you can find it in your heart to forgive me? Or are you about to kick my ass to the curb?"

With her eyes narrowed and chin raised, she said nothing. Just stared at him in a way that made his blood freeze solid in his veins.

Then her lips parted. "Maybe a little of both."

"Really?" He reached for her, but she backed away. He dropped his arms, but not the intensity of his gaze. "I'm in love with you, Sydney. That's all I need to know."

Her only comment was an indistinct smile. "Are you at all interested in what I know?"

"Of course."

Sliding closer, she brought her hand up to rest on one side of his face. "I care about you too much to love you."

The intensity in her eyes blurred behind a veil of tears. Suddenly, as far as Vince was concerned, billowing steam, lightning strikes, and raging, out of control flames held a certain appeal. For the first time since their argument started he was afraid he might have lost.

"That makes no sense."

"Maybe not to you. It makes perfect sense to me." She lowered her hand and started to slide away yet continued to look him in the eye. "That's why it's so hard to tell you I can't see you again. Ever."

He grabbed her hand, and when she twitched, he held on tight. "Look. I don't see that what I did was…deserves this strong a response. Never see each other again? Isn't that a little harsh?"

He was helpless to keep the astonishment from his tone. Why not just tell him to stop breathing?

"It's as much what you did as it is about who you are." She dropped her voice as well as her gaze.

He tilted his head to one side as he sought to get a glimpse of her face. "Who I—?" Letting out a sigh, he pulled back once and for all. "Even though your father was a police officer, you're one of those people who doesn't like cops? Is that it?"

The small laugh she emitted lacked anything resembling joy. "No. In fact, I'm one of those people who dearly loves cops. For the sacrifices they make."

"Sounds like I'm your kind of guy." This time he managed to flash some semblance of a grin.

She muttered something unintelligible under her breath. He was only able to pick up on two of many words. And could have sworn they were *I wish.*

Moving closer, he took both of her hands in his, brought them up in the narrow space between them, looked her in the eye, and smiled. "From my way of thinking, we don't have a problem we can't talk out."

"Your way of thinking is wrong."

His tightened hold thwarted her initial attempt to pull away. Then he relented and let her go.

"Why couldn't I fall for another bean counter like me? One who works for the IRS or something. Someone who holds a true nine to five position they serve by sitting behind a desk. It would be the rest of the world's job to come to him. He wouldn't be the one to go out the door day after day, risking his life for people who, for the most part, don't appreciate the effort." She stopped and swallowed, as if the bitterness evident in her voice had scalded her throat.

His instinct was to reply *because you didn't*, but he wisely kept his mouth shut.

Her mouth quirked down as she cast him a sideways glance. “Not only that, cops are lousy at long term relationships.”

Though from experience, he already knew the answer, he had to ask. “No exceptions?”

On a half-smile, she held his gaze. “No exceptions.”

“What if I said I didn’t believe that was true?”

“Then I’d say you’re more of a fool than I am. But that’s not the worst of it.”

He braced for another onslaught of coded information. “My being a cop is a terrible thing because why?”

“In addition to my father, both my older brothers are police officers. Maybe one of the reasons I’m giving you a temporary pass here, and not kicking your ass to the curb as you suggested, is because right now my brother is doing almost exactly what you are or were doing, and it scares me every day.” The picture of stoic determination fell, and her lower lip quivered.

He kept silent until she went on.

“Police officers’ families are as much a part of their job as they are. You know that as well as I do.”

“My mother has never been totally thrilled with my decision to join the force. I thought it was simply a maternal reaction.”

“Shows what you know. But, then, my mother never got the chance to have any say in either of my brothers’ decisions.”

He took her hand and squeezed. “I know that, and I’m sorry. But, if you’re going to worry about my safety, I can assure you, you don’t have to. I know what I’m doing out there.”

"That doesn't matter, either. We always worry." Her breath caught, and a sadness entered her eyes. "Whether we're a parent, sibling, cousin, friend."

"There are lots of cops I know who are in long term relationships." He made a stab at, sort of, changing the subject.

"Really?"

"Yeah."

To be honest, except for Jenny with Brad, who wasn't a cop at the time they got together, the only other example he could think of was Luke and Chelsea. Which wasn't all that encouraging either, since the last time he'd talked to Luke, their rocky relationship hadn't gotten any better. He scoured his memory for another, more positive example, and came up dry.

"I don't want to live without you, Vince, but living with you means living with the worry every day until you come home safe. I hid it when I could while I was growing up, but the anxiety is always there."

"The real life of a police officer isn't like the drama portrayed on television or in the movies. My friend Adam works as a technical advisor for some of them. He says the powers that be prefer to go with the drama and gore rather than the realism. It gives people a distorted view."

Sydney rested her head against the cushion. "That may be, but it doesn't change the fact police work is a dangerous way to make a living."

He called up ideas from all the survivalist reality shows he'd watched over the years on cable. "If you think about it, so is truck driver. What's that highway in Alaska covered in perpetual ice? People often risk their lives to make a living in different professions."

"Okay. I get the point you're making. That doesn't necessarily mean I agree with or accept your logic. Since the first day we met, you've known who I was. Who I really was." She paused to swallow before her gaze intensified. "I wasn't afforded that luxury."

"What I pretended to be on the outside had nothing to do with how my feelings for you developed in here." He pressed her palm to his chest over his heart. "Who Vince Miller truly is remains the same, no matter what."

Despite the smile she tried for, tears glistened. "I know you were doing what you had to do. I understand all about the undercover dynamics. It's all part of the job. Nothing personal." She glanced up then looked away before her gaze joined his again. "I do get that. Believe me I do. It's just that…"

"Just that what?"

"I'm not sure I can live day after day with the fear of losing you." She shook her head as more tears slipped down her cheeks.

A knock sounded from the front door, and they both turned.

Sydney glanced back at him. "Who could that be?"

"This is your house, not mine." Teeth gritted at being disturbed, he shrugged, then reached for his wine.

Swiping at her cheeks, she went to answer the door.

"Princess! How's my princess?"

There was no doubt about it, the stocky, gray-haired man who strode into the house and scooped Sydney into a bear hug had to be her father. For one thing, he had cop written all over him. Most notably, the way his gaze scanned the perimeter of the room he'd just entered over the shoulder of the daughter he still held on to. When his taking it all in gaze landed on Vince, the huge smile he'd come in with transformed to a definite scowl.

Vince nodded in greeting but refrained from lifting his glass.

"Daddy, what are you doing here?"

"Me?" At her question, his narrowed gaze flicked back to Vince, then cleared when his attention returned to Sydney. "Why? Is there a problem?"

"No! Of course not. Why would there be?"

"We did have this dinner date planned for a long time, I thought." Another pointed glance slid over Vince.

"You told me you had to cancel."

"You sounded so disappointed on the phone the other day, I decided to figure out a way to make it happen."

"What about your new job?"

"That's the beauty of being hired somewhere *after* you're retired. They need you more than you need them for a change. I told them I wasn't available for the next few days. They didn't argue."

"That's great. But instead of going out, why don't we fix something here?" Though she offered a smile, her voice dipped in confusion before she put her arm through his to lead him into the living room. "There's someone I'd like you to meet."

Vince had made sure to stand long before this. He always stood in the presence of a superior officer.

"This is my friend, Vince Miller. Vince, this is my father, Commander Andy Raines."

"Great to meet you, sir." As they shook hands,

Vince was the first to speak. "I've heard so much about you."

Actually, what Sydney chose to share was minimal at best, but he said it anyway.

"All good, I hope." The clichéd response was uttered with one brow lifted in expectation.

"Of course all good." Smiling, she pushed at his chest. "What other kind of information about you is there?"

"All good," Vince repeated.

"Daddy, Vince is a police officer like you. A detective." Vince picked up on the hint of sarcasm in Sydney's tone.

"Really?" At that bit of newsflash, the last ounce of wariness in his expression vanished.

"That's right, sir." He pasted on a smile as he released the large calloused hand. "Thirteen years and counting with my local department."

"And you made detective. That's good."

"Five years now." Vince made sure his smile remained in place as the small talk continued, though both were proving to be more and more difficult.

It wasn't that he minded meeting Sydney's old man. It was just that his timing *sucked.*

Chapter Sixteen

"Make yourself at home, Dad. Vince and I will go get you a beer."

Even before she finished, Sydney knew she sounded like an idiot. It sure didn't take two people to fetch a single bottle of beer. Her dad's odd look verified he too caught how ridiculous her statement was.

"I haven't touched my wine. I'll join you in having a beer." Vince stepped up to add to the absurdity.

"And some snacks." She grabbed her glass and Vince's hand. "Be right back."

"Take your time. I'll go bring in my overnight bag."

Her next step was a stumble before she recovered. "Fine, Dad. We'll meet you back in the living room."

She waited until she and Vince were in her kitchen with the door closed behind them. Even then, she had to lean against it before she could bring herself to turn and face him, as all the words she'd been forced to hold in for the past few moments gushed to the surface. Too bad she couldn't even spill them now. Lips pressed tight and eyes closed, she kept her back to him as she counted to ten. Then had to count all the way to twenty.

Vince had the good sense to remain where he was when she finally collected herself enough to turn around. "Say the word, and I'll leave right now."

The worry creasing his brow tugged at her heart.

She ignored its pull and shook her head. "Tempting, but no. You leave now, and I'll spend the rest of the night explaining why you did. Anyway, that's not why I brought you in here with me." She put a hand on his arm as he reached toward the refrigerator. "Do not say one word to my father about what Mark has done."

"You're not going to tell him about the break in?"

"No. I'm not."

"Why?"

"Trust me, you don't want him to know." When he stood there, obviously expecting more, she gave it to him. "For one thing, he and Mark never got along. Knowing my dad, he'd probably have my ex arrested, tried, convicted and on death row before lunch tomorrow."

Opening the refrigerator, she took out two cold beers to hand him.

"You're not joining us?"

She shook her head again. "I'll stick with my wine. For now anyway."

No one needed to know she was sorely tempted to go on an immediate week-long alcohol binge.

With her focus returned to the refrigerator for the wine bottle to refresh her glass, she wasn't ready when Vince set down the beer bottles to gather her into his arms.

"Are you kidding me?" Pushing at his chest only made him hold on tighter. "Not only is my father in the other room, right now I'm still very, very angry you lied to me."

"Just tell me at some point in the near future we can be alone to talk this out." He didn't seem to care when she initially stiffened at the idea. "Please give us that much."

A real sucker for the urgency in his voice, she relented. For a fleeting moment, a very fleeting moment, she gave into some unexplained need and leaned into his warmth. Only briefly.

"I'm not that heartless, Vince." As her gaze slid away from his deep and pleading stare, she picked up her glass and stepped away from him. "Really, I'm not."

"You two get lost in there?"

Her father's question came through the door and, fearing he'd come through next, she jerked upright. "Be right there." She projected her voice, then turned to Vince. "We need to get back out there."

Working fast, Sydney threw together some cheese, crackers, and fruit on a plate to take with her while Vince carried the beer. Once they were all settled back in the living room again, it didn't take long for the two men to strike up a congenial conversation sharing old war stories about their work.

"The perp took off on me and headed for a huge fence between two big backyards." Sydney's father set the beer Vince had handed over on the end table and leaned toward him. "I had no choice. My only option was foot pursuit. And me just back on the job after hernia surgery."

"Oh, no." Vince put his beverage beside her dad's. "Hate it when that happens."

Chin rested in her palm, Sydney sat on an opposite chair, and settled in for the long haul. What do you know? Her father and Vince were bonding. *Perfect.*

If she'd learned nothing else as the product of a law enforcement family, it was that police officers bonded on a level like no other. It never failed to amaze her. So many times she'd been out with her dad and or brothers when one or the other of them would nod in recognition to a perfect stranger. Who, of course, would turn out to be a fellow officer. This encounter of her father with Vince was no different.

"Had to scale the damned thing or lose him." Said father's next words broke into her thoughts. "Those stockade types are a bitch, too. Sorry." He glanced briefly at Sydney before his full attention returned to Vince. And totally missed her look of acquiescence. "Sheer wood panels with no real place to get a foothold."

"I feel for you, sir."

"I tell you, it wasn't pretty by any stretch."

"I can only imagine."

Sydney simply couldn't take any more. She'd heard this story recounted too many times. It was either join in the conversation or go screaming out of the room. "But you got him, right, Dad? The person you were after."

Some mutual chuckle the two men shared broke off at her intrusion. Neither one of them uttered a word as, straight faced, they glanced her way. Two sets of eyes stared as if they'd forgotten she was there.

"You're right, I did." Her dad paused to take a breath then immediately swung his full attention back to Vince. "Damn right I got him. Said a prayer then jumped that damned fence myself." With a deep, raucous laugh, he slapped a beefy palm flat on the chair arm. "I landed smack dab on top of the creep. He'd gone over then crouched down, figuring he'd lost me."

"Did you pull any stitches?" Shoulders hunched,

Vince winced as he dropped one hand to his lap.

"A couple. Probably would have been worse if the moron hadn't broken my fall."

Vince sat forward with a grin. "Nice when suspects cooperate like that."

"You bet."

More companionable laughter erupted into the room before both men fell silent.

Sydney took advantage of a break in the good old boy conversation. "So how did that cruise go, Dad? The one your retirees' group put together a few months ago to the Caribbean."

A scowl appeared. "Don't remind me. All couples. Most of them married for half a century or more." The dour expression became a cross between sadness and discomfort. "Felt like a fifth wheel the entire time."

"It can't have been that bad. The postcard you sent me said *having a wonderful time*."

His brow smoothed out. "That's only because I couldn't think of anything else to say."

"Maybe it's time you find someone." She spoke softly.

"Maybe." Her father picked up his beer and took a swig then glanced Vince's way. "Say, Vince, did she ever tell you about the time she tried out for the football team in high school?"

"Football? You sure you don't mean one of your sons?" Vince glanced over at Sydney who simply shrugged before they both looked back at her father.

"Nope. Her sophomore year, my girl worked out with the JV team, attended every practice."

Vince shifted his gaze over to Sydney. "You're kidding, right?"

"No, he's not kidding." She was about to add, 'why would you say that?' but clamped her mouth shut instead. Being a chauvinistic throwback was his problem, not hers.

Her father spoke up so she didn't have to. "You might think so. But then, you just met her, right?"

Vince cracked a smile as he glanced Sydney's way. "Must have lost my head for a minute."

"Happens to the best of us." He cleared his throat. "The new coach they hired had been let go from his previous job over some Title Nine brouhaha. Anyway, this guy obviously didn't learn his lesson. He figured he'd be able to humor my little girl. String her along until the actual season started. Then figure out a way to keep her off the team."

"Yeah? How'd that work out for him?"

A spurt of laughter echoed. "Not worth a shit."

Vince shared her dad's amusement with a smile. One that fell slightly as he gazed over at Sydney. "I don't imagine."

"Made her the kicker when he realized he couldn't keep her out of the game." Almost immediately, her dad launched into another reminiscence from before he retired.

Let the male bonding continue.

Sydney seriously wondered if she'd survive the mega doses of testosterone that had suddenly inundated her living room. She was standing before she knew it. Thinking quickly, she headed out to the kitchen. "I guess I'll go see about dinner."

The steaks she had planned to grill for the now scuttled private dinner for two would have to wait for another day. She returned those to the refrigerator and took out a bag of frozen chicken breasts. Baked potatoes and fresh asparagus would round out the meal. It was a good thing she had plenty of both. In no time, she had the chicken and potatoes in the oven and asparagus washed and stemmed. Wearing a frown so deep her head hurt, she closed the oven door, set the timer then leaned back against the counter.

Loyal, trustworthy and with enough caring and character to spare. On the surface, Vince Miller was everything she'd always sought in a man but never found. While at the same time, he represented the epitome of everything she swore up and down she would never allow to become a major part of her life.

Too late.

Refusing to succumb to more tears, she shook her head and straightened. When she returned to the living room, Vince had started in on a colorful this is what happened to me in the field story of his own. The polite thing for her to do was sit quietly and listen. Then she keyed in on Vince's expressions as he talked. Bright and animated, his face was lit up like a child's getting his first glimpse of a Christmas tree with a pile of presents underneath. Or a candy filled basket on Easter morning.

"There was no way we could just leave them there like that." He went on to describe an incident from back when he was a rookie. "The mother duck seemed to know we were there to help her babies not hurt them, so she didn't attack me when I started picking them up."

Sydney gave in to an actual smile as Vince recounted lifting out six little ducklings that were trapped behind the grate of storm drain.

"We took a little flak from some civilians because

we tied up traffic for so long. It was rush hour at the time."

Mouth grim, her father nodded. "You seem to always run into those who could care less."

"Didn't take long for me to find that out." Vince took a drink of his beer. "But no way was I going to let those helpless little creatures die."

"I hear you." His companion took a pull from his longneck as well.

Sydney swallowed a minor clog that suddenly formed at the back of her throat. "No. You couldn't do that."

Vince glanced over at her, and a smile lit up his features. "It felt pretty darned good to save them."

"I'll bet it did."

Her dad sat back. The look on his weathered face was one she'd seen many times when he talked with one of his sons. "Your father was on the force, too, you said before."

"He was for a brief time." Vince cleared his throat as his voice took on a low and even tone. "He never got the chance to serve as long as he would have wanted."

"Why's that?" Her dad's penetrating cop gaze trained in on Vince's face. "What happened? I get the feeling something not necessarily good."

Silence was the immediate answer. "You're pretty perceptive. My dad was gunned down his first time out alone."

Oh, Vince. I'm so sorry. Sydney's throat closed up so tight, the words never got beyond the thought. Hands rested in her lap and clasped together, she sat quietly to listen.

"He was hired right out of college by the

department where his father had worked." With his hands held together loosely in front of him, he produced an uneasy smile. "Right out of college is a little misleading. He was pushing forty when he earned his criminal justice degree. He and my mother had been married for almost twenty years. I was twelve."

Her dad nodded. "However long it took, sounds like he fulfilled his dream."

"That's what his father told him." A grin broke out, though sadness remained in his eyes. "Finally, he was going to work at what he loved."

"It is definitely a love." Emotion clouded her father's otherwise steady voice.

Sydney said nothing, her focus centered on Vince.

"Before he'd left for twelve weeks at the academy, we had a talk. He explained, though my mother was certainly capable of caring for both of us while he was gone, I needed to take care of her too."

"Your dad sounds like a man after my own heart."

Sydney didn't need to look over to know her dad was looking at her.

"Scared the hell out of me when the *what if* became real and I was actually faced with the prospect." Vince flattened his palms on his knees. "I didn't need to take care of her for long. She remarried a couple of years after my dad died. A lawyer who ended up being a state Supreme Court judge. They had three girls and a boy together. None of my siblings are even remotely interested in a career in law enforcement."

Why couldn't he have a twin brother who felt that way?

"How exactly did your dad die, son?"

Vince glanced away before he continued. "His first

call was to a domestic disturbance."

"Most dangerous." Her father shifted in his chair.

"You got that right." Vince looked up then nodded before he glanced back down. "Turned out he didn't realize that at the time. He, ah, seemed to believe once he had the badge in place on his chest he became invincible."

"It happens."

"At any rate." Straightening in his chair, Vince cleared his throat. "He never lived to file a report."

"Son of a bitch." The words emerged soft and low from her father's lips.

Unable to do much else, Sydney lowered her head in a moment of silent tribute.

"That had to be tough." Her dad brought a hand up to swipe across his mouth. "Even after a couple of decades, an officer killed in the line of duty is still mourned. What did your mother think when you went into the family business?"

"To her credit, she didn't try to talk me out of it."

"Probably knew it wouldn't do her any good."

Vince glanced up at him then over at Sydney. "Probably." Though the corners of his lips drew upward in a shallow smile, the lines of pain edging his eyes remained in place.

She sat forward to rub her fingers along Vince's forearm. "I'm so sorry for your loss."

His hand came over hers. "Thanks. It happened a long time ago."

"Doesn't mean it still doesn't hurt."

The doorbell rang, and her dad's beer bottle clanked on the table. "You kids sit tight. I'll get it." As Sydney continued to hold on to Vince, the chair creaked. Footsteps followed. The door opened. "Well, hello there."

She looked up to find Ida in the entrance and her dad smiling down as if he'd just won the lottery. With a quick glance at Vince, she let him go then stood to walk toward them. "Ida, how are you?"

"Just fine, dear, and you?" It took a moment before she pulled her gaze away from Sydney's dad.

"Good, Ida. Good. What do you need?"

"Neighbors don't necessarily need to have a reason to visit." Her dad cast an absolutely beaming smile down on their guest. One that virtually disappeared when his regard moved over to land on his daughter. "Do they?"

Sydney worked to find her voice. "No of course not." The necessary introductions followed.

"Actually, I do have a reason for dropping by." Ida rested a sparkling gaze on her father that dimmed slightly as she turned toward Sydney. "But I'll be brief. I wondered if you had the GPS thingy you mentioned I could borrow."

"Oh, sure. They're both here in my purse." She picked up her bag from the corner by the door. "I'll get it for you."

Ida eyed her dad up and down with a devilish smile. "Your daughter has mentioned you're a police officer. That must be thrilling."

"Well." Neck to forehead, his skin turned bright red. "At times."

"Why do I get the feeling you're just being modest?"

"Shall we have a seat?" With his smile so large, Sydney was afraid her dad's face would crack wide open. His hand came to rest on the small of Ida's back as he led her into the living room.

"Thank you." Sparse eyelashes fluttered over unusually bright eyes. "Your daughter may have told you about my cat Orson."

He blinked and shot Sydney a deer in the headlights stare as she handed over the small GPS device. Suddenly, she actually felt remiss she hadn't thought to fill him in on such an important issue.

The former commander recovered quickly. "You've owned him how long again?"

Sydney refrained from rolling her eyes. *Talk about fishing for information.*

"Four years, and he's a wanderer, as all males can be."

"That can be a problem."

"Tell me about it."

When he sat on the couch, she sat too. Then settled in close. Her father didn't seem to notice the invasion of his personal space. Nor did he move away from her.

"Anything I can help with?"

Ida reached into her pants pocket then dangled Orson's collar from two fingers. "Could you help me figure out how to put this on here?"

"Of course."

After a few false attempts, he had the small metal object attached to the cat's collar. "There you go."

"Oh, why thank you." She placed a hand on his arm as she gave him a starry-eyed stare. "You are so very, very good at that. And smart."

"He is that." Sydney was starting to go bonkers holding in another eye roll.

"Well, I won't bother you any more than I already

have. From the delicious aroma coming from the kitchen, you have dinner in the oven." Ida's gaze remained fixed on Sydney's dad as she rose.

"Would you like to join us? We have plenty to share, I'm sure."

"We certainly do." Sydney could only smile in agreement after her father issued the invitation. She certainly wanted her dad's happiness more than anything else. She truly did. But Ida? The woman had the morals of Orson. With sincere apologies to the cat.

"That's very nice of you." She quickly resumed her seat. "Maybe I will."

"Vince is a police officer too, Ida." Sydney spoke the first thing to come to mind then added a sarcastic jibe. "Who freelance writes on the side."

Ida's eyes widened and she smiled. "How very jack of all tradesy for you."

"I like to think I'm well-rounded." Vince dead-panned the response.

"You have another profession to fall back on. Good for you."

"In case this police officer gig of mine doesn't work out." He didn't look at anyone in particular as he mumbled the comment under his breath.

That didn't keep Sydney from hearing him. Did that mean if she asked him to, he'd give up a career he was devoted to? As much as she might want to, she knew quitting police work was something she could never, would never ask him to do.

Even if it meant, as a couple, they would never work.

"How long have you been a police officer, Vince?"

Sydney didn't bother to listen to Vince's response

to Ida's question. She simply watched his face light up as he answered.

It was nobody's fault she'd finally met a fabulous guy who provided definite possibilities of a bright and happy future…who turned out to be a cop.

Chapter Seventeen

Vince rolled up the sleeves on his denim shirt and sat forward at his desk. With his forearms resting on its top, he balled both hands into fists. Like it or not, this was shaping up to be one hell of a long day. Same as usual when the details of an unsolved case stuck in his craw.

Don't focus on what you don't know, concentrate on what you do.

Nighttime shadows of dusk had replaced any sunshine coming in through the police station windows. Incandescent lighting now shone down on the marred green walls. Even the day shift janitors had completed whatever cleanup they were assigned and left the premises.

Flexing his fingers, then wiggling the circulation back into them, he opened the file folder containing a variety of photos from the crash site he laid out in front of him. All his attempts to find out who owned the vehicle Brock Richardson died in had met with dead ends. The only thing he'd been able to determine for sure was the car was rented to a company, All Workings Incorporated, that existed solely on paper. Whose board of directors appeared to be figments of someone's imagination.

The only thing left to do was send the MO out to surrounding departments in Michigan and beyond with the hope someone, somewhere would contact him with information about a similar crime in their jurisdiction.

"Hey, Detective. I didn't know anyone from the day shift was still in here working."

Vince glanced up at the uniformed officer who stood in the doorway. "Just me, I guess."

Aside from the watch commander, this kid was one of two rookies who'd come on to cover dispatch on the night shift. They had been introduced, though just now, Vince didn't recall his name.

"What are you working on?"

Vince tapped the pictures. "Going over evidence on a case that has me bugged. A crash and burn in a rural area of M-53."

Coming forward, the rookie craned his neck for a better view of the upside-down photos. "What happened?"

A name plate on his shirt read A. Matthews. That was the name that eluded him. Matthews. Vince had solved that case easily enough. Now to tackle this other.

"A single car down a small embankment of a rarely traveled country road bursts into flames with the driver still inside. Plus, the vehicle was rented to a company that doesn't exist except on paper."

"What do the accident reconstruction people say?" The rookie picked up a side-view snapshot of the burned-out vehicle. Body removed.

"Nothing yet." Although he had requested the report STAT and been really, really nice when he did. "Hopefully, I'll hear soon."

"Must have been quite the explosion on impact."

Vince continued to study the prints. "That's just it. There's no evidence of any impact. No probable obstacles on scene."

Matthews set down the coffee cup he held. "Can it happen like that?"

"Appears it did."

"Puzzler."

Although Vince had never heard that exact term in the course of an active investigation, he nodded ready agreement. "It is that."

"Best of luck getting it solved."

"Yeah. Thanks." He glanced up again as the uniform retrieved his cup then backed out of the doorway and disappeared down the hallway.

I'm going to need it.

He massaged tense fingers across his forehead. What did he have so far? Brock Richardson, whom everyone thought had skipped the country, with his mistress in tow, was driving around the area, got lost or disoriented and ran his car off the road where it immediately burst into flames.

None of which made any damned sense. *Don't focus on what you don't know, concentrate on what you do.*

Slapping the file folder closed, he gave it a sideways shove to skitter across his desk with a flap and flutter. When it finally came to a stop beside a pile of many more just like it, he leaned back in his chair and clasped both hands behind his head. *What the hell am I missing?*

With his eyes closed to concentrate on pictures of the accident scene, images of Sydney floated up to take over instead. Brown eyes filled with caring and acceptance, mouth curved up in a definite smile of welcome. Without warning, the vision blurred then shifted. The smile fell as her eyes filled with contempt. Shock and anger contorted her features. All traces of her once loving acceptance vanished.

“The case be damned.” Opening his eyes, he whispered into his empty office.

What he was *missing* was her. What really bothered him was clear too. They had yet to resolve anything since he’d confessed who he really was.

Matthews was right. All his other colleagues were long gone. *Time for me to be long gone, too.*

He retrieved the file folder he shoved into what he termed his lock box, the bottom drawer of his desk, then grabbed his keys and cell phone.

After her father arrived, he hadn’t been able to get a clear read of her emotions. Hell, he probably wouldn’t get it right if she held his head in her hands and drew him a map. The resulting foursome ate dinner, with the older couple doing most of the talking. Which seemed to work since he and Sydney didn’t have a lot to say to each other.

Check that.

In his heart, Vince was convinced they had plenty more to say to each other. Problem was, his head didn’t have the slightest idea where to start. Not that he hadn’t tried. He’d called her once the next day. Monday. She was busy, or so she said, and promised to call him back. She never did. Then he got involved with as much as he could handle at the precinct and the rest of the week went by without contact.

Pushing upright, he was halfway to the door when his desk phone went off. He turned to retrace his steps. Could be the AI report. Mouth drawn into a grimace, he shook his head. Four o’clock on a Friday. *Talk about too much to ask.*

He hefted the receiver to his ear. “Detective Miller.”

“Hey, Vince. It’s Cindy from the coroner’s office.”

“You finished the report?” Reaching in the drawer, he retrieved the file folder he slapped down in front of him again as he sat.

A soft chuckle entered his ear. “Hardly. You know how slow those old procedural wheels turn. I sent the camera guy down to the holding area to take more pictures of the car. Plus, the official lab results won’t be available until next week. If you’re lucky.”

His hand remained motionless on top of the file folder he had yet to open. “You just called to frustrate me then?”

Out and out laughter sang over the line. “No. Although it’s tempting. You’re such an easy target.”

Tell me about it. Leaning forward, he rested his forehead between his thumb and forefinger. “So, you called because?”

“Because I know how concerned you were about the victim.”

“Hell of a way to die. Burned alive.”

“Which is probably how one would expect it had happened.” All traces of mirth in her voice had vanished.

Vince clamped his teeth together. “Damn.”

“Although the victim’s body was loaded with alcohol.”

“You think he was driving drunk, really drunk, went into the ditch, and the car ignited?”

“And our victim was too inebriated to climb out to save himself? Not a chance.”

Vince couldn't do anything more than shake his head.

"I take your silence to mean you're a little upset trying to take this all in. If it's any consolation, the flames probably didn't kill him."

"But I thought you said…"

"With all the windows rolled up, the smoke would have contained a huge concentration of carbon monoxide. The victim would be rendered unconscious and ultimately expire from suffocation within minutes."

"That's something." Whether this Brock character deserved it or not, it was good to hear he hadn't died as grisly a death as he'd feared.

"I know how basically sensitive you are, so I thought you'd like to know your victim didn't suffer, much."

He raised his gaze to the ceiling and leaned back. "I appreciate that."

"But if you share the information I just gave you with anyone before the official report comes out, I'll deny I even know who you are."

"Fair enough. Thanks for calling. I appreciate it."

"You're welcome." A measure of lightness had returned to her tone. "Not even I could make you agonize over the weekend."

"By the way. Thank whoever leaked the victim's identity to the press before telling us."

"If we knew who did that, they'd be long gone by now. I'm taking a chance calling you as it is."

"Don't think I don't appreciate it." He couldn't resist. "One more thing, though. Any idea how the fire started?"

"Not my job to figure out that part. I will tell you

we found adhesive residue on the victim's wrists. Matches traces of what we found on the steering wheel. Probably duct tape."

"Jesus." Vince went back to breathing deep. "I thought you said he was drunk."

"Probably to the point of being incapacitated."

"Someone didn't want to leave his demise to chance."

"You got it."

That metal fragment was part of a lighter. "So, while the papers are reporting a freak accident…"

"You have a murder investigation on your hands." She was quiet for a moment as if to let that sink in. "Just for kicks. Any suspects?"

"Only about three or four hundred employees who were left high and dry when all the On Trend clothing stores closed. And that's just from the list of local workers he screwed over. Nationwide, probably thousands."

"Lucky you."

"I think of these tough ones as job security." He couldn't even conjure up a smile at the irony of the joke he tried for.

"Although we both know, even if all crime stopped tomorrow, you're not going anywhere."

She may not know as much as she thinks she does.

"Nowhere else *to* go." Even as he said it, visions of Sydney reappeared in his mind to mock him. Shortly after they finished dinner that night, Sydney spent her time showing Ida how to go on line and configure the gps gadget. Next thing he knew, it was late. While her father was on his way to Sydney's guest room, Vince was headed for the front door. Not the scenario he'd envisioned when he was first invited over.

"As I said. I thought you'd want to know."

His inner reflections vanished. "Again, Cindy. Thanks."

"You bet."

He disconnected, then stood and tossed his keys up he caught with one hand as he headed toward the door. Thanks to Cindy, the weight on his shoulders he'd expected to carry around, at least for the weekend, had been lifted. *Some of it anyway.*

Outside, he'd just started his car when his cell went off. He hit the blue tooth switch on his steering wheel. "Miller."

"Vince, it's Sydney." At the sound of her voice, he immediately sat straighter. "I'm sorry I didn't call you back the other day."

"That's okay."

"I'm not going to kid you. I didn't know what to say." She spoke softly.

That makes two of us. "Are you up for company?" His voice held just the slightest hint of desperation and he could have cared less.

"Sure." Her answer was quick and direct. "It will give us a chance to…"

"…pick up our discussion where we left off?"

"I hope so. I'll see you when you get here."

"Yeah. See you."

The silver jeep practically drove itself to the Winsome Gate complex. As preoccupied as Vince was with how to continue to plead his case, he didn't remember driving there. Pulling into her driveway, he cut the engine, put the car in park, and sat back. Nervously drumming his fingers on the steering wheel, he could only think of one thing he needed to tell her. *I never expected to fall in love with you.*

He stared out the windshield. For how long, he had no idea when, with its wings fluttering madly, a butterfly dipped and soared in front of him on an early evening breeze. Light and delicate, its fragile wings propelled it with exceptional strength. Suddenly filled with resolve, he jerked open the car door and got out, powered his way up her back porch steps.

Sydney opened the door as if she'd been awaiting his arrival. "It didn't take you long to get here." With her hand resting on the frame, she stared back at him.

Everything in him wanted to haul her into his arms. To touch her, taste her. Pull her close. Instead, he stayed where he was and kept his hands to himself. "I came from work."

"I've missed you." She lowered her gaze before he could read any kind of message in her eyes.

If there even was one. "I've missed you too."

No judgement, no questions. Only total agreement.

"I appreciate you coming over." She took hold of his hand the second he crossed the threshold. Though nowhere close to the physical contact he'd envisioned on his way over, he'd take it.

"There's no way you could have kept me away." He allowed her to lead him through the kitchen to the living room and over to the couch.

The second they sat down, he rested his arm along its back. Anything to remain near to her. Merely to look for now. Not touch.

"You've given me a lot to process. I've been doing some rather heavy-duty thinking. About us."

At her serious tone, he nearly stopped moving,

afraid to even consider what she'd reveal next. Maybe a well thought out laundry list of reasons why they couldn't be together.

"I'm still the same person. Inside." He caught her gaze.

Brown eyes highlighted with golden specks stared back at him. Black as night, her pupils enlarged as he drew near. "I know."

"Then you also know I'm the same person you met and…became involved with." He'd stopped himself before the words *fell in love with* spilled out. Maybe she wasn't ready for that declaration.

She blinked but didn't look away. "Involved with is putting it mildly."

"Even so, I'm not going to rush you."

"That's just it, Vince. You already have. We have." Her gaze flicked away from his for only an instant before returning full force. "I guess I should have called you back right away."

"It crossed my mind you never planned to."

"I told you I wasn't that heartless. It's just…"

"What will it take…what do I have to do to make this right?" When he slid closer and she didn't back away, he took it as a meager victory.

"There's really nothing you can do, Vince. Nothing you do will change anything…make things become different."

"True." That his voice came out in a whisper didn't surprise him. Defeat never had been easy for him to accept.

"Not calling you right away wasn't intentional on my part." Her hand came to rest on his arm.

He was quick to cover its top with his palm and

hang on. "Then why didn't you?"

"Not only did I not know what to say." She let out a tiny laugh. "My dad didn't leave until Wednesday morning, although he spent as much time at Ida's as he did here."

"He left you alone?"

She nodded. "They went out to lunch and a movie Monday afternoon. She kept him entertained while I worked."

"Really." A silent string of expletives ran through his mind. Expletives not directed at her father, Sydney or even Ida. But at himself for a missed opportunity nearly a week ago to pick up where they'd left off.

She glanced down and ran her hand over the couch cushion. "What is it you want out of life, Vince?"

"You." Though her question may have surprised him, he answered without hesitation.

"Not about me. For you."

"Me?"

"Yeah." She lifted her head to focus a steady gaze on his face. "You."

To go on as I have been. Take care of citizens during the day. Come home to you at night. Tentative answers formed he knew she wouldn't want to hear.

"Do you even know?"

"Sure." A hurried response, but all he could come up with.

"Are you?" She was quick to call him on the out and out lie. "Sure?"

A definitive answer snapped into place. "To be with you for the rest of my life."

"Is that a proposal?"

"Do you want it to be?"

Dropping her gaze from his, she shook her head on a soft smile. "If it were, and I'm not saying it is. We could never have children."

Without even thinking about it, he scooted away from her. "Wow. You have all sorts of unreasonable caveats for us."

She glanced directly at him, and the hurt in her eyes stabbed him straight in the heart.

"The fact you use the term unreasonable speaks volumes, you know."

Her gaze dropped again, but not before he caught sight of the glisten of tears. More pain impaled his already tattered heart, and he slid swiftly over to gather her in his arms. That she came willingly provided a hint of encouragement. Even when she stiffened as he nestled her close, he refused to give in to her.

Or give up on them.

"Believe it or not, work really did intervene in my not calling you back."

Her voice brought him out of his reverie. "I believe you."

"Randall had a project that…" She sat up straight and stiff, scrunched her face and raised her voice. "…simply could not wait another moment."

"Your Curan impression needs a little work."

"Then Nancy had her own set of demands." She flattened her lips and extended her hand in a waving motion. "Don't get me started on her."

"A lot to deal with, I'd say." Before he was totally aware of it, he had his hand on her shoulder working his fingers to knead away some of her stress. "I imagine it's tough having to please two bosses."

"If only it were that easy." As his impromptu

massage moved to the back of her neck, she lowered her head and let out a true sigh of contentment. "It's frustrating trying to cover all the bases with those two."

He brought his other hand up as he continued the soothing touches to her neck and shoulders. "I can certainly relate." Horrific images of the accident resurfaced, and he steeled himself against their effect. "Although some of those I work with aren't exactly talking back."

"In what way?" The rigid set of her shoulders eased.

Why wreck her relaxation with his issues? "Just thinking about a case I was assigned."

Straightening, she turned, and he had no choice but to let his hands fall away. "One that bothers you. A lot. That tremor in your voice gives you away. Care to share? Maybe free up some of the tension that has you in its grip?" Concern melted to empathy as she settled her palm against his cheek. "Take some of the protect and serve weight off your shoulders?"

"It's really not…"

She slid her thumb over his lips to silence him. "Were you about to say, 'It's not really that bad?' Because I know better."

"I thought I came here so we could talk about us."

"Until I got the feeling you need to talk about you."

The urge was strong to do as she asked. Share. More like spill his guts about the whole, horrible crime scene. Somehow though, he couldn't. The need to protect her from the ugliness he dealt with daily was even stronger.

"Tell me, Vince. Give yourself permission."

Her whispered instructions finally penetrated the

barrier he kept around himself to shield the ones he loved from the horror of his job.

He took hold of both her hands in his and again held on. "That accident case I'm working on. The one you got a glimpse of the other day is the one involving your former boss."

"Oh my God. Not that. How awful for you."

He wrapped an arm around her to hold her against him. "By all indications, the vehicle crashed then burned."

"That's what the news report said."

"That's just it. Cars don't work that way. Fiery explosions happen to planes streaking in out of control high speed when they make contact with the ground or some other unyielding object." He sat straighter as memories of a motor vehicle burn school he'd attended came to mind. "Contrary to widespread belief, it's extremely difficult to ignite a vehicle. They simply do not go up in an explosion of flames like you see on television and in the movies. They're designed not to."

Sydney sat quietly with her mouth closed to simply listen.

"The accident I'm investigating was no accident. That fire had to be intentionally set. It's the only thing that makes sense."

"I must say, that's the first time that's ever happened to me before."

Those words made him look directly at her. "First time for what?"

"First time information about a case was shared with me. My dad and brothers would talk about their work when they were convinced, at times wrongly, I wasn't within earshot."

"Of course, I wouldn't trouble you with some of the less palatable details."

"Of course." Sarcasm laced her tone. "Don't pull me too deeply into your confidence."

Something flashed in resolute eyes, and he could have kicked himself for the comment.

"That's not how I meant it. I just…" He finished off with a shrug. She was basically right, so why argue? "His wrists were secured to the steering wheel with duct tape."

As he expected, she cringed in horror and closed her eyes. "Poor Brock."

"From what I understand from the lab, he didn't suffer." Without using her name, he shared the gist of what Cindy had provided.

"That's something." Her gaze remained level as she crossed her arms. "As awful as it was to hear some of those details, it's nice to have you take me into your confidence."

"I have to say, I appreciate the support."

"I also understand how work is on your mind no matter what. You rarely take a break from it. My dad and brothers couldn't either."

"Who says I can't?"

She pursed her lips and stared. "Can you?"

"I'll prove it." A flash of inspiration struck, and he leaned forward to pull her arms apart and down, then clasped her hands between them. "As the schedule would have it, I'm off most of this up-coming weekend, plus I'll take a personal day. I own a cabin a few hours north. Leaves are changing this time of year. The fall colors should be awesome. Would you like to go there with me? Spend some time alone? Provided you can get off work as well."

She tossed her head but didn't pull away. "Is that a challenge?"

"No. It's an invitation." He squeezed her hands with a gentle pressure. "A sincere invitation."

"Randall has promised me some comp time for all the twenty-four sevens I pulled on that out of town trip."

"Perfect. Call them in for a long weekend. We'll get away together, you and me. We won't deal with jobs or family legacies. No collective baggage to plow through. Just us. You and me. Two people who, I believe, have something special going on." He hurried to continue before she had a chance to ask him to define 'something special.' "The cabin is by Grayling in a quiet wooded area on Lake Papoose. I haven't had a chance to use it in a while. It's hardly a mansion, but we can still be alone."

Her gaze didn't waver the entire time he'd regaled her with the carefree joys of the backwoods getaway.

"You really think we have something special, Vince?"

"Absolutely. Don't you?"

She stared at him a moment before she opened her mouth.

Darned if he didn't find himself holding his breath.

"That sounds nice. I'd like that."

"That's great." Relief flooded into him and for the first time in a long time he flashed a grin. "Truly great."

As he stared into soft brown eyes, another thought came to mind.

Maybe things aren't so hopeless after all.

Chapter Eighteen

"It's not much, but it's paid for, and it's mine."

Vince ushered Sydney through the heavily lacquered knotty pine door and into the front room of his home away from home, as he called it. A true log cabin built in the 1950s on an inland lake in northern Michigan.

"It's beautiful. Cozy. With all the comforts of home." She scanned the interior.

A huge stone fireplace stood in front of them with its open hearth and wrought iron grate. Two plush and inviting recliners were situated on either side with an overstuffed leather couch directly across. Knotty pine walls reflected a bright, rustic sheen. The kitchen to their left contained an old gas range in avocado green, matching refrigerator, and white ceramic double sink. A butcher block table with four sturdy chairs around it sat between the two main rooms.

"It's nice to have for those rare times I can get up here." He walked by her to set the bags of groceries they'd purchased on their way through town on the table. Hands on his hips, he turned to survey the premises. "I paid the son of my nearest neighbor to come over and clean things up a bit. He did a decent job."

She set down their other purchase, two warm and aromatic bags of Chinese takeout. "It doesn't look like we have to do much of anything but unpack our suitcases and settle in."

"I'll go get them." He spoke over his shoulder as he headed out the door.

"I'll put our groceries away."

Making short work of that task, Sydney soon continued her inspection. Two doors spaced a few feet apart were off one side of the room. No doubt a bedroom and bath. Over in a far corner, four fishing rods with reels were mounted on wall hooks, and a worn covered wicker basket sat on a small three-legged stool on the floor. A black and white picture in a large wooden frame hung in the center of the display. She walked over for a better look and caught her breath. He was young, to be sure. Maybe ten years old or so, but Vince was definitely one of the three people in the picture. Those alert deep-set eyes of his were a dead giveaway. The other two occupants with him were older men, both with the same striking gaze. Probably father and son. Vince's father and grandfather?

"That's my Grandpa Miller. He built this place."

She glanced around as he walked over to set their luggage by one of those side doors then came to stand beside her. Already he carried a fresh, outdoorsy aroma.

Breathing deep, she let the comfort of his scent surround her. "That's what I thought."

"The other man is my dad." He paused to take a breath. "My biological dad. It's one of the last decent pictures I have of him except for his official department portrait. This one captures his spirit more." His voice faltered, and he cleared his throat. "That's me with the toothless grin."

"Holding up that fish as if it were a trophy whale."

"It was to me. The biggest fish I ever caught up here."

She stepped forward to study the well-preserved glossy photograph. "How'd you happen to have no front teeth? You look to be older than, what is it, five or six when those baby teeth first fall out?"

"Those weren't baby teeth I lost that year." He tapped his two straight, white incisors. "These are crowns. Had to have about three sets of them put in as I grew."

At the idea a youngster had to endure such procedures, her stomach lurched. "How'd you lose your original teeth?"

His eyes lit with something akin to mischief, and a smile emerged. "Got into a street fight and lost."

"With who? I mean whom?"

"Someone a lot bigger than I was at the time."

"How'd that happen?" She gazed from the picture to him then back again.

"Some new neighbors had just moved in next door to us. I was walking home from school one day when there was this commotion in their driveway. The lady was under attack by some guy. He turned out to be her husband, but I didn't know it at the time. She was on her knees cowering with both arms up for protection. He had this mean look on his face and stood over her with his fist primed to come down."

Her eyes grew wide. "What did you do?"

"Dropped my books then bounded over to push him away from her."

Why am I not surprised? She studied the face of the boy in the picture, smiling as if he didn't have a care in the world. More like he'd just conquered the world and was enjoying its spoils.

"Did you get hurt?" Twisting around, she looked up at him.

"A little. It turned out the guy was a true street fighter and fairly adaptable. Needless to say, the fist he had cocked and ready to strike landed on my face instead of hers when I jumped between them. He knocked my teeth out with his first punch."

A sparkle remained in his eyes as if, in his mind, that was exactly how it was supposed to happen.

She put her hand on his arm. "How old *were* you?"

"Ten or thereabouts." He stared straight ahead. "As I recall, my mother had seen me walking toward our house. When I didn't make it inside right away, she came out to see where I went. Or maybe she heard all the yelling. I don't remember much about that part. Being out cold and all."

"You were knocked unconscious?" She couldn't keep the disbelief from her voice.

He flashed a brief smile. Apparently, those memories weren't all that distasteful to him. "I guess there was blood everywhere. In addition to taking out my teeth, he broke my nose. Some other neighbors, one of them a big guy who worked on cars for a living, came out and managed to subdue the man until the police arrived. My parents pressed charges on my behalf. I was in the hospital for about a week. They couldn't restore my teeth until everything else around my face healed inside and out. I've since seen some pictures the investigating officer took at the time. With two black eyes and a ballooned out lip, I looked pretty messed up."

She said nothing, just shuddered at the thought of

an injured child in pain. Suffering because he cared enough to come to a stranger's rescue.

"I was toothless like that for about six months." He lifted his hand to rub along her shoulder. "The incident happened in June. I had to spend an entire summer and the first few months of the school year looking like I did."

"It must have been hard for you." Turning into him, she wrapped an arm around his waist. "Sounds like a lot for a ten-year-old to have to go through."

His initial response was a shrug. "Not really. We lived in a relatively small town at the time. Word of my heroics, as the mayor called it, spread rather quickly. Most of my friends knew what I'd done and why I did it."

"You were a hero." *Even then.*

"I considered the temporary disfigurement a badge of honor. My grandpa was beyond proud. My dad, too." His brow furrowed, and he lowered his voice. "For obvious reasons, they couldn't make a big deal about it in front of my mom. She was horrified I'd gotten hurt."

"Understandable."

"That was my first taste of how it felt to serve and protect. You could say I got the bug at an early age."

"Most of them do." She rested her head against his chest as his arms circled her from behind. *And there's nothing anyone can do about it.* "Maybe you became such a dedicated cop because you feel you have to fulfill a legacy your father couldn't."

"Maybe." Vince didn't take his eyes off the picture. "Grandpa is still alive. He and his second wife, Norma, live in Florida. They did the snow bird thing for a while, then packed up and moved permanently. He's in his eighties and still going strong. Still dabbles in police work. Provides advice to a special unit of the Pascoe County Sheriff's Department about evidence in cold cases."

"And you're obviously a chip off the old block. Rather blocks."

When he didn't respond immediately, she pulled away to look back at him. His mouth was drawn down at the corners. Something, a kind of concern she couldn't read, colored his eyes. "I'm sorry, Sydney."

The true remorse in his tone tugged at her heart. "For what?"

"Already, I've broken my promise to you. Hardly in the door, and already we're talking about what I do."

"Not exactly. We're talking about who you are." She couldn't keep the resignation from her voice.

After another shrug, he said nothing, simply held her. Vince Miller was a hero at an age when most kids were still hopelessly involved with video games and baseball. He'd grown into an honest, upstanding citizen. Strong, handsome, caring and kind. Who wouldn't be thrilled to call him friend? Or more? By all things sane, she'd be a fool to let him go. *But do I have the resilience necessary to be with him?*

"Are you hungry?" As if reading her mind and not wanting to 'go there,' he let his arms drop away from her, and headed over to the table. "After we skipped lunch, I know I am."

"Me too." She followed and sat down in a chair opposite the one he'd taken. "That food definitely smelled good all the way out here in the car."

"Whetted my appetite."

As he took the cartons out of the bags, she opened

their tops to release the inviting aroma of garlic chicken and fried rice. Her mouth watered.

Vince handed her a plastic knife and fork then took a similar set out of the bag for himself. "I don't have the patience for chop sticks."

"Me either."

"We need something to drink." Jumping up, he took a couple of plastic glasses out of the cupboard he filled from the faucet. "Best water in the state around here. A spring fed well."

She nodded her thanks as he set one in front of her. The paper plates supplied by the restaurant were soon filled with the savory rice and chicken dish, a crispy egg roll and three wontons each.

"Oh good. Fortune cookies." He brought the plastic wrapped cookies out then set the empty bag to one side. "We can have those later."

"I'll bet your mother was proud of you." She cut into her egg roll then put a forkful of cooked cabbage, spices, and shrimp into her mouth.

He glanced up, and his brow momentarily creased. "Once she got over the shock of it, she said she was. I mainly remember the worried look she carried once I came to and the whole time I was in the hospital. She kept shaking her head, asking me why I did it, but stopped short of saying I could have been killed." He scooped a large bite of chicken into his mouth, chewed then swallowed. "I overheard her whispering that to my dad a few days after I got home. When they thought I was asleep."

"My dad and brothers did that sometimes. Talked about my general well-being when they didn't know I was awake and aware." She gave him a small smile. It wasn't her intention to change the subject. She wanted to learn more about him. "But none of it stopped you from becoming a cop."

"Nope. It didn't stop me at all." He set down his fork and folded his arms on the table. "That is one of many great things about my mother, though. Once she realized how badly I wanted it, she accepted me for who I was. She didn't expect me to change to become something I didn't want to be."

She cut into her eggroll then stabbed another bite she held in front of her. "She sounds like a strong woman." *If only I could be that strong.*

He brought a forkful of rice to his mouth. "She's pretty neat. I think you'll like her."

"I'm sure I would…will." She blinked as she realized, if she and Vince did happen to stay together, she'd be meeting his family as he'd met her dad.

"For a while, and for her sake, I tried not to go into law enforcement. Worked retail for about a year." He winced slightly then shook his head. "Could not stand being confined to four walls all day. She came to understand that."

With her mouth full of rice, she nodded.

"She set a good example of what a parent should be. One I'm determined to follow. If I'm ever fortunate enough to have kids of my own." He paused to dig into his food, then held a forkful aloft. "So, what shall we do after dinner?"

She shrugged. "I don't know. You're the native. What do you suggest?"

He swallowed before he spoke. "How do you feel about walks on the beach?"

"I love them."

He set his fork down to take hold of her hand. "After all, our plan was to come up here to view the fall colors." Twining their fingers, he squeezed then brought her palm to his lips.

As the warmth of his kiss filled its center, heat spread up her arm to make a direct hit on her heart. "We did, didn't we?" A breathless quality came out in her tone. Retrieving her hand, she smiled at him. "Let's finish eating so we can get to that walk."

"Let's. We sure did get some nice weather for this week end."

"Warmer than usual temperatures and sunny skies." Sydney took care to steer their conversation to more small talk as they consumed the rest of their meal. She'd surveyed the lake as they drove in. Relatively large, its shores certainly weren't over populated. Unlike other lakes she'd visited where the cabins and other structures were as close together as tract housing in a suburban cul de sac. Another plus of their surroundings was the thick cover of trees that encircled them on three sides.

Putting down her fork, she wiped her mouth on a napkin. "Is there a public beach on this lake?"

He shook his head. "Other than a small one with no boat launch, there's not a lot of public anything on this lake. That's part of its charm. Grandpa knew a good thing when he saw it and bought up as much property as he could. I own about four acres on either side and behind this cabin."

"You don't have neighbors then?"

"A few here and there, but that's it. I'll show you around when we're done here."

Working together after they finished their meal,

they gathered up the debris from their take out to toss in the trash. At Vince's direction, she found some disposable wipes under the sink and cleaned off the table then tossed those away as well.

"We almost forgot our fortune cookies." Vince put the trash can back under the sink, then handed Sydney one of the cellophane wrapped treats.

Neither spoke as, papers rustling, they tore the sealed packages open.

Sydney broke her cookie apart and placed a sweet, crunchy piece in her mouth. "You first."

"Okay." Vince pulled out the tiny slip of paper concealed in his. "Take heart, your destiny awaits you." He glanced over at her with a smile. "Your turn."

Fumbling for a moment, she looked down at hers. "It takes courage to travel a different path."

His face was unreadable when she caught his gaze. "Sounds a little prophetic if you asked me."

Right now, she wasn't up to discussing what her fortune might mean. "I should use the bathroom before we set out."

"The left-hand door." He swept an arm out in that direction.

"Be right back." Sydney was pleasantly surprised by the bathroom, most certainly added after the fact. A full tub was in place along the back wall, with a toilet and sink, across from it. The blue and gray tiled tub brought to mind images of a time she and Vince had shared a shower at her townhouse and her cheeks heated. Along with certain other areas.

Which has no real relevance right now. A casual romp for sexual satisfaction wasn't what they were here for. Serious soul searching about their relationship was.

With a small sigh and renewed determination, she shut off the frivolous memories and got down to business. A few minutes later, she dried clean hands on a navy blue towel. After one final check in the mirror and a few finger motions to fluff out her bangs, she opened the door.

Vince stood from the couch. "Ready?"

She nodded. *As I'll ever be.*

"There's supposed to be a full moon out later tonight, but I'm taking a flashlight just in case we need it on our way home." He indicated the backpack he held in one hand.

"What else is in there?"

"Nothing much. A few other things we might be able to use."

"Are you always in ready for anything mode? I bet you were one hell of a Boy Scout." Sarcasm sometimes served her well when she was nervous. "Raised that old be prepared bar for the rest of them."

"I did what I could." He slung the backpack over one shoulder, shut the door behind them, then took her hand as they descended the porch stairs and walked toward a gravel covered trail.

Their path took them through a glorious canopy of sycamore, maple and birch trees, their tops bursting with all shades of red, orange, and yellow. She lifted her gaze to take it all in. "You were right. It is beautiful up here."

"Not to mention peaceful."

Hidden in the long grass on either side of them, crickets played their cheerful songs. Leaves rustled a mild rhythm high above, while pine needles below softened their foot falls to near silence.

Sydney breathed deep to fill her lungs with fresh, untainted air. “It is peaceful up here. You were right about that too.”

Vince squeezed her hand. “Are you enjoying yourself so far?”

Being with you, I am. “It’s nice to get away from the constant demands at work.”

“Exactly the reason I love the place.” He swung their clasped hands between them as they walked for a short distance in silence. “Careful. This part gets steep.”

He skillfully guided her between a couple of protruding branches, lifting one hanging at eye level out of their way so they wouldn’t get smacked. When the trail widened, he slowed to keep pace beside her as they approached Lake Papoose. The water, ruffled by the breezes of early fall, splashed against the shoreline with a gentle ebb and flow.

They came out on a good-sized clearing to a huge yellow sun lowering into the lushness of a horizon ablaze with crimson, orange, and gold. Hard packed gravel gave way to fine, white sand. A spectacular expanse rimmed by lazily swaying grasses. Sydney resisted the urge to take off her shoes and socks as her feet sank deep.

Vince pulled a compactly folded blanket of some kind from his backpack then shook it open to spread out. “I brought this for better star gazing. When the time comes.”

“Thoughtful of you.” She didn’t look at him as she spoke.

The sand beneath the blanket provided a cushion as soft as any bed. Reclined side by side, Vince and Sydney rested on their elbows as water lapped softly against the shoreline. Now and then more chirps of nearby crickets enhanced the absolute quiet. Across the blue-green water was another glorious mixture of red, orange, and yellow topped trees.

"You can't help but de-stress once you're up here." Moving to clasp his hands behind his head, Vince settled flat against the blanket.

Sydney closed her eyes as gentle breezes swirled around her face like a lover's caress. "It does tend to melt away any cares and worries you might have brought with you."

She slid down to lay the same way as Vince and rested both her hands on her stomach.

"Seems like we'll both be pretty mellow. At least until we leave here."

Though surrounded by serenity, Sydney considered her words carefully before she spoke. She knew exactly what Vince was getting at. Their agreement was to leave behind the jobs that always seemed to fracture their relationship to spend time alone together. Explore their true feelings. Discover whether what they had invested in each other was worth any necessary sacrifices to smooth out problems that would surely arise. Discuss possible compromises as they worked on building a future together.

If that's what we ultimately choose to do.

A tall order, because, right now she didn't want to make any life altering decisions. Right now, she just wanted to be with Vince at her side.

"Rest and relaxation can sometimes be addicting. Too much can fog up your sense of reason and mess with your rational mind." She whispered the concerns of her heart to him.

"Or force you to recognize what's truly important in life." The peaceful sounds of a forest at dusk blended with the whispered splashes of waves kissing the sand. As Vince drew her into a gentle embrace, Sydney shifted to face him and allowed his warmth to wash over her in much the same way.

As the last rays of sunlight filtered over them, creases of concern edged the corners of his eyes. He lifted a finger to trace a delicate line over her cheek and across her jawbone. Despite the warm air left over from an Indian summer day, she shivered at his touch.

"I don't have any reservations about the two of us becoming a couple. A permanent couple."

His breath drifted lightly over her skin as the import of his words crept into her mind. She held back a second shiver that threatened. Without conscious thought, she drew closer. "I appreciate that, Vince." Her voice was too emotion clogged. Shaky. "But, I—" His hand fell away, and she immediately longed for his touch.

"You have reservations, and it's up to me to convince you to see things my way."

She settled her head against her outstretched arm then gazed into his eyes. "How do you propose to do that?"

"For starters, like this."

Shifting ever so slightly, his face drew nearer until the warmth of his mouth covered hers, his lips moving in a slow and mesmerizing rhythm. Shifting again, he pulled her nearer. Caught up in her unending need for him, she let out a tiny whimper when his lips left hers. Then she closed her eyes on a moan of acceptance at the heated trail of his lips beneath her ear lobe and down her neck. His gentle hands moved under her sweatshirt, lightly over her rib cage then up to cup her breast. With a sigh and shiver she didn't try to hide, she clung to him as he showered her neck with delicate kisses.

Returning his attention to her face, he smoothed the hair back from her temple, then with his thumb and finger, toyed with a lock behind one ear. Her breath caught at the sweetness of his touch, and she closed her eyes to melt into him. Things were not supposed to happen this way. They weren't supposed to get sidetracked.

She forced her eyes to open. "We can't stay like this much longer. It's supposed to get cold tonight."

"That's what I heard. Although a few more minutes shouldn't hurt." He inhaled then released another sigh, and his chest rose then fell.

As she made a move to pull away, he held her tighter.

"I don't want to let you go, Sydney. Even temporarily, I can't stand the thought of it."

"I know. I feel the same way." Her response was so slight and low, the breeze could have taken it away before Vince had a chance to hear it.

"At least we're in agreement about that." He shifted to his back, holding her fast against him. "That's something."

The huge lump at the base of her throat blocked her from speaking right away, and she swallowed hard. As her head came to rest on his shoulder, she brought her palm up to lay over the strong and steady beating of his heart. Too soon tears dampened her fingers, and she blinked to dispel them.

You're right, Vince. At least we're in agreement about that.

At a rustling somewhere near in the bushes, he pulled away from her. A branch cracked then more leaves rustled, and Vince was already on his feet.

A large man wearing a plaid shirt and bib overalls entered the clearing. A small metal pail dangled from the hand at his side.

"Jason. What are you doing out here at this hour?" Despite the question, Vince kept his voice calm and low. Conciliatory.

The man stood with his feet spread apart and eyes reflecting a definite disorientation. They opened wider as he glanced around. "Addie wants me to pick some berries."

"Addie wouldn't send you out in the near dark to pick berries." With each word, Vince's tone grew from conciliatory to firm. "Why don't you let us walk you home?"

Before he quit speaking, Sydney had bent to gather then fold the blanket she held in her arms. "He's right, Jason. We'll take you home."

"Do you think Addie will be mad at me? I didn't mean to get lost."

"You shouldn't try to go off alone. It's not safe for you these days."

Vince hardly needed to explain the situation to her. She had no doubt the man suffered from a health condition, dementia or something similar. Without saying anything, she followed Vince, who now had a light hold of the man's arm, back down the trail.

It's not what he does. It's who he is.

After a few minutes walking in silence, they came

to a cabin set back in a shelter of trees. Vince had barely knocked on the solid pine door when a woman yanked it open, concern and anguish plastered on her face.

"Jason! Where have you been?"

With a shrug, he allowed Vince to lead him inside.

"I thought he was in bed." Though she spoke to Vince, her full attention remained on the man they'd just brought home.

"You might want to put a different type lock on the door. One he can't figure out. Ed from the hardware in town can help you with that."

The woman glanced over as Vince spoke and her gaze fell on Sydney. "Oh, hello."

He immediately drew her forward. "Sorry. Addie this is my, uh, this is Sydney Raines."

Sydney smiled, despite the awkward introduction. "Nice to meet you."

"Likewise."

"I'm glad we were out walking tonight."

Still tending to her husband as he sat on a dining room chair, Addie glanced over and smiled. "I am too. Thank you both for bringing him back to me."

"We'll let you get Jason settled in." Without looking her way, Vince took Sydney's hand and led them both out the door he closed securely.

The deep richness of the darkening sky filtered to lighter shades of silvery blue as the sun disappeared and the moon rose to take its place.

His arm came around her as they walked. "Too bad about the interruption."

"It happened." She circled his waist and hung on. "What else were we supposed to do?"

"Nothing, I guess."

"I think I figured out one thing today, Vince, if nothing else."

"What's that?"

"There's more good than bad in what you do."

And I need to remember that.

Chapter Nineteen

Vince's eyes were slow to open as he toyed with the idea of getting up. That was what it remained, thought with no action. Having Sydney with him in a bed that had been all too lonely of late, to do anything but remain where he was simply wasn't an option.

She lay on her stomach with one arm draped over his waist and her cheek resting, soft and warm, on his chest. The steady rise and fall of her breathing provided a reassuring echo in the bedroom they shared. His arm circled her body with a palm pressed flat against the middle of her back to hold her in place. Beneath the sheet, her smooth bare legs were in a wonderful tangle with the solid, coarseness of his.

He lifted his free arm to settle above his head, confident his plan to stay put was a good one. Especially since, in a few hours she'd be gone. Off on another damned scouting expedition for her boss. Their trip north had, in his mind, been a success. Alone for the rest of their time together with no interruptions, they'd talked, made love, then talked some more. Followed by more love making. All to complement their ultimate decision to stay together. Each doing their best to make things work.

A smile curved his lips as memories swirled. Sydney wearing nothing but moonlight as she walked across the room to join him in bed. The innocence of their growing love, striking a balance with an unending desire to explore. Each longing to discover all they could about how to bring the other pleasure.

Her limbs stirred as she roused and lifted her head. “Good morning.”

At the laziness so evident in her voice, he smiled. “Good morning.”

“How did you sleep?” She breathed the words against his skin.

It was impossible not to shiver at her touch. “Just fine when I’m beside you.”

“My thoughts exactly.” She rose up to scoot toward the pillows and him.

Perhaps her intention was to brush a light kiss on his lips, but he resolved to beat her to it. The moment she got there, he secured both his arms around her, determined to take her breath away. His mouth covered hers, sure and hard, before she had a chance to draw another.

At last, she drew back to gaze with fearsome intensity into his eyes. “I am going to miss you, love.”

“My thoughts exactly.” He brushed a thumb along her cheek.

Attuned to the same purpose, she straddled him at the waist as he stretched out on his back. Steadying herself with both hands on either of his shoulders, she lowered onto him, then worked her body and his in a slow and even motion. With his palms covering her hips, Vince matched her increasing speed with a hastening rhythm of his own. Soon, her breathing accelerated to match his. As she lowered her face in search of his lips, he pulled her tight, driving deeper and deeper until she whispered his name then convulsed around him.

She sat up and tossed back her head at the same second as he arched and released then pulled her nearer.

Still holding her, flesh against flesh, he stared into her eyes. “I cherish the day you came into my life.”

“Now it’s you who echo my thoughts.” She trailed her fingertips along his lips. “Something for you to remember me by when we’re apart this coming week.”

“Remember you, I will.”

With his arms still wrapped around her, Vince buried his face in her neck to savor the sweetly unique scent that belonged to the love of his life.

****

The sunlight of high noon filtered through the trees on either side of the highway once they finally got on the road. A bright blue sky overpowered a few hints of fluffy white, high flying clouds. Vince concentrated on the stretch of gray asphalt in front of him as it disappeared beneath the car. For now, traffic was light. As a result, they were making remarkable time. Too remarkable. They’d be at the airport before one. Her flight left at four-thirty. More than three hours lead time to get through security.

Two semis traveled side by side ahead of them. He let up on the accelerator to slow to their lower speed. He’d have to say good-bye to Sydney soon enough. No way did he want to rush it. Setting the cruise control on seventy-two, he guided the wheel with his left hand and set his right down on the seat. When Sydney’s fingers stroked a delicate pattern on his forearm, he looked over.

“Where are we going, Vince?”

“To the airport. You have a flight to catch.”

“Thank you.” Her hand slipped off him. “That’s very pragmatic of you. But, not what I wanted to hear. I’m talking about us. The long term us.”

He shot a glance in her direction. “You mean us as a couple?”

“Yes.” She dropped her hands to her lap.

“Where would you like to go?” He remained silent as he waited for her answer.

“The truth?” Her nervous laugh filled the empty space between them. “And nothing but the truth.”

“Nothing but the truth. It’s the least we both deserve.” He longed to place his fingers under her chin to steer her gaze to his but had to be content with the on and off glances her way his driving allowed.

“To be with you. Anywhere and anyway I can.”

It was all he could do to swallow before he responded. “Exactly what I wanted to hear. So where do we start?”

“From right where we are.” She looked away at something out the window, then glanced back at him and took a breath. “I love you, Vince. I can’t deny that any longer.”

“Another correct answer.” His voice lowered. “Not nearly as much as I love you.”

A contented silence folded over them.

Finally, he glanced over at her again. “So, what’s this trip for? Exactly.”

“Our itinerary is much the same as the last one. Though this time I meet Randall in California for a few days. We fly back to Grand Rapids for a night or two. Maybe three. Then home.”

Then home. He rolled the words over in his mind. “Where in California?”

"Palm Springs. This time."

"Do you have any idea when exactly you'll be back?" Once the words were out, he silently cursed himself. He'd promised himself he wasn't going to ask. Put more pressure on her for just doing her job.

"As soon as I possibly can. Randall plans to rent a vehicle. We'll fly the artwork from California there, then truck it from Grand Rapids, with what we bought on our last trip, to the gallery in Detroit."

Situating his hands at ten and two on the wheel, he accelerated to pass a half-ton pickup truck hauling a fifth wheel. Glancing right to make sure nothing was in his way, he pulled back over into his lane. "Sounds a little convoluted to me."

She shrugged. "Randall likes to cover all bases. I don't ask questions. It's his way of being ready for anything. My one consolation is that Nancy Parsons won't be going. Then hopefully, this will be my last trip for a while."

With a quick glance her way, he decided to take a chance and speak his mind. "Even with the woman who's given you so much trouble out of the picture, you're not as excited about this job now as when you first started, are you?"

"Does it show that much?"

"Maybe just to me." He brought his attention back to the road.

"Because you know me so well?"

"Possibly." His regard strayed her way again, and he covered her hand briefly before taking it back to steer toward the Merriman Road/Metro Airport exit. "Corny as it sounds, it's nice to hear you say that." He guided his vehicle through the circle drive to the airport entrance then followed the signs marked Departures.

"At least one of us loves the job they're in. That's something."

"You could always quit and find another. Move in with me while you look."

"And who would make the payments on my empty townhouse? The mortgage remains whether I'm there in residence or not."

He let out a sigh. "Guess I hadn't thought about that."

Approaching the McNamara Terminal on the right, Vince swung the car left to enter the Short Term Parking garage.

Sydney glanced up from whatever thoughts had consumed her the past few moments. "You don't have to walk me in. Plus, the hourly rate is ridiculously expensive."

"Too late. We're already here."

They parked then unloaded her bags in silence. With her carry-on looped over one shoulder and pulling her suitcase on its wheels behind them, he took hold of her fingers with his free hand as they entered the terminal then rode the slow moving foot tram inside.

Sydney glanced up at Vince and smiled. "Anyway, I can't make any more changes job-wise until I've had a chance to replenish my savings."

"That makes sense from a practical standpoint if nothing else." He held tight to her hand.

For whatever reason, seeing Sydney off, again, on yet another long business trip was turning out to be harder than he expected. Even so, he was determined to not let on how awful he felt as he stayed with her when she entered the maze of roped off stanchions to the check in desk.

She had her boarding pass and driver's license in hand and ready when her turn came to move forward. As luck would have it, they drew a super-efficient clerk who had her bag on the conveyor belt and Sydney registered in no time. Vince took her hand again as they walked away.

"We'll talk about this in more detail when I get home, Vince. Promise."

"I'll hold you to that."

"I won't back out on you." She briefly rested her head on his shoulder.

He brought his arm around her then squeezed to tighten his hold. "I know that."

When they stopped by the entrance to the security screening area, she turned to face him. "The line through here is growing. I'd better get at the end of it or I'll miss my plane." She laid her hands on his shoulders and moved in for a good-bye kiss.

"Have a good trip, and I'll see you when you get back." He flashed her the most encouraging smile he could come up with. *Safe travels.*

He didn't leave the terminal until she'd cleared TSA and disappeared up the escalator to the departure gates. When he walked outside, sunshine remained on his face all the way back to the car.

We'll talk about this in more detail when I get home.

Her words were his to hold on to until he and Sydney were together again.

****

Sitting at his desk, Vince continued to read the Accident Reconstruction report that had just been delivered.

Although the arms were bent at the elbow as one would expect to clutch the steering wheel prior to impact, the hands weren't in what would be the appropriate position. Instead of being closed around the steering wheel, they were open. Wide open. Fingers splayed. Identical adhesive residue was discovered on decedent's wrists and the steering wheel suggestive of duct tape.

He ran a hand through his hair and shook his head. It was finally official. The car crash that had claimed Brock Richardson's life was no accident, but murder by arson. The report also noted enough accelerant was used to make that a sure bet. They had a killer on the loose somewhere in the area. He had a community to serve and protect when all he wanted to do was concentrate on Sydney. Count the days, no make that hours, until she'd be home with him. So far, she'd been gone less than a week, but he missed her as desperately as if they'd been apart so much longer.

He clasped his hands behind his neck and leaned back in his chair then stretched his elbows out as far as they would go. When she did get home, come hell or high water, he'd figure out some way, any way to make it possible for them to move in together. His place or hers, it didn't matter.

"Uh, Detective?" Matthews appeared at his door before he had a chance to take his thoughts much further.

Vince sat forward with a thump. "What is it?"

"We have a woman here who wants to make a complaint." The rookie took a few steps in. "The chief thought you might want to handle it."

"A complaint about what?"

"An investment gone wrong. She says."

"Can't someone else handle it? I'm up to my eyeballs with a case involving a dead body with no clues about who made said body dead."

"Captain wants someone to humor her. Said you're the best one to do that. He said something about those super-duper bullshit skills of yours." A smirk quickly disappeared as he raised his hands in defense. "His words, not mine."

Vince grimaced at the reference to a reputation he no longer cared to live up to. "Oh, what the hell. Send her in."

"You got it, sir." Matthews was almost out the door when he turned back. "Oh, by the way, replies have been coming in on similar burned vehicle accidents like the one you're investigating."

"It's not an accident, but go on."

"They're printing right now. I'll bring them in when they finish." He paused for a moment. "After I bring you that complainant we have."

Vince glanced up briefly. "Do what you gotta do."

A few minutes later, spiked heels clicked with authority on the linoleum floor outside, then became no more than a whisper as they dented the carpet in his office. Vince lifted a brow at the sight of Matthews walking in beside her, having not heard his footfalls at all.

"Detective Miller." The rookie extricated his arm from a virtual death grip. "This woman would like to talk to you."

Wearing skinny jeans and black leather knee high-boots, spiked heels and all, she could have taken a wrong turn off a high fashion runway and ended up here in front of him. A white fur trimmed vest topped off whatever look she was going for.

He stood as she approached. “I’m Detective Vincent Miller. What can I do for you?”

She shook his hand lightly when he extended it over the desk then sat down in the chair opposite without being invited. “I’d like to make a complaint.”

Vince made sure not to crack even the slightest smile in the face of her dark-eyed stare. “Has a crime been committed?”

“Oh, most definitely.”

“Is there a victim?”

She reared back, her mouth set in a definite position of distaste. “What do I look like?”

“You’re the victim, then? Tell me what happened.”

“Someone obtained money from me under false pretenses.”

“Do you have a witness?”

“I certainly do.”

“Someone local?”

She drew down an already petulant mouth. “I would say so.”

Apparently, she wasn’t about to make this easy. He tried again. “Where exactly can they be found?”

“Right in front of you, Officer. The witness is me.”

“You?”

“Yes, me.” Her nostrils flared. “Do I have to spell it out for you?”

“Do you have any physical evidence? A signed contract?” Vince sat forward when she didn’t answer. “Any kind of formal agreement between you and the…uh…accused?”

Those highly padded shoulders slumped. “Unfortunately, no. My check is my receipt. I gave a donation.”

“Of your own free will?” Even he was having a hard time to play it straight with this one. “A donation in the form of a check you signed?”

She blinked then nodded again. “Well, yes.”

“That’s not a crime, ma’am. Not if there was no coercion involved. If it was your choice.”

Lips pursed and expression sour, the woman sat back and waved one hand in the air as if she swatted at an irritating bug. “You aren’t going to help me, are you?”

Swear to God I’m trying. “I’d like to if you’ll tell me what this is about.”

“You hear about people on the news being swindled all the time.”

“Unfortunately, most victims in those cases don’t recoup their losses.” He was careful to make eye contact and spoke as gently as he could. If this was a nut case he had on his hands, he sure didn’t want to send her off to take retaliation matters into her own hands.

The assured expression she’d walked in wearing faded. “You mean you really can’t do anything?”

“I can file a report.” Vince opened his desk drawer and shuffled through some file folders then pulled out a victim’s complaint form. After he filled in the date and precinct location, he glanced up. “Your name?”

“Nancy Parsons.”

The pen stilled in his hand before he jotted down what she said. With an unyielding sense of dread, he suddenly had a feeling where all this might be going.

Not to a good place. “The person you’re filing this complaint against?”

“Randall Curan.”

His insides knotted as he called on professional control. “Randall Curan.” He had to repeat the name. “You gave money to him?” This had to be a mistake. From all he’d learned about him, the guy operated the other way around.

“I did. Do you know who he is?” She didn’t wait for a yay or nay. “He’s the owner, the purported owner of the Argentile Gallery. He took my money. Did not honor the return he promised.” As if she couldn’t handle it any longer, she trained her gaze on the paper. “Aren’t you going to write this down as well?”

“What? Sure.” He scribbled the two well-known words on what he hoped was the appropriate line. “How much did you give him?”

Probably satisfied he got both names spelled correctly, she sat back then sniffed before answering. “A quarter of a million dollars.”

“Why?” Vince stayed upright when everything in him wanted to slump back in his chair.

Nostrils flaring, she drew herself up like an agitated Cobra as she met his gaze. “Why?”

He nodded, too dumbfounded to do much else.

She sized him up with a distasteful stare. “Because he needed it to fulfill his passion, and I believed in him. But that’s not the worst of it. That Howard Lancer creature caught me at the most inopportune time. Informed me he was owed thousands of dollars and actually expected me to make sure he was paid. As if I’m responsible for money squandered away before I came to Randall’s rescue. I mean really.”

"What about Curan's own wealth?" He'd ceased taking notes. The rest of this interview he could complete on his own. "It's almost a matter of public record, his family is worth millions."

"Billions actually." She lowered her gaze and sniffed again. "Not that their vast fortune will do Randall any good. He was cut off."

"When?"

"Five years ago." As if ratting out Curan was cathartic for her, she actually smiled, fleetingly, before she hurried on. "The situation was never made public."

"The family wanted it that way? Or he did?"

"I wouldn't know. He made some bad business decisions the past few years. Lost all the money in his annual allowance then sued to reach into his trust fund. A big no, no with that group."

"I can imagine." *Subject deeply in debt. Hounded by creditors.*

"Apparently the straw that broke the camel's back was his investment in the now defunct On Trend clothing chain."

The pen dropped from Vince's fingers, clattered to the desk top, then rolled to the floor. He stooped to retrieve it. "He was involved? It was his money that was lost?"

"Lost?" A disbelieving gaze met his. "It was stolen from him."

"How did you get this information?"

There was still a chance she'd gleaned what she knew from news reports and high society gossip. Though his gut told him that wasn't hardly the case.

"From Randall, of course. When he asked for my help." She pressed her lips together. "No one knows him the way I do."

"Is that a fact?" Though he wasn't sure he wanted to hear it, Vince had a feeling more would be forthcoming.

"We met in college. Hit it off immediately. Dated now and then the entire four years. We lost touch for a time and reconnected a few years ago."

Engrossed in the info she provided, something finally dawned on Vince he needed to set right. "As I understand, that Argentile Gallery is located in Manderfield. Why are you filing the complaint here in this jurisdiction?"

"Why?" Thin lips drew back in distaste. "Because here is where the crime occurred. I wrote the check I gave to him at the Country Club down the way. Where Randall and I had lunch."

Of course. Why didn't I realize that? He shook his head at the absurdity he'd become a part of.

"Then there are the women he…" She spoke up again before he had a chance to. Bringing a hand to her mouth, she cleared her throat. The tough as nails demeanor seemed to have hit a rough spot. "…takes up with when it serves his purposes. Then disposes of them just as quickly."

Her word choice made him wince. "You mean he breaks up with them."

"Of course." Taking a quick breath, she caught his eye and blinked. Then her gaze skidded away fast. But not before he noticed true pain filter into her eyes. "That's exactly what I mean."

"I thought so."

By now, Vince had dutifully written down darned near every word this woman spouted. Some of them made perfect sense. Most of them didn't. The hardest part was keeping a reasonable detachment. While Nancy Parsons watched every move he made, Vince stopped writing and sat back, not sure what to do next. It certainly wasn't a crime to be a piss poor businessman. Nor was it illegal to break off attachments with women you no longer care to see, romantically or otherwise.

Even if he wanted to, he could hardly put out an APB on Curan, marking him armed and dangerous. But, as the woman rambled on, flash bulbs exploded in Vince's mind with the strength to strike him blind.

"He makes sure to break up with them before they can leave him. Even the hint of rejection hurls the man into a rage. Though you wouldn't know it to look at him. He covers his emotions so very well."

Most psychopaths do.

"With his most recent endeavor, the clothing stores, not the gallery, he said he found out who did it and planned to make things right. But not before he went on a real rant, the man did. Threatened to extract revenge on everyone and their brother who was involved in that fiasco. I must say there are times I worry about his sanity."

Vince was losing his grip on a calm demeanor as she droned on and on. About what, he wasn't exactly clear. His mind had raced off to other things. Like how to get Sydney back home until this whole issue was sorted out.

Even if he had to fly to California and pluck her out of some overpriced hotel to do it.

Tap tap tap.

At the knock from his doorway, Vince glanced up.

Matthews came to attention when he did.

"More info came in for you." He held out a sheaf of papers as he came forward. "On the Brock Richardson murder case."

"Thanks. I'll take them."

His complainant twisted around, no doubt incensed at the interruption. Matthews must have agreed, as he beat feet for the door.

Vince set the pile to one side of his desk. "Now, Ms. Parsons. What else would you like to tell me?"

"Tell you?"

She stood so abruptly, he did too as if they were connected by some cosmic string.

"Surely I've given you enough. If you can't make a case out of all that." She indicated the note pad on his desk with a flick of one hand. "You don't know how to do your job."

Vince reared back at her insult but kept his expression neutral and his gaze steady. "You've given me everything I need here to put together a decent case."

"I certainly hope so."

"I'm certain you did." Lying through his teeth, he produced one of his most stellar smiles, even as his throat closed up so tight, he almost choked as he came around his desk. "We'll be in touch when we have something to share."

"See that you do."

To say that she spun on her heel would be an understatement. Except, when she started to walk out, her gait didn't resonate with quite the same confidence as when she'd strode in.

"Matthews! We're done here." He lowered his

voice from a shout when the rookie appeared. “Can you escort Ms. Parsons out?”

“Yes, sir. Right away, sir.” Taking the woman’s arm, he did as he was asked.

But not nearly fast enough. Vince could only shake his head as those boots she wore clipped and clopped their way down the hall.

“Sydney’s right. She is one hell of a piece of work.”

Back at his desk, he grabbed up the papers containing information on similar ‘accidents’ from around the country, to the one that claimed Brock Richardson. All women, some of the bodies had been identified, some not. None with a connection he could discern from the sketchy bios provided. As Vince studied the pictures of two of the victims, indistinct driver’s license photos, a familiarity flickered then vanished before he could get a firm hold on it.

Until…

Ripping open the bottom drawer of his desk, he rifled around until he got hold of the Argentile Gallery file he flipped open in front of him. After shuffling through the seemingly endless pages of FBI dribble, he finally found the newspaper from his first days on the case. Opening to page three, his fingers trembled as he laid the evidence photos over top of the newsprint pictures.

As vague similarities crystalized into positive IDs, his heart all but stopped.

Beverly Hartford. Elaine Queens. Shanna Martin.

Chapter Twenty

"Hi, Vince. It's Sydney. We're back in Grand Rapids safe and sound." She spoke into her cell when his voice mail tone sounded, amazed to have service in an elevator at the Amway Grand. "Though it was a horrendous trip, the good news is I got to fly home alone. Randall took an earlier flight yesterday at least as far as to here. An appointment or something came up. Though I want nothing more than to talk with you, I'm exhausted and going to try to take a nap." She let out a little laugh. "This is turning into a longer message than I intended. Just shows how much I truly miss you. Give me a call when you get this. It'll be worth waking up to hear your voice. I love you. Bye."

She disconnected and dropped the phone in her suitcoat pocket at the same time as the elevator arrived on her floor with a ping and a bounce. Juggling her purse, portfolio, and suitcase, she made her way down the carpeted hall. At the door to her latest hotel room, she slid the key card into place then turned the knob when the latch gave. As usual, a sophisticated electric eye of some sort sensed her presence the moment she stepped over the threshold. Soft lighting emerged, and the faint strains of music filtered down on the lavish interior.

Blocking out as much of it as she could, she kept walking. This artificial ambiance, nice as it could be on a limited basis, wasn't cutting it for her just now. After the last few hours she'd spent flying home in a crowded and bumpy jet, it was a toss-up which hurt worse, her feet or her back. She so needed the quiet and solitude of some down time and strode directly into the bedroom of the luxury suite then shut the door behind her.

Their trip to Palm Springs had turned out to be a royal bust. Worse even than their first California jaunt. Not only was this excursion more expensive, but a true exercise in futility. Though Randall probably wouldn't admit it in this lifetime, he'd grossly misread the market.

Mine is not to reason why. And so on and so forth.

"Or however the hell you want to term it. At any rate, not my problem." Standing her suitcase against the wall, she dropped her portfolio to the floor and her purse on top of that, then plopped down on one corner of the king-sized bed. She kicked her beige flats off first, then scooted toward the headboard. The plush down pillow she grabbed once she got there brought little comfort as she hugged it to her midsection. A poor substitute for the man she yearned for.

Whether Vince was fresh out of the shower and clean shaven, or newly home after a busy day on the streets with a five o'clock shadow to rasp over her cheek, didn't matter.

All I crave is a sweet and solid reminder of coming home.

"That's it." As an idea struck, she bounded off the bed and grabbed her phone to try Vince's number again. As before, the call went straight to voice mail. With the cell against her ear, she climbed back against the pillows.

"Hi, darling. It's me again. After I take that little nap I mentioned before, I've decided to rent a car to drive home. Randall wants to stay in GR a couple more days. I definitely don't, and I believe I can entice him to agree to let me go. I still have some major comp time coming. If I don't hear from you before, I'll call when I'm on the road."

She clicked off and lay the phone beside her on the mattress, rested her head on two more down filled pillows and shut her eyes. Settled deep into the comforter, she heard a door open and looked over. Vince was framed in the bathroom door. Blissfully naked and surrounded by frothy billows of hot steam.

"You're here." At his unexpected appearance, her pulse rate soared.

"I thought you were going to join me." His voice was low. "But this will work too."

"I've missed you so much." She opened her arms wide. "And now you're here."

He smiled in welcome as he approached the bed. "Not as much as I've missed you."

Shifting his way, she returned a wicked smile as she reached for the nightstand. "I have a surprise for you. It's…"

Bing. Bing. Bong. Bong. Bong.

The sing-song melody intruded on her brain. Her eyes popped open in response. Lifting her head with a start, she snatched the cell to her ear. *Vince calling back.*

"What do you need?" The smile in her voice blossomed on her face, and she closed her eyes as she waited to hear his deep, lazy chuckle. Just before he whispered, low and sexy…*You.*

"Sydney. Good I got you." Randall's higher pitched and decidedly agitated voice dove into her eardrum.

"Randall?" She pushed the pillow to one side and sat up. "I thought we were done for now."

"Change of plans. I need you to visit a client with me ASAP."

"Which one?" Unless he had an airtight and absolute good reason, she wasn't in the mood to relinquish her coveted alone time.

"We need to go back to the Somerset Galleria on 28th Street."

"The one we closed on the last time we were here." She provided a reminder their purchases from the venue were a done deal.

A huffed-out breath came over the line. "The one we *thought* we closed. Before that damned Nancy somehow stuck her big fat nose in it and managed to screw things up from afar. God, I wish that woman would leave things alone."

That makes two of us.

She knew better than to take sides. "Anything I can do to help?"

"Meet me in the lobby as soon as you can. If you wouldn't mind." He didn't give her a chance to respond, even if she'd wanted to. "We should be able to repair the damage she did and get the deal back on track within an hour. Shouldn't even take that long. Then I'll treat you to lunch."

The conciliatory air he used to cajole customers and clients alike didn't work on her. She scrunched up her face at the invitation. Yet another meal with an overbearing boss wasn't an item on her current to do list. Vince was.

"If we get done in time, maybe." She made a firm pass at rebellion.

"Either way, we have to eat." He snapped out the comment then cleared his throat. "May as well do so in the pleasure of each other's' company."

"I'll be down shortly." The low battery display immediately popped up when she set her phone on the night stand. "You might know when I'm in a hurry."

Rolling off the bed, she slid into her shoes. Surely Randall could wait a few moments. She didn't want to take a chance missing Vince's call. At the door, she dug in her luggage for the charger, then backtracked to pick up her cell. Before she left, and the phone died completely, she wanted to leave Vince one more message. That accomplished, she plugged everything in and walked out to the hallway.

The elevator descended quickly then bounced and chimed as it landed on the first floor. Sydney immediately took up a position front and center as the doors started to slide open. *The sooner we get there…*

"Oh! I…" Stepping out, she nearly bumped into Randall.

"The valet service is overwhelmed just now." He took hold of her arm and guided her toward a back stairwell. "There's a ten minute wait at best. I'd rather not take the time."

"Is this particular purchase that crucial?" If memory served, the deal he was so hell bent to restore hadn't been worth more than a few thousand dollars to the gallery, if that.

"In business, every deal is crucial."

He pushed through a heavy utility door that shut

behind them with a clang. She clutched the metal railing as he ushered her in front of him down a flight of cement stairs.

"We really need to hurry. Time is of the essence, as they say."

Sydney pulled free as they reached the ground floor of a nearly deserted section of the lower garage. Walking side by side, their footsteps echoed on smooth cement.

"The bell captain told me where they parked my car."

She was sure he meant head valet but wasn't about to argue or try to correct him. The sooner they got over to the venue, the sooner they'd be able to return.

"Why in the hell would they park it all the way down here?"

Randall's words echoed her thoughts, but she said nothing as he aimed the remote he held into the shadows. With a blip, car lights came on at one end of the next row over.

"There's the rental." Making a beeline for the driver side, he opened the door when he got there then paused. "Oh, crap. My briefcase is in the trunk." He glanced at her over the roof of the car, his face a distorted mask in the opaque glow of the dome light. "Get it for me, please."

Sydney stopped midway to the passenger door. "Of course, Randall." Irritation crept into her voice she had no compunction to hide. "No problem."

"There's a good girl." He aimed the remote again, and the trunk began to lift.

She gritted her teeth but made no comment. After the trunk lid rose to its full height and the interior light came on, she ducked her head inside. "There's nothing in here, Randall. The trunk's empty. Are you sure you didn't leave it in your room?"

"I'm sure." His muffled voice came at her from inside the car. "It has to be in there."

"Where would it be?"

"It may have slid to the back. You know how these parking jockeys drive." The tone he used took on an irritation similar to hers. "They probably slammed on the brakes once they got down here and thrust everything forward."

Whatever you do, don't get out and help. "I'm looking."

"Check way up under the cubby. Near where the back seat is. Please."

Keeping her lips pressed tight, she did as he asked. On her tiptoes, she stretched full out into the trunk to reach her arms all the way into a back corner. When she still came up empty, she pulled out and started to straighten. "There's nothing in here…ow!"

The colossal metal lid came down on her head with a sickening whack. She lurched further into the trunk as her chin hit her chest, and her front teeth sliced into her tongue. Weighty metal struck again. Its sharp edges dug into her back.

"Ahh!" Stars shot out from all directions in front of her eyes. She blinked, fought through the pain exploding in her mouth, then tried to raise her head and stand.

A solid object struck like an anvil against the side of her head. Rough bristles of carpet rasped over her cheek as she landed on the trunk floor and her world went black.

****

"It wasn't my fault I had to kill the damn woman."

The muttered voice, Randall's voice, pulled Sydney toward consciousness. The surface beneath her bounced and swayed. Jostled side to side, she flopped one way then the other at the mercy of some God awful bumps. She wasn't prepared when her body went airborne. As she struggled to spread out her arms, only her biceps flexed, and she glanced down. Her wrists were locked together in front of her. A hasty breath whooshed out of her nose as both shoulder blades connected with the floor.

About to be bounced in the air again, she rolled to one side to clutch the nap of a low piled carpet, then dug in her heels. Braced for impact this time, she rose then landed with less of a jolt. Though her eyes were open, she couldn't see much in the dark interior. All she could do was survey her surroundings as best she could through touch and sound.

The engine roar and hum of road noise told her she was on the floor of a moving vehicle. Except there were no horn honks of other traffic, no accelerations and slow-downs of a city commute. Just the constant side to side jostles and jerks of a car traveling at a decent clip. Probably down a country road.

An isolated country road.

Though nearly impossible, she had to maintain control. Keep her wits about her. *Once you lose control, you lose the battle.*

At some point, she'd been moved from the trunk to a back seat. If someone was desperate enough to knock her unconscious, no way would they leave the doors unlocked. Sheer survival instincts prompted her to check anyway. Deciding to risk it, she pulled herself up then lifted both hands together to curl her fingers around the door handle and yank. Nothing budged.

Dark eyes reflected in the rearview mirror to glance casually back at her. "Oh, I see you're awake." He tapped the steering wheel as if he'd just asked if she wanted to switch drivers.

Randall? What are you doing to me? She screamed the words in her mind. "Hjmmmjhh."

Duct tape across her mouth prevented coherent language. She kept her gaze trained on him as she squirmed and struggled to a sitting position and slid her butt onto the seat. Curan didn't seem to mind that she would become visible to anyone outside the car. Obviously because there was no one outside. Or anywhere else nearby. Remote country roads were like that. Desolate and deserted.

He glanced back at her again and lifted one side of his lip. "I see the tape held. Couldn't take the chance you'd wake up and scream until we were out of town. Sorry I had to bind your wrists. Can't have you grabbing at me from back there. We could get in an accident. Possibly get hurt. One of us, anyway."

She jerked her head to the side, determined to not look at him as he rattled on.

"I moved you to the backseat because I didn't want to take the chance you'd die there inside the trunk. That would be such a waste."

Why? The question repeated like a stuck record in her mind.

"Can you believe the gall of that Simms woman? After that boyfriend of hers was found dead, she called me to demand, demand, mind you, an actual half as her share. Said now there were two of us instead of three, it was only right."

Simms woman? Belinda? He killed Brock?

Sydney closed her eyes. As terror collided with desperation, hot tears seeped out. A sob filled her chest then rose up to escape from between her lips only to ricochet back down her throat. She gagged, then blew a rush of air out through her nose.

"She threw an absolute fit when I told her to go to hell. Said she'd report me to the authorities. Make it her personal mission to bring me down."

Fresh tears ran warm and wet down her cheeks. Another sob with nowhere to go scalded the back of her throat. She choked down the salty mixture. Her chest burned as fear and apprehension skidded in then came to rest in its center. The images she'd seen on television came back at her in a rush. Charred and twisted metal. Scorched remains of a brutal murder.

Sydney's heartbeat sped up as alarm tore through her and adrenaline surged. Another sour substance rose in her throat. She gagged against her bindings then inhaled long and deep through her nose to swallow the vile mixture.

"Brock was easy. Given his insatiable greed. But you already know that." Curan paused to glance into the mirror again as if he truly expected her to respond. "Insatiable greed, you know, is what ultimately did him in. It wasn't me alone."

His voice took on an edge of contempt as he continued with a mad man's confession. "'We'll split the profits fifty, fifty. I'll pay back the loan with interest.' He spoke in a low-pitched imitation of her late boss. "That was his meager offer when he first approached me to beg for the money he needed to keep his business afloat. I talked him down to sixty-five, thirty-five, plus jacked up the interest to serve my needs. To hell with his. But then what are brothers for? Brock and I were part of the same fraternity you know."

The car bumped and swayed. Soon, they turned down a more severely rutted dirt road. Sydney braced with her knees and flattened her shoulders against the seatback to remain upright then squeezed her eyes shut as more hot tears erupted to slide down her cheeks. Bringing both bound hands up, she swiped them away as best she could.

"It's too bad about your impending death. I must say you are one excellent employee. It will be a shame to lose you. However, like the others, it's time for you to pay."

Hot blasts of renewed terror shot into her bones as she kept her gaze trained out the window. Trees with thick trunks grew so close to the narrow dirt lane, they came together at their tops to form a natural canopy. Their bright colors blazing against the sky. Much like the woods surrounding Vince's cabin.

If only Vince were here.

As she thought of the man she'd hoped to spend the rest of her life with, a bitterly cold shiver shook her. Visions of his face appeared, and memories whirled. His gaze warm and loving, mouth curved up in a smile. Her heart filled with longing, and a whimper escaped around the tape covering her mouth.

"There was the satisfaction at seeing you sideswiped by that car near your apartment a while ago." He slowly raised his head to stare at her with vacant eyes. "When you walked across the street.

Pretending to be upset was a marvelous bit of acting on my part, don't you think?"

She kept her gaze averted, unable to stomach looking at him.

"Such a pity you'll be the last for a while."

They pulled into a clearing of sorts. The car rocked as he slammed it into park. Sydney's body lurched with the motion. She braced to remain upright. One car door slammed as he got out. The door beside her opened with a creak. He reached in to grab her by the arm and pull her out then shoved her forward as she struggled to maintain her footing. Her wrists may have been bound together, but her ankles weren't. She spun around to thrust upward with one knee. He dodged at the last moment, and she landed an ineffective blow to the top of his thigh. Something cold and hard came down on the side of her head just above her ear. Bright stars burst forth as she went down.

"Nice try, but no cigar! I'm obviously smarter than you."

Before she could get her bearings, tape squealed from the roll he ripped free to wrap around her ankles, then pushed off on her as he stood. Grabbing her up, he propelled her over to the car and into the driver's seat. The bottom of the dash raked against her knees. She twisted and fought in vain as more tape squealed and her hands were bound to the steering wheel.

"We don't need this anymore." He grabbed one edge of the tape over her mouth and yanked. "It'll probably do you good to scream some."

Hot pain tingled over her lips, as the adhesive tore at her skin, but she refused to make any utterance of protest. She gingerly moved her jaw from side to side to make sure it was still working as he wadded the tape he'd removed in his fist. Then he shut the door and left. Footsteps crunched and rustled as he walked away. Silence followed. After a moment the rustling returned. With her head twisted to one side, she caught sight of Randall piling dried twigs, branches, and other debris against the car.

Jaw tight with effort, she yanked and pulled against the bindings until her wrists throbbed. If she had to, she'd sacrifice a limb to avoid dying like this. Frenzied physical effort pushed her closer and closer to exhaustion as one scream after the other burst from her lips. Blood surged to pound in her temples, while tears of frustration blurred her vision. She ignored a dry, raw aching throat as she continued to shriek.

Someone, somewhere had to hear her. They *had* to.

Please let Vince somehow know I'll always love him.

She sent the message into the universe then closed both eyes tight, thrust her head back, and screamed some more.

Chapter Twenty-One

"Hey, Detective Miller." Matthews rapped on Vince's door then walked into his office. "More responses for your accident investigation."

"Really?" Vince was only capable of the single word response.

"Looks like you hit the evidence gathering jackpot." He handed over more faxes.

"Looks like it." The pieces of evidence were falling into place in neat little piles. Like harmless snowflakes combining to produce a dangerous avalanche. "I've since learned about quite a few like ours that happened across the country."

"Over what amount of time?"

"Looks like over the last three years. Maybe four."

Matthews let out a low whistle. "You think we got a serial killer on our hands?"

"That would be my guess."

"Good luck with it, detective."

"Yeah, thanks."

The young officer had no sooner left, when Vince's desk phone rang. He answered without looking up. "This is Miller."

"Vince Miller?" The man's deep voice spoke his name.

"That's right."

"I'm Captain Hollis from the Grand Rapids PD.

I'm calling about that car fire death you're working. We've just found one around here with the same MO. Given our close proximity to your area, I wondered if they're related."

"You think they are?" His grip on the receiver tightened as every ounce of blood drained out of him. He fought through the fog rolling into his brain as the rest of the conversation faded in and out past the roaring in his ears.

"We did luck out, however, over here on this one."

Vince massaged two fingers over his forehead. "How so?"

"Found some personal belongings that were in the trunk and didn't get torched."

"Any ID with it?"

"Naw. I'd never expect to get that lucky. This is toiletries mainly. Cosmetic bag. Not a purse. There is one thing, though, that's kind of a unique. Piece of jewelry."

"What kind of jewelry?" His voice was no more than a rasp.

"A necklace. Gold chain, with a single pendant. Blue, circular stone."

A vision flashed to mind. Sydney's necklace, laying on the flawless background of her throat. He blinked then shook his head. *Don't even think it!* "Would it be possible to send me a picture?"

"You think maybe you got a line on something?"

Vince squeezed his eyes shut. "I'm not sure. Probably not." *Please, God! Definitely not.* "Get that picture to me, will you? STAT."

"Right away."

"Thanks." Vince dropped the phone in its cradle

and sat back.

A jumble of theories and possibilities stacked into his head like a fifty car pile-up on the Interstate. Vince pulled out his cell and tried Sydney's number again. He'd responded to the voice mail from her as soon as he got it. For the umpteenth time, he cursed himself for not noticing her message sooner and damned the call he'd been on with someone else when he missed hers.

"Shit!" When his latest attempt to get a hold of her went to voicemail, he tossed the device aside to land on top of a file folder.

"Got a picture for ya, Detective." Matthews didn't have to come any nearer than the doorway for Vince to make out the image on the sheet he held up. "It's a necklace."

"Yeah. I see that." It was a miracle he could speak through a throat that was about to close up on him.

"Pretty one though." Matthews turned the picture around to study. "Gold chain. Nice looking stone. Wonder what kind it is."

"My guess would be sapphire." His body temperature dropped to zero as an icy chill crept across the back of his neck.

"More's coming in as we speak." Matthews stopped at the other side of the desk to hand the sheet over.

"Yeah. Thanks. I…" Vince cleared his throat as his voice failed him at last.

"You're welcome." With a quick salute, Matthews left him alone.

For the next few seconds, Vince couldn't move. Couldn't do anything but stare at the picture put in front of him. *Sydney's necklace.*

A crushing agony started at the base of his gut then shot out in all directions. As if he'd been shredded into a million pieces, then left, still alive, to suffer. Hands curled into fists, he pounded softly on the desk top. Once. Then again, and again.

Nearly done in by the battle between his personal grief and professional sense of duty, Vince reached for his desk phone and dialed. Hollis picked up on the third ring.

"It's Miller from Detroit…I'm pretty sure I know who your Jane Doe victim is." He didn't give his colleague any time to comment. "I'm going to call her next of kin. We'll be over your way in a couple of hours."

****

Vince pressed his foot down harder on the gas pedal as he fought to block out everything but the highway in front of him. A simple survival tactic as blind faith propelled him on. If he let his mind go where it wanted, all thoughts of Sydney would be front and center. He didn't want to deal with that much pain just now. To focus on the road was his best option. Straight, flat, predictable.

Until they got to the turn off to the hospital, more specifically, the morgue.

Terror and sadness, rage and impotence stabbed at him from all directions, tearing him up and threatening to destroy his heart.

Beside him, Andy Raines wasn't faring much better. "It's not supposed to be like this." He blew his nose then used the same handkerchief to wipe the tears from red rimmed eyes.

"It's a hazy connection at best, but right now it's

the only connection we've got." Vince didn't share the details of the other victims. Not yet anyway. "I just hope to hell I'm wrong."

"Children bury their parents. Not the other way around." He coughed into one elbow then dabbed at his eyes again.

Vince kept his lips tight and jaw clenched. The right thing to do was respond. Offer some words of…what? Wisdom? Sympathy? Commiseration? Pity he had nothing to give as they traveled to possibly identify a Jane Doe dead body as someone they each loved more than life.

"I read you the report. There's no positive ID. Yet." Vince's voice was about to break. He swallowed hard, then tried again. "I wouldn't have gotten you into this at this point, but I thought it would be helpful."

"To have next of kin on site. Just in case."

"Yeah." He spit out the word. For the first time it dawned on Vince the next of kin wasn't him.

Face in his hands, Andy let out a couple of wretched sobs.

Vince gripped the wheel, shaken to his soul. "There's a chance it's somebody else."

His companion lifted his head, pulled in a heavy breath then coughed. "You're a God damned idiot if you believe that, son."

Vince choked down a mass of emotional junk. "Then I'm a God damned idiot. Humor me."

"Consider it done. You idiots need all the help you can get." Andy's hollow laugh filled the space between them. "If it is her, I want to bury her by her mother. I'd purchased the plot beside Diana for me." On another sniff, he aimed his gaze out the window again. "I'll get myself another one."

Vince clenched his jaw. *Shut the fuck up!* His mind screamed words he couldn't utter out loud. To go with the tears pushing at the corners of his eyes he wouldn't allow himself to shed.

"You did try calling her cell." His gaze suddenly alert, Andy glanced over.

Vince nodded. "What do you think? Multiple times."

"Me too. Went to voice mail every damned time." He drew a shuddering breath. "My two sons were deep UC these past few weeks. Just before you called, I was notified they came out safe with their assignments fulfilled. Doug got information about a crooked councilman they're set to put away. And Reese took a couple of minor drug dealers off the streets."

"My congratulations to both of them." Vince responded on automatic.

"They're both good at what they do. Well trained with top notch instincts."

Vince struggled for a coherent response. "Makes it easier when they're out on the streets."

"Both boys understand what's expected and carry out their missions, but I still worry."

"I suppose you always do. I'm sure I would if I had sons in similar situations." Vince cast over a sideways glance at the same time as he veered right to take the exit Hollis had instructed.

"It's different with my little girl. Never thought…" Tears made his voice crack and he coughed again. "Did not see this coming."

"You usually never do."

"They found a gold and sapphire necklace in the

belongings of the victim you said."

"Yep." White knuckling the steering wheel, he pushed his foot on the gas and swung around a slower moving SUV. The sooner they arrived and got this over with, the better. If he didn't owe it to her father, he owed it to Sydney.

Andy pulled in a breath he released on a muffled sob. "I gave her that necklace for her sixteenth birthday."

"Yeah. She told me." He had to clear the emotion from his throat before he could speak again. "You must have paid a pretty penny for it too. You had it specially made, huh?"

He let out a soft snort. "Specially made. I wish. I lucked out and found the thing at a jewelry store. On sale. Put it on layaway for six months."

Vince whipped his head to the right so hard, the car veered with him. He straightened the wheel. "It's not a one of a kind?"

"Are you nuts?" Andy's look said as much. "I was a patrolman at the time with three kids to support. One of a kind, my ass."

His cell went off, and they both jumped. Andy pulled it out of his shirt pocket and fumbled to look at its face then slid his finger across the screen. "Hello. Hello? I can't hear on these damned things. How do you put this on speaker?" He jabbed a finger at the device.

"…didn't think about it before you left last night." Ida's voice came into the car. "I've lost Orson's finder thingy Sydney gave me. It's not on his collar."

"I'm a little busy right now." Andy spoke up as soon as he had an opening. "I'll help you find it when we get back."

"Where are you?"

He glanced up at Vince who shook his head. "Helping Vince with some case that's got him bugged."

"Oh, that's nice you two can work together." The tension in her voice disappeared. "Tell him I said hello."

"Will do." With the phone in his palm, Andy hovered his finger over its face. "I've got to go right now. Bye."

"If you must. I'll…"

Vince kept both hands on the wheel after he parked in the hospital lot. For the first few seconds, neither moved. Or spoke. Vince glanced out the windshield at the six-story, brown brick building in front of them.

"Well, shit. Here goes nothing." Finally, Andy released his seat belt to snap back with a click. "You coming in with me or not?"

Vince looked over but said nothing. Just cut the engine.

Andy opened his door then paused to turn toward him. "Or would you rather not?"

Vince hit the door handle on his side, when he really wanted to put his fist through the God damned vinyl and steel. "Why wouldn't I?"

"Let's get this over with."

"Yeah. Over with." He joined Andy on the wide sidewalk of the daunting structure.

Neither spoke as they walked, shoulder to shoulder through the glass double doors and went straight to the elevator that would take them to the basement. Even before the door opened after they landed, the smell of formaldehyde and God knew what else crept in through the cracks.

Vince touched Andy's arm. "You okay? You look like you're going to puke."

Sydney's dad kept his lips closed, then grimaced as he swallowed. "I feel like I'm going to puke. Nothing I can do about it."

The worst was the cold. Vince would never get used to the cold. Slipping both hands in his pants pockets, he stayed back to let Andy step off first when the elevator doors opened, then shivered as he followed close behind.

A uniformed security guard stood up from his desk, quick to intercept them. "Welcome, Gentlemen." He offered his hand to each in turn as Vince and Andy replied with their names. "You're here to view the DOA that just came in."

Vince nodded. "We are."

Beside him, Andy let out a shuddering breath.

"You'll want to go that way." He extended his hand behind him.

Vince mumbled his thanks then took Andy by the arm. Arrowed signs directed them toward closed double doors marked No Admittance in two-inch-high red block letters.

Andy stopped poleaxed when they didn't open automatically. "Jesus. Is there any way to not prolong this?"

Vince pushed his way through, then held the door for his companion. Another uniform, this one a police officer, waited at a second set of double doors.

He immediately straightened from his slouched position. "Miller, I'd guess?"

Vince nodded then introduced Andy and specified

him as next of kin.

"I'm Captain Hollis."

Andy put his hand on the man's shoulder apparently ready to push him aside. "Where do they have my daughter?"

The officer braced and stood pat. "That's just it, sir. It's not your daughter."

"It's not?" Mouth gaped open, he didn't finish as he splayed a hand over his face. Heavy sobs wracked his shoulders as he stepped back to lean, face first, against the wall.

Hollis turned back to Vince, his face awash in sympathy. "Your call may have been a tad premature. We came up with a tentative ID on the body already."

Beside him, Andy let out a gust of breath. "You what?"

For a split second Vince could only stare.

"You know how it goes. Dental records will have to be checked, but we lucked out on this one." The balding man looked down at the tops of his scuffed black boots then back at Vince. "Sorry you came down here for nothing."

Vince had a tough time correlating luck to a dead body. "How do you know?"

"We found a purse tucked under the back seat. Way under the back seat. My guys didn't see it until they took the damned seat out. Funny thing, it was near that cosmetic bag I told you about."

Andy wiped a hand across his eyes and strode over to stand beside Vince. "Go figure."

"Our victim's name was Belinda Simms. The good news is, she was dead before the fire."

Though Vince regretted a woman had lost her life,

like a long dormant volcano, immediate and total relief surged. Relief that didn't last long. They still didn't know where Sydney was.

He glanced over at Hollis. "If it's not who I thought it was, we're going to need your help on another one."

"Anything. As far as what?"

Vince took just enough time to fill his cross-state colleague in on the fact that Sydney could not be reached. "I realize missing persons cases need twenty-four hours, but given the circumstances I outlined, we may not have that much time."

Hollis pursed his lips and nodded. "Just tell me what you need me to do."

Back at the car a while later, Vince and Andy climbed in, then sat there and stared at each other.

"Well son of a bitch." Andy was the first to break the silence, then just shook his head.

"Couldn't have said it better myself." Vince put both hands on the wheel but made no move to start the engine.

He'd had his fill of these emotional climbs and dives. Tremendous highs because Sydney loved him. Tremendous lows when he believed he'd never see her again. Now he was soaring once again, and he'd do anything to avoid a crash landing. Needing to do something, he took out his cell and punched in her number.

"She's still not answering her phone."

On a hunch, he played back the last voice mail she'd sent him, hoping for a clue. Or maybe he just needed to hear her voice. The Bluetooth in his car picked it up.

"Vince, Sydney again. I may not be here when you call. My phone's about to die so I'm plugging it in at the hotel. Randall just called with yet another crisis. He wants me to go with him to help solve it. I'll call you the minute I get back." She paused to swallow. "I love you with all my heart."

Andy shot him an immediate glance as those last few words faded away. "Congratulations. My little girl doesn't love easily. She sounds pretty sincere."

"Yeah. Thanks." When his vision blurred, Vince squinted through the windshield and fired up the engine. "But now what? We still don't know where she is."

Andy stared at him a moment then snapped his fingers. "That's it. With any luck, that's how we're going to find Sydney."

The last thing Vince wanted was to get his hopes up for no reason. "How?"

"That homing device of Ida's." He spun in the seat. "Sydney gave her one of a pair. Let's hope the other one is still in her purse, and her purse is still with her." With each new suggestion, excitement rose in his voice. "And we can find it."

Vince said nothing as he aimed the car at the street and gunned the engine.

After a quick call back to Ida for the URL of the company and her user name and password, Andy punched some data into his phone, then stared at the thing for what seemed like hours.

"I got a hit." His voice trembled as he held up the cell. "I got a hit, and it's nowhere near Sydney's townhouse. But damned close to where we are now."

Chapter Twenty-Two

Sydney tasted salt and licked her lips as sweat mingled with tears to trickle down her face and drip into her mouth. After screaming long and loud for God knew how long, she must have blacked out. What she couldn't afford to do again. When she wasn't screaming, she'd desperately worked on her restraints. Unfortunately, the only thing she accomplished was to tear the flesh at her wrists.

A lone ray of sunshine came through the windshield to land on her face, and she put her head back then closed her eyes to savor its warmth. Immediately, the passenger door was jerked open. She twisted her head to the right. Randall glanced over at her briefly before he rummaged for something in the glovebox.

Long ago training from a self-defense class kicked in. Distasteful as it was, she needed to engage him. Somehow get him talking. Seek to find some semblance of mutual understanding.

"Randall." Her voice was raspy. She swallowed to soothe a painful throat. When it didn't help, she pushed on anyway. "I had nothing to do with you losing your money at On Trend. Why punish me? Why, Randall?"

Though he didn't look at her, his hands stilled as he drew out some folded papers. He shut the door on the compartment with a thump, then leaned further in until his face was inches from hers. "You betrayed me far more than either Brock or that bimbo of his did." His hot breath ricocheted off her cheek. "They stole my money and made me look bad to my family. Caused me to be cut off from what is rightfully mine."

"I had nothing to do with that. I've told you." "Brock swindled you. Not me."

"Don't you think I know that?" As if he couldn't stand to be close to her any longer, he pulled back to the doorframe. "Your sin had nothing to do with money."

Totally confused, she stopped speaking as she tried again to swallow. Reasoning with him was getting her nowhere. In fact, pleading her case only served to infuriate him more.

"The crime you committed was much worse."

"What crime, Randall? What did I do?"

A sneer emerged as glassy eyes caught her gaze. "You refused an offer most women would kill to receive. You tossed aside the opportunity to be my female companion."

Your what! She shook her head at the absurdity of this conversation. "I had no idea."

"No woman does that to me!" His voice grew louder before he stopped to produce a sickening smile. "When you think about it, it's really too bad I won't be able to kill you twice."

I'm simply dealing with a madman. Sorry she'd even started this conversation, Sydney shut her eyes, determined not to give him the satisfaction of seeing her fear. No longer looking at him, she couldn't shut out his voice spewing the plans he had for her demise.

"You definitely deserve to die." His voice became

shrill and nearly unintelligible before he pulled back fully then slammed the door.

Almost immediately, liquid sloshed against the side window. She gagged on the heavy stench of gasoline fumes. Coughing so hard she choked, Sydney pulled herself upright and opened her eyes.

Holding the red metal can aloft, Randall took his hand away from its spout to wave his fingers at her. His eyes glimmered wide and wild, and his mouth moved to form a litany of words she couldn't hear. Nor did she care to understand them. When she looked away, he pounded on the glass until she glanced up at him again.

He discarded the gas can to one side with a flourish, then held up two different items, one in each hand. A rolled-up piece of newspaper, and the silver-plated lighter she'd glimpsed before. The sobs she was determined to hold inside gathered in her chest until she was sure her lungs would burst.

Refusing to give up, Sydney thrashed against her restraints. The more she yanked, the duct tape at her wrists only tightened to cut more deeply into her flesh. With all the windows rolled up, the inside air around her was already growing warm and thick. No longer caring to hold in frantic sobs, she tossed her head back to scream her frustration.

Bang!

"Aahhhh!"

It couldn't be!

Sydney flinched at what sounded like a gunshot to peer out the side window. Emitting a shrill and gurgling scream, the madman fell sideways and disappeared.

"Stay down or I'll blow your fucking head off!"

More shouts and pounding footfalls shook the

ground as uniformed officers burst out of the surrounding woods. The whump, whump, whump of a helicopter grew louder then disappeared. Twisted to the right, she craned her neck as she strained to make sense of the commotion. The door beside her opened and she swung her head left.

"Sydney. Oh, my God, Sydney." She caught sight of Vince as he ducked inside.

Relief and gratitude rushed over her like a tsunami, and she momentarily went limp under its weight. On instinct, she moved to slide toward him, only to be held in place by her restraints.

No matter, he dove closer to her. "It's okay, sweetheart. I've got you."

"Check him for weapons!"

"Seal off this area!"

As all hell and more continued to erupt around them, Vince rocked slowly back and forth with Sydney wrapped firmly in his arms.

Softly and gently, he stroked the side of her face as he murmured phrases of assurance and comfort. "It's okay. It's okay. You're safe."

Knowing she *was* safe in his arms, she buried her face in his shoulder. Anguished sobs, too powerful for her to hold in, gushed out.

And all the while, Vince simply held her. Comforted her. Kept her safe.

Terrified and relieved. Exhilarated and exhausted, she leaned into him. When she had no more tears left in her, he reached toward the duct tape binding her wrists to the steering wheel. Though his hands shook, his expression was intense. With slow and deliberate motions, he carefully worked to peel the adhesive away from her skin.

"Tell me if I hurt you and I'll stop. Doing my best to be gentle."

He turned his face to hers, and she relished the simplicity of his presence as his breath caressed her cheek. Needing to maintain a physical connection, she nodded then rested her head on his shoulder. As he worked, she winced now and then, but didn't pull away when he accidently pinched her.

"There." He drew her wrists away from the last of the tape he left hanging on the steering wheel.

"Just hold me for a moment. Please." Lunging forward, she wrapped her arms around his neck. A whooshed out sigh was the only other sound to come out of her as she held on.

"If anything had happened…It would have…I wouldn't have been able to live without you."

Hot tears erupted to flow down her cheeks. She wiped her face on his shirt front, realized what she'd done, and offered him a timid smile.

"Let's get you out of here."

He released her only long enough to put one arm around her shoulders. With the other caressing her waist, he helped her out of the vehicle, then led her away from what would have been her death pyre.

"Where is he? I want to kill the bastard." Though her head throbbed, she didn't bother to censor herself and hissed out the words so only he could hear. She gingerly touched the duo of bumps she sported behind her ear. "He deserves to die and more."

"Don't worry. He'll get his." Vince let out a breath, then gently turned her head to study the wounds. "There's no blood, but you definitely need to get checked out. Hollis!" He raised his head to call out to a uniformed officer who stood nearby.

The man turned toward him. "Yeah?"

"You have an ambulance on the way, right?"

"Two of them. Should be here any time."

"Good. Thanks."

"Apparently, Curan scopes out his murder scenes ahead of time." Hollis glanced at Sydney, and his lips tweaked into an apologetic smile before he turned back to Vince. "We found a stash of a few more filled gasoline cans nearby, hidden under some brush."

"I think we'll find he's done this before." Vince pulled Sydney more securely to his side. "More than a few times."

"Captain Hollis. We need you over here, sir."

"On my way."

As the officer in charge hurried away, Vince led her over to a tree trunk that had long ago fallen into the clearing. Making sure she was comfortable first, he sat down beside her. All the while he never let her go. Despite the din of police activity going on in front of them, birds chirped, and branches swished in a calm breeze behind them.

She couldn't wait to lean against him again. "How did you find me?"

"We're both fortunate you have that forgetful streak." With his cheek rested against her hair, Vince explained briefly about using her mini GPS system then pointed to the sky. "Police helicopter took off shortly after we got a read out on your possible location. That father of yours has a lot of pull with the State posse around here."

"He's been at it a long time." She glanced down

and back at him.

"Hollis sent me a picture of your necklace recovered from another crash and burn site. I was sure it was you."

Sydney automatically fingered the one she miraculously still wore. "Brock somehow found one identical he bought for Belinda when she admired mine. Sad to say, I resented it at the time." She grew silent as an odd thought struck home. "How ironic. Here I was so focused on worrying about you being hurt on the job, and look what happens to me."

"On the job." He paused for a moment as if measuring what to say next. "During my investigation of Brock's murder, I discovered several other women who held similar positions to yours in Curan's companies…he…well…"

"I'm the only one he didn't succeed in murdering?" The mere idea of it made her shudder.

Vince tightened his arm around her. "Probably. And thank God for that."

Before she could respond beyond another shudder, his mouth brushed hers like a butterfly landing on a leaf. Warm and welcome, his lips covered hers again with a light, sweet pressure that left her breathless and needing more.

"I should have killed the son of a bitch when I had the shot."

At her father's husky, emotion charged voice, Vince released Sydney's lips but still held her as he glanced over. "You used sufficient force to neutralize the threat. Shooting him in the hand was all you had to do."

"Dad? When did you get here?" She left Vince's

arms, then stood just long enough to embrace her father.

"Vince brought me." He wrapped her up tight and openly sobbed. "My God."

She pulled back. "Where were you before this?"

"After I shot the bastard, I was detained by these damned local officers. But forget about that. You came so very close to dying." Tears glistened on his cheeks as he held her at arms' length and simply stared.

"But I didn't." Wriggling free, she retook her place beside Vince.

"No. You didn't. You sure didn't." Finally, he cracked a smile as he looked from her to Vince then back again. "Now that I know you're okay, and in good hands, there's another woman in my life I need to tend to." He punched a number into the cell he pulled out then put it to his ear and waited. "Ida. It's Andy." With a wink he turned his back and mumbled something low. "No. No. We're all fine. Now."

Judging by the spurts of conversation he allowed them to hear, he was doing all he could to assure Ida all was well. After he spoke again, the richness of his laughter echoed back at them.

Sydney snuggled closer to Vince. "It's good to hear my dad laugh again. Something he hasn't done for a very, very long time."

"I guess you could say the love of a good woman will do that for a man."

Lifting her head, she glanced up at him. "You really think my dad could come to love Ida?"

"The same way I love you?" He smiled and kissed the top of her head. "Stranger things have happened, I suppose."

"I'm not sure I'm ready for that."

Vince kept his eyes on her father as the man laughed again. "Too late. If I'm any judge."

"There, Ida's up to speed." Putting the cell away, her dad walked back to stand in front them.

Sydney opened her mouth to say what, she wasn't sure, so she remained silent.

"Commander Raines, can we talk to you a minute?" The unfortunate deputy who'd been sent to fetch her father cleared his throat and stepped forward.

He gave one of his trademark glowers as he glanced over. "Now?"

"Yes, sir. If you wouldn't mind."

"Hell yes, I'd mind."

The young officer blinked but didn't back down. "Procedure, sir."

Vince kept his arm around Sydney. "You discharged your firearm, Andy. Shot a civilian. You know the drill."

"I didn't kill the son of a bitch. That should simplify their damned investigation. Although, it did mess up that consultant job I had in the works. Can't be connected to a department in any official capacity until the investigations are complete." He dropped the magazine out of his Glock, then turned the handle toward the officer and surrendered the piece. "This better not take too long."

"The chief wants to talk to you first."

"Take care of my little girl until I get back." Though he looked at Sydney, he spoke directly to Vince.

"I'll do better than that, sir." Vince's gaze zeroed in on her and her heart warmed. "I'll take care of her forever."

As tears rimmed her eyes, Sydney met his gaze. "Is that a threat or a promise?"

"Both."

Sydney glanced over as one ambulance then another pulled into the clearing. "He confessed to me he killed Brock. And Belinda Simms. He said he was party to the On Trend swindle. Belinda tried to shake him down, demanding Brock's cut."

"When this comes to trial, I have a feeling your friend Nancy Parsons will corroborate any testimony you have to give."

"That woman is hardly my friend." She grimaced at the thought, then glanced at Vince in surprise. "Why would you say she'd back up my story?"

"Because I think she's as fed up with his antics as the rest of us."

Her mouth fell open as he gave her a summary of the recent conversation he'd had with the overbearing woman. She shook her head when he finished. "No wonder she detested me. And I thought Randall's touchy feelies were simply your typical sexual harassment in the workplace."

"Inexcusable in any form."

A few feet away, a squirrel poked his head out from beneath the log to survey the uproar taking place in front of him then quickly ducked back into shelter. A uniformed officer strung wide, yellow POLICE LINE DO NOT CROSS perimeter tape around what was now an active crime scene.

"I must say all this activity isn't helping a pounding headache go away."

The look he cast her was part shock, part disbelief.

"I'm sorry. I didn't even think of that."

"Only because all of this is simply a day at the office for you."

"In another few years, I can retire from the force. Even give us a decent pension."

She laid her head on his shoulder. "Then do what, Vince? A little gardening? Play golf?"

He shook his head and grimaced in distaste. "Never did develop the patience for either of those."

Her light laughter floated around them. "Me either." She glanced up at him, all traces of the smile gone. "I want you to do what you want to do. Not what you think I want you to do."

"We could compromise, and I'd get off the streets. Quit chasing taillights on a day to day basis. See if I can get promoted to a desk job."

"Only if that's your choice."

"My choice is to be with you." He pulled back and the soft, sweet expression of love she'd come to expect from him shone in his eyes. "And I'll do whatever I have to do to make that happen. I swear."

"It's going to take a lot more than the ups and downs of the job you have now for me to go anywhere." She reached up a fingertip to trace the outline of his lips.

Their corners twitched up at her touch. "Promise?"

"Promise. Comes with the territory. That's how it is when you fall in love with a cop." She let a mischievous twinkle light her gaze. "All I ask is that you be you. Promise me that?"

"Easy enough." Dipping his head, he began to close his eyes. "I do."

The twinkle remained as she drew nearer for his

kiss. "Maybe someday, Detective Miller. Maybe someday."

A word about the author…

Wife to one, mother to four, mother-in-law to four, and grandmother to four so far, Margo is a Detroit native who couldn't be happier now living in rural mid-Michigan. A communications specialist by trade, she has worked as a magazine editor, television producer, and speech and script writer. When not writing these days, she enjoys walking outdoors in every season, hates to cook, and loves to read. She can be found on line at www.margohoornstra.com

Thank you for purchasing
this publication of The Wild Rose Press, Inc.

For questions or more information
contact us at
info@thewildrosepress.com.

The Wild Rose Press, Inc.
www.thewildrosepress.com

To visit with authors of
The Wild Rose Press, Inc.
join our yahoo loop at
http://groups.yahoo.com/group/thewildrosepress/

www.ingramcontent.com/pod-product-compliance
Lightning Source LLC
Chambersburg PA
CBHW071511260626
47170CB00002B/339
* 9 7 8 1 5 0 9 2 2 2 1 4 8 *